A
TOWN CALLED
FURY

A TOWN CALLED FURY

AN EPIC SAGA OF THE AMERICAN FRONTIER

WILLIAM W. JOHNSTONE
with J. A. Johnstone

PINNACLE BOOKS
Kensington Publishing Corp.
www.kensingtonbooks.com

PINNACLE BOOKS are published by

Kensington Publishing Corp.
119 West 40th Street
New York, NY 10018

PUBLISHER'S NOTE
Following the death of William W. Johnstone, the Johnstone family is working with a carefully selected writer to organize and complete Mr. Johnstone's outlines and many unfinished manuscripts to create additional novels in all of his series like The Last Gunfighter, Mountain Man, and Eagles, among others. This novel was inspired by Mr. Johnstone's superb storytelling.

All Kensington titles, imprints, and distributed lines are available at special quantity discounts for bulk purchases for sales promotions, premiums, fundraising, educational, or institutional use. Special book excerpts or customized printings can also be created to fit specific needs. For details, write or phone the office of the Kensington special sales manager: Kensington Publishing Corp., 119 West 40th Street, New York, NY 10018, attn: Special Sales Department; phone 1-800-221-2647.

PINNACLE BOOKS, the Pinnacle logo, and the WWJ steer head logo are Reg. U.S. Pat. & TM Off.

ISBN-13: 978-0-7860-4206-7
ISBN-10: 0-7860-4206-0

First printing of A Town Called Fury: July 2006
First printing of Hard Country: April 2007
First printing of omnibus edition: September 2017

10 9 8 7 6 5 4 3 2 1

Printed in the United States of America

First electronic edition: September 2017

ISBN-13: 978-0-7860-4207-4
ISBN-10: 0-7860-4207-9

CONTENTS

BOOK ONE

A Town Called Fury

Chapter 1

Kansas City, Missouri, 1865

Jedediah Fury put down his paintbrush and bucket of whitewash, struck a match on the sole of his dusty boot, then set it to his pipe. Puffing in the sweet smoke, he sat down on a bale of straw and looked out over his future; more like, what his future had been reduced to.

He saw a house in town, small compared to the one he'd left behind back East, but still neat and tidy; three good saddle geldings, enclosed by the corral fence he'd just finished whitewashing half of; a milk cow in the tiny barn that had come with the place; a handful of clucking, pecking hens; a few newly purchased stoats, presently rooting and quarreling in their pen; and his old short-bed Conestoga wagon, the one that had made so many trips from the East Coast to the Western Shore and back again.

He really ought to figure out just how many miles he'd put under those wheels, he thought.

Or maybe not. He wasn't exactly sure he wanted to know how much time—how much blood, sweat, tears, and effort—he'd put into guiding pilgrims into the wilderness over the past twenty years. Well, not much the last few. Of course, people had wanted to go west, be shown the way, but he'd been more than a little pre-occupied with the War. He'd given it his heart and his soul, not to mention two sons and a wife.

His only remaining boy, Jason, had almost caught up with him on the other side of the fence. Jason made the last few strokes with the paintbrush and then carefully opened the gate and let himself out, placing his brush and paint bucket alongside his father's. He didn't join his father, however. He went to the pump and began to wash his hands.

"Nice job, son," Jedediah said around his pipe.

"Yeah," Jason replied without looking up. "Looks good." He paused and took a long look down the fence. "Your side, too, Pa," he added, a bit grudgingly.

Jedediah chuckled softly. Everything was grudging with that boy. Although he reminded himself that Jason wasn't a boy any longer. Twenty wasn't a boy, was it? No, at twenty, Jedediah himself had been trapping beaver and wolf in the Colorado Territory with Wash Keough, fighting off grizzlies and the frigid weather and the temptation to take a squaw to wife. He had managed to win out over all of them.

Jedediah sighed. No, twenty was no boy.

"Jason, after you finish up there, could you hike over to the mercantile and pick up a few pounds of flour for your sister?" He relit his pipe, which had gone out.

Finally, Jason twisted his head around. He'd just splashed his face with water, and it was dripping. Jason's mother, Jane, had always said that Jeremy had all the enthusiasm of the three, Jonathon had all the sweetness, and Jason had the good looks that would lead him either to prison or the U.S. Senate.

She'd been right, Jedediah figured. Jeremy, their eldest, had been so damned eager to please his senior officer that he'd led his squadron on a suicide mission into the swamps of Georgia and had died right along with the rest of them, probably to the shrieks and cackles of Rebel yells. Jedediah figured that if Jason had been in his older brother's position, he would have told his commanding officer to take a long walk off a short pier.

As for his youngest, Jonathon, well, the boy had been too kindhearted for his own good, God bless him. One afternoon, he'd invited a party of travelers to come in for some of his Ma's good cooking. Which was nothing that he hadn't seen his pa do countless times before.

But what Jonathon didn't know that day was that the very fellows he'd invited into the parlor were the same four that had, not three hours before, held up a bank down in Maryland and shot two men. They killed the boy and his mother before leaving the house. Little Jenny survived, but only because she had the sense to run and hide out back, in the woods.

"Flour? What for?"

Jedediah was jerked back into the present. "Your sister's making dinner."

A look of long-suffering martyrdom spread over the boy's face. "Aw, Pa! Why'd you want to go and let her cook again? Last time—"

Jedediah cut his son off with a wave of his hand. "We all have our unfortunate accidents, Jason. Don't go mentioning it in front of Jenny."

"Why not?"

"It hurts her feelings," Jedediah said, while throwing one of his *you-know-better-than-to-ask-that looks*.

It was wasted, though. Jason wasn't paying him any mind. His eyes were focused up toward the street, instead.

Jedediah followed his son's gaze to a small contingent of people marching up the graveled driveway. Could this mean a new trip to the wild country? He stood up and walked forward.

"Afternoon, folks!" he announced, in a voice that he hoped was authoritative, yet benign. "The Good Father" was the face he liked people to see, particularly people he was going to have to ferry across the wilderness.

"Don't get started yet," he heard Jason softly say behind him. "They might only be trying to get us to join the Baptist church."

And Jedediah thought, *No, by God, twenty isn't yet a man, not when it's that flip and sarcastic. . . .*

The tall man at the front of the group came right up to him and stuck out his hand, taking Jedediah's and pumping it vigorously. "Mr. Fury, sir?" When Jedediah nodded in the affirmative, the man continued. "I'm the Reverend Milcher, Louis Milcher, that is, and this is my wife, Lavinia." The small, tired-looking woman next to Milcher curtsied timidly.

"Reverend," replied Jedediah with a nod. "Ma'am. Pleased to make your acquaintance." Jason had been right after all: They were trolling for new congregational members. Even though he was pretty certain he knew what was coming, he asked, "What can I do for you folks?"

"I have been voted spokesman for our group, Mr. Fury," Milcher went on. "We are only eight wagons and a small gather of livestock, but I am certain that we can attract a few more fellow pilgrims when it's known that we have procured the great Jedediah Fury as our wagon master!"

Surprised yet not surprised, Jedediah scratched at his chin. "Where you folks planning on ending up?" By the looks of them, they'd be lucky to make it across the Missouri River into Kansas.

"Why, California, sir!" said Milcher, as if everybody in the world could have only one possible destination.

"Whereabouts in California?"

"I plan to go to southern California," confided Milcher. "I have already purchased land there, in a place outside the town of Los Angeles. Have you heard of it?"

Jedediah had heard of it lots of times and been there a few, and frankly, he couldn't see why anybody outside of a rattler or a family of scorpions would want to live there.

But he asked, "Why don't you folks step on into the house?"

and gestured toward the back porch. Over his shoulder, he called, "You go run that errand for your sister, Jason."

He heard Jason snort, but refrained from adding a word of castigation when the boy came immediately into sight, walking up the drive toward the street.

A few of the ladies actually gasped.

"Oh, my!" commented Mrs. Milcher, one hand to her rapidly coloring cheek. "What a handsome young man!"

"Thank you," said Jedediah as he led the party up the back steps, through the enclosed porch, and into the house. Since the age of fifteen, Jason had always had the same effect on females, whether he paid them any mind or not.

The Reverend Mr. Milcher had best reel his wife in—and fast—or this trip wouldn't be smooth *or* pleasant.

Jedediah swung open the door that led to the back hall and ushered the party inside, saying, "I reckon he's a good enough boy."

Try though he might, though, he couldn't keep some pride from seeping into his voice.

Jason walked the four blocks down into the beginning of the business district, and headed for the nearest dry-goods store. He wasn't any too fond of Missouri. Or Kansas City, for that matter. If he'd had his druthers, he'd have stayed back East and gone to college, the way his folks had always promised him he would.

But the War hadn't been their fault, after all—although he would have liked very much to blame them, or, at least, his father—and there was no money. Even the sale of their old family property had barely paid off their debts. He supposed he should be grateful that his father had an established trade of sorts to fall back on.

But Jason wasn't very grateful. All he could think of was those ivied halls that he'd never see, and the only thing he could feel was cheated and envious and hurt.

As he made his way along the street, he heard someone shout from down an alley, at his left. He stopped and looked, and there in the shadows, saw a fistfight in progress. One of the fellows in it was quite a bit smaller, and was suffering the brunt of it.

Never one to just mind his own business—as his father was fond of reminding him—Jason stepped into the alley's mouth and called to the punisher, "Hey, there, you! Let him go!"

The bigger fellow, one hand on the smaller's collar, turned his head toward Jason. And smiled.

It was a very unwholesome smile.

"Get lost," he snarled, and slugged the smaller boy again. Neither of them was past twenty-one. The boy getting the worst of it seemed quite a bit younger.

The smaller boy lost consciousness and slipped to the ground. Still smiling, the victor turned to face Jason. "And just what business is it of yours, Mr. Fancy Pants?"

Don't let him tick you off, Jason told himself, but he felt himself pulling up and standing taller, all his muscles tensed and braced for the onslaught.

"Get out," Jason said. The boy on the ground was still breathing, at least. And conscious again. Jason added, "Go on home."

The bully's head—now outfitted with a scowl—twisted to the side, and he said, "Just who the hell do you think you are, anyhow?"

"I'm someone who doesn't like to see murder committed for no reason but sport."

The bully appeared taken aback and said nothing for a moment, giving Jason the time to notice the initials M.M. embroidered on one point of his collar, and that he also wore not one gun, which Jason had seen from the first, but two.

"Go on," Jason said in a voice he hoped was calm and self-assured. "Don't be stupid."

But it appeared that the fellow wasn't falling for it. Or

perhaps, didn't notice. He shouted, "Stupid? Why, I'll—" as he suddenly ran toward Jason.

Jason sidestepped him at the last moment, and the bully's momentum took him out into the street and right into a mud puddle, which he promptly slipped and fell into. While he was cursing and picking himself up, Jason went to his victim and helped him to his feet.

The smaller boy stuttered, "Th-thank you. Be careful. That's Matt MacDonald!"

He said it, Jason thought, like everybody should know that name and be afraid at its mention.

Well, he wasn't.

And the bully was bearing down on him again, although he was slightly impeded by the mud soaking his pants and shirt, and the fact that he'd stepped into a bucket and it was stuck on one foot. He'd also lost one gun.

His first wild swing caught Jason square in the chest and sent him tumbling backward, into a stack of crates. But Jason rolled and came up on his feet fast, confusing the bully— who was undoubtedly accustomed to weaker and smaller opponents—and clipped him in the side of the head. The clip was followed by a sharp uppercut that laid the bully out flat— with his foot still stuck in that bucket.

"Gosh," muttered the smaller boy, who had fled behind the rain barrel.

Jason successfully fought the urge to laugh. "Duck your head in that water," Jason said to him. "You've got blood on your face. You don't want to scare your folks."

The boy obeyed, and when he and Jason walked out of the alley, leaving a cowed Matt MacDonald behind, Jason said, "What's your name, kid?"

The boy scrubbed water and blood from his face with a sleeve. "Milcher. Thomas Milcher. And I'm not a kid," he added, rather proudly. "I'm fifteen."

Jason smiled. "Sorry. Your papa a reverend?"

Thomas's hands automatically balled into defensive fists. "Yeah, what about it?"

"Stick close, then. I've gotta pick up something, then I'm going home. Your folks are there." He headed up the street again in search of a dry-goods store with young Thomas Milcher, a new acolyte, tagging at his heels.

Chapter 2

Jedediah was satisfied with the group clustered about his big dining room table and packed into the corners of the room. Seven couples in all, they were a good start on a wagon train. The Reverend Milcher had done most of the talking, but Jedediah had been able to pick up a few things about the others.

Hamish MacDonald was looking to become a rancher. At least he had announced, at least three times, that he had a dozen cows, with calves at their sides, and a prime Hereford bullock and four nice Morgan mares, and was looking for land: He didn't care where, so long as there was good grazing. MacDonald, a widower, also had a boy, twenty, and a girl, sixteen.

Young Randall Nordstrom had no children, but his wife, Miranda, was a seamstress, and he had a wagonload of foodstuffs and yard goods and geegaws. They were planning on opening a store, with Miranda doing sewing and giving music lessons on the side.

There were two Morton families. Well, three. Ezekial and his wife, Eliza, had two grown daughters who were also traveling with them. Electa was single and twenty-seven. Europa was thirty, and was now Mrs. Milton Griggs—and Milton was a blacksmith and a wheelwright. They used up two wagons between them.

The other part of the Morton family was elderly Zachary Morton, a gunsmith, and his wife, Suzannah. They had no children, at least with them, and Jedediah had at first thought that they were too old to make the trip. However, the Reverend Milcher had managed to convince him otherwise. And Zachary looked fit for his age. He sat at the far end of the table, glowering from beneath his gray and beetling brows while he fiddled with his pipe.

Next came Salmon Kendall and his wife, Cordelia. They hailed from Massachusetts, and were farmers. While Salmon had no special skills or merchandise upon which the train could count, he looked to have a strong back and a solid purpose. They had two children: Salmon Jr., called Sammy, twelve, and Peony, called for some inexplicable reason Piny, aged ten.

The Milchers themselves, he supposed, offered spiritual aid. The reverend and his wife, Lavinia, had seven kids ranging from five to fifteen. The wife seemed to have a bit of a harpy's tongue, but he supposed all those children would keep her busy. At least, he hoped so.

Altogether, the five families (counting all the Mortons as one) accounted for eight long- and short-bed Conestoga wagons; nine saddle horses and four breeding stock; a couple dozen cattle, assorted hogs, goats, two dogs, and a cat named Chuckles, which belonged to the Milchers.

It was a fine start.

"Well?" said the Reverend Milcher.

"Six or eight additional wagons, anyway," replied Jedediah thoughtfully. He really wanted at least twenty in the group. To take fewer could be foolhardy. They had plenty of hostile territory to traverse.

Eliza Morton looked crestfallen. "Where on earth can we find as many as we already are, Ezekial?"

Ezekial put an arm around his wife, comforting her. "I

shouldn't think it will be too difficult, Eliza," he muttered. "After all, ain't Kansas City the great jumpin'-off place, darlin'?"

Over the next few weeks, the wagon train grew and grew. Jedediah found a group of six wagons to join up, and the Reverend Milcher found two, then five, then seven. Milcher's were mostly farmers, but within the ranks of Jedediah's recruits were some folks he considered quite useful.

Michael Morelli was a country doctor. Well, not the go-to-school kind, but he was close enough. He, his wife Olympia, and their young son Constantine and younger daughter Helen would journey complete with a traveling surgery—something that Jedediah knew, from hard experience, would come in handy.

In addition, he picked up Saul and Rachael Cohen, and their boys David, Jacob, and Abraham. The Cohens were Jews and he expected some trouble from the Reverend Milcher along the line, but he figured he'd put up with it. The Cohens planned to open a store once they got to California, and brought two wagons to the mix, one of which would be filled to the brim with stock for their new mercantile.

True, the Nordstroms were well stocked, too, but most of their stuff was yard goods and notions and the like, while the Cohens carried hardware and hand tools. If forced to choose, Jedediah would have rather had the Cohens along any day of the week.

The rest of his recruits were farmers or potential ranchers, although Seth Wheeler had done some smithing in his time, or so he said.

The best he could say for Milcher's new folks was that one of the women had been a nurse during the War.

But still, he was glad for the bodies and the wagons. He thought they had enough, now.

Arrangements were made, money changed hands, wagons

were packed and repacked and loaded, and spirits were high. Always best to start off that way, Jedediah thought. The reality of the trip would take the wind out of their sails, but at least they were inflated with bright and airy hopes to start with.

That way, they had a lot farther to fall before they hit bottom.

As for himself, well, Jason was going with him, and Jenny was staying behind with Tom and Sally Norton, their neighbors, until he got back next year. Jedediah had arranged it all.

But Jenny wasn't having it, drat her. Right this minute, she stood before him in the front hall, her arms crossed over her chest—just like her mama—and a frown on her face.

"But I want to come!" she said for probably the fourth time. "I *am* coming!"

Jedediah let out a long sigh. "Jenny, I'll have no more of this. I told you, you're only fifteen and it's a long, hard trip."

"I know how old I am, Papa, and I know it's hard. But the boys got to go when they were only twelve!"

Jedediah opened his mouth, but she jumped back in right away.

"And don't say that they were boys!" she finished.

"Honey," Jedediah began in a measured tone, "they *were* boys. It makes a difference. You're just a young thing, learning to cook and bake and sew like your mama. Someday, you'll want to keep house for your man, and you'll want to keep it in a civilized place, not out on the wild prairie. Boys don't grow on trees out there."

She took a deep breath and looked up at him through lush, golden lashes, a glower on her pretty face. When her mama had worn that look, Jedediah knew that he was in trouble.

"Papa, I'll be safe. After all, you and Jason will be there. Why, I could get shot by a bandit or kidnapped into a house of degradation right here in Kansas City!"

She smiled a tad when she said that last bit. Her mama would have, too.

He shook his head. "What about school?" he asked, even though he knew full well that Electa Morton intended to teach school on the trip west. He just hoped that Jenny didn't remember it.

But she did.

"Oh, radishes, Papa! I spoke with Miss Morton, and she says I can help her. I've already got my eighth-grade certification, as if you didn't know."

She had been at him so much lately that he knew he was beaten. Or would be, very shortly.

He gave in to gravity.

"All right, Jenny," he said, shaking his head. "You wore me down." She squealed and literally gave a leap up into the air while he added, "You can go along, I reckon, but you'll have to do your share, just like anybody else. You'll walk behind the wagon, do the cooking, and help with the livestock. You'll have to learn to reload in case there's trouble, you know."

"I'd rather you taught me how to shoot."

He slapped his hat on his head. "Don't press your luck, daughter," he said, and walked around her, to the front door.

Jedediah rode the half mile down to the Reverend Milcher's current place of residence—the double lot behind Barker's laundry—on his old blue roan saddle horse, Gumption. Milcher and several of his group had set up temporary camp there, and Barker was charging them a pretty penny for the pleasure.

Milcher saw him coming, and lifted a hand.

"Hail, Brother Fury!" he cried.

The greeting annoyed Jedediah a bit, but he didn't let it show on his face. "Morning, Milcher," he called. "How are you folks coming along? Ready to go in the morning?"

As Fury dismounted, Milcher walked out to meet him. "Indeed, indeed," the reverend said, nodding his head. "We could leave this evening, if you desire."

"Tomorrow will be soon enough."

Jedediah cast a gaze toward the corral, where there stood a number of milk cows, horses, oxen, and goats. He noticed the absence of Hamish MacDonald's livestock, though, and mentioned it.

"Oh, he's moved them out to graze. Somewhere north of town." Milcher sniffed, as if he didn't approve of such consideration being paid to one's livestock. "They'll be back in time, though." He checked his watch. "I hope."

"Those cows of yours could use a little grass," Jedediah said softly. They were fair ribby and dull-eyed. "They'll get some starting tomorrow, though."

"My opinion exactly!" Milcher said, loud enough that a woman walking down the opposite side of the road heard him and stopped to stare.

Jedediah ignored Milcher's overeagerness and asked, "Where's Jason? I don't see him." Indeed, all he saw were people packing wagons and fiddling with livestock, and children playing in the spaces between the wagons.

"He went to load the water barrel wagon. He and Matt MacDonald. And Milton Griggs." Milcher pointed down the street.

Matt MacDonald? Ever since the day that Milcher had showed up on the Fury doorstep, Jason and Matt had been avoiding each other like a case of the smallpox. He hoped they were mending their fences.

"Well, then," Jedediah said, just as he noticed a stack of crates sitting beside Milcher's wagon. "Let me help with those crates, Milcher."

"Be obliged, Brother Fury."

Jedediah wouldn't stay long, though. He had his own Conestoga to pack yet again, now that Jenny was going along on the trek.

Dad blast it, anyway!

Chapter 3

Jason sat his mare on the far bank of the Missouri, mopping his brow. Who would have thought it would take this long to get them all across? But only two of the ferries were operational, the cattle had decided to go downstream a mile before crossing all the way over, and the Milchers' cat had developed a sudden urge to go swimming.

He thought one of their kids had likely tossed the cat over the side, but he kept his peace and fished the poor thing out of the drink. He'd like to get his hands on that kid, though.

The cattle had been brought back upstream by his father's three hired men—Milt Billings, who Jason was surprised his father had hired, because Jason didn't trust him any farther than he could throw him; Gil Collins, who at twenty-four was the youngest of the three, and something of a cipher; and Ward Wanamaker. Jason liked Ward. He was good with livestock, good with people, and seemed to be looking forward to the journey.

The men were holding the cattle in a tight group about a hundred yards from where Jason sat his palomino, watching the final wagon roll off the ferry. Later on, the three would serve as jacks-of-all-trades, everything from Indian fighters to roustabouts to baby-walkers.

Farther out ahead, his father was lining up the rest of the wagons, making sure everybody had made it across the river high and dry. Jason doubted the Milchers' cat was faring as well as the rest of the Milchers.

He looked for Jenny, too, and spied her, the third wagon from the front, high on the driver's bench of the family Conestoga. He couldn't help but quirk his mouth up into a smile. He'd bet she hadn't figured on driving a six-in-hand when she'd begged her way into this.

Well, she'd be walking soon enough. His father had brought along extra trade goods this time, and all those mirrors and blankets and geegaws weighed as much as two fat steers, and that was in addition to their personal things. He'd also brought extra ammunition in a wagon currently driven by Tommy Milcher, and another filled with extra water for the livestock. Ward Wanamaker had left the livestock and was presently taking the ferry back to drive it over. Jenny'd have to get out and lead their team sooner or later. His father would insist.

On the road west, horses and oxen were more important than people. Unless you were starving to death.

And even then, it was iffy.

He'd noticed that the Reverend Milcher, in addition to all those kids, had brought along a piano. Probably to accompany all the hymns he'd be leading in that new church he planned to build. Jason figured that piano would probably end up somewhere beside the trail about halfway into the Indian Territory. As would the Nordstroms' big old breakfront, and Milton Griggs's anvil.

People brought the craziest things along.

He heard his father's familiar whistle, and reined his horse around, while taking a last, longing look at the eastern horizon. Good-bye to college, good fellowship, and good things. Hello tumbleweeds and wild country and sudden death.

Well, his path was set now, in the hot, dry caliche and baking sun of the land to come. He'd just have to live with it.

He gave the men a friendly wave to move up the herd, then

goosed his horse into a slow lope and caught up with the plodding wagons up front.

Ten miles from the Missouri, and Lavinia was already having second thoughts about that piano. Louis had purchased it, secondhand, in Missouri, and it had seemed like a good idea at the time. Music to bring the godless back to the fold, silky songs of praise to unite the congregation into one big family.

· But it weighed too much. It took up the room where three of their children could have slept, and Lavinia had left behind one hundred pounds of flour and another fifty of cornmeal to make room.

She was happy to defer to her lord and master, but not when he was being an idiot. And only an idiot would cast her children outside, to sleep beneath the wagon with the snakes. It was bad enough that they had to walk behind or alongside the wagon, that they'd have to stay there for what—fifteen hundred miles? Two thousand? They had been mad to give in to Louis's wanderlust, mad to leave their comfortable farm and their rightful place in society.

Louis had insisted there was more, though. Greener pastures, he'd said. If only his greener pastures weren't so very far away!

And now here she was, only ten miles into the wilderness, with stinging feet and throbbing thighs and aching calves and ankles swollen like the fabled elephants. Her head hurt, her eyes burned, and she could only imagine what her children were feeling.

At least Seth, at twelve, had been deemed mature enough and lightweight enough to do the driving. Her littlest, Hope, rode beside him on the bench, and her next-to-youngest, Charity, clung to her hand and bravely tried to keep up, although Lavinia carried her half the time.

Young Thomas drove one of the communal wagons for Mr. Fury, but the rest of the children walked.

She felt a rivulet of sweat make its way down her back, underneath the stays of her corset. Perhaps Suzannah Morton had been right. This was no place for the niceties of society.

And it was no place for these shoes. The blisters rising on her heels, she stopped, putting Charity on the ground beside her. Charity didn't understand, and held up her arms with a pleading look.

Lavinia shook her head. "Mother's feet are sore, darling. She can't carry you any longer until they're bandaged. Run and ask your brother to let you ride on the wagon with Hope."

The little girl's pretty face lit up. "Yes, Mother," she said, and scampered off ahead.

Lavinia stood exactly where she had stopped for some time, letting wagon after wagon pass her, group after group of walking women and children, until the Morellis' wagon came into view. She didn't know the Morellis very well, since they were Catholic and her husband frowned on papists, but she knew that he was a doctor, and that was what she needed.

She waved at him, up there in the driver's seat, and called out, "Dr. Morelli? Dr. Morelli, I have a medical problem!"

He slowed the wagon, then pulled out of line and stopped completely. "Mrs. Milcher?" he asked, cocking a brow. He slid down to the ground and approached her. "What seems to be the problem?"

Suddenly, she was embarrassed. What if her husband should find out she'd gone to a papist for help? He'd be angry sure enough, but still, she didn't feel she could walk another step without some sort of aid.

"My feet," she said, pointing to the ground.

He slipped an arm around her and helped her hobble to his wagon. "Those are no shoes for walking, Mrs. Milcher," he muttered. "Does one of your boys have a spare pair of boots?"

Horrified at the suggestion, she gulped and said, "Boots?"

"Yes, good, sturdy, roomy boots." Dr. Morelli was already

at work with the button hook. What he produced when he pulled off her shoe shocked her. She had thought she was blistered only on her heels, for they hurt the worst, but instead, her foot was a mass of blisters, bruises, and contusions.

Morelli clucked as he removed the other shoe. He looked up and gave her a stern frown. "Women," he said. "You lame yourself for fashion."

Then he handed over her shoes and got to work with antiseptic and bandages. When he was finished, he lifted her up onto the wagon's tailgate and said, "Stay put, you hear? I don't want you on your feet for at least two days. I'll drive you up to your own rig."

Cowed and embarrassed, Lavinia Milcher simply nodded.

When they circled the wagons late that afternoon, Lavinia Milcher wasn't the only walking wounded. Three other women and girls had so damaged their feet that they'd have to ride for the next few days. Young Jacob Cohen had made the mistake of trying to play with the Milcher kids, and had taken a beating for his trouble to their gleeful cries of "Jew boy! Jew boy! Jew boy!"

Jason, torn between drowning the lot of the Milcher kids or just poleaxing their father, had settled for hollering at them, then hoisting the battered and weeping eight-year-old Jacob up into his saddle and taking him to his mother.

Fortunately, they were traveling right in front of Doc Morelli's wagon, and Mrs. Cohen whisked the boy back to the doctor before Jason had a chance to apologize for those idiot Milchers. She abandoned her wagon entirely, and Jason had to take over the driving for about a half hour.

He honestly didn't know how anybody could take sitting on those damned seats all day! By the time she got back, with a bandaged Jacob in tow, Jason's backside had bruises on its bruises. He was glad to turn the rig over and get back up on

Cleo again. After that torturous ride, the palomino's smooth gait seemed like heaven.

By the time everybody was in place and the wagons were circled for the night, the sun had slipped beneath the horizon. Men turned to stripping the harness off their horses and oxen, and the woman started to fix dinner. Jason had a few words with his father, telling him of the Cohen/Milcher battle.

Jedediah simply nodded and said, "Figured it'd happen. Just didn't figure so soon." He placed a hand on Jason's shoulder. "You did the right thing, Jason. I'll take care of it. Don't know why these folks can't just get along for as long as it takes to make the goldurn trip!"

The livestock was put up, dinner was prepared, a fire had been built in the center of the circled wagons, and most folks sat round it, plates in their weary hands. Jedediah stood up slowly, dreading his speech.

He walked over to the fire, and said, "Folks? Can I have your attention?"

Gradually, the buzz of conversation died away, and all eyes were on him.

"Just wanted to say a few things," Jedediah began. "First off, you all did real well for a first day on the trail. We made twelve miles, by my reckoning."

Scattered applause broke out around the fire.

"Of course," he added, "that was all on the flat. We won't do as well later on. But by the same token, some days we'll do better. Now, most of you know that I hired us some help for the drive. Milt Billings—stand up there, Milt—is an ace horseman. He speaks Piute, Comanche, Crow, and Apache. And that's gonna come in mighty handy."

Some of the women began to whisper nervously, but Jedediah put the kibosh on that directly, saying, "We're gonna need to trade with the natives, and that takes communication, folks."

The whispering stopped.

"Next, there's Ward Wanamaker and Gil Collins. Ward, doff your hat so's they can tell who's who."

Ward did, and smiled wide. Gil just stood there, twitching nervously.

"Ward and Gil are both as good with their guns as they are with livestock or a shovel. You get into a bind and need somebody to help with your livestock, or you need a spare driver for a spell, you call on Ward or Gil. Sit down, boys."

He paused a moment. "Now, there's something else that's been preying on my mind. Folks, we have all throwed in together in order to make this difficult trip across the wilderness. And that means leavin' our petty bigotries behind us. We've got somebody from practically everywhere in the world in our group. Folks from the north, and folks from the south, folks from the old country and the new; Protestants, Catholics, and Jews. Now, I heard about some trouble breaking out today, which is pretty damned soon for trouble. You parents, you school your young'uns to be more tolerant, else you're going to be in for a world of hurt. Everybody got that?"

The group was shocked into silence—which he'd hoped would be their reaction—and Jedediah made his way back to his place and sat down, between Jason and Jenny. "Good dinner, honey," he said, and forced down another bite of Jenny's overdone rabbit.

Chapter 4

Jenny started the next day as she had started the day before. After she got herself ready, she piled every blanket and quilt she owned on the driver's bench, then waited while her papa and Jason hitched the team. It was beyond her how those other drivers made do without padding.

Jason must have seen her padding her perch, because he actually smiled at her—something he didn't do very often—and said, "Smart girl."

It was enough to plaster a smile on her face for the next two hours.

By that time, they had made another four or five miles, and her papa had ridden down the line, saying that there was a town about six miles up the trail. Jenny knew that could mean only one thing—they'd camp outside it, and some of them would be able to go in and visit. Or buy things!

Megan MacDonald, who was fast becoming her best friend, had told her there'd be gooseberries ahead, or so she thought, and ever since, Jenny had been set on getting hold of some canning jars and paraffin. The Nordstroms had some in their spare wagon, but the cost was too dear.

Well, she'd show them. She'd slip into town and get her own. The trip, meanwhile, was baking hot. She was glad she'd worn her bonnet. It kept the sun off her face, anyway, but she knew her hands were turning brown as walnuts. Papa had given her driving gloves, but the reins were so soft and old that she hadn't needed them. Until now. She began to dig through her bag.

"Hello!" called a familiar voice.

Jenny smiled and turned to spy Megan, walking up alongside the wagon.

"Hello, yourself. Want a ride?"

Megan's pretty brows knitted. "You sure? I mean, that it's not too much load?"

"Don't be silly. Besides, I need to find my driving gloves."

"Okay," Megan chirped, and placing her foot on the step, swung up into the seat beside Jenny, who handed her the reins. "You're not blistering," Megan remarked.

"No, but my hands'll be as dark as a red Indian pretty soon."

Megan laughed. Although Jenny was two years Megan's junior, the two had hit it off right away. Megan was nothing like her overbearing father or her bully of a brother, Jenny had decided within three minutes of their first meeting. She had all the humor in the family, and a cleverness to match it. And besides, both girls had lost their mothers at an early age.

They were fast becoming sisters in spirit.

And Jenny had seen Jason watching Megan. Not overtly— that wasn't Jason's style—but just in quick glances. He appeared to like what he saw, and Jenny was glad. Perhaps, if she was lucky and said her prayers faithfully, Megan could become her sister in more than spirit.

She hadn't broached the subject to Megan, though. That would have been bad luck.

"Like what you've done to the seat," Megan said, as Jenny pulled on the first glove. They were men's gloves and she swam in them.

Jenny laughed. "Don't know why everybody didn't think of it."

"Oh, they will before too long," Megan said. "If you know what I mean."

Jenny followed Megan's gaze up the line, where Europa Griggs could be seen, fresh from driving duty, rubbing her backside as she limped along.

Jenny laughed. "Guess so!"

Up ahead, Jason had more pressing matters on his hands.

Salmon Kendall's wagon had run over a rock—a big one—and broken an axle. Jason had the Kendalls unpacking their wagon, and Jedediah had hastened the other wagons in the train around the Kendalls, in order to keep the time lost to a minimum. Jason was helping Kendall to lighten the load while he waited for the Griggs's wagon or the Wheelers to arrive.

At least, Seth Wheeler had said he'd done some black-smithing and wheelwrighting in the past, and Milton Griggs was a smithy. Jason hoped that included some axle work, too.

When the Morellis passed them, Doc hollered, "Can I help, Jason?" but Jason waved them past. That was all they needed—a wagon falling on their only medical man. He noticed that the MacDonalds passed them by without a word. That figured. Even the Milchers called, "God be with you!" And the Nordstroms offered their help, but not so much as a look from Hamish MacDonald. Or Matthew, who actually could have been of some help.

But no, he just rode that big flashy pinto of his right on past, as if Jason and the Kendalls and half their cargo, spread out in the grass, weren't there at all.

Bastard.

When the boys driving the cattle and horses came up close, Ward Wanamaker rode over and pitched in, and together, he and Jason and Salmon got the wagon unloaded at just about the time that Seth Wheeler drove his team up.

When he asked if he could help, Jason sure didn't turn him down.

"Wagon's got a busted axle, Seth," he said, while Wheeler climbed down. "I'm hoping you can do something about it."

Seth gave a scratch to the back of his head. "Lemme take a look," he said, and got to it.

After five minutes of making sounds to himself and peering from various angles, he stood erect. "Can't fix 'er," he said, and Salmon's face fell. "But I can shore her up long enough to make the town. Your papa said there was a town not too far off, right?" he asked Jason.

"Sure did."

"Good. Don't supposed anybody in this train has an anvil? And supplies?"

Jason brightened. "Milton Griggs does, I'm pretty sure. He's comin' up now."

Through the dust came the Griggs wagon, with an uncomfortable Milton driving, his lank blond hair flopping beneath his hat. Jason flagged him down and explained the problem, and he and Milt and Seth wrestled the anvil out of the back of the wagon.

"You're lucky that thing didn't go straight through the bed," Seth remarked.

"Bottom's reinforced iron," Milt replied with a grunt.

"The whole thing?" Jason asked. He wondered that the horses could haul it. That is, until he took another look at the team. They were Belgian draft horses, as big and muscular as the man who owned them.

"Whole thing," Milt said. "Somebody got a fire goin'? I got my bellows and stuff in here somewhere. . . ."

"Not much to it, Mr. Griggs," said Seth. "We've just gotta strap her together with some iron. They can replace the axle when we get to the town, I hope. This thing's pretty much shot."

"Call me Milt," Griggs replied. "Let's get that fire going. C'mon, boys, somebody dig me a pit."

* * *

Salmon Kendall's wagon, jerry-rigged axle and all, fell into last place in the train an hour later. His load had been split out between Milt Griggs and Seth Wheeler—and Saul Cohen's extra rig—and the wagon slowly limped along, eventually catching up with the others.

Jedediah rode back to see how they were doing, and was pleased to see that Jason had handled the situation. "How's that axle look?" he asked as they rode along, bringing up the rear.

Jason thumbed his hat back. "Not good. They'll have to replace it once we get to town. Either that, or buy a whole new rig. If I didn't know different, I'd swear that Conestoga of Kendall's was a hundred years old. Damn thing's full of dry rot."

Jedediah made a disapproving face, then shook his head. "Idiots," he muttered.

Jason knew exactly what he meant, and didn't reply.

They pulled into the tiny prairie farming community of Bliss, Kansas, just as the sun was setting. Jedediah ordered the wagons lined up along the outskirts of the tiny town, and the herd bedded down farther out.

Jason rode in ahead to see if they had a carter or a smithy who could either fix the wagon or replace it. He was hoping for the first, and he knew Salmon Kendall was, too. Wagons cost dear, and Salmon didn't look as if he was any too flush. He'd sweated all through the repair work, and Jason was pretty sure it wasn't from the heat.

He found Bliss Livery right off, and as it turned out, he was in luck. The proprietor had nothing of the sort handy, but he knew of some folks that had come out from Iowa not too long ago, and were trying to sell their wagon. When Jason tracked them down, it turned out they were just as willing to sell the whole shebang as the rear axle. He guessed they weren't doing too well, by the look of them.

He rode the palomino out to meet Salmon Kendall, and directed him out to the wagon, then sent Milton Griggs after him, just in case. They might need another pair of strong shoulders, and frankly, Jason wasn't up to it.

He'd yanked his neck, back, and shoulder clear out of kilter back there, while they were shoring up the axle. So far, he'd managed to hide it from his father and the others—who wanted a ramrod who busted his own body during the first days out?—but right now, all Jason wanted was a hot bath in town, to soak in for maybe six or eight hours.

That, and about a quart of liniment.

Jason wasn't accustomed to hurting himself. Oh, he'd been shot during the War, but that had been an accident of friendly fire, seeing as how he was attached to the Department of War in Washington. Just a glorified paper-pusher, that's all he'd been. Not a hero, like his brother, butchered in the swamps of Georgia, or a hero like his father, who'd spent the last few months of the war in that hellhole, Andersonville Prison.

No, just a pen-pusher, a paper-shuffler, a requisitions expert—a big, fat nothing.

The man who'd shot him was a private, cleaning his mostly-for-show service pistol in the next office over.

Life wasn't fair, Jason thought grimly as he rode into town and found the barbershop. No, sir, it just wasn't fair at all.

Jedediah was just sitting down to his supper, and wondering what the devil had become of his son, when he heard a wagon rolling in, and saw Salmon Kendall on the driver's bench. Salmon reined in the team and jumped down, a grin splitting his face.

"What do you think, Mr. Fury? Isn't she grand?" He swept

an arm back toward the big Conestoga, which was quite obviously a different rig than the one he'd been limping along in.

"Why, I think she's a beauty, Salmon," Jedediah replied, and fought off the urge to scratch his head in wonder. Salmon and Cordelia Kendall hadn't a pot to piss in nor a window to toss it out of. How on earth could he have afforded a new rig?

"Mr. Kroeger, the man with the wagon?" Salmon went on, all in a rush. "He and his folks are havin' hard times, said that if he couldn't sell the wagon, they were going to burn it for firewood this winter. Wouldn't sell just the axle. So I traded him, my wagon for his, and I threw in a hog for good measure. What do you think of that?"

Salmon's hogs were fat and would make a lot of bacon and chops, and Jedediah knew the Kendall kids had named them, but he kept his counsel. "That's fine," he said, "right fine. Griggs look her over for you?"

Salmon gave a quick, happy nod. "Yes, indeed, and he pronounced her trail-worthy—a good deal better than my other rig, he said later on. I mean, after we left the Kroeger place. Why, he said my old rig was full of dry rot."

Jedediah nodded. "Happens. You'd best get your things unloaded from the other folks' wagons and into your own before they start to take a dislike to you, though."

"Certainly, certainly!"

As Salmon Kendall climbed back up to the driver's bench, Jedediah called after him, "You haven't seen my boy, have you?"

"Not since about five. He rode off toward town."

Jedediah nodded, as if that was exactly where Jason was supposed to be—blast him, anyway!—and waved to Salmon as he pulled out.

"Papa?" asked Jenny, sitting at his side. She had perpetrated the so-called stew on his plate. He probably could have sold it for axle grease, if it had a little less salt in it.

"What, baby?"

"What's Jason doing in town all this time?"

"I'm sure he's got a good reason, honey." He held out his plate. "Now, serve me up some more of that cornmeal mush."

Jenny sighed. "Corn bread, Papa. Corn bread."

Chapter 5

Jason was slouched in the steaming tub, half asleep, his back and shoulder having already been tremendously eased, when the voice broke into his consciousness.

"You the wagon man?"

He opened one eye, surprised to hear the female voice in the men's bathing house, but not entirely shocked by it. During the War, even lowly paper-pushers were welcome in Washington's bordellos. And it was precisely the tone of voice he'd expect to hear in one of those places, too.

The woman standing at the door way was dressed like a saloon girl. Probably was one, too, in those bright green spangles. And all that red hair, piled up on her head. She couldn't be much older than he was, even under all that makeup. Which she didn't really need, he caught himself thinking.

He opened the other eye.

"Yes, I guess I am," he said. "Miss . . . ?"

"Miss Krimp," she said. "Abigail Krimp. And you are?"

"Jason Fury, Miss." He caught her gaze flicking to the tub, trying to peek beneath the water, and set his sponge drifting to cover a strategic part of his anatomy.

She looked disappointed.

He smiled. "And may I ask what brings you . . . here, Miss Abigail Krimp?"

"My man would'a come, but he was busy. Sort of. So he sent me."

She was pretty enough, but if she didn't come to the point pretty soon, he was liable to toss that wet sponge at her. "About what?"

"About joinin' up!" she said, as if he should have read her mind.

"With the wagon train?" he asked. She sure didn't look like any pioneer he'd ever seen.

"Well, of course." Rather than showing signs of leaving, she sat down on the bench and crossed her arms stubbornly. She cocked her head. "You're a handsome devil, ain't you? And we wanna go to California, me and Rome. Be nice, havin' you along for scenery the whole way."

"And Rome is?"

"My man, you fool. The one playin' cards up at the Red Garter."

Now, Jason didn't have anything against gamblers, personally, but he knew his father did. Jedediah vowed, quite often, as a matter of fact, that they were all larcenous ne'er-do-wells and he wouldn't have one within five miles of any of his wagons.

So Jason pursed his lips for a second, then said, "I'm afraid you'll have to find yourself a different party to join, Miss Krimp."

This time, she shot to her feet. "Why?"

"Because my pa is in charge, not me, and he doesn't take to gamblers of any sort. Or fancified ladies," he added.

Suddenly, she looked stricken. "But there hasn't been a wagon train through here in two years! They all go down through Hastings!"

"Then I suggest you get yourselves down to Hastings, wherever that is."

She yanked a folded towel off the shelf behind her and

threw it at him. "Well, I guess that 'handsome is as handsome does' is the truth, after all!" she spit. "Thank you very much, and good luck with your journey!" she added snidely before she flounced out of the bathhouse, emerald skirts flashing.

He caught the towel before it could land in his bathwater, and set it on the little tub-side stool that also held an empty shot glass and a half bottle of bourbon.

"Thanks, Miss Abigail," he said to the place where she'd been, then closed his eyes and sank back down. "I'll probably be needing it. Sooner or later."

Women. Were they all crazy, or was it only the ones he ran into?

Roman LeFebvre sat back and watched the rube in the blue shirt scrape up the pot. Rome was having a bad night, and he should have bowed out of the game a good hour ago. Really, he should have gotten out years ago, but if a man was born stubborn, he couldn't help but hold onto it.

He was going to have to let go, though. All he had left was the hundred-dollar bill pinned inside his vest, and he'd need that to pay the hotel bill and get the rig out of hock, down at the livery.

He was saved from having to ante up again by Abigail's entrance into the saloon. He stood immediately when she stepped in, bowed out of the game, and made his way over to her through the crowd.

But when he got to her, she didn't have good news for him. He knew it by the look on her face, which he promptly backhanded.

Holding a hand to her cheek, she flushed red and looked around, embarrassed, then said, "It wasn't my fault, Rome. He said they didn't take gamblers."

He slapped her again, although no one in the bar paid any mind to it. This time, she fell back against the bar and began to cry. "I'm sorry, Rome," she sniveled. "It wasn't my fault, I tell you."

He raised his hand again, but this time withheld it when she cowered. "Get packed," he said. "Everything. Swipe the hotel linens, too." He started toward the door.

"Wh-where you goin'?" she whined.

He should have traded her off to that whoremonger down in Louisiana when he had the chance, he thought. But he hadn't, and now he was stuck with her.

"To do some business," he said. It was none of her nevermind, anyway. She ought to be happy he was going to take her along with him.

Midnight at the sleepy line of wagons, and Salmon Kendall was still too excited to sleep. Carefully, he slipped from under the drowsing Cordelia's arms and crept from the wagon, careful not to wake the children.

The night air was cool and crisp, so cool that he almost needed a jacket. He would have gone back up for it, too, except he saw a fire still burning down the line. Someone else couldn't sleep, either. He headed for it. Perhaps they'd have a spare cup of coffee.

To his surprise, he found Saul Cohen crouched near the fire, intently gazing into a small book. Cohen looked up. "Evening, Mr. Kendall," he said.

"Evening, Mr. Cohen," Salmon replied, then gestured with his hand. "May I?"

"Sit, sit!" said Cohen, and closed his book. He tucked it in his pocket. "And what keeps you from sleep this night?"

Salmon smiled a little. "My new wagon. Still can't believe it."

Cohen shrugged. "Why not? All the way since Maryland, we've seen them rotting in the fields. Once a man has got to where he is going, he does not have much use for a

Conestoga. Unless, of course, he's in the freight business . . ."
He stared into the fire, as if he were considering just that.

For a moment, Salmon felt a little cheated. And stupid, because now he did remember seeing all those wagons left out in the fields, in various stages of disrepair and decay. But then Cohen said, "So, you'd like coffee?"

"Yes, please, Mr. Cohen. If you wouldn't mind." Salmon like the way Cohen talked. It was kind of singsongy, sort of like German but with more of a thickness to it. Or something. He couldn't quite peg it.

"My name is Saul," Cohen said.

"And I'm Salmon."

The two men shook hands before Cohen handed over the mug, which Salmon took happily. He said, "Well, I s'pose I ain't the best businessman. I'm just happy I got the problem solved. Mr. Griggs said my old wagon would have just . . . *disintegrated* before we got to Colorado!"

Cohen nodded. "Dry rot?"

"How did you know?"

Cohen shrugged. "It's a gift."

Salmon laughed nervously, then sipped at his coffee, more to keep his mouth busy than because of overwhelming thirst. He didn't know quite how to respond.

Saul Cohen, who didn't seem aware of his discomfort, said, "You are a brave one, coming to drink coffee with me, even in the middle of the night. Don't you think that Milcher will be cursing your milk cow tomorrow?"

Salmon blinked in surprise. "We only have the one, and he's a bull."

"Still, he would try to curse him. Or maybe your chickens . . ."

"Why?"

It was Cohen's turn to blink. "Salmon, my friend, don't you know that I am a Jew?"

"You are?"

Cohen said nothing.

"But we used to live down the road from some Cohans, and their people came from Ireland!"

"Cohen, Cohan, so much difference one little vowel makes. . . ."

Salmon shook his head. "Well, I'll be dogged. I'll be double dogged!" He had never before known a Jew, but Saul Cohen didn't look like he ate babies or anything. If a body listened to Milcher, well . . . Then he mumbled, "Aw, that Milcher's an idiot. 'Tween you and me, I don't even think he's a real man of God."

"I am inclined to agree," Saul said, adding, "Sometimes, on these old Conestogas, the linchpins give out. You have a problem like that, you come see Saul Cohen. I'm no good for axles, but linchpins, I can replace. And for you, wholesale." He waved an arm toward his spare wagon, the one Salmon knew was loaded down with hardware.

"Thank you, Saul. I'll keep that in mind."

The two men smiled, having come to an unspoken agreement of friendship. It was the first, on the trip, for Salmon. He'd bet it was for Saul, too.

Salmon leaned back and took another swig of coffee, but this time it had nothing to do with nervousness. "That chicken your wife fried up for my family tonight? It was right good. Like for you to thank her for me. Those potato things were real tasty, too."

Saul nodded. "It was for her own happiness. She knew all your family's cooking things were spread out in other wagons. Besides," he added with a tip of his head, "you go to all the trouble to kill one chicken kosher, you might as well kill two."

Salmon chuckled, although that *kosher* part had him stumped.

"And of course," Saul continued, "they were your hens. We should be thanking you."

Salmon's chuckle turned into a roar that was broken only

by his wife's hissed, "Salmon Kendall! What are you doing out here in the middle of the night?"

He looked up and there she stood, cloaked in her old wrapper, her night-braid looped over her shoulder, glowering at him.

He scrambled to his feet. "Sorry, Cordelia," he whispered. And then he remembered himself. "Saul, this is my wife, Cordelia. Cordie, Saul Cohen."

Cordelia nodded. "A pleasure, Mr. Cohen. I've met your wife, Rachael. She's a wonderful cook."

"Saul," Cohen said. "And yes, my Rachael knows her way around a hen." He, too, got to his feet.

Cordelia smiled and said, "As you were, Mr. Cohen. I just came to rope my husband and bring him back to pasture."

Cohen slid back to the ground gratefully. He lifted a hand and said, "Good grazing, friend Salmon." Then the hand went to his pocket, and he pulled out that slim volume again.

"You, too, Saul," Salmon replied as he walked away, backward, with Cordelia resolutely pulling him along. "See you tomorrow!"

They were nearly to the wagon before Cordelia hissed, "You're making friends with him?"

Salmon put on his brakes, which nearly hauled Cordelia off her feet. He was a good foot taller than she.

"Why not?" he asked.

"Well, they're Jews, Salmon!"

"So?"

"Reverend Milcher says they killed our Lord!"

"I don't know about that, honey. And I'm pretty dang sure Saul Cohen didn't do it personally. Why, his wife made us dinner!"

"But the Reverend Milcher says—"

"You know, I'm pretty sick of the Reverend Milcher and his sayings. He's not even a good Baptist! He's not anything that I can figure. And he's tryin' to run everybody in this group."

"He's a good Christian man, Salmon."

Salmon sighed. "Not if he's holdin' it against the Cohens that a bunch of Romans crucified Jesus nigh on two thousand years ago. That's just plain stupid. Besides, I like Saul."

"But—"

"Stop bein' silly, gal." He patted her fanny. "Now, get yourself up in the wagon before you wake the whole camp."

Chapter 6

Two days out of Bliss, Kansas, Jedediah waved Jason to his side. He'd had a gnawing feeling that somebody was following them, but he'd only just seen the trace of a dust cloud on their back trail. Whoever it was, there weren't very many of them. However, he didn't like anybody riding his coattails, be it for good or for ill, and he intended to find out what was going on.

Jason rode his palomino up alongside Jedediah's roan. "What is it?"

No *Papa,* no nothing. No respect!

But he didn't take the time to jaw out the boy. He pointed to the low ridge they'd just traversed. "See that dust cloud?"

Jason squinted and shaded his eyes with the flat of his hand, scouting along the horizon. Finally, he stuck out a hand, pointing. "There?"

"Right. Somebody's dogging us. Take a man off the herd and ride back. See what it is they want."

"And if they want to rob us and take our livestock?"

"Guess you'll have to stop them, won't you?" Jedediah wheeled his horse and took off at a slow lope, toward the head of the train.

* * *

Jason sat there a moment, shaking his head. Everything was so cut and dried, so black and white, with his father. What was he supposed to do, just ride back and shoot whoever it was? That would make Papa proud, now wouldn't it?

Sniffing disdainfully, he at last turned his horse toward the herd, which was traveling off the wagon train's right flank. He loped on out to its edge, to Ward Wanamaker, who was riding a sorrel today. Ward reined the gelding in as Jason joined him.

"My father thinks we've got company coming up behind," Jason said without preamble. "Ride back with me and take a look, okay?"

"Sure," Ward said amiably. "But I can tell you right now what it is."

Jason cocked a brow.

"Buggy," Ward replied to the unspoken query. "Fella and a gal, and the back's packed full of their stuff, includin' three crates of chickens and a goose, and about six pink trunks."

"Pink?"

"Pink."

"Redheaded woman?"

"Yup." Now it was Ward's turn to arch his sandy brows. "You know who it is, Jason?"

"Think so," Jason said, disgust dripping from his voice. His pa wasn't going to be happy about this. He reined his palomino around and said, "C'mon."

The two men rode down the line of wagons at a soft lope, until they left the caravan behind and headed out over the open, empty prairie, toward the distant ridge and its thin skyward trail of dust.

Jedediah rode up next to the Kendall wagon, spotted Salmon on the driver's bench, and called, "How's the new rig working out for you?"

Salmon's face lit up just like a kid with a new toy. "Just fine, Mr. Fury, just dandy! She's sure a lot smoother, though

I suppose these help some." He pointed down to the folded blankets, quilts, and coats upon which he sat.

Jedediah said, "You're catching on, Kendall."

He let Kendall pass him while he looked back down the line. He saw Jason and Ward in the distance, heading back toward whoever was trailing them.

He figured it was somebody looking for a little free protection.

Probably not Indians, who wouldn't trail them for so long or so openly. The same went for raiders. Anyone counting on doing harm to the group would have done it long before now, and they sure wouldn't have been so dumb as to give themselves away by sending up a careless cloud of dust.

No, Jason and Ward would be all right.

He dug his heels into his roan and urged it up the line again, past Salmon Kendall, past Saul Cohen's two wagons, past the MacDonald rig, and up to the Milchers. Mrs. Milcher and all the kids were on foot, and the reverend was driving one-handed, smoking his pipe.

"Afternoon, Milcher," he called, tipping his hat.

"Good day to you, Brother Fury," came the answer.

Briefly, Jedediah ground his teeth. He'd just about reached the end of his rope with Milcher's affectations. He said, as evenly as possible, "Why don't you let your two littlest gals ride? They can't weigh much." Their mother was practically dragging them through the prairie grass.

"No, it's good for them, brother," Milcher replied. "Children need their exercise, just as young animals do. Makes them strong in their bodies, and strong with the Lord! Have you thought any more about Sunday?"

"I told you before, Milcher, this train doesn't stop for a whole day for anything, not even God."

"But the spiritual needs of—"

"You can meet those in your own time. Mine is going to be spent moving this train west."

He didn't bother to say good-bye. He simply let his roan

drop back to poor, beleaguered Lavinia Milcher and reached down. "Hand 'em up, ma'am," he said, nodding to the girls, and one at a time, she lifted them up to him.

"Thank you, Mr. Fury," she said. "They're exhausted."

"It's a long walk for a little mite," he said as he got the girls adjusted behind the saddle. "Hang on tight, now!"

He dropped back farther, to the MacDonalds' wagon. He wasn't fond of Hamish or his son, Matthew, both of whom were on horseback, at the head of the train. They were already hard at work establishing themselves as "community leaders," Jedediah thought with a snort.

But Megan was driving their rig right now, and she was as unlike her father and brother as a strawberry was from two sour pippins. Jedediah didn't think she'd mind the two little ones.

He was right. She accepted them with open arms, and let them crawl back inside the wagon, where they could lay down. They were asleep almost before their heads were down on the pillows.

"That reverend!" she whispered, so the girls couldn't hear. "He's just too pious to breathe!"

"I wouldn't argue that, Miss Megan," Jedediah said, gave one last glance toward Jason and Ward's diminishing figures, then rode off to fill in for Ward with the herd.

"I told you, lady, you're not welcome. Not you *or* your gambler friend."

The girl—Abigail Something-or-Other, he remembered—stared up at Jason dumbly. The slicker at her side was looking pretty annoyed, though. They didn't even come close to having a proper rig.

"But here we are," said the man, finally. He gripped his buggy whip like a cudgel. He was fairly tall, dark, and good-looking in a way that would have done him quite a bit of good on a riverboat. But not out here.

"That doesn't have anything to do with it," Jason insisted. "Turn around and go back while you still can."

"No," the man said, and he said it like he meant it.

Ward wasn't being any help either. He just sat there on his sorrel without saying a peep, and his attitude seemed fairly sympathetic toward the pair in the buggy.

Jason leaned forward in his saddle, elbows out, palms crossed on the saddle horn. He could sit here arguing with them all day, but he could see this fellow was so set on westering that they'd still follow along. He supposed he could just shoot the man, but then that would leave him with the gal on his hands and probably no way to get her back to a town. So he did the next best thing.

"All right," he said. "I'll let you talk to the wagon master." He wheeled his horse and set off at a gallop toward the train, which was out of sight. Ward came right along with him, and he heard the rattle and bang of an overstressed buggy trying to keep up behind them.

He allowed himself a little smile. The jolting ride up to the train ought to knock some of the pioneer spirit out of them. He glanced back just long enough to glimpse the woman holding onto the armrest and seat back for dear life, and the man braced stiffly—only his feet, pushing against the footrest, and his mid-back, pressed as if his life depended on it against the backrest, were still—both of their faces filled with sheer terror at being jolted skyward at any moment.

Smugly, Jason urged his mount into a faster gallop.

Within a few minutes, they were even with the train and had come up even with Jedediah, who had dismounted and was staring very unkindly at the newcomers.

"Get them the hell out of here," he said.

It seemed to Jason as if his father had taken all of fifteen seconds to evaluate the pair of interlopers. It was longer than he'd expected, actually.

"Told 'em, Pa," Jason said with a shrug, "but they wouldn't take no for an answer."

"That's right, Mr. Fury," Ward added. As if Jason needed backing up.

Still, he was glad for the words. His father looked uncommonly angry, which was very angry indeed.

"We don't want your . . ." His father trailed off, interrupting his famous "We-Don't-Need-Your-Kind-Around-Here" speech, and Jason noticed that his gaze had been momentarily distracted by a passing wagon. Milcher's wagon. And Milcher was staring down at the girl and her spangled dress like the very wrath of Judgment itself.

Jedediah seemed to gather himself. He looked the man in the face and asked, "What's your name, boy?"

"Roman LeFebvre," came the reply, "and my lovely companion is Miss Abigail Krimp. And I am hardly a boy, sir, although I thank you for the compliment."

"None intended. Everybody under forty is a kid to me." Jedediah idly scratched at the back of his neck, which Jason knew meant his pa was brewing up something.

"Tell you what, Roman LeFebvre," Jedediah finally said. "You fall in behind the last wagon. Once we camp for the night, we'll let the group decide whether you stay or go. Their decision's final, no ifs, ands, or buts. Fair by you?"

"Delightful, and fair as a Kansas court. And call me Rome, sir."

Jedediah stepped back up on his roan. To the complaint of saddle leather, he said, "Last wagon, Rome."

His father rode off in one direction, Ward rode off to join the herd, and LeFebvre turned his wagon around to meet up with the end of the line, which left Jason sitting there on his horse, watching the line of Conestogas move on by while he slowly shook his head.

Chapter 7

The Reverend Milcher took center stage after dinner, just as Jedediah had thought he would. As for himself, Jedediah leaned back against the wheel of his wagon and lit his pipe, getting ready for what would pass as his evening's entertainment.

"Now, you all know me, my dear friends," the reverend began, sweeping his arm toward the crowd in a semblance of humility. "I have brought most of you from the eastern shores of our great country. I have ministered to your needs and seen to your wants."

A few heads nodded in agreement, but nobody said anything.

"And I say unto you that these newcomers have no business amongst us. We are stalwart and godly men and women, pioneers all! We have no need for spangles and cards, for games of chance and ribald song."

Fewer heads nodded this time and a few folks frowned, but he wasn't getting any argument from anyone yet, Jedediah noted. He wondered if Milcher thought that the gambler was going to turn his wagon into a traveling honky-tonk, while his women played "Belly Up to the Bar" on Milcher's wife's damned piano.

"And I say, so long as we are cleansing our ranks, we should divest ourselves of the members of the Hebrew race amid our ranks. Let these crucifiers of Christ and these . . . entertainers . . . be cast out together, so that they may have each other's company on the return trip. I am not an unkind man, my friends. I would send no one into the wilderness alone."

There was a profound silence, during which you could hear only the stomp of a horse's hoof and the soft grunting of a pig.

And then Salmon Kendall, shy and quiet Salmon, stood up.

"Brother Kendall!" announced Milcher, obviously expecting a second to his motion.

"Excuse me, Reverend, but I don't know what you got against the Cohens here. Why, Saul and his Rachael have been good friends to me and mine!"

Thus began a heated debate that delineated—for Jedediah, at least—the two major camps among his pilgrims. Namely, those who wished to cross the land lugging a cross and the New Testament, and those who just wanted to get there, period.

Now, the MacDonalds—two of them, anyhow—were staunchly on Milcher's side. Surprisingly, so were the Wheelers, the Widow Jameson and her brood, and Milt Billings, although as a hired man, Milt had little say-so in the actual proceedings.

Dr. Morelli and his family kept their mouths firmly closed—afraid, Jedediah supposed, that if the Jews and the "fancy women" and gamblers were being picked on now, the Roman Catholics couldn't be far behind.

He probably wasn't wrong.

When you came right down to it, Jedediah was rooting for the gambler and his woman. Oh, he didn't like them. He didn't have to, he supposed. But it'd be worth the extra bother of taking the gambler along if it knocked the Reverend Milcher down a notch.

Jedediah would like that. In fact, he'd enjoy it more than he'd admit, even to himself.

They went on and on, these hearty pioneers of his, these escapees from civilized society. They argued and yelled and preached and hollered as if they were debating the course of the world instead of just one lonely wagon train of outsiders, of dreamers. And that was it, wasn't it? No matter what each one thought, no matter from whence he or she had come, they were all outsiders now. Outsiders, wherever they went.

And at long last, the outsiders voted to keep the Cohens, to keep the gambler and his woman, and to ignore Reverend Milcher's protests to the contrary.

Jedediah had good reason to smile.

He stood up, brushing his hand on his britches. "Glad that's settled," he said. He knocked his pipe's bowl against the palm of his hand. "One more thing before everybody turns in for the night." He threw a glance Milcher's way, to make sure he was paying attention. This was mostly for his benefit.

"I noticed a lot of little kids really dragging today," Jedediah said. "This is probably my fault for not saying something sooner, but I make it a rule on my drives that all kids under the age of ten walk only half days. It's too hard on them, otherwise. Everybody got that?"

The Reverend Milcher sniffed and disappeared into his Conestoga. But he'd heard.

"LeFebvre!" Jedediah shouted, waving a hand at the gambler.

LeFebvre, a winner's grin stretching his face, came at a trot. "Yes, Mr. Fury! What can I do for you?"

"You can pay me your share of my fee," Jedediah said, and stuck out his hand while he looked over the man's poor excuse for a rig. "That'll be eighty dollars, flat."

Abigail hummed to herself as she finished cleaning the supper things. She'd listened to the debates earlier, and was more than pleased that they wouldn't have to turn back, although she was more than a little miffed by Milcher's use of the term "ribald song."

She wasn't exactly sure what that meant, but she figured it couldn't be good, not judging by the tone he'd used.

Rome was still up there, talking to the wagon master, Mr. Fury. She'd learned he was the pretty boy's father, and she sighed without realizing it. That was one fellow she'd like to take a little buggy ride with, if it weren't for Rome.

Oh, well. Things were what they were. Rome couldn't keep her from looking, though.

Suddenly he was behind her, grabbing her around the waist.

"Oh!" she gasped.

He chuckled into her ear. "Oh, indeed, Abby!"

She relaxed a bit. He was in a good mood.

He let go of her just long enough to turn her about to face him. "You got any pin money, sweetheart?" he asked with a smile.

"There's thirty-five cents in my pocketbook," she replied.

His grip on her arm tightened. "No, I mean real money. It's gonna cost us eighty bucks to tag along with this crew. After I paid the hotel and the livery, I've only got forty left. And that's just barely."

Her arm was already throbbing, and her eyes welled with tears. "Rome, really, I—"

"You must have something stashed, honey. Something put by. How'd you buy that new dress? The green one? I sure didn't shell out for it." He began to slowly twist the gripping hand, and now her arm burned as well as throbbed. She thought she might faint.

"In my carpetbag," she whispered, afraid that at any minute she'd scream and give them away.

"That's my girl," he said, dropping her arm like she were nothing more than a rag doll. If she hadn't had the corner of the buggy to catch herself on, she would have fallen like one.

"Why do you have to be so mean to me?" she asked, rubbing her arm.

He already had her carpetbag, and was dumping its contents out into the dirt. "Because you don't tell me the truth, angel," he said, distracted by the bag. He pawed through her underwear and shoes and stockings until he found her little change purse, the one made out of soft deerskin with silver fittings.

He opened it and smiled as he counted out the money.

"You been holdin' out on me, Abby," he said at last. "Seventy bucks, even." He stuffed the whole roll in his pocket, then stood up. "I'm gonna go pay Fury. You clean this mess up, you hear?"

As he strode off, out across the circle made by the wagons, she heaved a sigh, then bent to pluck her clothing from the dirt. And as she did, her tears finally spilled. He'd taken her money, her savings. She'd never be free of him now. At least, not before three or four years more of working in saloons and brothels.

She'd been barely sixteen, orphaned, and living on the street when he found her and introduced her to the life, and she knew nothing else. It was a rough and cruel existence, and she had secret dreams of leaving it behind, of marrying, of becoming respectable. Now she'd be too old for anyone to want her. At least, by the time she saved up enough money to slip out of Rome's clutches.

Blast him, anyway.

She stuffed the last items into her bag, realizing that tomorrow she'd have to figure out how to do laundry on the move. She looked out, into the open circle, and saw young Jason Fury talking to another man, the one with whom he'd ridden out to their buggy. Ward Something? It didn't matter. The two of them were standing before a fire, and the light washed up over Jason, all golden and warm and enticing.

It wasn't difficult to imagine him making love to her, being tender and gentle and caring and . . . nice. Yes, nice.

He was looking better and better.

"Well," Ward was saying as they watched the gambler walk past them, "I guess they're stayin'. Your old man sure surprised me!"

"You're not the only one," Jason said. The only thing he could figure out was that his father was, in some way, using Rome and Abigail to put the Reverend Milcher in his place. If so, it had worked as far as he could tell. Milcher sure had his drawers in a bunch.

Which was just as fine with Jason, if the truth be told. He couldn't abide the man.

But then, he didn't like much of anybody on the train. There was an open, ongoing aggravation between him and Matt MacDonald. It was only a matter of time before it would come to blows, and everybody knew it.

He found Mr. Nordstrom haughty and stuck up, the Mortons—every single one of them, including Milton Griggs—too boring for words, and Eulaylee Jameson (and all three of her grown kids) too bigoted and narrow-minded to live.

And the rest of them, he didn't know well enough to dislike. He figured he would in time, though.

But he thought he kind of liked Ward Wanamaker, and he knew he liked the oldest Milcher boy, Tommy—probably because he was a frequent target of Matt MacDonald—and he was certain that he liked Megan MacDonald. The girl was pretty, with long, shiny, setter-red braids, sparkling green eyes fringed with russet lashes, and a fair, freckled face. And she made him laugh.

She was only seventeen, though, and so he hadn't made any overtures. Only seventeen, and bound to stay with her family out West, once they got there. He'd be headed back East. To college. Which was no place for a married man.

"What?" he said. Ward had been saying something or other, and Jason had completely lost track of it.

"Indians?" Ward said. "Where were you? Rhode Island? I asked if we should we count on a fight anytime soon."

Jason shook his head. "Hard to tell. Before the War, we could buy most of 'em off with cattle or trade goods. That's been years ago, though."

Ward nodded. "So you know 'bout as much about it as I do."

"I'd say you nailed it, Ward."

Saul and Rachael Cohen lay snug in their quilts, having tucked their three boys into the spare wagon and seen them safely asleep. Saul was pleased about the evening's goings-on, although he was sorry the subject had come up. Again.

"Will it ever stop, Saul?" Rachael asked, echoing his thoughts.

"You expect it to stop?" he replied. "How can it stop while these *goyim* are still so ignorant? Since the beginning of time, they've been ignorant. You think anything will change that?"

"I suppose you are right," she said, and snuggled closer to his side. "But still, I will pray for them."

He smiled. "Now you're sounding like Reverend Milcher, Rachael, always praying for people. Who don't want to be prayed for, I might add."

"Possibly, Saul," she said, cocking a brow. "But I have a more direct route." Before he could speak, she closed her eyes, and whispered, "No middleman."

Chapter 8

Three weeks, one broken leg, a busted collarbone, and one Piute episode later, the wagons found themselves cutting down into Indian Territory.

Electa Morton had tripped in a gopher hole and broken her leg below the knee, and was now teaching school from the back of her parents' wagon. Young Tommy Milcher, Jason's friend and admirer, fell from his horse and broke his collarbone.

As for the Piute, they had been a small band of stragglers, and had been bought off with the offer of three of Jedediah's "eating steers" from the herd, two blankets, and one hand mirror from Jedediah's box of trinkets. They'd ridden off, happy as larks.

But Jason was concerned. The wagons would be going through Comanche territory, and nobody but him seemed the least bit upset about this. Even his father, usually a most careful guardian, seemed unconcerned. Maybe Jedediah knew something he didn't.

He sincerely hoped that was the case.

They were two days into Indian Territory, and their surroundings had gradually changed from the endless grasslands of Kansas, where they had gathered buffalo chips for fuel to burn and bumped across seas of buffalo bones, to a rugged kind of half-desert, half-plains. The kids were more often riding than walking, even more than his father had decreed the night he had the blowup with Milcher.

Well, not a blowup, really, Jason corrected himself. It had been more like a quiet victory, without a threat made or a single blow struck.

But Milcher had been halfway quiet ever since, with the exception of Sunday mornings. Roman and Abigail had been left alone, and the Cohens had been unmolested, insofar as he knew, by either hand or word.

Hamish MacDonald, however, was becoming more and more of a problem. He had his own map, and it was his dogged persistence that had them taking this particular route. Jedediah had wanted to stay either farther north or cut down farther south—mostly to avoid the Comanche threat—but Hamish swore up and down that he had it on good authority—from his brother-in-law, who had settled in Houston some years ago—that lately, the whole Indian problem was much exaggerated, and mostly a fabrication of the Eastern newspapers.

Jason was surprised his father hadn't fought harder against Hamish. But he hadn't, and for the first time, Jason wondered if perhaps his father was getting too old for these trips.

Jason was out riding with the herd, and they were slowly moving over a hill of red earth about two hundred yards north of the wagons. Grazing had been good for the livestock so far, and they were all fat and sleek. He knew that wouldn't last long, though. The grazing was growing sparse, and would continue to grow thinner and thinner.

He swung farther to the north to bring in a stray calf when he caught a movement from the corner of his eye.

It wasn't much. Just a patch of color that shouldn't have been there. And he could no longer see it.

But he'd been well trained by his father, and he immediately called to Ward. "Get the herd down the hill!" And then he bolted down himself, toward the train, chasing the errant calf before him.

He came down so fast that his mare nearly skidded into the side of the MacDonalds' wagon, and he immediately shouted, "Circle the wagons in tight! Men, get your firearms ready!"

He cantered down the line shouting the same thing, over and over, to the shocked faces of the pilgrims, but they all sped up and made a halfway decent circle up ahead. He heard his father shouting instructions, too, while the herd of horses and cattle and such climbed down the hill and headed for the circle. The men left a gap between two wagons just wide enough to funnel the herd through, three and four at a time, then closed it tight as Jason galloped back.

It was just in time, too. He heard the whoops of attacking Indians breasting the hill's crest just as he jumped his palomino over the traces of Rome LeFebvre's silly little buggy. Leaping from the saddle and slapping his palomino on the backside, he crouched down beside Rome. His pistol was in one hand and his rifle was in the other.

All Rome had in his shaking hands was an old Colt Navy and a derringer. Abigail was crouched beside him, white with terror.

Jason saw their attackers now, and too clearly. They came boiling down the hillside in full battle regalia, with very serious looks on their painted faces.

Jason had met up with Comanche once before. He hadn't liked it.

He pulled up his rifle and drew a bead on one of the front riders. He fired.

And missed.

He cranked another shot into the chamber and aimed again. This time, his slug hit home.

By now, the suddenly formed camp was in a panic. Some of the men were doing as Jedediah had instructed back in Missouri—firing while their wives or kids reloaded. Others, including Roman, were simply frozen.

Jason wasn't one to waste time. He slugged Rome in the jaw, just hard enough to get his attention, and said, "Shoot, you idiot!"

When that didn't work, he shouted, "You know what a Comanche'll do to you if they get in here? They'll tie you to a wagon wheel, cut a hole in your belly, string your guts out while you watch, and let the pigs eat them while you're still living!"

Rome went to work with his gun. Abigail fainted.

Jason just kept on firing.

He fired, in fact, until he ran himself out of ammunition and had to make a run across the circle to the ordnance wagon. On his way, he dodged confused cattle and spooked horses, jumped over a dog, snatched up a wandering Milcher kid, and took a stray arrow just above his left elbow.

He handed over the Milchers' spawn, then reached across his body and broke the arrow off, so that only an inch of it protruded from his flesh. It was bleeding like a butchered hog, but he didn't have time for it now.

His father, who had obviously run dry himself, was at the ordnance wagon, and tossed him down a box of the right ammo for his rifle. His eye flicked to Jason's arm and he opened his mouth, but Jason shouted, "It's all right, Pa! Watch yourself!"

And then he headed back across, to the sounds of Indian whoops and cries, shouted curses, kids and women crying, and cattle and horses dying. He ducked down behind Salmon Kendall's rig. Salmon needed some help.

His wife, Cordelia, lay behind him, struck by a Comanche lance. Dead. His daughter, Peony, lay across her mother, sobbing. Salmon and his boy, Sammy Jr., both had rifles and were firing with a grim purpose. Sammy Jr.'s face was streaked with tears, but his expression was resolute.

Salmon just looked like he was in shock. Load, fire. Load, fire. Load, fire.

But he was accurate. Before him lay four dead Comanche,

one of whom had made it halfway past the wagon's whiffle bar. It was likely the Indian's lance that had killed Cordelia, Jason thought.

Quickly, he knelt beside Salmon, shouldered his rifle, and took a shot at the swiftly circling Indians. "Should have got yourself a repeater!" he shouted.

"No money!" Salmon shouted back as he reloaded. And fired again. He was a good shot, all right. Another Comanche dropped from his pony.

"Sorry about your wife," Jason added lamely.

Salmon paused, mid-reload. "Yeah. Those red sons of bitches!"

All business once more, Jason shouted, "Your kid isn't hitting anything. Have him load for you instead."

"Sammy!" Salmon barked, and it was done.

Across the circle, Jedediah had located Milt Billings, the only man of them who spoke any of the Comanches' lingo. Milt was emptying his handgun into the swarm at the time, so Jedediah waited until he stopped to reload.

"Milt!" he roared, to be heard above the noise of the battle. "Milt! Can you talk to these Indians? Tell them we'll give them cattle!"

But Milt, concentrating on loading his gun, simply shook his head. He looked up and shouted, "No way these boys are gonna settle for anything but the whole herd, goats, pigs, and all. And the girls."

Jedediah's blood ran momentarily cold. He'd known what the Comanche were after, but hadn't wanted to admit it to himself, hadn't wanted to believe their luck could be that bad. Why had he let Milcher and MacDonald talk him into taking this bloody route, anyway? If they got out of this, he was going to ride into Houston, Texas, himself, and take a good, hard kick at Hamish MacDonald's brother-in-law's backside.

Maybe his head.

And then he felt a sharp pain in his side.

"What?" he asked, much more softly than he'd intended.

He tumbled backward, and was lucky that his fall was broken by a steer who didn't step on him, once he was down. Suddenly, he couldn't see very well, which was strange because he'd always had eyes like an eagle.

Maybe it was later in the day than he'd thought.

Maybe it was getting dark.

That was good, wasn't it? The Comanche would break off their attack, come nightfall.

Vaguely, distantly, he heard someone shout, "Mr. Fury! Somebody get Dr. Morelli! Dear God, Fury's down!"

And then he heard no more.

Jason was over by Carrie English's wagon, helping Carrie and her daughter put some sort of system in place, when Morelli came for him. He had just about decided to send Gil Collins, one of the hired men, down to help her. She was a widow, and she was a lousy shot.

Someone put a hand on his shoulder, and he wheeled, nearly shooting Morelli in the chest. Morelli quickly blocked the rifle's barrel with his forearm—his quickened reflexes arising from the heat of the battle—and said, "Come with me, Jason."

When he added, "Now," Jason took him seriously, and shouted his apologies to the Widow English, adding that he'd send her some help.

Morelli said no more, just shoved his way through the milling, excited herd, leading a puzzled Jason. If there was something wrong, why hadn't his father taken care of it? He stopped following Morelli's relentless path when he spotted Gil Collins, who was helping the MacDonalds, who probably needed the least help of anybody. Both Hamish and Matthew were firing, taking down their share of the redskins, with Megan reloading like a maniac.

He shouted until he got Gil's attention, then told him to go help out down at the English wagon. And then he stood there, being shoved around by crazed cattle and spooked horses, until Gil got on his way, taking Megan along with him. Gil was a cipher, and Jason suspected he was a bit of a slacker, too, something they could hardly afford right now. But Megan was a fine shot, when she was allowed to do something besides reload.

Quickly, he caught sight of Morelli, who had paused and was waving at him frantically to hurry along. The roar of battle assaulted his ears as he pushed forward again, leaping over dead and dying livestock, shoving the living ones out of his way. He fervently hoped they weren't losing as many people.

And still, the whoops and screams and battle cries came. He suddenly realized he had no idea how long the battle had been raging.

Forever, maybe.

When he caught up with Morelli, he was standing over a prone, blanketed figure, and the bottom dropped out of Jason's stomach. The toe of his father's boot protruded from one end.

He said, "It's not . . ."

Morelli had the grace to look uncomfortable as well as saddened. "I'm afraid so, son. Your father took a lance through the lungs. There was nothing I could do."

Jason barely had time to absorb this—that his father, who had joked that he'd been through things that would have killed most men twice, yet lived to tell the story, could actually die—when a great roar and cry arose from the east side of the circled wagons.

Jason saw that the circle had been breeched beside the gambler's rig, and that there were Comanche inside their camp, driving out livestock, and taking captives. Women screamed in terror, girls cried hysterically as they were snatched up into the arms of mounted heathen, as men and boys alike tried their best to hold back the seemingly endless horde.

A tomahawk swung, and young Tommy Milcher, the boy that Jason had saved from a beating by Matt MacDonald, back in Kansas City, fell dead, his head nearly separated from his body. A lance split the air, and fatally pinned Miranda Nordstrom to the side of a wagon. Her husband, Randall, screamed and ran to her, putting a slug squarely through the neck of the brave that had killed her.

By the time Jason, Dr. Morelli, Hamish MacDonald, and Saul Cohen hastily worked their way through the terrified livestock, the Comanche were already riding off and had cut off their attack. They had a small herd of horses and cattle—"Got three of my goddamn Morgans!" Hamish shouted—and a small number of the older girls that had been at that end of the circle.

"I'd think you'd be more concerned about your daughter, Hamish," Jason said, clipped and hard, and began searching for Jenny. His sister had been wearing a yellow dress, he remembered. Where in that milling mob of confused and heartbroken settlers could he glimpse even a flash of that color?

Hamish set in to search, too, shouting, "Megan! Megan, girl, answer your father!"

Jason could find that yellow color nowhere in the camp. But as the Indians breasted a distant hill, he saw it. She was slung across an Indian pony, and as far as he could tell, she was still fighting her captor.

Good girl.

Good Jenny. She was a Fury, after all. And it was up to him to save her.

Chapter 9

Jason barely gave Morelli time to get the arrow out and patch up his arm before he was in the saddle. The weeping of women was all around him, and the silent tears of the men he felt, more than heard.

Lord knows, it was all he could do to keep his own tears back. He had lost his father and his sister, all that remained of his entire family. But he wasn't alone, he kept reminding himself. Nearly everyone had lost someone—man, woman, or child—either to the lance or the arrow or the blade, or to the kidnapping.

Milt Billings, the man who spoke Comanche, came along, as did Ward Wanamaker. They had to go along, because they worked for the Furys, which meant they now worked for Jason. And, oddly enough, Saul Cohen tagged along. Jason couldn't figure what Cohen was trying to prove, but he wasn't about to turn down any volunteer.

Except Matt MacDonald. Jason didn't want to ride with anybody who'd screw it up, which was something Matt was bound to do.

Instead, he told Matt and Hamish that he needed them both at the wagons. They were both good shots, and the Comanche could well come back.

And they bought it.

But Jason knew there wasn't a chance in hell those Indians would return. They'd gotten what they wanted.

He gave orders that the dead be buried, the injured be taken to Dr. Morelli's wagon, which was serving as their hospital, and that the dying livestock be put down as painlessly as possible.

He also gave orders that somebody get the dead steers dressed out and start them to roasting. He didn't want anything to be wasted. They'd need that meat.

Through the twilight, Jason and his group rode over the same hills the Comanches had traveled with their prisoners. Through the night, under the moon and the stars, they followed the savages' trail.

And then finally, at about three o'clock in the morning, they were just breasting a rise when Jason whispered, "Down! Everybody get down!"

He had spotted the camp.

Ward took the horses back down the rise and out of sight, while the other three men lay on their bellies, scouting the camp with binoculars or spyglasses.

Down below, all was quiet. Only a couple of small fires were still burning themselves out. There were a few teepees set up, but it didn't look to Jason like any sort of permanent camp. Probably just a raiding party.

"There's our stock," whispered Saul, at Jason's right. He pointed quickly to the northeast.

Sure enough, their cattle and horses, along with the Comanche ponies, stood quietly, dozing within a crude corral their captors had tied together from the plentiful tumbleweeds. It was staked, at intervals, by lances thrust down through the thickest part of the sage.

As Ward Wanamaker joined them, Milt Billings said, "This is gonna be easy."

Jason, lowering his spyglass, twisted toward him. "Easy? Just how is that?"

Milt looked at him like he was an idiot. "We just sneak down and drive off all the livestock."

"And what about the girls?" Saul asked.

"Oh," Milt said, and looked away. "I forgot about them."

Jason turned back to the camp and raised his glass again. "You've got too much of your mind on MacDonald's Morgans, Milt. You'd best be thinking about his daughter, instead."

Saul Cohen asked, "So, is anyone hatching anything close to a plan? I'm thinking that maybe we should just ask them nice, but then again, I'm thinking that's probably the best way to get them mad again."

"Don't take much," said Milt.

"Nope," echoed Ward, who was obviously at a loss, too. "Maybe Milt didn't have such a bad idea, Jason. I mean, Mr. Fury." This last part he added quickly, as if he'd just remembered Jedediah was dead, and now Jason was the top boss.

"It's still *Jason*." he said. "And you mean we should use that as a diversion?"

Ward nodded.

"Been thinking the same thing, myself."

"It could work," Saul said, sounding very unconvinced. He shrugged. "Or not."

"Guess I ain't so stupid after all," Milt muttered beneath his breath as the four of them backed down the slope.

Twenty minutes later found them creeping along the outside fringes of the camp. So far, so good, other than the camp cur that had started barking. Milt's cranky, growled "Shut up, dog!" in Comanche had quieted him, though.

Jason was in the lead, and he had just reached the makeshift corral. He pulled the knife from his boot and cut the first thin strip of buffalo hide that held the brush together, when he heard a scuffle behind him.

He wheeled to see Ward Wanamaker down on the ground,

fighting off a Comanche warrior. He ran back toward Ward, knife in his hand, when he was bushwacked by yet another brave and went sailing to the side. He hit the ground rolling, and brought the point of his knife up just in time. The young brave who had bowled him over stopped his attack quite suddenly, and stood there, a rifle in his hand and just out of reach, smiling.

Jason didn't think that smile of his was any too wholesome. Neither was the rifle, come to think of it.

He heard a yelp behind him as Saul Cohen was taken down—not permanently, he prayed. He could see Ward and Milt. Ward was on the ground. Milt was kneeling, head down. A Comanche blade was at his throat, and he looked like he was waiting to die.

He was likely the only sensible one among them.

Jason's pa had always said he didn't have much sense, though, and he wasn't ready to give up. To the young Comanche standing guard over him, he said, "Speak any English? You savvy American?"

The brave remained silent. "Milt!" he called.

Haltingly, a knife pressed to his throat, Milt repeated his question in the Comanche tongue.

Jason's guard barked something back to Milt, who answered him carefully. Then Jason's guard lowered the muzzle of his rifle, just a touch.

"You are Fury?" the brave asked, and Jason realized that as big as the brave was, he wasn't just young, he was a kid! And then he realized the boy had spoken in English.

"Jason Fury," he said, trying not to let all the surprise he felt show in his voice.

"A relation to the Fury called Jedediah?"

"My father," Jason replied, and couldn't keep the bitterness from his voice.

The brave didn't seem to notice, though. "I am son of Peta Nocona, Chief of the Quahada Comanche. My father knows your father, and is friend to him." The rifle's business end dropped a tad lower.

All of a sudden, Jason's future didn't seem so dark. He said, "Then you must be the one called Quanah Parker. My father spoke of you and your father. He traded with you often." In fact, Jedediah Fury had been one of the only white men who could ride in and out of Peta Nocona's camps, and keep both his hair and his intestines intact.

Quanah stared at him for what seemed like hours—but was probably mere minutes—then waved his rifle. "Why did he not come?"

"He's dead. Your raiding party killed him."

A few minutes longer of staring. No remorse, no apology, just that blank stare. Then Quanah said, "Stand up, Jason Fury. You are in no danger. Yet."

Once Jason got to his feet, he saw that although tall and imposing in physique, the boy was about sixteen or seventeen years old—and had light eyes. His father had mentioned those disconcerting eyes more than once. They were a steely gray, a legacy from his white mother—Cynthia Ann Parker, Jason thought it was. She'd been a captive, too, just like their girls.

Jason started to sheathe his blade back in his boot, but Quanah shook his head. "Drop it to the ground. Your guns, too." He barked a command at one of the other Comanches, and they all motioned their captives up, too, and divested them of their weapons.

They were making enough noise that the camp was waking. A few braves appeared at the flaps of their teepees, ready for action, but Quanah made sure they knew everything was under control.

"Why have you come here tonight, Jason Fury?" he asked. "Why have you come to steal our horses and cattle? You come to revenge your father, maybe?"

"I came to retrieve what was stolen from me," Jason said. He knew that if he gave in, even an inch, he'd be seen as weak.

"I've come for my cattle and my horses and my sister. My father's life cannot be taken back."

Quanah's brows shot up, and his smile widened. He swept an arm toward the slowly milling animals in the corral. "All these are yours? Will you play for them, Jason Fury?"

"Play what?" If this Indian thought he was going to sit down at a spinet and play "My Old Kentucky Home," he was out of his mind.

Quanah started walking, and motioned Jason along. They were of a height. "I have learned a new game," Quanah said, "from our friends in Mexico."

Jason's mind was suddenly flooded with what might define a game for Quanah, and his blood nearly froze in his veins. His father had told him plenty of stories about the Comanches' penchant for cruelty as sport, even cruelty to their own dogs and horses. He shuddered, but he followed Quanah inside a tent anyway.

Quanah motioned for him to sit down on the buffalo-hide rug that made up the floor, and it was only once he sat that he noticed Saul, Milt, and Ward come into the tent behind him. They squatted down next to him, in a line to his right.

Poor Ward looked like Jason felt—terrified. Milt looked resigned, as if he'd already given in to destiny and just wanted to get it over with. Saul, on the other hand, seemed fascinated with everything he saw, from the feathered headdress hanging back against one curve of the teepee's side and the scalp locks depending from Quanah's spears, to the tent itself. He seemed to be making mental notes on its construction.

The warriors who had been guarding them followed them inside, making for a cramped tent, and sat down behind them, still holding their own guns on them.

Not the most auspicious setting for a parlor game, Jason thought.

While Quanah threw some sticks on the little fire that had been dying in the center of the tent on a broad stone hearth of sorts, he said something in Comanche, and all of a sudden

Milt smiled a little. The braves behind them lowered the weapons they held, and seemed to relax. One even stifled a chuckle.

Well, Jason thought, at least it wasn't going to be a blood sport. The man behind him would have allowed himself a big belly laugh for that.

Quanah turned to Jason. "You play the game called craps? Blanket dice? Do you know it?" He gestured with his hand, as if he were throwing dice.

A few years in Washington, D.C., had taught Jason a lot of things his father wouldn't have approved of. He nodded. "I've played once or twice."

"Good," Quanah said. "I find it most amusing." He spoke quickly in his tongue to the other Comanche, all of whom hurried from the teepee.

Milt leaned toward Jason and said, "I'll be a badger's butt. He's sent 'em to wake the others, in case anybody wants to make side bets."

"You have dice?" a smiling Quanah asked, as if he were under the impression that all white people carried them by the bushel basket.

Most whites of Quanah's acquaintance probably did, Jason realized. The Comancheros, whites who were known to trade with and raid along with the Comanche, were a pretty rough bunch.

"You could be holding your horses for a minute?" said Saul's voice.

Chapter 10

Jason looked down the line. Ward shrugged. Milt shook his head. Saul rooted in his pockets.

"Saul?" said Jason.

"No. I have no dice," he answered. "But maybe I have something almost as good." And with that, he produced three sugar cubes from his pocket. "These will do, no?"

"Aw, there ain't no dots on 'em!" Milt sneered.

"There can be," Saul said, inspecting the cubes and discarding the one with the most wear on the edges. He held the remaining two out to Ward. "You'll hold, please? Lightly, so they shouldn't melt?"

Ward reluctantly took the cubes, and Saul went back to patting his pockets—this time, the ones on his vest. He finally came up with a few toothpicks, and smiled. He took the sugar back from Ward, and proceeded to go to work, drilling shallow, precise holes in the cubes with the end of a toothpick, then gathering a tiny bit of ash from the edge of the fire, and inserting some in each hole. Not much. Just enough to darken it.

When he was finished with the first, Jason held out his hand. "Can I see it?" he asked, and then turned it over in his hand, inspecting it closely. "Saul, this is a work of art."

Saul, working intently on the second cube, simply shrugged and said, "My Uncle Amos, he was a jeweler," as if that explained everything.

By that time, there was quite a crowd gathered outside the tent's flap. Jason heard muted voices muttering in Comanche, and an occasional chuckle. His gut tightened. He'd already lost his father this night. Now, he was gambling his sister and Megan MacDonald on the roll of a couple of sugar cubes.

Someone had brought the girls, too. They were shoved into the tent behind Jason and his three companions. Jenny, true to the Fury family temperament, looked mad as hell, but that didn't stop her from giving him a quick hug and whispering, "I knew you'd come. Where's Papa?"

He said, "Later, Jenny," and chanced a glance at Megan. She looked confused and a little teary, but not beaten. Good girl, he thought. The third captive was Deborah Jameson, youngest daughter of the widowed Eulaylee Jameson, and Deborah was the next thing to hysterical.

"These three are my first wager," said Quanah Parker, now deadly serious. "What do you have to match it?"

"All our firearms," said Jason.

"You forget, Jason Fury. We have already taken your firearms."

Jason acknowledged that with a brief nod. He didn't have a single thing on him worth trading. He looked at the men. Even Saul, who he was beginning to count on to get him out of rough patches, held his hands to the side, palms up. Nothing.

And then he had something akin to a stroke of genius. "We rode here on four horses, and one of them is a palomino mare. Only four years old, top stock. Will they do?"

Quanah nodded. "Is good enough. I would like to see this mare."

Jason shook his head. "Not unless you win them."

Quanah laughed, surprising Jason. "You are smart, like your father," he said at last. "You roll first."

Saul handed Jason the sugar cubes, saying, "They're not ivory, you know. Don't toss them too hard."

Jason nodded.

He took the homemade dice and shook them gently in his cupped hands. Then he closed his eyes, said a short prayer, and tossed them down in front of him.

He heard a shout go up outside before he was able to pry his eyelids open. Quanah sat, shaking his head slowly, while Saul and the others grinned from ear to ear, and Jenny suddenly hugged him from behind. One die read six, the other five. He'd won.

Thank God.

He whispered, "Jenny, is there anyone else?"

"No, just us three," replied his demolisher of kitchens and ruiner of meals. "Jason, you're wonderful, even if you're my brother!"

"And now I shoot," Quanah said, collecting the sugar cubes. He looked frustrated, and a little angry. It was not a handsome expression on one so young. "This time, it is the . . . stolen horses against your women."

"Cattle *and* horses," Jason said, "against our horses. Just our horses."

"No." Quanah's cold, gray eyes narrowed. "The women, too."

Nothing was more important to Jason than getting those girls safely back to camp. Not even Hamish MacDonald's fancy Morgan mares. "I guess we're done, then," he said, and started to get to his feet.

But the point of a spear against his shoulder sat him back down again. He didn't know who was holding it, but it didn't matter.

"This time, I roll," Quanah said, and Jason prayed fervently for a two, three, or twelve. You lost automatically if you rolled one of those.

The dice stopped rolling on the buffalo hide. A four and a two: six.

Quanah Parker shouted something in Comanche, and there was a lot of noise outside. Milt leaned toward Jason and muttered, "He said, the point is six. Or somethin' like that."

Quanah waited for the noise, presumably of side bets being made and covered, to die down, then gently shook the sugar cubes again. Jason heard Saul mumbling, "Seven, seven, seven, seven . . ." as though praying. Seven would be the only automatic loser Quanah could roll.

But Quanah heard it too. "Quiet!" he roared, and the spear point that had been pressing against Jason's shoulder suddenly arced overhead and landed next to Saul's throat. He gulped audibly and his eyes grew round, but he shut up.

Quanah threw the dice again.

Ten.

The warrior with the spear called the news outside, and again there was a noisy roil of voices.

Finally, Quanah called for silence, and rolled the dice again.

Eight.

This went on for some time, with Quanah trying to roll his "point" of another six, and failing each time, between bursts of activity outside the tent flap, while Jason and his men all silently prayed he'd roll a seven.

After rolling his third ten, Quanah threw the dice down and leapt to his feet. "These are loaded! You try to cheat me!"

Jason, to whom he'd made the accusation, forgot about the brave with the spear, and jumped to his feet, too. Once he was standing, though, he felt its tip press hard into his back. But one shouted, angry word from Quanah, and it pulled away. From the corner of his eye, Jason saw the spear-holder back out of the tent.

"Back with the women!" he said, and the men rose and began to back up. "All except you!" He pointed to Jason.

"You think I loaded sugar cubes?" Jason asked. "How the heck could I do that? They weren't mine, and playing craps was your cockamamy idea in the first place!"

From across the tent's tiny fire, Quanah launched himself at Jason. He landed with the force of a charging bull, and Jason was knocked to the ground, narrowly missing Megan, who scrambled aside and sent Milt sprawling into Saul.

Quanah's hands were round Jason's throat, throttling him, and Jason did the only thing he could think of: He brought up one knee, hard, between Quanah's legs. The pressure of Quanah's fingers immediately left Jason's throat as Quanah doubled up with pain.

Still gasping for breath, Jason took advantage of the situation and pulled Quanah back down by his beaded neck-piece, rolling atop him at the same time. Then he hauled off and punched him in the face, just as hard as he could.

"Jason, don't!" he heard Jenny cry out, but he hit Quanah again.

Quanah wasn't out, though, and when Jason came in to deliver the third punch, Quanah blocked it with a massive forearm, which then drove upward to clip Jason under the chin. It hurt like hell.

The blow knocked Jason upward and halfway out of the teepee, and when he looked up, he found himself surrounded by at least twenty angry braves.

From inside, he heard Quanah bark a command, and the crowd stepped back. Jason barely had time to make a sigh of relief before the gray-eyed brave was on him again. The two rolled about in the dust of the camp, slugging, slapping, kicking, and generally trying their best to murder each other, when Jason caught a glimpse of the opening of Quanah's teepee.

What he saw only made him madder.

Here he was, getting beaten to a bloody pulp and creating the world's greatest distraction, and there stood his entire party, girls included, watching the fight and cheering him on, when they could have been sneaking off to the horses.

He slammed Quanah with a hard right to the ear, and Quanah rolled him farther, catching him in the temple at the same time. One of the braves threw a knife down to Quanah, who snatched it up and held it at Jason's throat. Jason felt it break the skin, felt rivulets of blood flow down the sides of his neck.

He did the only thing he could think of. He smiled and said, "Your point was a six, Quanah?"

Suddenly, the blade eased away and Quanah barked out a laugh. He sat up, still holding the knife—which was, at least, now pointed to the side—then slowly stood up. "You are right, Jason Fury. It was a six."

He tossed the blade to the side, then held a hand down to Jason, who gratefully took it. When both men were on their feet, they dusted themselves off and checked their body parts for serious injury, and Quanah was still laughing. Jason couldn't help himself from joining in, although in his case, it was the sheer ridiculousness of the thing. Why Quanah was laughing was anybody's guess.

Maybe he was thinking of all the good, clean fun his boys would have later on, torturing them.

But instead of throwing Jason on the fire, he escorted him back to the teepee they'd tumbled out of, and resumed his former position. Jason and his people did the same.

"Jason, are you hurt?" Jenny asked.

"Are you all right?" Megan echoed.

Deborah Jameson didn't speak to him. She was too busy weeping.

"I'm fine," he replied, even though his throat stung like the devil and it felt like his jaw was broken.

After a few moments, Quanah found the dice again and inspected them for serious damage. Fortunately, they were the only things in the teepee that had escaped it.

With a grunt, he threw them again.

An eight.

He frowned, then gathered them again. Jason noticed that all this tossing and the friction with hands and the buffalo hide had worn the sharp edges of the sugar cubes away. There weren't many more rolls left in them.

Quanah muttered something, then threw the dice.

Jason held his breath.

"Seven!" shouted Saul, then clamped a hand over his own mouth.

"Seven it is," muttered Jason, who couldn't believe his luck. Now, of course, he had to be even luckier to get everybody, along with the livestock, out of the village and home safely.

It wasn't difficult at all, though. Quanah was a man of his word. They gathered the horses and cattle, including Saul's bullock, which his kids had named Mr. Cow—and which Saul greeted with a happy hug—and MacDonald's Morgans, and Jason left three of their meat steers behind. In the end, they had about fifteen horses and cattle to drive back to camp.

They rode out of the Comanche enclave fully armed and with no problem, gathered up the horses they'd ridden in on, and started back to the camp. It was coming dawn by then, and Jason was discovering new bumps and bruises every minute.

The girls were asleep on their horses by the time they came in sight of the circled wagons, but the drifting scent of roasting beef brought Megan around first.

"Food?" she asked, her pretty face soft and fresh with sleep.

"Likely more of it than you'll ever want to see again," Jason replied. He saw kids and women turning four steers on long spits over roasting fires in the center of camp, and men hitching a team to a dead horse, presumably to drag the corpse out of the camp, where they'd already dragged three others.

Dr. Morelli was still hard at work. He looked to be setting one of the Milcher kids' legs. Jason also saw Reverend Milcher out south of the wagons, presiding over the burials of the butchered whites.

Milcher was good for something, anyway.

Chapter 11

In the privacy of their wagon, Jason held Jenny tightly against his chest. She wept as if her heart was broken, which it most probably was.

"Hush," Jason soothed. "Shh, shh, baby girl."

"But why!" she cried. "Why didn't you tell me?"

"Because I thought it was best, honey," he whispered. He had been exhausted last night, and they'd never have made it back to the wagons if he'd told her about Pa. He was exhausted now, but didn't have any further to go. He just had to comfort her the best way he knew how.

"Jenny, you've got to be brave," he said, although he didn't alter his embrace. "We've all got to be."

"Why?" she beseeched him. "Papa's dead, Jason! Papa's dead. . . ."

She fell into another fit of weeping, and still Jason held her, trying by his actions to let her know that she still had somebody, even if it was only her lousy older brother.

Megan MacDonald, red-eyed and looking overly hugged and squeezed after her reunion with her father and brother, poked her head over the tailgate's edge.

"Excuse me, Jason," she said softly, "but you should come."

He still cradled his sister's head. "What is it, Megan?"

She climbed up into the wagon and made her way to him and Jenny. "Go see Dr. Morelli," she said, taking a sobbing Jenny into her own arms. "Now."

Once she'd given Jason time to get well clear of the Conestoga, Megan held Jenny away, at arm's length. "Jenny, listen to me," she began. When Jenny, lost in sorrow, paid her no mind, Megan shook her roughly, then slapped her across the face.

This finally got her attention.

"Ow!" Jenny exclaimed, holding a hand to her damp cheek. "Why did you do that? How can you be so mean to me?"

"Jenny, you're not the only one," Megan said, her voice soft. "We all lost someone, be it friends or family. And Jason, who was in here comforting you? Well, he lost his daddy when you did. Did you stop to think of that? Did you stop to think that he might miss him even more than you do? That the weight of being in charge and the responsibility of all of us is on his shoulders, now?"

Jenny slowly blinked.

"I don't mean to scold, Jenny," Megan went on gently. "I just think you should look at things from, well, a broader perspective, that's all."

"I-if I'd stayed in Kansas City, like Papa wanted, I wouldn't know about this. I wouldn't have had to know until Jason came home."

Jenny's voice was getting a little too floaty and far away, just like Mrs. Halliday, back home, right before she went crazy and took an ax handle to the family cat.

Megan said, "Don't you go getting ax-handle crazy on me, Jenny."

Jenny squinted at her curiously.

"I need you to get your grieving over with. *Jason* needs you to be done with it, or at least put it aside for a while, and come help up clean up after those blasted Comanche. The horses and cattle kicked everything to pieces last night. And the Comanches will be riding in here in a couple of hours to pick up their dead. Jason's going to need all the help he can get."

"But I'm so tired," Jenny croaked.

"Me, too."

Slowly, Jenny nodded.

"I'm going to leave you alone now, all right?"

Jenny whispered, "Yes. Thank you, Meg."

"You're welcome, honey," Megan said, and brushed a kiss over Jenny's forehead before she climbed over the seat and back down to earth. She heard Jenny's renewed weeping from inside the wagon, but at least it was more controlled, less wild, than it had been before.

It was true that Megan had lost friends in the raid, but no family, thank the Lord. But then, it was also true that Mr. Fury had been like a kind and good father to them all.

She looked across the circle to see Jason, Dr. Morelli, and the Reverend Milcher engaged in discussion, and set out at a brisk clip to join them. Or at least get within eavesdropping distance.

This ought to be a scrap worth hearing.

"You know, Milcher," Jason said in a conversational tone, "I've been trying to be nice to you on account of your losing Tommy, who I had a high regard for, myself, and your two younger boys getting hurt. But I'm just about ready to haul off and slug you."

Milcher had the audacity to look both surprised and offended. "Whatever for, sir?"

"You know damn well what for. You are not going to pile up those dead Comanches like so much kindling and set fire to them!"

"They're heathen," Milcher said firmly. "Murdering, thieving heathen at that. It's all they deserve."

Jason paused for a moment, his jaw muscles working overtime.

"Now, Reverend," interjected Dr. Morelli, "Jason said that the other Comanche were coming to pick up their bodies. We can't have them find a pile of ashes, now can we? Why, there's likely to be another massacre!"

"We're all shook out of shape, Milcher," Jason said, under control again. "We don't want to do anything that we'll be sorry for later. Quanah showed himself to be a fair man, last night, and I—"

"A fair man?" Milcher shouted. "Since when are any godless redskins fair men? Since when do those who murder and steal qualify as men at all? They killed my son. Do you hear me? My *son*! The one who did it could be right out there!" He swept his arm around the circled wagons, to where the corpses of the Comanche lay.

"When you find the one who did it, do you want to carve him up a little?" Jason asked. "Maybe take his scalp? Maybe hack off his balls?"

Milcher suddenly looked horrified.

Morelli muttered, "Now, Jason . . ."

"Go back to your wagon, Milcher," Jason said, "and think about turning the other cheek. Either grab some of that beef that's roasting, or comfort your wife—she lost Tommy, too, you know—or get some shut-eye. But when those Comanche show up to gather their dead, I do *not* want to see your face."

When Milcher climbed back up into his wagon, he immediately embraced his grief-stricken wife.

He looked about him as his children, who were mostly whole—other than the nine-year-old boy with a broken arm and the seven-year-old boy with a bandaged calf where a heathen arrow had found home and the fifteen-year-old boy who would never be with them again, never see the distant shores of California, never again join him in prayer—and the

Reverend Milcher collapsed into tears, muttering, "Oh God, my God . . ." into his wife's shoulder.

Alone, his hat in his hand and the noonday sun beating on the back of his neck, Jason slowly walked down the line of fresh graves. Someone had made crosses and simply written the names of the deceased. No niceties like dates of birth or death, no "beloved son" or "devoted wife." Just last name, first initial.

Here lay, now and forever, T. Milcher—plucky young Tommy; M. Nordstrom—quiet, plain-faced Miranda, who sewed like an angel; C. Kendall—Cordelia, wife of Salmon and mother to Sammy and Peony; R. LeFebvre—Rome, the down-on-his-luck gambler; S. Wheeler—Seth, part-time blacksmith and wheelwright, who had dreamt of opening his own saloon; M. Griggs, who had died from his wounds while Jason was playing dice with Quanah Parker; and, at the end of the row, his father.

J. Fury, the marker said. Except, in Jedediah's case, someone had taken the time and care to carefully write "Wagon Master & Good Shepherd" underneath in tiny, precise letters.

Obviously, someone who also had not thought highly of Hamish MacDonald's all-knowing brother in Houston. Or maybe it was his brother-in-law. At this point, Jason didn't much care.

All he knew for certain was that what he was left with was at least as many injured as killed, wagons with nobody to drive them—although he figured to leave Abigail Krimp's buggy behind and have her drive the Nordstroms' second wagon, the one that the late Miranda Nordstrom had been driving.

A picture flashed through his head, that of poor, plain Miranda, pinned to the side of a wagon by a Comanche spear, the life draining from her face.

He shook his head like a retriever fresh from a pond, as if he could shake that picture, all the bad pictures, from his head. He couldn't, though. He knew he'd live with them for the rest of his life.

"I suppose I should thank you, Fury, for gettin' my sister back safe," said a voice to Jason's left. It belonged to Matt MacDonald. When Jason looked over, there was a smug smirk on Matt's face.

"Consider it said," Jason said, gruffly. A conversation with Matt MacDonald was the last thing he needed right now.

But he quickly learned he was wrong when Matt said, "Pa sent me to get you. We're havin' a meeting. About who should take over now that your pa's dead."

A rush of anger surged through Jason's veins, momentarily replacing his sorrow. He slapped his hat on his head, pushed past Matt, and headed back toward the circle of wagons. "Take over, my Aunt Fanny!" he mumbled.

That big bag of wind, Hamish MacDonald, was behind this. He was certain of it.

Chapter 12

Jason was right.

When he hopped over the whiffletree of Salmon Kendall's wagon to enter the clearing inside the circle, there was Hamish, standing on a box—which he most likely carried around with him, just to orate from—sweeping his arms back and forth.

Quite a crowd had gathered around him, too.

As he angrily strode out to the center of the circle, Jason flicked his eyes from wagon to wagon, looking for Megan. Surely *she* couldn't be in on this!

He spotted her—sitting beneath Nordstrom's second wagon, knees hugged to her chest and her head bowed. In embarrassment, it seemed. It couldn't be easy having a father like Hamish. It could also be simple exhaustion.

". . . led us into the veritable mouth of disaster," Hamish was saying. He hadn't seen Jason yet. "Don't we need someone trustworthy? Don't we need someone seasoned? Don't we need—"

"Somebody who knows the way?" Jason broke in, from the edge of the crowd.

Chuckles and titters erupted across the throng.

"And somebody who don't have a know-it-all brother-in-law down Texas way," shouted Zachary Morton, their eldest member and head of the Morton clan. His brother's son-in-law had been injured in the fight, and at this moment lay in his wagon, suffering from a stab wound to the chest.

Morton's wife, Suzannah, slapped his arm, but she broke out in a grin anyway. At least, she covered her mouth with her hand, to keep from showing her picket-fence teeth. But her eyes sparkled like a leprechaun's.

"Jason Fury, you're only a boy!" Hamish shouted, and pointed a work-gnarled finger at him.

"Boy, maybe. A fool, no." Jason's temper was about to boil over, and he heard his father's voice in his head, saying, *Calm down, boy, just take a deep breath.* . . .

And so Jason shut up, letting his last comments hang there, in the air. The whole camp had gone quiet, waiting for Hamish's rebuff.

But before he had the chance to formulate something cutting, Jason said, "Everybody, I'd like your attention, if you please. In case you haven't heard, I gave the Comanches leave to come pick up their dead this afternoon, and I reckon it won't be long before they're here. Men, I want you to keep your firearms close at hand, but I don't want anybody flashing them at the Comanches. I want this to go quick and peaceable."

The Comanche arrived within the hour, and so silently that no one was aware of their presence until Milt Billings trotted over to Jason, who was helping Abigail Krimp move her few belongings to Randall Nordstrom's extra wagon.

"They're here," was all Milt said, and Jason looked up to see about fourteen or fifteen braves outside the circle, lifting the bodies of their fallen comrades onto the backs of the extra ponies they'd brought along. Several of the Indian ponies were still aimlessly wandering the scene from last night, and the braves rounded them up, too, and put them into service.

Quanah Parker was with them, which Jason hadn't expected.

This was a job you sent your minions to take care of, not one on which you went yourself.

But he was there just the same, mounted on a tall, Medicine Hat pinto, overseeing the others. He caught Jason's eye, and lifted a hand in greeting.

Jason reluctantly waved back. He could tell his men were getting antsy. Even a few of the women looked like they were ready, willing, and able to take on one of those braves with nothing but a couple of darning needles and a frying pan.

When he saw Matt MacDonald slowly pick up his rifle and, from the cover of a wagon, draw a bead on Quanah, he stole up behind him and banged him over the head with the butt of his pistol. Matt crumpled to the ground like a bag of brass doorknobs.

Which got Hamish all bent out of shape. He came charging over, shouting and blustering. Jason turned his gun on Hamish and hissed, "Shut up, you."

Fortunately, Hamish was shocked enough to do it.

The Indians slowly began to make their exit, leading their dead and wounded behind them, but Quanah rode closer to the circled wagons. Right up to Jason, in fact.

"Greetings, Jason Fury," he said, his face like a stone.

"Greetings, Quanah Parker," Jason replied. And waited.

"My braves say your doctor treated the few who still lived after the battle."

He did? thought a surprised Jason. But he didn't let it show on his face. He said. "Our Dr. Morelli is a good man."

"You will give him my thanks, Jason Fury. Until we meet again." Quanah reined his horse in a quick circle and galloped off to join his men.

"Which I hope is the twelfth of Never," Jason muttered.

"When?" demanded Hamish. Jason had all but forgotten him.

"When what?"

"When did that low sawbones sneak out to help those filthy redskins?" Hamish hollered.

Jason realized he was still holding his gun on MacDonald. He said, "Hamish, I haven't slept since yesterday morning. I'm tired and I'm cranky, and if you don't shut the hell up and stop causing trouble, I'm going to pull this trigger and damn the consequences. Do we understand each other?"

Hamish, a glower on his face, remained silent. Which, lucky for him, Jason took for an affirmative. He holstered his gun. "Now, if you want to do something useful, you'll put a party of men together and gather enough kerosene and brush to pile over those dead horses."

"Brush?"

"Yeah. Then set fire to 'em. No sense in drawing in any more predators than we have to. We're not leaving until tomorrow morning."

Dr. Morelli was leaning against a wagon wheel, dozing, when Jason walked up.

"Morelli?"

He cracked open an eye. "Ah, Jason! How goes it?"

"Not too good. Can you take another look at my arm before I go to my wagon and catch some sleep?"

Worry furrowed Morelli's brow. "It's worse? What in the world did you do to it, anyway?"

He asked Jason to remove his shirt, took a look at the wound, and frowned. "Been scrambling around in the dirt?"

"Exactly that," replied Jason wearily. "Plus a few other things."

"Why in heaven's name were—?"

"Don't ask," Jason cut in.

Since Jason looked no more eager to tell him than he did to swim the English Channel, a silent Morelli went to work. At last, after he'd removed the bandages and cleaned the wound with water as best he could, he picked up a bottle of alcohol.

"This is going to sting like hell," he warned, then watched Jason nearly ram his first through his own forehead when he splashed some on the open wound.

"I hear you helped the wounded Comanche," Jason said through clenched teeth.

"Yes," Morelli said, unsure of just how Jason had reacted to that news. "I took an oath to help all those who need my services."

"That was real kind of you, Morelli," Jason said, "and also real stupid. You've got Hamish MacDonald against you now. And more than likely, whoever else he's told."

"I know. I've already had words with Mr. MacDonald." Morelli wouldn't repeat those words for all the money in the world.

Jason seemed to understand. "Erase 'em from your mind, Morelli. I'm in charge, and I say thank you. You did the right thing."

Morelli couldn't help smiling. He tied off the new bandage and quickly fitted Jason with a sling. "Not neccessary. Now, get some sleep, son. And throw out that bloody, filthy shirt."

Saul Cohen, who'd slept through the entire day, woke quite pleasantly at ten that evening to find Rachael waving a plate of beef, peas, and potato pancakes under his nose.

"Ah, my beauty!" he said with a yawn.

Rachael smiled. "You're meaning me or the food?"

"I can't mean both?" he replied, and kissed her before he took the plate from her hands.

The boys, all three of them, were curled like dozing puppies at his feet, Rachael was with him, no one was hurt, Mr. Cow was tied to the wagon's tailgate, and the camp was quiet. The past day and a half seemed like some horrible nightmare.

He hoped he'd never have it again.

He and Rachael repaired to the driver's bench while he ate his meal, and afterward, they stayed for a while and just stared up at the moon, drinking some of the sweet wine she'd brought along. They held hands.

"Was it horrible, Saul?" she asked him softly. "Getting the girls and the horses and cattle back, I mean. When you had to go into the Comanche camp."

"Yes and no," he said.

"Why so?"

"Yes, because, my darling, I was so frightened that I almost soiled myself."

She giggled softly. "I think I can understand. And why no?"

He reached into his pocket and produced two much-used sugar cubes.

"Sugar?" She waved a hand at him. "Throw those things away, Saul. They are full of dirt specks from your pocket!"

He held them closer to her. "You're noticing anything out of the ordinary about those 'dirt specks'?"

She took one and held it to her eyes as she twisted it in her fingers. "No, I . . ." And then her brow furrowed.

"Saul Cohen! You were gambling?"

He leaned back against the puckered, gathered edge of the wagon's canopy, pulled her close to him, and said, "It's a long and very strange story I'm going to tell you, Rachael Cohen, so you might as well be comfortable."

Beneath her father's wagon, Megan MacDonald feigned sleep. A few feet away, on the other side of the man-height wagon wheels, her father, her brother, and the Reverend Milcher were having a discussion that she was most interested in hearing.

Normally, she wasn't one to eavesdrop, but here she was, doing it twice in the same day. But they'd woken her, and how could she be expected to go back to sleep, especially considering the topic they'd woken her with?

"Well, something's got to be done," the Reverend Milcher was saying. "The boy has no respect for his betters. Absolutely none!"

This had been going on for at least the half hour Megan had been awake.

"I'll agree with you there, Milcher," her father said. She could tell he'd lit a cigar by the meter of his pauses, and also because of the stench the wind wafted her way every once in a while.

"He's an ass," muttered Matt.

"Shut up, Matt," her father snapped. "You got any bright ideas, Milcher? I already tried it the *American* way. Tried holding a meeting and a vote, and what did I get for it? Sass, plain sass, I tell you! It puts me in mind of when I was a lad, in Scotland. Jason Fury's puttin' on a bit of the English, I think!"

Megan knew what he meant by "puttin' on the English"— that Jason was acting like he was better then everybody else— but she didn't agree. Jason *was* better than they were. Out here in the wilderness, at least, and probably anywhere. That wavy, yellow hair and those blue, blue eyes, those dimples and that cleft in his chin and . . .

"You know I would not willingly wish harm on any man, Mr. MacDonald," Milcher said. "It is not the Christian way. And I know that you wouldn't, either."

She heard her brother make a muffled snort, and her father say, "Course not, Reverend. I had nothing so drastic in mind. After all, he saved my darlin' lass, sleepin' there beneath the wagon, from those filthy redskins. And wipe that smirk off your face, Matthew."

"I'll be bidding you good night, then, MacDonald. I'm afraid that for now, we are in the grips of an ethical dilemma that can't be settled by three men in one night. And I must get some rest. It's been a long day."

"That it has, Milcher."

"May God bless you both, then." The reverend walked away, his footsteps scuffing softly off into the distance.

Megan knew that her father wouldn't do any serious physical harm to Jason. He just wasn't that kind. Oh, he might try to undercut him at any and every given opportunity, and he might even get mad enough to hit him. But he wouldn't kill him. She doubted the Reverend Milcher would even take a swing at him, despite all his complaints. He was too much of a coward.

They just didn't like taking orders from somebody younger than they were, that was it. They were men accustomed to being in charge.

Matt, though, he was different.

Megan loved her brother, but she knew that at heart, he was a bully. And, she thought, he might just be a dangerous bully.

Deadly, even.

Jason had to be warned, and it looked like it was up to her to do it.

Chapter 13

Jason sat his mare on a ridge not far above the plodding wagons, watching their progress. He was glad they'd left the plains of Kansas far behind. There, one wag had said, you could look farther and see less than anywhere else in the world. Jason had to agree with him.

Kansas, then the Indian Territory, and now New Mexico— beautiful and bleak at the same time.

Since early in the trip and the trouble with Salmon's axle, Jason had been able to avoid stopping near any towns. He did this for two reasons: His father had tended to avoid them, saying that introducing strangers to the mix made for trouble. The second reason was some paperwork that had inexplicably floated across Jason's desk during the War—probably from somebody's attempt to effectively "lose" it.

These papers had told of a wagon train headed west that had cut through the Utah Territory and stopped by a town. A short time after they moved on, they were attacked by what was alternately reported as a band of Indians, or settlers disguised as Indians, or both.

At any rate, the pilgrims were slaughtered, probably by radical Mormons, although the case had never been fully looked into due to the more pressing issues of the War with the South. That had been the Mountain Meadow Massacre.

Jason wasn't taking any chances.

Despite their problems with the Comanche, they were still what would be considered a rich wagon train. They had more than their share of livestock, and between the cloth and so on in Randall Nordstrom's extra wagon and the hardware in Saul Cohen's, the train would be prime booty for any plains pirates that happened along.

There hadn't been any more talk of replacing him since a fortnight past and that Comanche business, although Megan had come to him the next morning. She'd warned him to watch out for her brother, Matt—as if he needed anyone to tell him that—and she'd repeated the conversation she'd overheard between her father, her brother, and Milcher.

He made note of both, however, although he had to admit that he took more notice of how pretty she looked that morning. That, at least, was real and visible. And touchable.

Although he hadn't. One hand had started toward her shoulder, but he'd stopped its movement. There was no future in it, was there? And he was a man intent on realities, on things that were tangible. So he hadn't touched Megan. Not a friendly hand on shoulder, not a tender, brief brush of her cheek, nothing then, nothing since, because she didn't fit into his plan for the future, the one in which he took these people where they wanted to go, made his way back East, went to college, and then on to big, important things.

But lately, he was having a harder and harder time keeping his hands off her. Hell, he couldn't stop thinking about her. He even dreamt about her, about his lips on hers, about the softness of her throat and the thin, velvet skin of her eyelids. Tantalizing, disturbing dreams of his arms about her, in the night, and what they would do together.

He gave his head a shake, trying to rid it of such thoughts. He had no business thinking them. What he ought to be thinking about was Jenny.

His little sister hadn't been the same since they'd lost their father. The sparkle was gone from her eyes. He hadn't expected it to return this soon, but he'd thought that he would have seen some hint, some vestige of it at odd, unguarded moments. But no, nothing.

Oh, she went through the motions. She drove their wagon every day, helped make camp at night, helped with the cooking—which, fortunately, had turned into a more communal affair—but she wasn't anywhere near the same boisterous, opinionated, curious, girl-brat Jenny he'd known all of her life.

He was beginning to think that perhaps she'd be better off if he just dropped her off somewhere. He knew a few people along the route, people that he'd trust to keep his only sister safe until he came for her.

Of course, that had been before the War, years ago. There was no telling if any of them were still alive. It was a hard life, west of the Mississippi. And the farther west you went, the tougher it got.

He comforted himself that they'd be out of Comanche territory soon, but then, that only meant they'd be going into Apache country. The Apache weren't that much of a threat, unless, of course, you were a Mexican, a race of people against whom the Apache seemed to hold a special grudge. The wagons would travel south of Tucson through Apache Pass, which was the heart of Chiricahua Apache territory. His father had told him plenty of stories about them, none of them too appetizing.

They were in the New Mexico Territory now. They had just forded Ute Creek with no problem, and were in sight of the Sangre de Cristo mountain range, which at this far distance looked misty and insignificant. He figured to make Santa Fe, just past the southern end of the Sangre de Cristos, within ten days. That is, if they kept moving as fast as they had.

This was his one secret pride—that he was making better time than Jedediah ever had made when ferrying settlers over the Santa Fe Trail. Of course, outside of that incident in the panhandle of the Indian Territory. That had been a piece of really bad luck. Or good luck.

Jason guessed it all depended on how you looked at it. He'd been tremendously aided by good weather and a distinct lack of Comanche, which he was beginning to think might have something to do with Quanah Parker. They had also been fortunate to find water when it was needed, when their reserve barrels were nearly dry, and had been able to find not only enough to drink and water the livestock, but to refill their barrels completely, every time.

But he knew that his father would be proud of him. And for some reason he didn't entirely understand, because he and his father had spent most of their time disagreeing over nearly every conceivable subject, this gave him a great deal of pleasure.

He'd put Ward temporarily in charge of leading the train. Milt and Gil could handle the livestock for a while. The animals were fat, still, and not inclined to be spooky or stampede. He watched the wagons pass him, swinging south, followed by the herd and remuda.

He sat a moment longer, his thoughts drifting back to Megan MacDonald, all red hair and freckles and Celtic charm, and then, finally, he nudged the mare with his knees, cantering to catch up with the wagons.

The rain started at about three in the afternoon, and Jason had to choose between trying to hurry the wagons along and thus beat the rising waters to the next ford, that of another branch of the Canadian River, or stopping exactly where they were in an attempt to let the waters go down again before they reached their banks.

He chose the latter. Wisely, he hoped.

There was no shelter of trees, the terrain being rocky and open, the substrate gravelly, with most vegetation no higher than a bush. Jason circled the wagons as best he could, in the face of what had rapidly become a hard pelt of rain, and brought the herd within the circle. Lightning had a tendency to spook cattle, but when they were firmly surrounded by a comforting fence, or in this case, a circle of wagons, they wouldn't be tempted to bolt.

Rounding up the entire herd tomorrow, if they were hidden in every nook and cranny for three miles around, was the last thing he needed.

He helped a few folks unhitch their draft animals, gave Olympia Morelli a hand with her wagon's canopy, untying it on one side and stretching it out overhead and mooring it by poles to make a covered porch of sorts. It had fallen upon Olympia, along with Rachael Cohen, to do most of the cooking since they were both extraordinary cooks. Oh, the other women helped with stirring or chopping or basting things, but it was those two who kept them fed, preparing the big evening communal meal.

Beneath this canvas-canopied area, Rachael and Olympia set out a large table—packs of cleavers, big wooden spoons, skillets, and cook pots—while a few feet away, out in the rain, Jenny tried to get a fire lit.

Jason meant tried, because the sage she was using was green, and the rain wasn't helping matters. They'd used up the last of their buffalo chips a few days ago, but even that wouldn't have helped. When damp, they were unlightable, and nobody would want to handle them, anyway.

Jason was about to go to her aid when, from across the camp, Megan came out of the rain, bearing a burning torch of twigs beneath her duster, which she held over her back and head and outstretched at arm's length to shelter the flames. He watched as she and Jenny then worked the twigs beneath the pile of brush and brought it to a hissing blaze.

This happened at roughly the same time that various members of the party began to arrive with chickens—one here, two there—already dressed out, and vegetables.

He smiled at the sight of those chickens. Saul Cohen had said that Rachael put her foot down. "If your cooking Olympia and I are going to do, the least you can do is make the food ready, and by that, I mean you should clean it on the inside *and* outside!" she'd announced to the other women.

From that day forward, vegetables had arrived peeled or chopped or washed. Chickens had arrived plucked and gutted, and goats, deer, and antelope had arrived skinned, gutted, and either already on the spit or cleaved into quarters.

Out of respect for Rachael, Olympia requested that no hogs be slaughtered. None were.

For folks that the Reverend Milcher had wanted to leave behind at the side of the road, the Cohens were turning out to be real leading citizens.

Jason was thinking this just as Lavinia Milcher showed up with a pot of sliced carrots and what looked like chopped onions. She stayed on while the other women just dropped off hens or vegetables or bags of flour or cornmeal, and proceeded to fix the dish herself. Jason figured it must be something her kids liked, though God knows why. When he was a kid, it would have taken the militia to get him to eat carrots.

Rather than being pressed into kitchen duty—Rachael already had Saul cutting up chickens into pieces for frying— Jason walked over to his wagon, leading his palomino mare. Once there, he stripped her of saddle and bridle, and fed her a rasher of oats and barley, topping it off with a handful of corn. While she munched her supper, he walked out through the herd and found his father's roan, Gumption, which he led back to the wagon. He filled Gumption's nose bag with the same mix he'd just fixed for Cleo.

He patted her sleek, golden neck. "Gonna give you the day off tomorrow, Cleo," he said to her before he turned toward Gumption. "'Cause *you're* getting fat." He patted the roan's rump, then climbed up into the wagon.

Jenny was inside, hunched over a book.

"Hello, daredevil," Jason said with a hopeful smile.

She looked up. "Daredevil?"

"Saw you and Megan lighting the fire earlier. Good job."

"Thanks," she replied, without expression, and turned back to her book.

Jason tried again. "What you reading, Jen?"

She held it up, showing him the spine at the same time she said, *"Moby Dick."*

Jason grinned. If she was reading, she was feeling more like herself. Maybe he wouldn't need to leave her off in Santa Fe after all.

Rain pelted the canvas overhead now, and he heard thunder in the distance. He found himself a place to sit, then took off his hat. "Gonna be a goose-drownder."

Jenny said, "A toad-floater."

He grinned back. "We've got to get you started on Jane Austen, Jenny."

She looked up, head cocked. "Why?"

Jason closed his eyes and shrugged. "Just think you ought to be reading some 'girl' books, that's all."

"What?"

"Don't holler at me. I'm sleeping. And wake me for supper."

He heard her let out an exasperated groan, but then it was over, just like that. He fell asleep to the sound of raindrops pelting overhead.

Chapter 14

Three men stood on the banks of the raging creek, now grown to a full-blown river after last night's rain. The rain had stopped hours ago, but it seemed there was no end to the runoff from the Sangre de Cristos.

"They look so far away," Saul Cohen said dreamily.

"Not so far as they did yesterday," added Salmon Kendall.

"Near or far, doesn't matter," said Jason bitterly. So much for his record-making trip to Santa Fe. They could be stuck here for days, and he said so.

"Days, Jason? That long?" Saul asked. "It's moving pretty fast. Seems to me it ought to empty out those mountains in no time."

Salmon shrugged. "Mayhap it's not that deep?"

"Oh, it's deep, all right," Jason said, "and it's running fast. You're right about that, Saul. We'll make camp here, well back from the creek." He turned and pointed farther from the shore, to a line where the grass and brush weren't bent over and slicked with mud. "I don't want anybody closer than ten feet from the other side of that flood line, and have everybody set a rock behind their wheels."

Saul's brows flew up. "The water, it was up here, wasn't it? But that's a good thing, no? See how far it has gone down?"

Salmon shook his head. "Looks to me like it only had to go down two or three inches to back its way down there, Saul. This here's pretty flat land, where we're standin'."

"What're you bunch of old hens doin'?" came Matt MacDonald's voice from behind them. He was riding up. "Let's get to fordin' that thing." He jabbed his finger toward the swollen banks of the creek.

Jason, as usual, was highly tempted to yank him down off that horse and just plain haul off and slug him. But, also as usual, he held himself back. His back to Matt, he just said, "Can't be done."

"Did you try? Did you even try to ride across?"

"It's very deep, Matthew," said Saul. "He should know, shouldn't he?"

Matt snorted. "Yeah? Well, when was the last time you were through here, Fury? Eight, ten years ago?"

"Six," Jason said.

"Well, a lot of things can change in six years," Matt said. "Hell, that's more than half a decade!" And with that, he goosed his horse into a quick trot, heading straight toward the edge of the water.

Jason hollered, "Hey!"

Saul and Salmon both shouted, "Stop!"

But Matt entered the water, which quickly rose from his horse's fetlocks to knees and hocks. *Any time now,* Jason thought. Then, quite suddenly, it was as if the world had dropped from beneath Matt's horse.

They were both in the rapidly moving creek, with the horse struggling to keep his head above water while Matt tried to stay in the saddle.

"Oh, cripes!" Jason swore softly, then yelled, "Get off! You're drowning him! Get behind him and grab his tail!"

Matt acted as if he were deaf and continued to cling frantically to the horse's back.

"Matt! Matthew MacDonald!" Hamish came thundering up behind Jason and the others. "Jason, get him out of there!"

"Been trying," Jason said. Matt was in the current now, and he and his floundering horse were moving swiftly away. "He won't listen."

"Matt, boy! Can you hear me?" Hamish called. If he could hear, Matt gave no sign. "Dammit, Fury! Do something!"

Jason said, "Give me your horse, Hamish."

Hamish got down and handed over the reins without question.

Jason swung up into the saddle, and took off at a lope, parallel to the swollen creek bed, silently cursing all the while. He knew why he was the one everyone counted on to save this idiot, but wished he'd been at the other end of the forming camp. And then felt guilty for thinking it.

When he came up even with Matt, he pulled Hamish's rope from the horn and shook out a loop. He'd try for the horse's head, but he'd be happy to just get a rope on Matt. The horse could make it out by himself without Matt impeding him.

But his loop snagged the horse's head. He quickly tied the end of it around the horn, and then, praying that Hamish had paid somebody better than he or Matthew to train it, commanded, "Back! Back, old son!"

Lo and behold, the rope grew taut. Matthew's progress was halted, and his horse began to turn in the water, and then slowly began to swim diagonally against the current, toward Jason.

"Good boy. Back, back . . ." Jason kept on talking calmly to Hamish's horse, and the tall gelding kept doing his best to please.

And then Matt's horse began to struggle. Jason knew he was having a hard time kneeing his way over the crest of the bank and carrying Matt's weight, too. So he tried again.

"Matt! Get off him and grab his tail! He'll pull you up right after him!"

Matt shook his head vehemently. Mr. Big Man Matt MacDonald was scared to death, and Jason knew it—and if he didn't get over it pretty damn quick, he was going to get both himself and his horse killed.

"Can I help?" huffed an out-of-breath Hamish, who had apparently run after him.

"Yes," said Jason. He quickly slid down off the horse and told Hamish, "Don't let this horse move until I tell you, got it?"

Hamish gave a quick nod, and Jason took off, running downstream toward Matt and his horse. Once he hit the water, he grabbed the rope to help him keep his balance. He knew that the water would be about waist high on him, unless he went over the invisible bank that Matt's horse was struggling against. He didn't plan to get that far.

Fighting the current, he waded out to about ten feet from the horse's head and called to Matt again. "Get off the damned horse, you fool! He can't make the bank with you on him!"

Nothing. No response.

He walked five feet closer, halving the distance between them. "Matt! Turn your head toward me and look."

Slowly, Matt's head came around. He appeared to see his father, because Jason thought he saw just a touch of relief on his face.

Jason said, "If you're afraid you're going to get kicked, dismount and work your way forward till you can get you hand on the rope, okay?"

This time, Matt nodded. He let go of the reins, much to his horse's relief, and grabbed a handful of wet mane instead. Jason could tell that he'd freed his feet from the stirrups when his backside bobbed to the surface and he began to pull himself forward.

He nearly drowned his horse in the process, but at last he had the rope in his hands and hauled himself forward, hand over hand, to Jason, who said, "You can stand up, now."

Matt did, and seemed surprised when the water was that shallow.

"Get back up to dry land," Jason said. "Tell your father not to let that horse of his move a muscle."

Matt, who was feeling well enough to grumble, threw Jason a sneer and worked his way around him. Jason waited until Matt was halfway back to his father before he moved forward, toward the horse.

He managed to grab one of the reins, snaking along the top of the water, and softly said, "It's all right, old boy. You're safe. Calm down, easy, easy." Slowly, the terrified animal relaxed a bit. Although his hooves still churned the water.

"All right, fella, now this is going to take a little work from both me and you, but we can do it, can't we?" Jason kept on, holding his tone even and light and comforting. "Sure, we can. We won't let that dumbhead be the end of us, will we, boy?"

He snagged the other rein. "All right now, I'm going to let go of this rope. Things are easier when you can breathe, aren't they? And I'm just praying that I won't get swept down in there with you. Now, when I jerk your reins, you just come along with me, just like coming out of a stall that's dug down a mite from constant cleaning, right?"

Jason closed his eyes for a second in silent prayer, then braced himself against the current and let go of the rope. He jerked the reins. "Hup, boy, hup!" he cried.

And the pinto clambered over the crest of the bank, just as easily as a cat running up a tree.

With the horse's bulk to keep him from floating off downstream, Jason threw his arms around the beast's neck. "Good boy!" he cried, then added, more softly, "Atta boy. We weren't going to let that idiot kill us, were we? We're made of tougher stuff than that."

Behind him, on the bank, he heard Hamish applauding and his cries of, "That'a boy, Jason! Good job!"

And then another burst of applause broke out—Saul,

Salmon, Dr. Morelli, Megan, Jenny, and a few others had gathered to watch the little drama in the creek.

Jason flushed, grinned, tipped his hat, and began to lead Matt's horse out of the water after he removed the loop he'd tossed over its head. He noticed that the more shallow the water grew, the less the horse shivered—and the more he did.

He shook his head. Jenny would have him smothered in quilts and drinking tea for the rest of the afternoon, if she was truly back to being the old Jenny.

Piled with quilts and grudgingly sipping at the hot tea she'd forced on him, Jason sat silently in the back of the wagon while Jenny sat on the driver's bench, the closed copy of *Moby Dick* beside her.

He was quite the hero, her brother, although he'd never see it that way, let alone admit to it. She was proud of him, truly proud. He had saved Matthew's life. Even Matthew admitted it, and he had more than his share of pride. This she knew. But she couldn't help but admire him, anyway. He had other qualities that more than made up for that tiny shortfall.

Oh, but he looked commanding when he rode that big spotted gelding of his. And he was handsome, too, handsome as the day was long, with those flashing blue eyes and those cleanly chiseled features and that devilish grin. He'd been so brave to try and ford the creek by himself.

And he was going to be very rich someday. Not that a thing like money mattered to a girl like her, she reminded herself.

But it never hurt, did it?

She wondered . . . If she begged and pleaded with Jason long enough and hard enough, would he leave her behind once they reached their destination?

True, she was only fifteen, but plenty of girls her age were already married and had children.

Which was exactly, although she hardly dared admit it, even to herself, what she was hoping would come about, if she could just figure out how to get Matthew's attention in that way.

She knew that Jason didn't much care for him, and that the feeling was mutual. But then, they were of an age, weren't they? She supposed it was natural for jealousies to arise between them.

Mrs. Matthew MacDonald.

Mrs. Matt MacDonald.

Jenny MacDonald.

Well, a girl could dream, couldn't she?

Chapter 15

Megan MacDonald carried another pot of coffee to her wagon, and her brother, the idiot. Honestly, how could anyone be so blind? And stubborn.

It amazed her that he had lived to see twelve, let alone twenty. Always doing exactly what he'd been told not to do, always disobeying orders since the time he knew what orders were. And he always suffered for it, which meant that she always had to take care of him in the aftermath.

She half-wished he'd break his leg or something, some injury that would keep him immobile and out of trouble, for a while at least.

But he didn't, so she just kept patching him up and pouring him coffee and bandaging his blisters. He wanted to be in charge, he wanted to be the one everyone trusted. He wanted to be Jason.

What he didn't understand was that trust like that wasn't given, it had to be earned. And Matt did his best to earn nothing except the occasional sneer. She loved him, but . . .

After she dropped off the coffee, for which she received little more than a grunt from the still-shivering and quilt-wrapped Matt, she went to check on his horse. Jason had stripped him of tack, or maybe it had been her father, but the gelding still needed a rubdown. Even in the sunshine, he was shivering.

She went to work on him with a couple of old burlap bags, and soon had him fairly dry and looking a good bit more comfortable. She looked around for Jason's palomino mare, and saw her tied to the Fury wagon, her nose bag on and moving rhythmically with the gentle grinding of grain against molars.

Leave it to Jason to think of his horse first.

Leave it to Matt not to think of his horse at all.

Her smile turned into a scowl. She was embarrassed enough by Matt's actions, but there stood her father, bragging to the Reverend Milcher on his boy's idiocy.

"Rode right out there," Hamish was saying loudly, while he waved his arms about. "Wouldn't take that upstart's word for nothing. Says he would have made it across, too, if Jason had warned him about the current instead of yelling at him to get off his horse. Trying to get my Matthew kicked to death, that's what Jason Fury was up to."

Now, even Megan knew that you should slip off a horse that was going down under you in the water. Slip off and grab his tail, out of reach of those pummeling hooves, and just float along after him. She'd done it herself once, when she was younger and certainly more stupid. And she'd done it out of instinct.

Apparently, Matt couldn't do the right thing even when he had specific instructions.

But then she felt bad. She shouldn't think such things about her only brother, even if he acted like a lunatic half the time.

Well, three quarters.

She turned Matt's horse free and started back toward the wagon. But then she remembered that Matt was in there, and went instead to the Fury wagon. She could use a visit with Jenny.

It didn't hurt that Jason was inside, either.

* * *

"I'd stop with the talking young Fury down, Mr. MacDonald," Saul said as he led his draft horses out to graze.

"Matthew did a foolish thing," he went on. "I know. Wasn't I there? And I think that most of the other people think so, too, and that what Jason did—going out there after him, I mean—was truly brave."

Hamish answered him with a sneer, and then, "Aw, mind your own beeswax, Jew."

Saul said nothing, just gave his head a slow shake and proceeded with the horses. He'd given up on Hamish.

Some had suggested to Saul that oxen would be better for pulling his merchandise wagon, but he liked his Shires. They were sure-footed, very strong, and gave him no trouble. Rachael could drive them all day without incident, and ten-year-old David had no difficulty controlling them, either.

Perhaps Saul would be sorry later on, but at the moment he was glad he didn't have two teams of oxen to deal with. Let alone one. He supposed it would be like having two teams of Hamish MacDonald to contend with each day.

This, he could do without.

"Good for you, Saul," said a voice. It was Salmon Kendall's. He'd led his team of mules and horses out to graze, too. "I overheard what you told MacDonald. He's sure a piece of work, ain't he?"

Two at a time, Saul let his big horses free. The ground practically shook as they trotted away!

"And he reproduced in kind," Saul said, still staring after the Shires.

Salmon laughed loudly as he loosed his mules. "You can sure say that again. Matt's a skunk's behind if ever I met one."

"They're getting set up for dinner," said Saul, who had turned around. He watched his Rachael carrying a bowl of something or other over to Olympia Morelli's cook tent. "I wonder what it will be this evening."

"Sure as hell ain't gonna be nothin' as exotic as pronghorn," Salmon replied. "At least, I ain't been out huntin'. Doubt anybody else has, either."

Saul caught sight of Hamish, leading a party of four men and armed with a big knife: what he'd heard several of the other men refer to as an Arkansas toothpick.

"It will be beef," he said, just as his attention was diverted by the sight of a pretty, young blond woman with a six-year-old girl and a terrier pup tagging at her heels, walking down toward the shoreline. She carried a blanket and a long pole. He pointed. "Isn't that Carrie English?"

"Beef? How do you know? And danged if it ain't, and she's got Chrissy and Rags with her, too."

They watched as she spread out her blanket, sat down on it, summoned Chrissy away from the water's edge, and baited her hook.

"She gonna fish for her dinner?" asked Salmon, as if he'd never seen a woman fish before.

"I believe she is," replied Saul.

Rachael had told him that the petite midwife was running short on supplies already, and it was likely she was trying to keep up her end by supplying a major portion of at least one supper.

He added, "I'll go see, shall I?"

And then, when he'd walked ten feet, it suddenly occurred to him that Salmon had lost his wife, and just recently. It wouldn't hurt for Salmon to go help a pretty widow, would it?

"Salmon!" he called. "Hey, Salmon!"

And as Salmon turned around and approached him, he thought, *Better her than the Widow Jameson, at least.*

Eulaylee Jameson and her daughter, Cynthia—just as plain, dark, and beetle-browed as her mother—were, at that moment, carrying a basket of canned goods to the cook tent. There were home-canned tomatoes and peas and potatoes in this haul. Yesterday had been strawberry preserves, apricot jelly, and enough dried apples for three pies.

Eulaylee, Cynthia believed, was getting more than a little sick and tired of this community cooking business. The way Eulaylee would see it, her preserves were hers, period. According to her mother, nobody could cook or can as well as she could, anyway, so why should she be forced to share with a bunch of people who didn't know which end of the ham to keep for yourself, and which one to send to the church poor drive?

"Philistines," Eulaylee muttered under her breath.

"Yes, Mama," said the long-suffering Cynthia. She didn't have much more charm than her mother, but she was at least relieved that somebody else was doing the cooking without demanding that she be pressed into service.

Her sister, Deborah, had been in a state ever since the men brought her back from the Comanche camp, and their mother was doing nothing to make things any better. To hear their mother tell it, you'd think that Deborah had held up her arms and said, "Take me!"

And their brother was no help, either. A mama's boy to the end, Elmer was the one who'd planted the idea that Debby has been a more than willing captive.

The peckerwood.

Sometimes, she'd just like to punch him. Except that wouldn't be very ladylike, would it? Cynthia was constantly concerned about being a lady. After all, she was practically an old maid, and she'd thought that perhaps she could find herself a man on the trip west.

So far, she wasn't having much luck. Jason Fury and Matt MacDonald were too young, although they were both highly attractive. Hamish MacDonald was too old and too gruff and reminded her too much of her mother.

Salmon Kendall and Randall Nordstrom had both lost their wives in the Comanche attack and were both of about the right age, but she didn't think it would be proper to single one of them out quite yet.

She'd give it another week or two, although her mother had been nudging her toward Randall Nordstrom since the very day they shoveled the first grave dirt over his poor wife.

And then there were the hired men. But somehow, Cynthia felt she was a little above Milt Billings and Ward Wanamaker and Gil Collins, even though she found herself fascinated by Gil. He had such nice blond hair and such a clean, straight nose. . . .

"Cynthia! Honestly, girl. Get your head out of the clouds!" her mother snapped. They were at the cook tent already, and she helped her mother swing the basket of preserves up onto the table.

Olympia Morelli—who was getting far too big to be decently out in public, Cynthia thought—took the jars from their basket, thanking them effusively for each one. That Jewish woman was there, too, and smiled at her.

Cynthia looked away, embarrassed to be noticed.

Her mother had refused to eat any supper the first couple of nights that Rachael Cohen helped with the cooking, but all those good smells finally got to her. She finally ate. But she still wouldn't admit it was any good, even though Cynthia had caught her scraping her plate more than once.

"Roast beef tonight, Mrs. Jameson," a smiling Olympia Morelli said to Cynthia's mother. "Mr. MacDonald is slaughtering a steer. Your tomatoes, peas, and potatoes will make wonderful side dishes."

Eulaylee grunted a response, then abruptly turned and walked back toward her wagon. Cynthia curtsied, said, "Thank you, I'm sure," to Mrs. Morelli, and trotted to catch up.

Eulaylee glanced up the bank, then froze. Cynthia nearly ran into her.

"Well, would you take a look at that!"

Cynthia followed her mother's pointing finger to the figures on the creek's bank, about a hundred yards away.

"Why, I believe that's Salmon Kendall with Carrie English! And his wife's not dead a fortnight!"

Actually it had been more than three weeks, but Cynthia knew better than to open her mouth.

"Why don't you have Salmon Kendall following you around?" her mother wanted to know.

"I didn't think it was proper to—"

"Proper, my bustle! Well, it's probably too late now. You're going to stay an old maid all of your life, Cynthia Ann Jameson, unless you start baiting your line for Randall Nordstrom! He's probably a better catch anyway."

They had reached their wagon.

Eulaylee climbed up first, wagging her large backside at a frowning Cynthia, who followed, muttering, "Yes, Mama."

Chapter 16

It was ten in the morning before Milt and Ward rode back into camp with the news that although the water had significantly retreated, there wasn't a decent place for fording within miles. Ward's horse was covered with drying mud up to his belly, and Milt reported that the meadowland on either side of the creek was all in the same condition—waterlogged.

For the first time, Jason was at a loss. The main part of the creek bed itself was probably eight to ten feet deep with a sharp drop-off on either side, worn that way by all the rainstorms since he'd last been through with his father. There was barely a trickle of water going through it today, although a few muddy sinkholes existed where large carp, washed down from somewhere upstream, gasped their last.

"What you thinkin', Jason?" Ward asked. "Build a bridge?"

Jason smiled momentarily. "Out of what?"

Ward looked around at the featureless landscape and gave a sheepish grin. "Oh, yeah."

But then Jason recalled a story his father had told him, about taking a train of settlers out to Oregon, in which he was faced with a similar problem. Jason said, "On the other hand, Ward, you may not be far from wrong."

"Huh?" Ward scratched the back of his head, bobbing his hat up and down.

"You feel like digging?"

Ward's nose wrinkled. "I must be feeble, Jason, 'cause I don't know what in tarnation you're talkin' about."

Jason said, "You will, Ward. You will."

By two in the afternoon, Jason had put together two gangs of men for the work.

Hamish MacDonald wasn't happy.

"If I wanted to wreck my pants and boots, I could've just stayed home and dangled 'em in the creek," Matt said as he slipped into his oldest trousers.

"That blasted Jason Fury," Hamish grumbled. "This whole thing is his fault. I saw a map. We could have swung farther south and crossed the Canadian River all at once, but nay, we have to ford every bloody branch of it. And what kind of fool calls a river 'the Canadian' this bloody far from Canada, anyway? We're practically in Mexico!"

Matthew jerked a boot on. "Damned if I know," he said without expression.

"And now that little brat of a lad has us *digging* our way out! Might as well try digging to China, I say!" Hamish grabbed a shovel and tossed it to Matt, then grabbed the other one for himself.

"Tell him, then, Pa. Or tell your friend Milcher. I already know how you feel about it."

Hamish glowered at his son good and hard, but those parental glowers didn't work like they used to. Honestly, he didn't know what was going on with his son. Or the world in general, it seemed.

Digging! Manual labor. The hired men should be doing this, not every man in the bloody camp.

It offended Hamish's entire sense of class structure.

"Pa?"

He turned toward Matthew. "What?"

"This time, aren't you the one putting on a little too much of the English?"

Before he realized it, Hamish did something that he had often had the inclination to do, but never had. He slapped his son across the face, just as hard as he could.

"Sass!" he roared as Matthew picked himself up off the floor of the wagon. "You're as bad as Jason Fury, sassing your betters."

Matthew, his cheek red with the imprints of his father's fingers and palm, merely smiled. Which only made Hamish madder.

"I don't know what this world is coming to." Hamish climbed down out of the wagon, leaving his ungrateful son to his own devices.

By three in the afternoon, the two teams of men had dug down the near slope of the bank. Jason had them start well back at a narrow angle, digging their shovels into the sodden earth and emptying them down into the creek itself.

By the time they pitched the last shovelfuls down into the creek, the earth they'd uncovered was dry and the creek bed was a quarter filled with earth.

Then they started on the walls of the opposite bank, digging down the muddy water way and casting the refuse at their feet. Jason planned for them to dig the path two wagons wide, and on a shallow slope both down and up, filling the creek itself halfway to the top of its original bank.

Things were going along quite handily, too, aside from the grumbling from Hamish and Matt MacDonald, when he heard sounds approaching from the way they had come.

"Everybody, get your guns. Get back to the wagons and your families." It didn't sound like marauding Indians, but it could very easily be brigands and thieves. They were driving wagons. At least, it sounded like they were.

He had only reached his own wagon when they came into sight: a wagon train, just like theirs. It was somewhat smaller and battered. Some of the wagon canvases showed signs of burning and they had no herd or remuda.

Jason, his rifle over his shoulder, jumped down from his wagon and walked forward, holding up a hand. The incoming wagons stopped, and a middle-aged fellow, his graying head bandaged and one arm in a sling, rode out to meet him.

"Had some trouble?" Jason asked.

"Comanche," the wounded man said. "They killed nigh on half of us—men, women, kids, it didn't matter—before they ran off our herd. We're half-starved, mister. Best we've done since the attack was a deer, three days back."

"Well, settle your wagons here, friend. We'll feed you, and we've got a doctor, too."

"Bless you, son, may God bless you all," came the broken-voiced reply. Jason could see tears brimming in the man's eyes. "What are you called, son?"

"I'm sorry," Jason said. "I'm Jason Fury, sir."

"Well, by God." The man took off his hat and slapped it across his heart. "You any relation to my good friend Jedediah Fury?"

"His son, sir."

The man let out a happy hoot. "He here, or are you leadin' this whole shebang by your lonesome? Oh, and I'm Colorado Gooding, leadin' what's left of this tattery crew to Santa Fe."

"I've heard my father speak of you, Mr. Gooding," Jason said, and held up his hand, which Gooding shook. "But I have bad news. My father was killed on the trail a few weeks back. Comanche, possibly the same band that attacked you."

"Lordy," breathed Gooding as he bowed his head. "Ain't nothin' good in the world anymore? The great Jedediah Fury, dead and gone."

Jason suddenly realized that he felt much the same. There

had been so much to take care of, so many people to handle and manage, that he hadn't had time to mourn. He hadn't thought he needed to. But right now, in the presence of this stranger, he found himself crying just like a kid.

He wiped his eyes with his shirt sleeve, but that didn't stop the tears from falling. Before he realized what was happening, Colorado Gooding had dismounted.

"We're all gonna miss him terrible, son," Gooding said, and he was crying now, too. "Somethin' terrible."

Jason didn't know how long they stood there, in the middle of that meadow, weeping. All he knew was that when it was done, he felt better. And he was pretty damned glad that Hamish and Matt MacDonald hadn't been there to see him.

"Sorry," he said as he finally backed up and stood erect. He gave a final wipe to his eyes. "Didn't mean to go all blubbery on you, Mr. Gooding. My pa always taught me that men don't cry."

Gooding actually chuckled and sniffled at the same time. "Well, Jason, even your pa couldn't be right about everything. And call me Colorado. Now tell me. What are you folks doin' stopped out here on a nice day like this?"

They moved Gooding's wagons around half of Jason's, in a semicircle, and then Jason showed Gooding the dig. Gooding immediately added what few able-bodied men he had left to the project, and then sent the others to Dr. Morelli, who was obviously thrilled to be able to put down his shovel and pick up instruments more suitable to his profession.

The digging was finished by nightfall, and once again, the men butchered a steer and the womenfolk put together a meal. Gooding's people ate ravenously.

Jason, Saul, Morelli, Salmon, Hamish, Colorado Gooding, and a few of Colorado's men all sat near the main campfire, eating good barbecued beef, hot corn bread with butter and jelly, and a variety of canned vegetables from practically every wagon in Jason's train.

"You sure it was Comanche?" Hamish was asking.

"Sure as the day I was borned," Colorado replied. "Filty bastards."

"I wonder why they let us off so easy," Hamish mused as he helped himself to more coffee.

"I'd hardly call it 'easy,'" Jason said. "And we had quite a few more men with guns."

"That knew how to use them, anyway," Colorado said with a shake of his head. "We was damned lucky to keep our scalps."

One of his men, a big Swede called Thorson, nodded in agreement. "We are lucky to be eating this good meal with you, to have lived this long. I lost my brother and his wife, and even I took a spear in my leg."

"Lucky I caught it when I did, Thorson," said Dr. Morelli. "You were pretty close to gangrene."

"Didn't your people have a doctor in their number?" Saul asked in amazement. "Or sugar cubes?"

Colorado blinked, then shook his head. "Closest we had to a doc was a midwife. But she got killed right off. And what's sugar cubes got to do with anything?"

Jason said, "Long story, Colorado."

"You say you knew Jason's papa?" Hamish asked.

"Me an' ol' Jedediah Fury go way back to forty-nine," Colorado replied. "You know, when everybody and his brother went gold-crazy? Why, practical every other feller in the country was off to see the elephant, and it was folks like me and Jedediah what took 'em there."

"Elephants? There are elephants where we are going?" Saul asked, his eyes wide.

Salmon, sitting next to him, whispered, "Not really. I'll tell you later."

"More than once, me and Jedediah met up somewhere and hooked our caravans together," Colorado went on. "Strength in numbers and all that. By God, this is fine beef, Jason. My regards to the cook."

"Cooks," Jason corrected him, catching Megan's eye.

"In fact, I was thinking—if Jason ain't got no objections— that mayhap we could tag along with you as far as Santa Fe."

"That where you're headed, then, is it?" Hamish asked.

"Yup. All right with you, Jason?"

"Fine by me," Jason said.

Chapter 17

The two trains, now one, crossed the creek the next morning, saving the Widow Griggs, whose late husband, Milton, had installed a cast-iron bottom in his wagon, and had carried an anvil in it, for last, right before the livestock were run across.

By the time the last goat bleated its way across, water was already beginning to seep across the lowest part of the built-up, artificial path they'd made to bridge the creek. Jason knew, because he stayed behind, watching to make certain that every single wagon, ox, horse, cow, pig, goat, and dog made it across without problem.

Colorado Gooding was somewhere up front, he supposed, taking much pleasure in heading up such a large train of wagons. And Hamish MacDonald was probably right beside him, talking up the beauties of the lands beyond Santa Fe, at least what he'd heard or read about them.

Jason reined Cleo around and loped her up past the herd to catch up with the wagons. People actually looked happy this morning, where they had appeared sharp or cross or simply dejected before. Maybe it was because they were finally moving again. Maybe it was because the rain was over, and the sky was clear.

Whatever the reason, he was just thankful. Even Eulaylee Jameson, her cat, Boots, dozing in her lap, waved and smiled when he passed her rig. He was so surprised, in fact, that it took him a second to return the gesture and add, "Fine morning, isn't it, Mrs. Jameson?"

"Lovely, Mr. Fury, just lovely," she replied with a genuine grin before she turned her attention back to her team.

Jason dug his heels into his mare before Eulaylee had a chance to think of any other questions, but slowed down when he reached the Cohens' rigs. Saul was driving the one behind, the rig that carried the merchandise for his hardware store.

"Mornin'," Jason called.

Saul waved. "Nice day, isn't it?"

"That why everybody's in such a good mood?"

Saul said, "I believe so. This troubles you?"

Jason thumbed his hat back. "Only insofar as Eulaylee Jameson smiled at me, Saul."

Saul laughed. "I supposed that might trouble me as well, but then, I have the safety of my Rachael's skirts to hide behind, don't I?" He wiggled his eyebrows comically. "And I am not such a fine figure of a man as you, Jason. Rachael says you make all the girls' hearts beat a little faster."

Jason made a face and waved his hand at Saul. "These women don't have enough to do that they've got to gossip all day?"

Saul said "We men brag about the animals we hunt or the men we best." Saul shrugged. "Maybe it gives them something to do while they cook. While they do the things that women do." The grin faded from his face, and he said, "Jason, you watch out for that Alabama man."

"Who?"

"Montana. Utah. Whatever his name is."

"Colorado?"

Saul nodded.

"Why? He was a friend of my pa's, Saul."

Saul shook his head, then said, "Something bothers me.

Perhaps it is just that he is too friendly with Hamish and the reverend. Perhaps it is only that I do not believe he has bathed in too long a time. I don't know. Don't listen to me."

"No, Saul, no," Jason said. "I've been concerned about Colorado, myself." He didn't say how much. All he knew was that he wasn't going to go suspecting the man he'd blubbered all over last night of . . . what? Commandeering his wagon train? That was just crazy.

Still, he waved Saul good-bye and goosed his mare ahead, toward the front of the train. It was getting on toward afternoon, and he'd best be up front when Hamish found out there was another branch of the creek to ford.

It looked to him like Colorado Gooding had added nine wagons to their force. Most were driven by women, but he saw a few strange men on horseback. To these, he rode up and introduced himself.

He met Paul Hartung, Garth Witherspoon, Mel Sanderson, farmers and ranchers all, and Raul Chavez, a native of Santa Fe, who had ridden all the way to Kansas City to pick out new pigments for his stained-glass business, and was now hauling them back with Gooding's caravan.

"The other hombres, they were killed by Comanche," he said, in a thick Mexican accent. "My own brother, Luis, was among the dead."

Jason nodded. "I guess we've all lost somebody."

"Mr. Gooding, he tells us of your father. I am sorry, amigo."

"Thanks. Sorry for your brother, too. Were you two in the glass business together?"

"*Sí*. He was learning the trade." Chavez suddenly looked ahead, staring. "*Dios mio*. Is this yet another creek to be forded?"

"Probably," muttered Jason. He tipped his hat and loped on ahead, leaving Chavez behind.

* * *

"Damn it!" Hamish roared. He was off his horse and pounding his thigh with his fisted hat. "Damn it, I knew it."

Jason figured there had been quite a bit of swearing that came before, and was glad that he had only just ridden up. He, too, dismounted.

He looked down, and said, "Well, it looks like we've got another hole to start filling, Hamish."

Colorado burst into laughter while Hamish grumbled. The Reverend Milcher, who had ridden a few feet off to the side, probably so as not to sully his ears with Hamish's profanity, rode closer and stopped.

"Dear Lord," he muttered, just loud enough to be heard.

"There you be right on the money, Reverend," cackled Colorado.

Hamish turned an irate face toward Jason. "If you'd done the sensible thing and taken us farther south, we would've only had to ford this bloody thing one blasted time."

Actually, it would have been twice, but Jason wasn't about to quibble. He was more inclined to punch Hamish right in the middle of his furry red face. But he didn't. He stood his ground and clenched and unclenched his jaw, and then said, "Hamish, if you don't want to dig, then why don't you take a couple of men and go shoot us a couple of deer or antelope for supper?"

Hamish gritted his teeth and swung back up on his horse and, without a word, rode back along the line of wagons toward the remuda. Jason noticed that he pulled his boy out of line to follow him.

Good riddance, Jason thought, and turned his attention back to the gaping hole that ran the length of the creek bed.

This branch carried quite a bit more water than the previous passage, and was wider and deeper. The banks were only six or seven feet above the water, although there was no telling how deep that water was. Not without going in.

With a sigh, he tossed his reins to Colorado, who said, "Hope you can swim, boy."

Jason looked up. "You want to volunteer?"

Colorado waved his arms. "Wouldn't dream of robbin' you of the pleasure."

Muttering, "I didn't think so," Jason walked to the edge of the bank and slid straight down it, on his butt. Upon landing, he found himself knee-deep in water, and called up, "You'd best toss me down a loop, Colorado, or I'll never get back up."

In a matter of seconds, a rope sailed down and landed in front of him in the brown murk. He picked it up and waded out to the middle, then the opposite bank, then ten feet upstream and back across. The water, at its deepest, was only waist-high on him—a depth that, under normal circumstances, could be easily forded by both livestock and wagons. The bed was gravel and seemed solid enough. The problem would be getting the wagons and livestock down to it.

Well, it wasn't like he was new to digging.

He snugged the rope around his middle, sloshed back down to where the horses were waiting above, took a steady grip on the rope, and cried, "Start hauling, Colorado!"

The second dig wasn't as bad as the first.

For one thing, they had a few more men on the crew, right from the start. For another, all the dirt could be thrown to the side instead of carried to, and thrown into, the creek itself. Still, it took them until well after dark, and they were not finished, even then.

Jason called a halt for the day, and they all trooped back to the now-circled wagons and the cook fire.

Dinner was a little sparse, Jenny thought. Hamish, Matt, and their men hadn't been able to scare up more than one thin buck for their dinner, but the women had stretched it by making venison stew with plenty of home-canned okra, peas, potatoes, onions, and tomatoes. And one of the Cohen's goats.

The goat's name was Nellie, and Jenny was sorry to see her butchered.

Saul sat next to Jason and Jenny while they ate, his wife having taken charge of the children, and every once in a while, tired though he was, he said, "Well, now, I believe that was a piece of my Nellie. Not so gamy, you know?"

And Jason would laugh through his fatigue, Jenny would smile, and Saul would shrug his shoulders.

And they all would think very unkind thoughts about Hamish and Matt MacDonald. Except for Jenny. She was still thinking kind thoughts about Matt. More than kind, as a matter of fact.

Just that morning, he had kissed her behind the shelter of his father's wagon. There was no particular reason for it, which made it all the more exciting for Jenny. He had simply led his horse up to her, after Megan, to whom she'd been talking, went up front. He grabbed a pair of gloves out of the back of the wagon, smiled, leaned over, kissed her square on the mouth, mounted up, and rode off.

All without a word.

She'd been thinking about it all day long. And she hadn't told anyone, not even Megan. Not even her diary. And especially not Jason.

Jason would throw a fit, wouldn't he?

Especially now, as exhausted as he was. He was practically falling asleep while he ate, although she had been able to coax him into changing out of those muddy clothes. That was something, anyway. Usually, she couldn't get him to do anything that was even halfway good for him.

But even now, tired and dirty, he was still remarkably handsome, she thought. If she'd been an artist or a sculptor, she couldn't think of any other subject she'd rather paint or model than her brother. Or Matthew MacDonald. Either one would do quite beautifully.

She realized that the little group had gone silent, and looked over at Jason and Saul. Saul had fallen back against the wagon's wheel, and was asleep with his mouth open. Jason dozed with his chin on his chest.

"Some wagon master," she muttered, and stood up to step over her brother. She put her hand gently on Saul's shoulder, and when he opened one eye, said, "It's time to go to your wagon, Mr. Cohen."

As she helped him to his feet, she heard a distant rumble of thunder and muttered, "Wonderful. Just what we need."

When Saul had sleepily stumbled off a good twenty feet and his wife came out to make sure he got all the way home, Jenny bent to Jason.

She had him, in fact, clear up into the wagon and had his boots pried off before the skies opened.

Chapter 18

Jenny didn't know how she'd fallen asleep. But she must have, for the next thing she knew Jason was gone and there was a lot of yelling outside, mixed in with the battering of rain on the lightning-brightened canvas roof.

Quickly, she poked her head outside. She might as well have poured a bucket of water over her head, the rain was that fast and thick. But through it, she was able to see men rushing from their wagons and toward the creek. Mr. Kendall was going from wagon to wagon, right around the circle, waking them up, and it wasn't long before he came to hers.

He was trotting through the mud, going to go right on past, but she flagged him down. "Mr. Kendall! What is it? What's wrong?"

He looked wild-eyed. "It's Carrie English! Her wagon's goin' in the creek!" He was off and running again before the last words were out of his mouth.

After glancing back to make certain that Jason had heard, too, Jenny jumped down from the wagon without thinking about a coat or hat, even in the cold rain, and began slogging her way toward the creek. She couldn't imagine why the Widow English had moved her wagon so near the stream that it could slide in. It had been a good thirty feet from the bank this afternoon, while the men were digging.

Jenny picked up her pace. There was little Chrissy to think of, and Rags.

Carrie English, soaked and sobbing, was now sheltered in Hamish MacDonald's comforting grip, and the last thing Jason heard, when he ran for his horse, was Hamish saying, "Don't you worry, lass, Jason'll get her." He prayed that Hamish was, for once, right. He leapt into Cleo's saddle—which had been put in place by Ward—and loped along the water's edge, signaling Ward and Saul and Morelli to get a move on, too. It was black as pitch, save for the lightning that flashed all too near, and he felt as though he were standing in a shower bath. A cold one.

But as he neared the wagon, floating downstream in the current, he pulled his rope off the horn, tethered one end of it there, and leapt down off Cleo's back, carrying the rest of the coil.

"You know what to do!" he called to Ward before he waded out into the current, letting out rope as he moved closer to the wagon.

Ward nodded at him, and that was the last time he looked back.

The wagon was still floating, but he didn't know how much longer that piece of luck would hold out. And he mentally kicked himself for the thousandth time. He should have reminded Carrie to block the wheels of her wagon. Hell, he should have blocked them himself. Her wagon had been well up from the water's edge, but on a slight incline.

But who could have known it would rain so blasted much and so hard? Who could have known the water would rise so fast, and that the ground beneath the wagons would turn to slick, slippery mud?

He should have, that was who.

The water, having gone from ankle- to thigh-high, was suddenly over his head. He fought to pull himself to the surface—and also, to remember to hang onto that rope. Just as he thought his lungs would burst, his head cleared the water. He began to swim for the wagon, aided by the current, and finally grabbed the driver's bench with one hand. He heard a cheer go up behind him, on the bank, but didn't look back. He wasn't done yet.

He quickly looped the rest of the rope around the bench, tying it off hard, while he shouted, "Chrissy? Chrissy, you in there?"

A tiny, drowsy voice answered, "Yessir?"

Wasn't that just like a little kid, to sleep through something like this?

"You just hold still, baby," he shouted before he turned back to Ward. "Toss me another!" he called.

Ward's loop sailed out and just about settled over Jason's head. It would have, too, if he hadn't shot a hand out to catch it. This one, he tied to the whiffle bar, diving under water to do so. When he came up, Saul was ready for him. Just like that, another loop rocketed out from the bank. It landed on top of the driver's bench, which he tied it round.

He signaled the men, and one by one, the ropes went taut and the wagon stopped moving. Thank God. A glance over his shoulder showed him that Morelli had switched horses, and was sitting on Cleo now, holding her steady.

Then, at last, Jason said, "Chrissy, honey, come here. We're gonna take a little swim."

Her head popped up and she blinked. "Is that you, Mr. Fury?"

He nodded and held out a hand. "Come on, baby."

"Where's Rags?"

The dog. He hadn't seen hide nor hair of it. He said, "He went on ahead of us, Chrissy. He's all right." He hoped to hell it wasn't a lie.

At last, he felt the little girl put her tiny hand in his.

* * *

Rags had indeed jumped from the wagon, but swum the wrong way. Now he was a hundred feet downstream from the wagon, swimming desperately for the bank.

Jenny kept pace with him, encouraging him. "Good boy, Rags! You can do it." She had run past Jason, who had already been tying the first rope on the wagon seat. There was nothing she could do there. But she'd heard a faint, terrified yip from downstream, and had followed the sound.

Her skirts felt like lead, weighing her down, holding her back, and she stopped to strip out of them. Nobody would see her clear down here.

Rushing ahead in nothing but her chemise and pantaloons, she splashed into the muddy water. Rags was tiring, she could see it. He'd stopped barking, and was now stroking only intermittently.

"Rags!" she shouted. "Don't you dare die! What will Chrissy do without you?"

The water was up to her waist, but she kept moving forward. For not the first time, she blessed her papa for throwing her into Folger's Creek one spring afternoon, long ago. Her mother had been fit to be tied, but she'd learned how to swim. Even if she had got her new Easter dress soaked through.

A few more steps and she reached the drop-off. She went under the surface, but unburdened by a rope and guns and heavy boots, she bobbed right up to the surface, blinked muddy water from her eyes, and began to swim for the now-limp puppy.

Jason made his way slowly up one of the ropes, with Chrissy clinging to his neck, and giggling. He was glad somebody was enjoying this.

As he pulled his way toward the bank, which seemed a lot farther off when he was trying to get to it than when he'd swum out to the wagon, the men on the ropes slowly backed their horses, helping him a little.

"Mr. Fury, I don't see Rags," came Chrissy's voice. "Where is he?"

"Let's worry about Rags later, all right, sugar?" he said, just as he felt his boot touch the bank. He stepped up on its spongy surface, and was suddenly in water that was only hip-deep. Ward whistled his admiration, and Saul and Dr. Morelli both broke out in big grins.

As Jason shifted the little girl into one arm, he wished he could be as happy as they seemed. They might haul that wagon a piece, but sure as anything, the tongue was going to sink in and stick it, and keep it stuck.

At last, Jenny reached the pup and latched onto him, pulling him toward her. He let out a weak yelp, letting her know he was still alive. His curly coat, usually black, tan, and white, was now a sodden, solid, dirty brown from the water, and his usually hard, muscled body felt like a dishrag.

Still, she clasped him to her and began to stroke, one-armed, for the bank. Progress was slow, and she feared she was far from the wagons by this time. She was tiring, too, and each pull toward the creek's edge took more and more out of her.

She began to wonder if she'd ever set her feet on the earth again.

One stroke. Another. The bank seemed just as far away.

And then she felt something, something wet, but warm. Rags, licking her cheek. "We'll make it, boy," she whispered, and got a mouthful of water for her trouble.

And then she heard a faint whistling sound, and a *plop*.

And Matt's voice. "Put it around you, Jenny!"

Suddenly, she realized what he was talking about. His rope floated only a few feet from her. She stroked again, and managed to get her hand on it, then her wrist through the loop. She hung on for all she was worth.

"Got it!" she shouted weakly.

The rope began to pull her toward shore with what seemed like magical swiftness.

"Let go of the damned dog and grab it with both hands!" Matt yelled. "I'm gonna pull your arm off!"

"Just keep going," Jenny called back, and tightened her grip on the puppy.

Matt said something she couldn't make out, but he kept pulling. And he was right. By the time she made the bank and was able to stand up, her arm felt as if it had been wrenched from its socket.

"You all right?" Matt asked, once she had walked clear of the water. "You're naked!"

"I'm fine, thank you, and I am *not* naked! I have my underwear on."

He said, "Could'a fooled me."

She looked down at herself just as the lightning flashed overhead. The water had made the cotton of her underthings clinging and nearly transparent. In shock and shame, she figured that at least he couldn't look at her if she was behind him.

She shifted the puppy to her bad arm and held the other up to Matt. "Give me a ride back to my clothes, please."

Matt reached down and hauled her up behind his saddle. "Real shame, if you ask me," he said, then clucked to his horse.

And despite herself, Jenny felt a strange and not unwelcome tingle zipper its way up her spine.

Chrissy having been delivered into the hands of Dr. Morelli, Jason took the last rope and prepared himself to go back into the water.

"What are you *doing*?" Saul asked, over the thunder.

"Gonna dive down and hook up the tongue," Jason said. The wagon's tongue was the pole that came off the whiffle bar and extended up, between the two pairs of horses that pulled the wagon. And it was stuck in the creek's bed already. They had made no further progress on getting the wagon out.

Ward hopped off his horse. "Lemme go this time, Jason."

Jason shook his head. "I need you out here, Ward, holding pressure on the wagon."

"But—"

"Doc, give me your rope, and snug up the other end around your saddle horn."

Morelli hesitated a moment, but then did as he was told. Jason tossed him one end of the rope, uncoiled several loops to give him sufficient slack, and then waded in.

When he made his way to the wagon's bench, he took a deep breath before he dove down. He knew he wouldn't be able to see anything, so he felt his way down to the whiffle, then along the tongue until he found the closest ring to the end.

Quickly, he threaded the rope through it, but ran out of air before he could tie it off.

He broke the surface gasping and sputtering, but before he could dive down again, he heard Saul call out, "Tie it there, Jason! Tie it at the surface!"

At first, he thought Saul was crazy, but then he realized that the end going to the saddle horn was taut. "Right!" he called back, and pulled on the other end of the rope until it, too, was taut. He pulled so hard, in fact, that he felt the wagon's tongue come free from the creek's bed.

"Hold that horse still," he shouted to Saul, and kept on pulling until the end of the tongue broke the water's surface. Then and only then did he tie it off, at the ring, then turn for shore to the shouts of the men and the giggles of a little girl, who was having the time of her life.

He made it out of the water just as that terrier pup of Chrissy's came galloping up the side of the creek, barking and yapping and carrying on. He looked like he hadn't had such a happy time of it, but he was delighted to hear the little girl's laughter.

"Rags!" she cried gleefully. "Rags! Mr. Fury, you were right!" Morelli let her slide to the ground, and the pup flew into her arms.

"I'll be danged!" Ward muttered.

"Miracles happen all around us," said Saul, with a shake of his head.

"All right, everybody," said Jason as he swung up on Dr. Morelli's horse. The battering rain was punishing them all. "We don't have this rig out of the soup yet."

Chapter 19

The next morning found the men digging again—or at least as much as they could, the water still being high—most of the women washing out muddy clothes, and Carrie English's belongings all sitting out in the sun to dry.

As for Carrie, she was grateful. Grateful her child had been saved—which she was told was due to Jason Fury in its entirety—grateful her possessions were only damp, not lost forever, and grateful that her daughter's only companion, a little terrier mix, had survived.

Matt MacDonald had told her she had Jenny Fury to thank for that. He'd said she'd swum right out, brave as you please, caught the floundering dog, and brought it safely to shore.

She wondered if he was sweet on Jenny. Of course, he was the only man, outside of her brother, who was of a suitable age for Jenny. What was she? Fifteen? Sixteen? And she certainly was pretty. She had her brother's wheat-blond hair and good looks and elegant carriage.

And his good heart, it seemed.

Carrie hoped the creek wouldn't go down too fast. After all, some of her things were still dripping. Her mother's breakfront was going to be all right, too, she thought with a sigh of relief. It had been her grandmother's before that, and had made the trip, by sailing ship, all the way across the ocean from Ireland. A great many hopes and dreams were tied up in that old piece of furniture.

Rags ran past her, followed by Chrissy.

"Mr. Kendall's coming, Mama," Chrissy said as she went by.

Instinctively, Carrie's hand went to her hair, to straighten it.

"All right, baby. Go play," Carrie said.

Jenny sneezed again, and snuggled down farther into her quilts. After all, hadn't Dr. Morelli told her to stay in bed today? He hadn't said she couldn't read, though, and *Moby Dick* was under her pillow.

But somehow, she found she couldn't concentrate on Captain Ahab and Starbuck or the great white whale this morning. All she could think about was Matthew MacDonald.

She loved him, and she couldn't tell a soul, although she was bursting to.

There was a knock on the wagon's tailgate, and then Megan's head appeared above it. Megan said, "Morning!"

Jenny said, "You'd best keep your distance. Dr. Morelli thinks I'm getting a cold. You know, from last night."

"We all ought to have one, then," Megan replied. "I've never been so cold and wet in all my born days."

Jenny couldn't stand it anymore. And Megan wouldn't tell, would she? She said, "Megan, I have something to tell you. But you've got to promise that you won't tell a living soul, that you'll take it to your grave!"

Megan cocked a brow. "Well, that sounds important!"

"It's the most important thing I've ever had to say in my whole live-long life!"

Megan sat down and leaned forward. "Well, I promise then. Cross my heart and hope to die."

"Megan, I . . . I'm in love with your brother." There. It was out.

Megan blinked, but otherwise there was no change in her expression.

A scowl came over Jenny's face. She had expected quite a bit more than that! "What?" she demanded.

"Jenny, you're my very best friend, and I love my brother, but . . ."

"But?"

"But I don't think he's the kind you ought to fall in love with, that's all."

Jenny's hands twisted her quilt. "And just what kind is that?"

"Morning, ma'am," Salmon Kendall said with a tip of his hat.

"Won't you sit down, Salmon?" Carrie replied, pointing to a barrel set out to dry.

Salmon sat, looking generally nervous, and took off his hat. He passed its brim, over and over again, through his long fingers.

Carrie waited and waited, and finally broke the silence. "And what can I do for you this morning, Salmon?"

"Nothin'," he said, then quickly added, "Well, quite a bit."

"Yes?" she urged.

"Well, it's just that last night, when you . . . you know . . . I got to thinkin' 'bout . . ." Suddenly, he stood straight up. "I . . . I gotta go." He slapped his hat back on his head and turned on his heel.

Carrie watched after him. If he wasn't a man with marriage on his mind, she'd eat her hat. Maybe his, too. But she wondered if it was her he really wanted, or just another woman to take his wife's place. It was very soon, she realized. Perhaps too soon.

She would wait and see.

Megan hopped down from the Fury wagon, feeling terrible. She was a traitor to her brother and a traitor to her best friend, all at once. To her brother, because she should have stood up for him instead of talking him down—even though he deserved it—and to Jenny, because her feelings were real and true, and Megan had dashed her tender hopes.

Or at least, she thought she had. Hoped she had. And hoped she hadn't.

She walked back to her own wagon, then changed her mind before she reached it, altering her path to take her down by the creek. Jason would be there. It did her good just to look at him. Maybe, if she stared at him long enough, she could think what to do.

When she reached the creek, Abigail Krimp had a blanket all laid out, and invited Megan to join her. Megan was grateful for the chance at a dry perch.

Abigail proved a little too chatty, though. Mostly, about Jason.

"Isn't he just the handsomest thing?" Abigail said, so close to a swoon that Megan was embarrassed for her.

"Who?" she asked, although there could be little doubt about whom Abigail had spoken. She was staring straight at Jason.

"Mr. Fury, of course!" Abigail replied, and stifled a giggle.

Megan, disgusted, started to stand up to leave. If anybody had a right to gush over Jason, it was her. Not some Johnny-come-lately floozy, which was what her father called Abigail.

But Abigail grabbed her sleeve and pulled her back down. "You don't have to go so soon, do you? I think he's about to take off his shirt."

Jason splashed water over his face, then wiped himself as dry as he could with his sweaty shirt. It was past noon, and they weren't done yet.

The water had receded nearly back to yesterday morning's levels, which gave him hope, but the men were tired and sore and out of sorts, and weren't moving as fast as they had the previous day.

Still, he held out hope that they'd finish by mid-afternoon. He wanted to get across this creek today, by God.

Wiping his brow on a bandanna, Saul Cohen came up next to him and momentarily rested his shovel against a rock. "I didn't think it was supposed to be so hot this early in the season," he said.

"It's not," said Jason. "We just got lucky."

"We're lucky with both heat and water," Saul mused. "It could be worse. There could be more snakes."

Jason said, "Yeah, I suppose there could." Just that morning, Rachael had killed a rattler hiding in their temporary woodpile.

Saul helped himself to a dipper of fresh water from the bucket. "How many more?"

Jason cocked a brow. "How many more what?"

"Branches of this river?"

"None."

Saul pursed his lips. "But other creeks, other rivers?"

"Yes."

Saul picked up his shovel. "With fords or ferries or bridges already there, one could hope. Just so it shouldn't be boring."

Jason lifted his shovel, too. "These treks rarely are, Saul. Boring is what you pray for."

"The Good Lord didn't have his ear turned toward you on that one, Fury," broke in Mel Sanderson, one of Colorado Gooding's men. "Appears he didn't hear any of us." Sanderson picked up the dipper that Saul had just put down and helped himself to the water.

"I couldn't say, Sanderson," Jason told him. "But so far, we're alive, aren't we?"

"At least, most of us are," cut in a sweaty Matt MacDonald, who had just stepped up for his turn at the fresh water.

Jason didn't answer him. "Back to work, men," he said, and started back to the dig.

Behind him, he heard Sanderson say, "Don't believe that Jason feller likes you much, son."

And Matt MacDonald's growled reply: "The feeling's mutual."

Chapter 20

By four o'clock, most of the wagons had successfully forded the creek, and were setting up a new camp about one hundred yards from the point of crossing. Jason was still busy at the ford, though, helping the remaining wagons across the stream, then climbing back up the muddy slope they had dug down to it.

Last of all came the Wheelers' iron-bottom wagon, which managed to sink into a creek bed that had held up under the previous wagons just fine. Jason had to run and borrow a couple of oxen from one of the other wagons to help pull it up.

But he got the job done, then brought the herd and remuda across. They were the easiest, although the hogs and goats were a little cranky about being asked to ford something that was deeper than they were tall.

Everybody made it fine, though.

By five, the women were cooking dinner. Mel Sanderson had produced a harmonica and proved to be pretty darned good with it. When she felt the song was godly enough, Mrs. Milcher accompanied him from inside her wagon, on the piano.

Jason leaned back against the side of his wagon, where

Jenny and Megan sat on a blanket. "Three hundred yards in a day," he grumbled, shaking his head. "Pa would be plain embarrassed."

Jenny looked up. "Papa would be proud, and you know it, Jason."

"He thought seven miles a day on the flat was bad."

"That wasn't counting digging fords," she said. "How long til we get to Santa Fe?"

"A week, maybe, if we're lucky. We've got the Sangre de Cristo foothills to contend with."

Mrs. Milcher stopped playing, for Sanderson had turned to playing a lively jig and Colorado had pulled out a fiddle and was playing along, with a great deal of enthusiasm if not much talent. Several couples were dancing.

Megan stood up and shyly held her hand toward Jason just as Abigail Krimp came up from the other side and grabbed his arm. "Let's dance, Jason," Abigail said, pulling him toward her.

He didn't have much choice. He followed her out to where the other pilgrims were dancing, and joined in. When he turned back toward the wagon, Megan had disappeared.

The trail, which had become frequently used enough to show ruts, split into a Y in the foothills. And about six feet from that very spot, Hamish MacDonald and Jason were having a difference of opinion.

"I say we go up," Hamish insisted, pointing toward the right hand arm of the Y. "Right is over the mountain. We'll save time."

"It'll take us over the foothills, all right, but it's tricky. We're bound to lose some wagons, maybe people. I won't chance it, Hamish."

"You're loony, lad. Look how deep those ruts are! It looks to me as if more than half the travelers that have passed this way have taken that route!"

It was all Jason could do not to slap the old man right across his ruddy whiskers. He said, "We're taking the low road, Hamish. Around the foothills, not through them. You can do as you damn well please. I'm sick and tired of fighting with you."

And then he just rode off, shouting to the wagons directly behind to follow him, and left Hamish sitting his horse in their path.

He didn't look back for quite some time, being content to ease along the trail followed by the clanks and rumbles of wagons and the rhythmic plods of hooves. But when he did glance up, he caught sight of something that made his stomach turn over—Hamish MacDonald's wagon, driven by Hamish himself, with Matthew up front on horseback.

It didn't make him ill that Hamish wanted to chance killing himself, and it certainly didn't bother him that Matthew was up there—but Megan . . . Had Megan followed her father and taken the mountain trail? Was she in that wagon?

Leaving Ward to lead the caravan, he galloped back to his own rig, only to find Jenny deep in conversation with Megan.

"Megan," he cried in relief. "You didn't go with your father and brother!"

Megan said, "They're crazy. I told them that if I couldn't stop them from killing themselves, I could at least save myself." Then she added, "They won't get killed, will they? I mean, not really?"

"They had a big fight over it, Jason," Jenny interjected. He didn't understand why, but Jenny acted as if she'd rather they hadn't left the rest of the train. Jenny knew what a pain in the butt Hamish had always been, and the trouble Jason continually had with Matt.

Megan said, "You've got to stop them, Jason! I know they're both bullheaded, but . . . I mean, I was only trying to . . ." And then she doubled over and began to weep.

Before Jason realized it, he had leapt from Cleo's back to

the wagon seat and taken Megan into his arms. Jenny, sitting just beyond Megan, arched her brows, glanced heavenward.

"Megan, it's too late," he began.

She sobbed harder.

"Megan, I didn't mean . . . what I meant to say was that it's too late for them to turn their rig around. They'd have to back the Conestoga down that narrow trail, and that's a lot more dangerous than just going on ahead. They'll be fine up there if they're careful."

Sniffling, she lifted her face and looked into his eyes. "Really?" she asked.

Her eyes, cheeks, and nose were reddened with weeping and moist with tears, and for some reason he couldn't help thinking that she'd never looked more beautiful. He couldn't help himself. He kissed her.

Her lips were soft and warm. He heard his sister hiss, *"Jason!"*

Blinking rapidly, he pulled away. Megan's face was filled with questions, Jenny's with outright shock and surprise. He felt heat shoot up his neck and fill his cheeks.

He scooted away to the very edge of the bench, then dropped down and off the wagon. It was a miracle he landed on his feet, he was shaking so hard. The big wheels rolled on by him. Megan's head appeared briefly, peeking around the edge of the canvas roof. And then somebody jerked her back. Undoubtedly Jenny.

He whistled for Cleo, and the palomino came trotting up. He remounted, wondering why just kissing a girl would have such an effect on him! But this was no Washington-soiled dove or Kansas City whore. This was the girl he was going to marry.

Marry? Where had that come from?

"Megan MacDonald!" Jenny scolded as she jerked Megan back, momentarily incensed that her best friend had allowed Jason to kiss her in public. Especially when that same best friend had been so unpleasant about Jenny's confessed feelings for Matt.

She was still mad about it, even though she had pretended to forgive Megan. It just made things easier, that was all—it wasn't as if Jenny could just find a new best friend in the little community of the train.

But this new affront was too much!

"What do you mean by kissing my brother?" she asked. "I mean, right out here in front of God and everybody?"

Megan had a slightly dazed look on her face. She said, "I didn't kiss him. He kissed me." And then she smiled, just like a cat in the cream, and leaned back. "He kissed me!"

"You sure stopped crying quick."

Megan didn't answer.

Jenny frowned. "Maybe you'd better fill me in with the rules for this sort of thing. I'm probably too young to understand," she added sarcastically, "but I'll try."

Megan turned toward her. "Understand what?"

"Why it's all right for you to make eyes at my brother all the time, and for you to kiss him right out where anybody can see you, but it's not all right for me to do the same with your brother. Don't you think I'm good enough for your precious Matthew?"

Megan said, "Just the opposite, Jenny. I don't think he's good enough for *you*."

"Jason, oh, Jason!" Abigail Krimp waved her hankie at him from the driver's seat of Nordstrom's spare wagon and, reluctantly, he made his way over. She was all dolled up today—looked like she'd just walked out of a saloon, actually—in spangles and sparkly things and cheap jewelry.

"Hello, Miss Abigail," he said, and tipped his hat as he rode alongside the wagon. "What can I do for you this afternoon?"

"Oh, nothing, nothing at all, Jason," she said. She dabbed

the hankie at her own neck—and chest, most of which was exposed. "I just wanted to tell you what a fine dancer you are. In case I didn't last night, I mean. Because you really are. A good dancer, I mean."

"I, uh . . . Thank you," he said, flustered. "Well, I'd best get back up front."

"Oh, don't go quite so soon," Abigail said, before he had a chance to show Cleo his heels. "Did you know that we had such talented musicians in our very midst?"

"My pa said something about Colorado playing the fiddle." Badly.

"I thought he was just grand, didn't you?"

"I really have to—"

"Jason!" Ward Wanamaker galloped toward him from the front of the train. "Jason, come quick!"

Grateful for the excuse to turn his back on Abigail Krimp, Jason pushed Cleo from a walk directly into a lope and rode up to see what was agitating Ward.

When they met, Ward looked as shook up as a bottle of overwarm sarsaparilla, ready to explode. "You've got to come up front!" he shouted.

Jason held his hands over his ears—Ward was only a couple feet from him, but he was yelling like he was still six wagons away.

"Sorry," Ward said, still excited, but less loud. "There's been an accident."

Hamish had fallen off the damned mountain. That was the first thought that came into his head.

But Ward followed up with, "It's the Milchers. They busted a wheel all to smash!"

Well, that was just wonderful, wasn't it? "I don't suppose they've got a spare?"

Ward blinked. "You know, I didn't think to ask 'em."

"Well, get up there and do it." Ward galloped off, and Jason turned his attention to slowing up and halting the other wagons. When he came to Salmon Kendall's rig, Salmon asked if he needed a hand, which Jason gratefully accepted.

Salmon untied his saddle horse from the rear of his wagon, tightened its girth, and swung up into the saddle. "If they don't got a spare, I do, and so do the MacDonalds and Saul," he said as they jogged forward. "There's probably more, but I don't—"

"The MacDonalds' spare wheel is probably halfway up the mountainside," Jason said, "but I'm glad to know that you and Saul both have one." More like, he was pleased to hear that a couple of his employers weren't complete idiots. But he didn't say so.

Instead, he said, "I thought an extra wagon wheel was on Pa's 'necessities list' for each wagon, right along with a rifle and water."

"It was, Jason, it was."

Chapter 21

As it turned out, an extra wagon wheel was one of the "frills" the Reverend Milcher had thrown out so he could fit his new piano in the wagon. And Saul Cohen had the misfortune of being in the wagon right in front of the Milchers, and thus was deprived of his spare.

"Sorry, Saul," Jason said as they watched Milcher, Salmon, Colorado, and Milt Billings lever Milcher's wagon up onto a makeshift support consisting of Mrs. Milcher's marble-topped dresser. Milcher had done a job on his wheel, all right. If he had tried to find the biggest, most jagged boulder to run over, he couldn't have done a better job. Jason had Ward slapping whitewash on the offending rock, to mark it out for the following wagons.

Saul was philosophical about the whole thing, though. He shrugged and said, "It's good to help the man who hates you. He might come in handy later on. At least, that's what my Uncle Nathan used to say, and didn't he die the wealthiest Jew in New Jersey?"

Jason thumbed back his hat and said, "Guess I never thought about it that way. But you're right."

The humiliation of it was written all over Milcher's face. It must be eating him up inside to think that he and his kin were going to make it only because a heathen Hebrew had done him a favor.

With a loud thud, accompanied by numerous groans and the discordant hum of piano wires, the wagon was dropped on its support. Jason said, "I sure wish that Seth Wheeler was still with us. At least he knew something about being a wheelwright."

"I haven't had a chance to see Mary since the attack," Saul said. "How is she holding up?"

"Fine, I suppose," Jason replied. "Well, as good as anybody else under the circumstances. She was a big help to Dr. Morelli. She was a nurse during the War, you know."

Saul nodded. "And, I'm told, a dance hall girl before that."

This was news to Jason. "Where'd you hear that?"

"Rachael. These women, they gossip," Saul said, staring straight ahead. "Well, they gossip and my Rachael, she keeps her ears open. Anything you want to know about the private affairs of anyone we have lived near or known or *almost* known in the past nine years, you bring yourself to Saul Cohen and ask. I'll ask Rachael for you."

The men had Milcher's old wheel pulled off. Well, it wasn't really a wheel anymore. It was just splintered wood and a bent, broken, rusty rim, which they tossed to the side in pieces.

The land they were currently stalled on had taken what Jason's father would have called "a turn for the worse." Trees, when there were any, had gone shrubby or stunted and twisted. The color of the earth varied, but was mostly the color of powdery, dried blood, and the farmers in the group had been remarking on it since they passed through Indian Territory.

Snakes were more common, as were spiders. A week earlier, Jason had called everyone around him and explained the importance of watching where they walked, a lecture that was brought on by Europa Morton, sister to their schoolmarm, having been struck by a rattler.

Usually, she was driving, for her husband, Milton, had been injured and later died during the Comanche raid, but for some reason she was on foot. She had explained that she'd heard somebody's teakettle hissing and had gone to investigate. And of course, the "hissing" she'd heard was a warning rattle from a rather old and large diamondback.

The snake was so old, in fact, that it hadn't injected enough venom to hurt anything more than her pride, but after Ezekial killed it, Jason had stretched and tanned its skin. He thought Europa might like to have it to display. Or that her father might like it for a hatband.

It turned out that neither one of them wanted the thing, but Salmon Kendall had expressed his admiration for it, so the hatband went to him. It looked a little funny on that floppy-brimmed hat he always wore, but he didn't seem to mind.

They got the new wheel in place and levered the wagon back down, although Jason thought that the "sawhorse"— Mrs. Milcher's bureau—was forever going to be the worse for wear. And they started moving again. By this time, it was nearly five, and Jason figured they could travel for perhaps another hour before they stopped for the night.

Which they did, at a wide spot on the trail that Jason had remembered. Other wagon trains had used it, too, for there were a couple of graves, marked by crude crosses, near the edge of the place, and someone had left behind an old rocking chair. Saul's eye landed on it right away, and after giving it a kick to ward off snakes, he scooped it up, vowing to repair it later.

There was still no sign of the errant MacDonalds, but Jason didn't expect it. Either they'd meet up later, in Santa Fe, or Hamish would get himself killed, regardless of anything Jason had said to Megan.

He felt oddly embarrassed by that kiss. If he'd been

thinking, if he'd been in his right mind or she hadn't looked so vulnerable, he would have restrained himself—both from the action itself, and the self-recriminations that followed. But he hadn't been and she had, and he didn't.

And it was done.

Dinner that night was a hodgepodge of game and tame animals, canned vegetables—and beans, beans, and more beans. Everybody would be glad when they got to Santa Fe and could restock their mobile pantries. Once again, the harmonica and fiddle came out for some music, or at least, something vaguely akin to music, but the piano was silent, Mrs. Milcher having said she wasn't up to playing.

Jason figured that was probably the truth. She was still embarrassed about her husband having abandoned their spare wheel in favor of the piano, and likely didn't want to be reminded so soon.

As for Jason himself, he was keeping to the shadows, huddled in conversation with Saul or Salmon on the opposite side of the circled wagons from his own wagon and Megan MacDonald. He hadn't spoken to her since making that grave error earlier in the day. At least, that was how he thought of their kiss now: his grave error.

They could have absolutely no future together. Hers lay with her father and brother, in California. His lay on the opposite side of the country. She should marry some other erstwhile pioneer. Not him.

No, not him.

Still, he couldn't help feeling drawn to her like iron filings to a magnet. How could he feel she was so right—that she was the *one*—when she was so obviously wrong for him?

His head was in danger of losing out to his heart, and he knew it. What he didn't know was that, being young, he was unintentionally callous, and this was why he avoided her now.

"What?" he muttered, vaguely aware that Saul had said something.

Saul looked confused. "Nothing. I just asked if you need more coffee."

Jason shook his head. "No, thanks."

"We keep eating beans like this, and Rachael, for once, will be glad to be sleeping in an open wagon."

Jason smiled a little.

"It's a girl, isn't it?" Saul asked. "The reason you're acting so strangely, that is. For a minute, I thought maybe you were mad at me for volunteering my spare wheel. But now I'm thinking that maybe you've got woman trouble. Why else would you hide over here, with a couple of old married people?"

It took Jason a moment to realize that the "old married people" Saul referred to were himself and Rachael.

"Don't be silly," Jason said. "Unless you want to get rid of me?" He started to stand up, thinking he'd overstayed his welcome.

But Saul put a hand on his arm. "No, no. Sit and make yourself comfortable. And tell me—who is she, this girl who has you tied in such knots? Is it the lovely Miss Krimp?"

Jason snorted.

"I take it this is a *no*?"

"You take it right."

"Ah. Megan MacDonald, then."

Jason turned toward him.

"Didn't I know it? Rachael," he called. "We were right."

Jason snapped, "Keep your voice down!" before he realized his mouth was moving. And then he muttered, "Sorry, Saul."

"No apology is needed. I remember what it was like with my Rachael, and I wasn't trying to keep twenty-some wagons safe on the way west. You have quite a lot to handle, Jason."

More than Saul knew, Jason thought. "I can't. Not right now."

"You can't fall in love *now*?" Saul's eyebrows went up.

"Love isn't something you can give yourself permission for. You can't pick the time and place, or the girl. Love is God's gift to you and a woman, forever and always."

"Well, He sure picked a bad time to give it to me."

Saul threw his arms into the air. "The young," he said, shaking his head. "So ungrateful."

"Jason?" Jenny's voice.

"Over here, Jenny."

She came from the next wagon in line, her skirts held up in clenched fists and swishing angrily before her, and Jason thought, *I'm in for it now!*

"Jason Fury!" she began. "Have you been over here all the evening? I've been looking for you. *Megan's* been looking for you!" Just then, she saw Saul and said, "Good evening, Mr. Cohen."

Saul nodded and said, "Good evening, Jenny," adding, "Please, don't let me stop your conversation. I'm not here." He leaned back against the wheel spokes and straightened his legs out before him.

Jason barely heard him. He said, "Megan?"

"Well, no, not actually," Jenny admitted angrily. "But if I were her, I would have dogged you all over camp!"

"You did," Jason said.

"Oh. Well . . . can we go somewhere and talk?" Her eyes slid toward Saul, then back to Jason again.

But Jason had no intention of going anywhere. "No. Just tell her . . . just tell her I'm sorry if I embarrassed her."

"Embarrassed her!"

Clearly, if Jenny got any more steamed up, she'd whistle like a teakettle.

"Jen, it's none of your business!" he said. "Now, go back to the wagon."

"None of my business? It's none of my business when my own brother—?"

"I said, go back to the wagon," he snapped, cutting her off. "Now, Jenny. I mean it."

She must have taken his glower seriously, because she stood there a moment, her mouth hanging open, then turned away. But she stopped walking for a second, just long enough to turn back and hiss, "Coward!" at him.

Jason stood there, watching her march back across the circle, before he gratefully slid back down and landed beside Saul.

"Sorry," he said.

"Women," Saul said.

"Exactly. Women."

Saul paused for a few moments before he said, "Whatever it is, you'd better fix it tonight. Be a *mensch*."

Jason still hadn't looked at him. "Yeah. I guess so." Jenny'd been right. He was a coward. All she'd done was point it out.

Damn it. Belatedly, he looked over at Saul and raised a brow. "A *mensch*?"

"Be a man, Jason. A human being."

Chapter 22

Be a mensch, he told himself as he rose and walked, like he was heading for the gallows, to his wagon. Megan was nowhere in sight, but he couldn't think where else she would be staying other than with Jenny, what with her pa and brother having taken the upper trail.

Hell, half the time she spent the night with Jenny, anyway. Jason had been sleeping under Salmon Kendall's wagon.

He reached the Conestoga and stood there for a moment, wondering what to do next—other than turn tail and hoof it back to the East Coast, which was his first thought.

"Welcome home." Jenny's voice. He turned toward it. She hung out of the back of the wagon, off the tailgate, and her face was as stern as her voice. For a moment, she wasn't his little sister at all. She was his mother.

"You were right," he said, attempting to keep his voice flat and even. He sure didn't feel that way. "Where's Megan?"

Saul shook his head as he watched their young leader. "I wouldn't wish to be in his boots tonight for all the cream cheese in . . . where do they make cream cheese, Rachael?"

"Where they have many milk cows. Saul, don't you think you're taking too much on yourself?"

"Because I am curious about cream cheese?" He shrugged. "I would like some right now. From New York City, where there are no Indians."

She felt his forehead. "Why are you talking crazy, all of a sudden?"

He reached up, took her hand, and held it in both of his. "Is it so crazy to wonder about a boy wooing a girl when it's possible that he's let her family stray into the hands of the heathen horde?"

Rachael rolled her eyes and withdrew her hand. "You're talking of the MacDonalds?"

"Who else?"

Rachael pulled over her little milking stool and sat down on it. "And the Comanche?"

Saul nodded.

"We haven't seen them for weeks," she said. "Why should we see them now?"

"Perhaps we are too many. Perhaps young Quanah Parker spares us, for some reason known only to himself and God. Who's to know? But out there, one wagon, alone?"

"You shouldn't even mention it, Saul," Rachael said with a shudder.

"Why not? You think, from my lips to God's ears?"

"You don't think it's bad luck to joke about such things?"

He took her hand again and patted it. "All right, Rachael. Don't be worrying your head."

There was a long silence, during which they sat there, him holding her hand. And then, at last, she said, "Saul?"

"What, my love?"

"Saul, I am in a family way again."

He looked up at her, looked up at this beautiful woman whom God had chosen for him, the woman who had left all she knew to come west with him. How had he ever deserved her?

He put his hand on her belly. It was still very flat. At least, by what he could feel through all the layers of clothing that women wore. "How soon?"

"Seven months, perhaps seven and a half. We will be settled in our new home by then. I am hoping for a girl this time. A girl is all right?"

Megan couldn't believe what she was hearing. It didn't make any sense. It was all she could do not to burst into tears, but she hung on, hung on because it seemed to confuse him so much when she cried. At least, that was what he was blaming for kissing her this afternoon.

Blame?

How could such a wonderful thing, such a perfect and sublime thing, need somewhere to lay blame?

"Do you understand, Megan?" he asked. He hadn't touched her, not with the tiniest tip of his finger. He'd purposely stayed at the opposite end of the wagon from her. There was only one lamp lit, and she could barely make any of him out except for a glimmer of his profile. It danced with his every movement.

"No, I don't understand, Jason. Explain again how your kissing me affects some college back East?"

Once again, he bumbled into a long, convoluted explanation that made no sense whatsoever. But she understood that she was listening to a young man desperately trying to talk himself out of loving her. Without much success, it seemed.

She clasped her hands in her lap and said, "You love me, Jason. And I love you, too."

Far away on the upper trail, Hamish MacDonald poured himself another cup of coffee. "And Megan said we couldn't feed ourselves without her!"

Sitting across the small fire, Matt lit a cigarette. He hadn't been much for smoking before, but ever since he'd learned that Nordstrom's extra wagon carried an ample supply of ready-mades, he'd gone to town on them. He threw the twig he'd used to light it back into the fire, and said, "She was just about right, too."

His father said, "I'll grant you, I've had better jackrabbit on this journey—"

"Didn't help that it fell in the fire," Matt cut in.

"—but not all that much superior."

"Also didn't help that you didn't notice it for a good fifteen minutes."

His father shot him a glance that fairly blistered, and Matt quickly added, "Or me, either."

Hamish's scowl evaporated. "That's right, by God. You didn't notice it, either, laddie."

"No, Pa." His father had been touchy all day. No use in baiting him now.

"That's more like it," Hamish said in a grumble, and pulled out a cigar.

"When you think we'll make Santa Fe?" Matt asked.

Hamish searched the edge of the fire for a twig, then gave up and pulled out a match. "Your guess is as good as mine."

Hamish puffed at the cigar, lighting it. Why did he have to smoke that smelly tobacco? Lord knows, he could afford better. Judging from the fumes, it had to taste awful, like a mouthful of pig swill, Matt imagined. But if it was the cheapest possible but looked good, his pa would buy it.

That was how his pa did everything—shit on the inside, gold foil on the outside.

Except for those Morgan mares of his. They were bred to the nines, each and every one. Matt had nearly wet himself when he learned what his father had paid for just one mare. Funny, him leaving them behind with the herd and the main wagon train when he was so sure he had found a superior route.

Superior route? Hell, Hamish and that damned wagon had nearly fallen down the mountain at least three times today.

Once, Matt had to hitch his saddle horse to the front end of the team to help get the Conestoga back up on the trail. It was the last thing that Matt wanted to admit, but he wished his father had listened to Jason Fury this time.

The trail was terrible—narrow and rocky and rutted—and they had several times seen the traces of scraped earth left by some long-ago, ill-fated wagon that had tumbled over the edge, dislodging rock as it went. If it weren't for his father's wishes—and the fact that he knew it would tick Jason Fury off—he'd be down below, taking the easier trail with the rest of the party. And to tell the truth, he had come more to irritate Jason than to please his father.

Too bad that Jenny had to be a Fury, Matt thought. She was a little young, but she was sure a looker. If you liked the wholesome type, which Matt usually didn't.

But he figured he could make an exception for Jenny Fury.

Sooner or later, that stuck-up, pigheaded brother of hers would head back East to go to some fancy college, and Matt figured that by the time that happened, Jenny would be more than willing to stay behind. With him, and as a MacDonald.

"What are you thinking about?" came his father's rumbling voice. "You look like the cat who swallowed the canary bird."

"Nothing," Matt said, embarrassed to have been betrayed by his own expression. "Just thinkin', that's all."

"Well, don't look so damned smug."

Matt exhaled his last lungful of smoke through his nose in two jets of yellowish air. Smug, indeed! He *ought* to be smug. Pretty soon he'd be in California, set with a wife, rid of Jason Fury, and first in line to inherit enough good cattle and horses to make him a big man, no matter where they settled.

That is, if his father didn't get them both killed on this mountain trail.

Chapter 23

Olympia Morelli saw it first, and screamed. Dr. Morelli, driving the wagon, saw where she was looking and immediately hauled back hard on the team's reins, crying, "Look out, look out!"

Having managed to halt his wagon in time, Morelli leapt down to see to Olympia. She was mere days away from giving birth, and had only just climbed down from the wagon to stretch her legs. Now she stood about twenty feet away from the wagon, hands over her mouth, and she would not stop screaming.

Other women took up the cry as Conestogas hastily pulled out of line to avoid the hail of wagon parts and tumbling livestock and broken furniture and stray rock that came down the mountainside like so much confetti, thrown by a careless giant.

When it was all done, Hamish MacDonald was in their midst again, although only his scraped and twisted corpse. He rolled and bumped to a halt against the off-lead horse of Salmon Kendall's wagon, spooking the animal so badly that Salmon nearly lost his rig, too.

Dodging flying chunks of wagon, Morelli left his wife and

ran to the body, but there was nothing that could be done. Hamish's face was pulp—raw flesh, decorated here and there by cactus thorns—and he no longer breathed.

For not the first time in his career, Morelli saw death as a blessing. He could tell with a quick glance that aside from the surface damage, Hamish had sustained two broken arms— both compound fractures—and a leg broken so badly that it was twisted like a licorice stick.

Morelli didn't have time to look very long, though. Salmon Kendall grabbed him by the arm and yanked an instant before part of a wheel landed on the corpse, followed by a broken axle.

"Thank you, Salmon," he yelled. All that debris coming down the mountainside made a deadly rumble and racket.

Salmon nodded at him, then pulled him farther toward the back of the wagon, around it, and then off the trail. Olympia was still there, although she wasn't standing any longer. She was on the ground. He ran toward her.

"I'm sorry, Michael," she said when he got there. "My water broke."

As the last of the debris thudded and skittered down upon them, he helped her to her feet and to their wagon, where their children waited, huddled and afraid.

"Pa!" Matt called down the mountainside.

No answer, except for the retreating noise of torn rock and a wagon turned into toothpicks. Everything that was his and Megan's in this world, including their father.

To him, the wagon had simply disappeared after its outside wheels slipped off the trail. The Conestoga skidded and tumbled, turning twice over and spewing its contents like a burst canning jar before it went over the abrupt edge of a cliff.

From then on out, he only heard its progress.

Roughly, he wiped at his face, but he was still shaking

from the shock, his burning eyes still brimming from the loss. He swung down off his horse, but his legs didn't hold him up. He sat down on the trail, just where his boots landed, and he began to sob.

This is that damn Jason Fury's fault!

Below, the wagons had finally pulled clear of the section of trail where the remains of Hamish MacDonald's wagon rested. A grave had been quickly, if not easily, dug, and Hamish himself had been buried and spoken over, and the grave marked by a crude cross.

His dead and battered draft animals had been covered over with kerosene and brush and set alight, and a weeping Megan—aided by Jenny and a few of the women—had picked up the precious few items not ruined and stowed them in the Furys' wagon.

But Hamish's belongings weren't the only ones to suffer. Carrie English's wagon had been plowed into by the front half of Hamish's Conestoga, crushing her front wheel, and again they had a wheel to change. Fortunately, she was carrying a spare.

One of Hamish's dead horses had slammed into the Milchers' team and broken the leg of the off-wheel horse, necessitating its being shot. Assorted wagon debris had landed on Randall Nordstrom's second wagon and broken two of the wooden hoops that held the canvas up. Nordstrom had tried to figure how to fix them for the longest time, then given up and just strapped the canvas down, over the load.

And Jason kicked himself. Why had he dared Hamish to go up there in the first place? He should have just knocked him out and thrown him in his own wagon, then let Megan drive it. By the time Hamish came around again, they would have been well enough along that he wouldn't have turned back.

Everybody would be safe and sound.

And they wouldn't be stopped again, here in this clearing, trying to put themselves back together while Hamish's horses sent up pillars of blackish smoke in the distance, and Mr. Morelli delivered his wife, and the Widow English nursed a broken arm.

And where the heck was Matt MacDonald? Not that Jason really cared. He supposed Matt was still up there, someplace. Alone.

And for a moment, he *did* care about Matt. He knew what it was like to lose your father. He wouldn't want to be alone at such a time as this.

"Jason?"

He turned his head. "Yes, Jenny?"

She looked overly tired and washed out. "The Morellis. They've had a little boy. His name is Rubio. Mrs. Wheeler helped midwife."

"Congratulations to the Morellis, then," he replied, although he lacked enthusiasm. Somehow, he couldn't drum up much for a new life when so many people were leaving this world in such a hurry. Hell, if he hadn't known better, he would have thought there was a going-out-of-business sale up in heaven.

"How's Megan doing?" he asked.

"She'll be all right," Jenny replied. "She usually is, though I don't know about a time like this."

"Jenny, I've been thinking. Papa had a good friend in Santa Fe, Wash Keough. Been thinking that maybe I ought to leave you there till I can come back for you."

Her head snapped up again. "What?"

"I said, I've been thinking that—"

She pushed away his arm. "Oh, I heard you, Jason Fury. You will not drop me off along the trail, you hear me?"

"But I thought you might be happier if—"

"Since when is anybody concerned about *my* happiness? I won't stay, I tell you. I'll grab the first horse I see and take out after you."

He slid his arm around her stiff little shoulders. "Now, now, Jen. Can't have you hanged for a horse thief. Guess I'll have to take you all the way with me, then, just to keep you out of prison."

Some of the stiffness went out of her, and she said, "You promise? You know, they hang horse thieves."

He nodded. "I know. And I promise, Jenny, you won't hang."

Night fell.

Matt MacDonald crouched in front of his fire, alone, missing his father's company.

No, not really. Not missing his company. Just . . . regretful. And put out.

Yes, put out. It was all so damned inconvenient. Well, he did feel a little sad about his father, but was it only because he was supposed to? Was it just because he was used to him? After all, Hamish was the only father he'd ever known. He was the only grown man he'd known all his life. He supposed he should feel sorrow.

But mostly, he felt put upon for having to ride up this damned mountain in the first place, and for having to watch all his belongings tumble down all to Hell. Also, for the knowledge that he was going to have to navigate this lousy excuse for a trail all the way to Santa Fe, and all by himself.

And for the fact that he had no dinner. He hadn't seen hide nor hair of a bird, let along a jackrabbit, all damn afternoon. All he had along was some hardtack, in bits in the bottom of his saddlebags, and he'd eaten the last crumbs by about four o'clock. He was thinking very fondly of beans and beef. He'd just have to do without. Tomorrow he could find something to shoot and eat.

He wondered if the train had come across what remained of his father and the rig. He wondered if it had even rolled and fallen that far, or if it had crashed behind them. Nothing could have survived that fall. Not a horse, not his father. Not the wagon. Nothing.

Stomach growling, he lay down in the middle of that rutted trail and tried to sleep.

Chapter 24

Several days later, when Jason and the wagons pulled into the dusty town of Santa Fe, Matt was waiting for them. He waited until he saw Jason dismount. Then he walked out into the open, right up to him, tapped him on the shoulder, and slugged him in the jaw when he turned around.

Having rehearsed this scene in his mind over and over, he had expected Jason to go down. Maybe even fly back a couple of feet.

But not only did he not go down, he punched back. Hard. The blow to his stomach sent Matt back, doubled over and staggering and waiting for Jason to strike again, but he didn't. He just stood there, glowering and rubbing his face.

"What's your problem, MacDonald?" he half-shouted.

Men from the other wagons were running up by this time. Through the pain, Matt heard Saul Cohen shouting something or other. He hoped it was, "Jason's gone crazy! Get him!"

But apparently, it wasn't, because when Saul's boot steps reached Matt, he felt arms wrestle him to the ground, and finally realized that Saul Cohen and Salmon Kendall had him down and pinned. "You idiot," Saul hissed into his ear.

"Let go!" he shouted. "I'm gonna kill you, Jason Fury!"

He heard, more than felt, somebody slip the revolvers from his holsters, and then arms yanked him to his feet.

"Señores," came an unfamiliar voice, "is there a problem?"

The voice belonged to a big Mexican, complete with badge. "Must I repeat myself?" he asked, and this time he looked a little perturbed.

"There's no problem," said Jason, as Kendall and Cohen slowly released Matthew. Matt shook himself out.

"No," Matt said, glaring at Jason. "No problem at all." *That you need to butt into.*

The deputy stood there a moment longer, until he was satisfied there wasn't going to be a fistfight, Matt supposed, and then he walked on without further word. When he passed out of sight, Kendall and Cohen released Matt, although they both stood too close. Matt took a step forward, toward Jason.

"My pa's dead because of you," he said. "That's something I won't forget. Ever. You get me?"

Jason said, "Don't suppose you will. Even if it's not true."

Saul Cohen butted in. "Now, Matthew, your papa made his own decision. Didn't we all hear him, Salmon?"

"I sure did," Salmon Kendall agreed. "Heard him plain."

"Just be thankful you were with him," Saul added. "He might not have lasted so long as he did without his blood beside him."

Jason remained silent.

Matt pretended he hadn't heard a word out of either Saul or Salmon and grumbled, "You'll pay for this, Fury. Sooner or later, you'll pay and I'll be there, takin' the toll."

After getting the last wagon in place and seeing that each family was settled in, Jason set out to see the dusty little town of Santa Fe and look up his father's old friend, Wash Keough. Saul tagged along, with a shopping list from Rachael tucked into his pocket.

Santa Fe was a wonderland to Saul. Most of the buildings

were made of a clay mud—which, Jason informed him, was called adobe—which was whitewashed to glimmer in the sun. Some buildings were plainly Spanish in their architecture, and others were, well, American. Plain. A little dirty-looking.

Saul was shocked at the dead animals left to rot in the streets, though Jason seemed to pay them no mind. He was aghast when they passed a cantina that looked to be a brothel, too, and when he stopped to watch a wheelwright at work, crafting spindles for a buggy wheel, Jason had to tug on his arm to get him moving again.

"This is some strange place," he said. They passed a beautiful señorita, dressed all in black and followed by an older woman and two men carrying guns.

Jason saw him looking and said, "That's Miss Constanza Corboda, with her companion and her bodyguards. Rich, really Old World Spanish, if you know what I mean."

Saul didn't, but nodded his head anyway. He was too busy taking everything in to be distracted by explanations.

At last, Jason turned into the front walk of a small white house, adobe in construction, and rapped on the turquoise-painted, chipped front door. Red, dried, and hard fruits of some kind hung on it in a huge bunch.

"That's called a *chile ristra*," said Jason.

The door opened and a smallish, gray-haired man with his hair in a long horse tail—nearly to his waist—a face like an ax blade, a big grizzled mustache, and a little potbelly under his long pink underwear stood there for a moment, then cried out, "Jason? Jason Fury?" and latched onto the boy like a starving tick to a passing dog. Saul noted that the horse tail was so long that the very ends of it were still shot through with a little brown.

Jason slapped the old fellow on his back, crying, "Howdy, Wash. How goes it?"

"Fine, fine," said the man, who Saul guessed to be Wash

Keough. "Well, come in! What you doin', standin' on a man's front stoop all the day?"

Saul followed Jason in, although he had yet to be introduced. However, Mr. Keough didn't seem too inclined toward the formalities, so Saul decided he needn't be, either. He waited until Keough led them to the kitchen and put on the coffeepot before he stuck out his hand and said, "Saul Cohen, sir. It's an honor to make your acquaintance."

"Well, I'm sorry there, Mr. Cohen," Keough boomed happily. He was short, but he filled the room, and Saul could see why he had been a friend of Jedediah Fury. Both of them were larger-than-life characters. "I'm right pleased to meet you," he went on, still pumping Saul's hand. "Any friend of Jason's is a friend'a mine. Where's your pa, anyhow, Jason? That ol' mule skinner owes me a game'a checkers."

He let go of Saul's hand, and Saul fairly collapsed into a chair. He tried not to listen while Jason told Keough about his father's death. The words of it washed over him, but he heard the thickness in Jason's voice, and the sorrow in the voices of both men.

He fervently hoped that no one would cry, and then said a quick prayer for forgiveness. He shouldn't be worried about being embarrassed at a time like this.

But no one cried, thank God. In fact, no one so much as spoke a word once the news had been passed on. Keough poured out the coffee, or at least, what was passing for it, then joined them at the crude table.

"That's tough," Keough said at last. "That's mighty tough for you, Jason. But it had to happen sooner or later. A man pushes his luck with redskins too much, he's bound to get arrow-shot sooner or later. You're damn lucky they didn't take off with all your womenfolk, too."

Jason sighed, and then launched into the story of trailing Quanah Parker, and the subsequent dice game for the girls and the livestock.

Despite his sorrow over Jedediah's death, Wash Keough seemed to find this part hilarious. He laughed and laughed, and Saul found himself wondering if the man would think it so amusing if he had been there.

"Jason, you say Saul here thought up makin' the dice?" he boomed.

Saul nodded weakly, just remembering how scared he'd been. How scared they'd *all* been.

Suddenly, Keough slapped him on the back. "By God, Saul, that was some kind of quick thinking! Jedediah would'a been proud of the both'a you! So, where you headed this time, Jason? California? Arizona? Maybe up Denver way?"

As it turned out, it didn't much matter to Wash Keough where their destination was. He was passing fifty, had not one cent to his name, and he was ready for a new start. Jason figured it was about the fifteenth new start Wash had undertaken.

Jason was happy for him to tag along. Hell, he was delighted to hire him and pay him thirty dollars and found. Wash was as close a thing to a mountain man as they were likely to run across, and he'd traversed the trail west more than most. Probably about as many times as Jedediah had, if not more.

But there was one thing—Wash had to "test out the grub" before he made his final decision.

"Be proud for you to," Jason said as they all three walked back through town, to the place where Jason had left the wagons. "We've got a mess of really good cooks. You'll be surprised."

"Hope so, Jason," Wash said.

"Oy!" Saul said suddenly. He stopped and put a hand over his heart. "Rachael's list!"

"Better take care of that, Saul," Jason said with a smile. "She'll have your guts for garters otherwise."

Saul wiggled his brows. "I assure you, Mr. Keough, the

ramifications would not be so terrible." He plucked the list from his pocket. "But almost." Saul ducked into the nearest mercantile.

"Hope he don't forget sugar cubes," said Wash, trying to appear philosophical, "in case we run into some like-minded Apaches."

"Good thinking," said Jason.

They had walked to the southernmost part of town, where the wagons waited, before either of them spoke again.

"Got a sizable herd there, boy," Wash commented.

"It's smaller when everybody's hitched up," Jason said, before he thought.

"Well, of course it is," Wash snapped. "You take me for an idiot?" Then his mood lightened considerably. "Say, what's that I smell? Is that fried taters and onions?" He sniffed the air again. "Is that beef? I ain't had beef in a coon's age, let alone woman-cookin'!"

Jason said, "You'll have both tonight, Wash. While we're waiting, let me introduce you around."

"Just don't go 'specting me to recamember half the folks I shake hands with. Never was good with names, and I find I'm gettin' worse in my old age."

Jason introduced him to nearly everyone in the caravan, and spent the time walking between wagons to give him a quick rundown on everyone he'd just met.

"That's gal's mighty sweet on you," Wash said after they left Abigail Krimp's wagon.

"The feeling's not mutual."

"You got somebody else?"

"No. Yes . . . I mean, no."

Olympia Morelli, the newborn strapped to her back like an Indian papoose, was up and around and directing the meal preparation. Rachael Cohen shot Jason a questioning glance when the introductions were made, and Jason quickly said, "Saul's at the mercantile."

"So where else should he be?" she replied with a shrug.

"Them wouldn't happen to be dried apple pies bakin' in them covered skillets, would it?" Wash asked. His nose was working again, and he wiped away a little drool at the corner of his mustache.

"Yes, they would, Mr. Keough," Rachael answered. "I shall be sure to save you a large piece."

Jason had never seen the old desert rat beam so wide.

"What happened, Wash?" he asked. "Why are you so broke?" It appeared as if Wash hadn't eaten a decent meal in a month of Sundays with a couple of Saturdays tossed in.

"Thieves," was what Wash said. "Thieves and miscreants." He said it with a "that's that" air, and Jason didn't press him further.

Later, Wash ate with Jason, Saul, and Salmon, and Wash told Jason that he'd been eating nothing but snake for the last two weeks.

"Hell, I murdered the last jackrabbit in Santa Fe months ago," Wash said. "And I was about to run outta snake."

"Run out?" Salmon asked.

"How could a man run out of snakes in this country?" Saul asked.

Wash drew his gun and opened the chamber. "Only two slugs left, see?"

Jason said, "Don't worry. I'll supply the ammo."

"Fair 'nough." All of a sudden, he sat straight up. "That your woman I see comin' there, Saul? The one with that good apple pie all plated up?"

Again, he licked away a touch of drool at the corner of his mustache.

Chapter 25

The wagon train stayed over in Santa Fe for the next day, too. Jason figured that folks needed some time to get their land legs again, and the women were especially glad for the chance to stock up for the remainder of the journey. The men took care of all sorts of little repairs that they'd let pile up, and then collected in the nearest cantinas for beer and gossip.

The women weren't the only ones who liked to talk.

Matt MacDonald wisely kept his distance. Jason didn't see him, although he heard that the few surviving possessions that were Matt's or his father's were being carried by Nordstrom, and those of his sister were being carried by, well, *him*.

Jenny at work again.

But he overheard snatches of whispers when people thought he couldn't hear. They told him nothing new, just reinforced what he already knew.

That Matthew MacDonald was planning on killing him.

There wasn't much he could do about it, save for walking up to Matt, bold-faced, and shooting him through the heart. All he could do was just wait and see what happened, try to keep an eye on the slippery son of a bitch in the meantime, and above all, stay alive.

By the time the wagons were ready to pull out and head

west once more, Wash Keough had regaled the entire camp with stories about Jedediah, running back to when he was a trapper and ranged the Rocky Mountains. Jason noticed that the entire camp also knew about Quanah Parker and the sugar-cube dice game now, too.

Actually, Jason was growing a little embarrassed about it.

He caught sight of Matt about a half hour after they pulled out. Matt was on horseback, riding alongside the Milchers' wagon and deep in conversation with the Reverend Milcher. Jason preferred to think that the reverend was counseling Matt on the loss of his father, but he couldn't help but wonder if Milcher was in on the plan to do him harm.

But that was just stupid, wasn't it? There wouldn't be a plan, not an organized one if he knew Matt, and even if there was, Milcher wouldn't be in on it. He was too much the pacifist. He could barely kill an animal for the supper table.

Still, just the fact that Matt and Milcher were talking made Jason a little bit mad.

And the fact that Megan was still there, constantly in his thoughts, frustrated him no end. He had made a point of steering clear of her.

But now they were moving again. Now they'd swing southwest, traveling down through Chiricahua Apache territory, and then up to Tucson. Then it would be north a few more days until they came to the north end of the Santa Rita range, then west over to California.

It all sounded so simple when you just thought about the route or saw it on paper. Deceptively simple.

There were the White Mountain Apaches to get by, then the Chiricahuas down around Apache Pass. Apaches left and right, as thick as proverbial thieves. The Maricopa and Hopi Indians he wasn't too worried about, nor the Pimas, seeing as how they were fairly peaceable by nature. But the Yaqui tribe, over by the California border country, he was very much concerned about.

And Wash was no help. Oh, he was full of stories about white men being burned or flayed or skinned alive by Apache; men having their privates hacked off—women, too—babies impaled on spears, and torture beyond any measure of reason. Jason had to warn him not to tell those tales around the other parties in the train, particularly the women.

"Aw, goldurn it, anyhow, Jason. Why you gotta take the fun outta everything?" Wash had complained. He grinned when he said it, though.

Conversely, Wash had himself been filled in on every action, idea, overstepped boundary, and implied insult suffered by each and every member of the train since they'd left Kansas City.

Now, he liked Jason and had admired his father a good deal, and he had a hard time believing that Jason had sent Matt's daddy up that hill just to fall off it. Or that if Jason had taken the southern route over the little patch of Indian Territory, they wouldn't have run into Quanah Parker and his murdering thugs. Or any number of other things that Matt MacDonald told him.

The Reverend Milcher seemed to be a troublemaker, too. Bad-mouthing Jason every chance he had, that one, then invoking the name of the Lord, like that would make everything all right. And talking bad about those folks of the Hebrew persuasion. His woman was a bit of a snob, too. She seemed offended by Wash's manner of dress. Also, his talk and his hair and, well, everything about him.

He scratched at his neck. Well, there was no pleasing some women. Maybe she thought he was Hebrew, too. Hell, all he knew about Hebrews was that the Bible talked about them a lot, and that Jesus was one. You'd think that would be a good thing to a Bible-thumper like Milcher.

They were about four days out of Santa Fe, and Jason had

put him up front, as the scout. This was fine by him. He was up here all alone, with no women to pick at him or scold him for not taking baths. Nothing but the very faint rumble of wagons behind him, nothing but the warm air and skittering critters and soaring birds before him.

It was good to get away from civilization again. To escape the hodgepodge that was Santa Fe, with its fancy Spanish self-proclaimed aristocrats and its riffraff. And everything in between. He had liked it at first, but the town had grown old on him.

He thought of himself as a man of the wild places and a man of action, not some loiterer on the fringes of civilization. He had got to feel more and more like a camp dog.

So now here he was, on the ramble once again, and with cash in his pockets, thanks to Jason Fury. He felt like a new man.

He'd been jogging along, thinking and whistling, then thinking some more for about four hours, when he saw the dust up ahead. It was a good ways off, but it was in a line, the kind that a bunch of galloping riders might make. He stared at it a couple of seconds longer, then wheeled his horse and went back to the wagons.

Better safe than sorry.

Jason gave the command to circle the wagons in tight. He figured that what Wash had seen might be Apache, but then again, it might have been a herd of wild horses or cattle, or a line of troopers. But one out of four chances was reason enough to be prepared, no matter how inconvenient for certain members of the wagon train.

Milcher, for one. He had broken a buckle on his harness, and complained about having to untie the ends.

"You should have taken care of that back in Santa Fe," Jason said.

"I couldn't," Milcher stated, in between working at the leather straps with his fingers and teeth. "It was Sunday."

This time, the circle was formed in no time, complete with the livestock in the middle, and the men also pulled the wagons snugly head-to-butt, once the teams were unhitched. Men armed themselves, women took their positions, and children and pets were tucked away in safe hiding places.

And they waited.

After what seemed a long while to Jason, the line of rising dust came into sight. It moved north of them, paralleled them for a bit, then turned north and disappeared.

"Is that all?" Saul finally asked. "Are they gone? Are we free to move again?"

Jason scratched the back of his head. He wanted to say that he was damned if he knew, but instead, he turned toward Wash. "What do you think, Wash? They go on past, or is it a trick?"

"I think I'd wait a mite if I was you, Jason. They's tricky."

"Who's tricky?" called Milcher, who had just picked up part of his buckle-less harness again. "Comanche again?"

"More like Apache," said Wash. "Course, in this country, could be either kind'a redskin."

"Either kind?" Milcher's face, already lower than a well-digger's boot, fell even further.

Salmon Kendall had walked up. "What's the deal, Jason?"

Jason straightened his hat. "Looks like we're going to wait here a little longer, Salmon. You know, to make certain they haven't circled around."

"You know best," Salmon said, and headed back to his wagon.

"Wish I did," Jason muttered as he started toward the horizon where the dust cloud had disappeared. "I wish to hell that I did."

* * *

Two hours later, there was still no sign of marauding heathen, and Jason decided to move on out again. They might wring another mile or two out of the day if they hurried. Each man or woman hitched his or her team once more, and off they set.

This time, Jason rode up front with Wash. Not because he wanted to keep an eye on the horizon—Wash was capable of that—but because he wanted to put as much distance as possible between himself and the still-complaining Milcher. As if it was *his* fault that the reverend hadn't replaced that lousy buckle.

He supposed he'd have to hear about it until they reached Tucson. Which, he fervently hoped, would not be on a Sunday.

"You're awful quiet, boy," Wash said.

"Guess so." The comforting creak of leather rode the silence, filling it.

Wash asked, "Want I should shoot us somethin' for supper?"

"We're still eating the steer we butchered last night." And then he quickly added, "Thanks for the offer, though, Wash." It was more than he was getting from most of the others.

Silence again. It began to grow dark, and Jason reined his mount in. "Enough, Jason?"

"Reckon." They turned their horses around and began to walk back toward the wagons. "Wash, you figure those really were Indians in that dust cloud?"

"Hard tellin'," Wash said with a shrug.

"Well, next time you see something suspicious, you just do exactly what you did today."

Half-hidden beneath his scraggly mustache, Wash's mouth quirked up into a grin. "Even if it puts your Reverend Milcher out a mite?"

"Even if it puts him out a whole bunch. Especially, in fact."

Wash said, "That's the Jason Fury I recollect."

Jason didn't remember having been so, well, *petty* before, but he didn't say anything. He just let it pass, and tried to think kind thoughts about the Milchers. Maybe he was being too hard on them. Well, hard on the reverend, anyway.

In fact, when the new camp circle was formed and everybody was busy uncoupling their draft animals, Jason made a point to go over to Milcher and let him know that Saul Cohen had the hardware and skill to fix his broken harness.

As he had imagined, Milcher turned him down.

The blamed idiot.

Chapter 26

They traveled down through Apache Pass, into the land that would one day be officially called Arizona but was still a part of New Mexico. The landscape grew more and more rugged, and the Reverend Milcher was overheard to say that the crags and spires of Apache Pass were surely the work of the Devil.

A few miles after they traveled out of it, they came across signs of a massacre. They discovered the burned-to-charcoal remains of a wagon and three charred bodies, which apparently had been tied to the wheels.

Apache arrows were stuck in the low scrub that ringed it.

"Glad Chavez isn't with us anymore," Jason commented when they found a chunk of unburned board with a bit of a sign on it, in Spanish.

"Who?" asked Wash.

"They joined us on the other side of the Sangre de Cristos with Gooding's group," Jason answered. "They got off the trail in Santa Fe."

"Oh. The same Chavez what does the stained glass and ironwork?"

"That's the one."

"Thought they both went back East to pick up stuff for glassmakin'. Him and his brother, I mean."

"They did. Comanches got the brother."

Wash shook his head. "Damned shame. Y'know, I got half a mind to take off and go buffalo huntin'. Sooner or later, we'll starve the bastards out if we can't get 'em to play nice no other way."

Jason doubted it would make much difference to the Apache. You'd have to kill every steer, goat, hog, rabbit, badger, snake, horse, mule, and burro in the countryside to put a little bit of a rumble in their larcenous stomachs.

He didn't think much of the Apache race. Not as a whole, and not as individuals.

He pulled up his horse and dismounted.

"Whatcha doin'?" asked Wash.

"Better bury these bodies," Jason said, pulling the folding shovel from his saddlebag. The corpses looked like they'd died hideous deaths. Their blackened, shriveled mouths were stretched open in twisted, silent screams. He didn't want Megan or Jenny to see them.

Wash dismounted, too, and found his shovel. "Better hurry, then," he said as he, too, drove his shovel into the hard caliche soil. "Wagons'll be comin' along pretty soon."

Aside from the mystery riders and the hapless Mexicans, they had no more trouble with the Apache, and for this Jason was very glad. They rumbled through Goose Flats, which was little more than a collection of the tents and shacks of miners. They traveled north, the days growing hotter and the nights growing warmer, and came in sight of Tucson and its presidio a few days later.

Jason had the wagons pull directly into the presidio, for safety's sake, and there they set up temporary camp. Jason remembered Tucson as a place where the mosquitos were thick and the swampland even thicker, but it seemed the town had used up most of the old swamp water for irrigation. He didn't even see a mosquito.

By this time, he figured that Matt MacDonald had given up on killing him, since he was still breathing. In fact, he'd only caught a couple glimpses of Matt since Santa Fe. A coward was always a coward, he'd decided.

Megan, on the other hand, was ever present. He'd taken to walking with her in the evenings. Those evenings when it was safe, anyhow.

He'd also explained that he couldn't stay. That he wanted to go back East, to college. To live back East and never see the West again.

She said she understood, but somehow, he had a hard time believing her. He was having an increasingly hard time believing himself.

His pilgrims took full advantage of Tucson, even if they didn't speak any Spanish. Personally, he found it difficult to get around without speaking Spanish, but Wash spoke it fluently, and did the linguistic navigating for him and Saul and Salmon.

Their first stop was Cantina de los Lobos, where Salmon had far too much tequila and Wash practically took a bath in beer, or *cerveza,* as the locals called it. They all partook of the cuisine, which turned out to be enchiladas, enchiladas, and more enchiladas.

By the time they left, Saul and Jason were carrying Salmon between them while Wash staggered along behind, weaving and farting his way down the street.

"Jason Fury!" Jenny scolded when they finally stumbled back into the presidio. "Have you been drinking?"

"Wash and Salmon drank it all up before I had a chance," he said.

Her eyes narrowed, as if she didn't quite believe him. "Well, Megan's been looking for you."

"Figures," he said, and let Salmon slide to the ground.

"Thank you," huffed Saul, who'd been holding up Salmon's other side and was plainly tired.

"Welcome," said Jason. "Where is she, Jenny?"

"Over at our wagon."

"What's wrong?" Jenny seemed nervous and upset, not at all like herself.

But she said, "Nothing. Go see Megan, all right?" And then she turned from him and toward Salmon, on the ground. "Saul, you should have know better than to let him get like this. He's going to feel awful in the morning."

As Jason walked away, he heard Saul say, "Better he should feel awful in the morning than I should have a broken jaw tonight."

When Jason reached the wagon, he called, "Megan?"

Teary-eyed, she emerged from the tail end of the Conestoga and climbed down. She was still dressed, though she had pulled a quilt about her, like a cape.

"What is it?" he asked, suddenly concerned. "What's wrong?"

"It's Matt. I'm so sorry to bother you with this. I mean, seeing as how the two of you are like water and oil."

"What about him?" he asked, without denying her charge. It was common knowledge, after all. "I haven't even seen him, except for a snatch here and there, for days."

"He's in jail, in town, and nobody will go and get him out." She burst into tears, and he pulled her close despite his reservations to the contrary.

"It's all right, Meg, don't cry," he whispered into her setter-red hair. "I'll get him out."

"But it's serious." She wept against his shoulder. "H-he killed someone."

Jason had no words to reply to her. He knew that Matt MacDonald would come to no good, but this was pretty early for him to turn from a schoolyard bully into a cold-blooded killer.

At last, he said, "They're wrong, Megan. I don't believe it. Where is he?"

* * *

He took Saul and Wash with him. Wash was sobering up faster than anybody could have expected, and Jason thought they might need him to breach the language barrier.

When they reached the jail, however, the sheriff turned out to be an Irishman named Clancy—or so said the little sign on his desk—and he sure enough had Matthew locked up in a cell. Matt didn't look any too happy about it either. And neither did he act overjoyed to see Jason, Saul, and Wash come in the front door.

"Can I be of assistance to you gents?" asked Clancy, rocking forward with a thump to put all four legs of his chair on the floor.

"As a matter of fact, you can," Jason said with the friendliest smile he could muster. He stuck out his hand. "I'm Jason Fury, sir. Wagon master of the train parked over in the presidio?"

The sheriff shook his hand. "Sheriff Clancy. I heard about you folks. Believe I've got one of your company under custody, as a matter of fact." He nodded toward Matt's cell. "You come to see me about him?"

"What's he charged with?" Jason asked.

"Well, seems he picked himself a fight up at the Purple Garter. Picked it with the wrong fellow, too." Clancy leaned forward and whispered, "Y'know, your boy here isn't too smart. I'd be keepin' him under lock and key if I were you."

Wash farted loudly, then collapsed into a chair. "'Scuse me," he muttered.

Nobody paid him any mind other than Saul, who turned red and cleared his throat.

"How much is his fine?" Jason asked, pretending Megan hadn't so much as breathed the word "murder." He knew the MacDonalds were well fixed—although not so well fixed as they had been before Hamish came tumbling down the mountain—and Matt could pay him back later.

"No fine," said the sheriff. When Jason looked puzzled, he added, "See, he decided to knock out Jose Vasquez, then take a knife to him. The son of Miguel Vasquez? Oh, hell. The Vasquez family's been the big muckety-mucks around here since who laid the rail."

"The big what-whats?" piped up a puzzled Saul. In the corner, Wash let loose another round of gas.

"Well, what's it going to take to get him out of here by morning?" Jason asked.

The sheriff sat down again and folded his arms. "Sorry, boys. Can't help you. Got to go to trial. Unless . . ."

Jason leaned forward. "Unless what?"

"Unless you can get him clean out of the territory. I don't care much for the Vasquez bunch, myself. Old Miguel holds himself pretty damned high, if you ask me. But I think that's going to be tough, considering that your friend here called him a stinking Mex and tossed a near-full spittoon over him before the fight even started."

Jason looked over at Matt, then back at the sheriff. "Aw, crud."

With the still-half-drunken Wash along for linguistic support, Jason and Saul set out for the Purple Garter in search of Miguel Vasquez, father of the murdered boy. Try though they might, however, he was nowhere to be found.

After going to the Purple Garter and four other saloons, they bumped into one of his cronies, a man who swore that Miguel had ridden home after the incident. And that furthermore, his *compadre* Miguel had still been angrier than a sack full of wet bobcats. He'd wanted to lynch Matt right then and there.

From the tone of the speaker, Jason decided that he wouldn't want Miguel mad at *him*. But what could he do? Like it or not, Matt was his responsibility. Additionally, he was Megan's brother.

He had no choice.

He and Wash and Saul went back to the presidio, where

Wash passed out, Saul went to be with his family, and after making sure the water barrels were all refilled, Jason went to his wagon, to face Megan and his sister.

He had a feeling they weren't going to be any too keen on his plan. He wasn't, either.

He got them together and urged them inside the wagon, where he joined them.

"Listen up, you two," he began. "I can't get him out before we leave. In fact, I don't think I can get him out at all. Legally, that is. He killed a man in a bar brawl."

Megan's face fell, and Jenny didn't look too good, either. He'd had suspicions that something was going on between Matt and Jenny, but then again, he didn't really want to know. He'd just been hoping he was wrong, but Jenny's face told him otherwise, damn it.

"I'm going to break him out," he said. But he tried to sound as if it didn't even strike him as breaking the law, just as if Matt was his lifelong friend, just as if Jason was invincible.

He sounded a great deal more secure than he felt.

Chapter 27

At four o'clock, he roused the camp. They were a little cranky about being awakened before the dawn, but he managed to get everybody moving. They started to hitch their teams and eat their breakfasts.

He slipped into town, taking Ward Wanamaker with him. Ward had volunteered, saying that Jason was a fool if he thought anybody, man or women or sheriff, could see him once and forget him, and that was just the way it was.

Ward went into the sheriff's office first, found a groggy deputy on duty, managed to crack him over the head, then called for Jason.

Together, they tied and gagged the luckless deputy, found the key to Matt's cell, and locked up the unconscious deputy in his place.

Matt, who had said nothing during the entire procedure, finally spoke just as they were leaving. And then, only one word. A growl on his face, he looked at Jason and said, "Why?"

"Because you paid my pa to take you to California," Jason said. "Now, shut up."

"Huh?"

"Quiet!"

"Listen, you son of a bitch, if you're gonna—"

Ward stepped between them and grumbled, "If you two are set on killin' each other, I'd suggest you wait till we get clear of town."

They slipped out, the streets still being mostly devoid of people except for the occasional dozing drunkard, and walked quietly toward the presidio. When they reached it, the wagons were ready to go. In fact, Salmon and Saul, both of whom knew what Jason and Ward were up to, had already lined the Conestogas up and started them out the presidio gate.

Jason saw someone waving at him, squinted, and realized it was Jenny.

"Come on," he said, grabbing hold of Matt.

Ward grabbed the other arm, and they fairly dragged Matt, kicking and hollering, to the wagon. Halfway there, Jason had finally had enough. He slugged Matthew on the jaw as hard as he could, and as he'd hoped, Matt crumpled.

"That's better," Ward said.

They dragged Matt's limp body the rest of the way to the wagon, and tossed him up into its bed. Jenny covered him over with quilts—"In case anybody gets nosy," she said—while Megan drove on. Saul had already tacked up Jason and Ward's horses, and they sprang up on them and went immediately to work—Ward with the herd and remuda, and Jason with the wagons—and Jenny ran to drive Salmon Kendall's wagon. Salmon was still passed out in the back.

Saul flagged Jason down when they were about a half mile out of the presidio and asked, "Why didn't you take me along? I never helped in a jailbreak before."

"That's why," Jason said. "Didn't want to start any new habits."

Later that day, while they were slowly working their way north in the shadow of the Santa Rita Mountains, Sheriff Clancy caught up with them. Jason saw him coming and met him at the middle of the caravan.

"Well, what brings you up this way, Sheriff?" Jason asked.

The sheriff reined in his horse next to Jason's. He was not smiling. The opposite, in fact. "I think you know that answer to that, Fury. I want him back. Now."

"What? Who?"

"Don't play games, Fury. I'll search every single wagon in this train if I have to."

Jason propped his hand on his saddle horn and shook his head. "Think you might have a hard time convincing folks to do that, Sheriff, seeing that you're out of your jurisdiction, and also seeing that you arrested one of our most popular members last night. How's Matt doing, by the way? Have you set a trial date?"

Clancy glared at him.

"I'd like to know," Jason went on. "A few of us would like to come back for the hearing. You know, make sure everything's on the up and up?"

Clancy said, "Cut the horseshit, Fury. You and I both know you've got him."

Jason's eyes widened. "We do?"

But Clancy was adamant. "You know damn well that MacDonald broke outta jail early this mornin'. Just before your wagon train pulled out. That's too big a coincidence, Fury."

Jason sighed. "Well, then, I guess we've got a problem, Sheriff. Now, I wouldn't mind you searching my wagons. Wouldn't mind it a bit, personally, although I can't speak for some of the ladies in our party. But see, I've got to get these people to California in a hurry, and we already lost several days trying to get across the Canadian River during a thunderstorm."

"That's not my problem."

"I think it is."

They sat there, their horses dancing nervously between them while the wagons slowly passed. And then at last,

Sheriff Clancy turned his horse and rode back toward Tucson, without a word.

Jason sat there on Cleo, watching him go and thanking the Lord for allowing the sheriff to buy into his bluff. Especially when it was done to protect a cowardly murdering jackass like Matt MacDonald.

Two days later, they swung west again along the Old Mormon Trail and entered a flat, endless plain of desert scrub and blooming cactus called El Despoblado, a wild, ummapped part of the territory. They made steady progress, although Jason posted several men as scouts. They looked in every direction for Apache, who could use the low cover in their favor.

The talk around the campfire, in the evenings, was turning toward farming, and most of the men agreed that this wide plain would make for fine crops. All it needed was water.

Jason pointed out that it would also most likely produce trouble with the Apache, but folks were too excited about the land to listen to him. Additionally, it had been a while since they'd had Indian trouble, and they seemed to have pushed the reality of it away.

Jason pointed out that there were no trees, and therefore, no shade.

Saul said that they could plant some.

Jason pointed out that the Milchers already had purchased land in California.

The Reverend Milcher remarked that he could get his money back, and didn't his flock here need him?

All of this was pointless, Jason figured. There was no water, period. Of course, there was water underground here and there, but he didn't mention it. He just wanted to get these folks across the Colorado River and into California.

But the next day, they came to a small stream thickly lined with cottonwood trees for as far as the eye could see. The

Reverend Milcher proclaimed it a sign from on high, akin to manna in the desert. Privately, Saul told Jason, "I wish he'd stick to his half of the Holy Book."

Jason pointed out that in California, trees had already been planted, and towns—hungry for new citizens—had already been founded. And he was fairly sure that the rivers and streams there ran year round, something he couldn't say for Arizona streams.

Salmon Kendall looked up. "They disappear?" He had been keeping company with Carrie English of late, and sat beside her at the campfire, whittling a little model of Rags for Chrissy.

"They still flow," Jason said, "but they do it underground. Least, that's what I'm told. It'll be pretty hard to irrigate your fields when there's no aboveground water to do it with."

"I've seen it done," piped up Ezekial Morton, the senior member of their group, and usually the most taciturn.

That captured Milcher's attention, and he was on Ezekial like a duck on a June bug. "Where, Brother Morton? How?"

"In Tucson," Morton replied. "While you young bucks were out painting the town, I took a little sightseeing tour. They got them big, deep wells dug down there. Got a sort of augerlike contraption in the center of 'em that brings up the water, and two mules run it. Day and night, the man told me." He scratched at his beard. "Course, I suppose they change the mules out two or three times a day. . . ."

"Well, there you go!" exclaimed the reverend. "We'll build one of those for the dry season!"

Jason shook his head. "You know, the only reason I can think of for you folks staying here instead of going on to California and some sort of civilization is that you'll have to buy land in California, and here it's free for the taking."

The resounding calls of "That's right!" and "Yes!" and "Durn tootin'!" almost knocked Jason off the hay bale he was sitting on. These people were not only cheap, they were crazy.

Wash, apparently the only other sane one in the bunch,

said, "What you gonna build them auger things out of? Cottonwood?"

"That's correct, sir!" Milcher answered confidently.

Wash shook his head and clucked his tongue. "Don't you know you can't kill cottonwood? Hell, fence posts made from it sprout in the ground and give you a fence fulla trees in no time! Cain't imagine what kinda bushy nonsense you'd get if you was to stick 'em down a well!"

"He's right," said Jason.

"We can get other kinds of wood," Salmon Kendall said. "And we've got our wagons. There's plenty of wood in them, and I'll bet it isn't cottonwood."

A murmur of agreement spread over the group.

Jason sighed. He couldn't fight them on it. He said, "All right. Those who want to stay here, can. Those who want to go on to California, I'll lead them. Anybody?"

He looked out over the crowd. There wasn't one taker among them. Against his better wishes, he said, "Fine. I'll stay and help you get your town started, then. I owe you that much."

The Reverend Milcher stood straight up and raised his fist. "Hoorah!" he shouted. And then most everyone rose as one man, and echoed his cry.

"Tomorrow," he said, once everyone had quieted down, "I shall consecrate this land. And we shall also name our new town."

"Well," Matt MacDonald said, stepping from the shadows, "it looks like decent grazing land, anyhow."

"I vote we name it for Jason's daddy!" said Salmon.

"A wise idea," Saul said.

The Reverend Milcher frowned. It looked as if this wasn't going the way he had expected. "Is that a second?"

"What else would it be?" Saul responded.

"Very well, then. All those in favor?"

The small crowd thundered, "Aye!"

Hopefully, Milcher added, "Opposed?"

Not one word was uttered.

Except by a puzzled Jason, who asked, "You're going to name the town Jedediah?"

Saul slapped his shoulder. "No, boy! Fury! And we'll build it right here, right where we are standing."

Heads nodded all round.

Jason was beaten, and he knew it. These fools would try to build their town right here, and the newly christened Fury would fall to the Apache or just plain dry up and blow away.

He said, "If you're set on it."

Chapter 28

Jason and Megan were strolling around the inside of the circled wagons, because Jason didn't want to take a chance on Megan getting snakebit out there in the brush and grass. Since Tucson, he had given up on trying to keep their mutual attraction private, and they strolled openly, arms linked.

"You don't like this idea, do you, Jason?" she asked. "The whole thing about the town, I mean."

"No," he said firmly.

"But why not?"

He looked down at her. "Weren't you listening earlier?"

"Yes, but I thought you were just trying to paint the worst possible picture to dissuade the Reverend Milcher from giving up his land in California. And let the others know that it won't be easy."

Jason didn't say anything.

"We know it won't be easy, Jason. But we're here, we have water and land—land forever! And it's just here for the taking!"

"You realize you're probably going to build right in the center of somebody's range land?"

"But nobody owns the range, Jason."

"True. But some people like to think they do. And then there are the Apache."

She gave a little sigh. "They haven't bothered us yet."

"Not yet. But that doesn't mean they won't. We're sitting in the middle of their home range, too."

She looked down for some time, while they walked the length of three wagons. "You're not going to stay, are you?"

"Not any longer than I have to." He felt bad about leaving her, but he had to tell the truth. He was leaving eventually. "I'll stay long enough to help get the first buildings up and make sure you're settled in, but then I'm going."

Megan turned her head away and whispered, "All right. I understand, I guess. Will you take Jenny with you?"

He hadn't ever thought of *not* taking Jenny. "Yes."

"Does she know about this? She's pretty stuck on my brother, you know."

Jason stiffened. He hadn't wanted to know about it, had tried to ignore it, push it from his mind. And now here it was. He said, "Tough."

Megan stopped walking, and he stopped, too. Her hands, curled into fists, were cocked on her hips. "Tough? That's all you have to say?"

He tried to save it by saying, "What I mean is that it's going to be tough on her. But she's young. What does she know yet? And Matthew doesn't strike me as the type to want to settle down."

She set her pretty jaw. Through clenched teeth, she said, "And I guess you don't strike me as that type, either."

"But Megan—"

"Good night, Jason," she said before she turned and ran for the wagon she shared with Jenny.

"Saul? Saul!"

"Yes, Jason, what is it?" Saul looked up from his work, which, at the present, was digging a hole.

"What's the hole for?"

Saul shrugged. "For a well, you dig a hole."

Jason grinned despite himself. "I think maybe you'd better start again, about twenty, twenty-five yards over. You're right in the middle of the trail. What are you digging it for, anyway?"

"Why, the town's water supply! For when the stream dries up."

This time, Jason couldn't hold back his laugh. He said, "Saul, you'd best make it farther than that, then. If we're going to grow up an entire town around your well, we'd best leave it room enough to grow without every wagon train coming west going right through somebody's front garden."

Saul nodded. "Again, wisdom beyond his years . . ."

"And get somebody to help you," Jason called over his shoulder as he walked away. He had other fish to fry.

Everybody seemed to be of the same mind as Saul in thinking that nobody would ever again use this trail. The wagons were still circled smack on it, with the shallow trail ruts running right through the circle.

Actually, this gave Jason a modicum of hope. Other trains would come through here, and could pick up those who became dissatisfied with their choice to stay. There was a back door, after all.

But folks had already begun setting up shop, right where their rigs sat. Canvas wagon covers were untied and pulled out and staked up for shade, just like Olympia Morelli's was each night to make the cook tent. People were spreading out, freeing up possessions they'd kept squirreled away since the start of their journey.

He was looking for Megan, hoping to clear up their little misunderstanding of the previous night, but was told by Ward Wanamaker that she was gone. And his horse, too!

"Yeah, Matt was headin' off to scout a good place to headquarter a ranch," Ward said. "Megan went with him, and your sister, too. She took your Cleo. Said you wouldn't mind."

Actually, he did mind quite a bit. If Matt wanted to wander around on the plain and act as Apache bait, that was his choice. But he had no business taking the girls with him.

Jason pulled a horse from the remuda, borrowed a saddle and bridle, and made ready to go and bring them back. "Which way did they head?" he asked Ward, as he swung up into the saddle.

Ward pointed. "Southeast. They were followin' the creek. You want I should ride along, Jason? Wash is right over there, too. You might want a couple'a extra guns."

"Yeah." Jason nodded curtly. "Be glad of your company, Ward."

The men spotted the Apache before the Apache spotted them. There were two braves, and they seemed to be trailing somebody. Probably Matt and the girls, because they kept to the cottonwoods along the stream.

Wash pulled out his rifle and started to take aim, but Jason shot out an arm and shoved the barrel aside. "No," he whispered. "Let's see if we can take care of this without any bloodshed."

"But they's only Apache!" Wash hissed, disappointed.

"You shoot two, and you'll have two hundred down here looking for them. And finding the train."

Wash swore under his breath, but shoved his rifle back into its boot. If Ward had any feelings one way or the other, they didn't show on his face.

The Apache had stopped, and so did the men. At a signal from Jason, the men dismounted. Jason, the only one tall enough to see over the slightly rolling scrub and grass, kept the Indians in sight.

"What?" Wash said. "What do you see?"

Jason shook his head. "I figure that Matt and the girls've stopped up there, somewhere. The Apache are either just waiting them out, or looking for a chance to attack. Or, hell, maybe they don't think it's worth it for a kid and two girls. . . ."

"Worth what?" Ward asked.

"Worth possibly getting shot." Jason kept his eyes on the Indians. They were still mounted, and he could make out their heads and shoulders. "They'll have to have seen that Matt's armed. And if I know Jenny, she's got Papa's shotgun on her."

He just hoped that if she saw those braves on their trail, she'd hold off on blasting them. While they stood there, he ran scenario after scenario through his mind, but all of them ended in blood. Mostly theirs.

At last, he quietly said, "Mount up, boys."

"What you thinkin', Jason?" Wash asked, his eyebrows knitting and relaxing, then knitting again.

Ward, jumpy as a cat in a room full of rockers, said, "Yeah, what?"

"We're gonna charge those Indians, men. Charge 'em full out, yelling and yelping and hollering. There are three of us and two of them, and they know there are more of us ahead of them. What I figure to do is split them off to the east at high speed, then pick up Matt and the girls and hightail it back to camp."

He didn't wait for either of them to respond. He just kicked his horse and took off, screaming at the top of his lungs, and screaming some more.

Ward and Wash followed him, thank the Lord. They all three hooted and hollered at full volume, and the Indians, shocked and surprised, did exactly what he'd hoped they'd do. They took off at a gallop, heading east over the prairie.

And not one single shot was fired by either party. Jason was proud of that.

The three kept up their hollering until they came in sight of

Matt and the girls. Matt was on his feet, trying to see what all the noise was about.

Jenny and Megan had taken shelter behind some weedy cottonwoods at the timber's edge. Jenny had her shotgun raised and ready.

"Don't shoot, Jenny!" Jason called, and they came out of hiding immediately.

"What the hell are you doing, Fury?" Matt demanded. The remains of a picnic, hastily abandoned, were scattered at his feet.

"Saving your butt from Apache," Jason said, and then ordered the girls up on their horses. Matt remained where he stood, clenching and unclenching his fists.

"They're going to come back, MacDonald," Jason said. "No two ways about it. I'd get out of here fast if I were you."

Jason took off the other way—Wash, Ward, and the girls behind him—before Matt had his foot in the stirrup. He started his horse running while he was still trying to gain his second stirrup.

Jason would have found it funny, but he was too busy trying to keep an eye on the girls, watch the east for returning Indians, and guide his horse back to the circle of wagons. When they came skidding in, Jason leapt from the saddle and tossed his reins to Ward, then immediately yanked Jenny down from Cleo's saddle.

"Jason!" she cried.

"What were you thinking?" he demanded. "Don't you know you could have been killed? Or worse?"

When she just stared at him, mouth open, he pushed her away and began hollering, shouting, "Apache, everybody! On your guard!"

Folks grabbed their guns, tucked their children away, dropped whatever they'd been doing before, and waited.

An hour passed before Jason allowed them to let down

their guard, but he still assigned Ward and Wash to keep watch.

The people under his care might think he was crazy, but he didn't care. He was still responsible for them.

And they were, by God, going to keep breathing so long as he was around, whether they liked it or not.

Chapter 29

Night fell and the Indians still hadn't returned. Saul and Salmon and Milt had managed to dig deep enough to find water. Salmon immediately threw his hat in the air and climbed up out of the hole, certain that their work was done.

But Saul knew they'd have to go deeper. The stream was running now and the water level was high. It would go lower. How much lower, he didn't know. All he knew was that he had forgotten how much he hated well-digging.

Saul also knew that Milt Billings had been hired by Jedediah to care for their livestock and help them across the western expanse, but somehow, Saul didn't believe that Jedediah could have known Billings very well. The whole day long, Milt had complained about Jason seeing Indians where there weren't any.

As far as Saul was concerned, if Jason said there were Apache out there, there were Apache. No two ways about it. And he found his anger with Milt slowly coming to a boil. First off, the ground was too hard. Well, they were all three having to dig it, weren't they?

The next complaint on Milt's list was that Jason had taken Milt's horse when he galloped off into the scrub, and when he'd brought him back, he hadn't even walked him out.

Well, Saul had seen Ward Wanamaker walking out four horses while they were all arming themselves for the supposed Apache attack, which, he was extremely glad hadn't come.

By the time they crawled up out of that hole, the usually peaceable Saul was ready to whack Milt Billings over the head with a shovel.

But he didn't.

As the three of them sat there, dangling their legs over the edge and watching the water level slowly rise, Saul's boys came out to join them. David, the oldest at ten, said very formally, "Good evening, Father," and helped himself to a little square of ground next to Saul. He dangled his legs over the edge, too. Jacob, eight, and Abraham, six, came next, and both tried to sit on Saul's lap at the same time. Unfortunately, Saul didn't have enough lap, and scooted the larger Jacob to his other side.

"Mother says dinner will be ready in a half hour," David said, then made a face.

"What? You don't like what we're having?"

"Mrs. Jameson gave canned beets again." His voice turned to a whisper. "Even Mr. Cow won't eat them!"

Saul smiled. "Well, we'll see what can be done, David."

The boy visibly relaxed.

"If he was my kid," said Milt, "he'd eat 'em whether he liked 'em or not."

The hairs on the back of Saul's neck went up. "Lucky for him, he is not yours."

"Don't get uppity. All's I meant was that out here, you gotta eat what you're given, when you're given it. 'Cause you ain't likely to be given much of anything again."

"Speak for yourself. I will see to my own."

"Stop it, you two!" said Salmon, just as the alarm rose.

Wash Keough, atop the Kendall wagon, shouted, "Apache! Everybody in! Apache!"

Saul scooped up his boys and ran for the wagons, with Salmon hard on his heels.

"I thought Indians weren't supposed to attack this close to night," huffed Saul as he slid down next to Jason, rifle in hand.

"Don't believe everything you read," was all Jason said. Jenny was beside him, ready to reload.

Rachael, having secreted the boys in the bottom of their wagon, joined Saul.

"Sorry if your meal is ruined, Rachael," Jason said. He could see the cloud of dust rising, now, growing nearer.

"It will do the stew good to wait a little," she replied stoically. "And Olympia had already taken the biscuits off the fire."

Jason tossed a box of cartridges toward Saul. "In case you run out."

But Saul was staring out at something much closer than the approaching cloud of dust. "Dear God," he whispered. "It's Milt! He fell in!"

Jason shifted his gaze and saw the well that Saul had been digging, and saw Milt trying to pull his way out. The water must have risen, and it looked like he was having a hard time gaining any purchase on the muddy walls.

"Stay put, Milt!" Jason shouted. The cloud was getting closer. "Keep your head down!"

"I keep it down, I'm gonna drown!"

Jason stood up, muttering "Damn!" and made a run for Milt.

He heard his sister shouting behind him to come back, but he was already halfway there. When he reached Milt, the dust cloud was almost upon him, and he was vaguely surprised that the Indians weren't screaming war cries, weren't scream-ing anything at all. But he reached down and gripped Milt's hand, and yanked with all his might. Milt came up out of that well like a catfish on a hook, and scrambled back toward the wagons on Jason's heels, spraying well water as he went.

They both skidded inside just as the forms of the men within the cloud could be made out.

Not Apache.

Not Indians at all.

The party reined in about twenty feet from the circled wagons, and a single rider emerged from the yellow mist of dust still surrounding the rest of his comrades. "Hello the wagons!" he called. He was dressed in an ordinary way, with Levi's, boots, and a flannel shirt. And he had a badge pinned to his belt.

Jason stood up. "Who's that out there? Be careful, there's a newly dug well about five yards from where you're sitting that horse."

"Thanks for the warning, friend. I'm Deputy U.S. Marshal Bill Gordon, with a party of deputies. We've been out after Juan Alba and his band. Finally picked up tracks, and here we are. Good thing, too, because we were about to lose sight of 'em."

"How many men you got with you, Marshal?" Jason called.

"Fifteen."

Jason leaned toward Rachael. "Can we feed fifteen extra?"

She nodded in the affirmative and Saul said, "They can have David's beets."

A muffled, "Hooray!" came from deep within the Cohens' wagon.

"Come on in, Marshal," Jason called with a wave of his hand. "We were just about to have some dinner."

Nearby, Jason heard a still-sodden Milt grumble, "Apaches, my butt."

There was plenty of stew to go around, and one of Marshal Gordon's men gobbled up David's detested beets and asked for more. Mrs. Jameson was visibly pleased, but offered no seconds, which came as a surprise to no one.

While they ate, Gordon regaled them all with the flamboyant—and sometimes grisly—exploits of Juan Alba, or, as the marshal frequently referred to him, the Scourge of the Borderlands. The kids, from little Constantine Morelli and Abraham Cohen to Sammy Kendall and Seth Milcher, were transfixed, and Gordon played to his audience.

Jason had the feeling that this Alba was someone akin to the outlaws of Kansas and Missouri—blamed for most of the deeds done by other gangs, whether they were in the area or not.

Milt Billings was still drying out beside the fire, and still grousing about getting dunked in the well, and the Apache alarm being raised, and having hired on in the first place.

Finally, Jason couldn't stand it any longer—he was enjoying Gordon's stories, too—and quietly stood up. He walked over to Milt and said, "You can leave any time, you know. Nothing's holding you here."

"I just might," Billings said. "These people are daft! Wanting to build a town in the middle of nowhere, in the middle of Apache country!"

"I agree with you, Milt. But this is the place they picked."

Milt picked up his socks from the edge of the fire and shook them out to see if they were dry. He was barefoot, because he'd propped his boots upside down on sticks a little farther from the flames. "Well, it sure ain't my choice for a quiet neighborhood."

"Like I said, Milt, the door's open. Marshal Gordon's pulling out in the morning. You can go with him."

"Where's he headed?"

"Prescott."

Milt appeared to mull this over for a moment, and then said, "I'll take the last of my wages tonight, if you don't mind, Jason."

Jason paid him on the spot. He was sorry to lose Milt's gun, but that was all.

"You were horrible to Jenny this afternoon," Megan said as they walked around the inside of the circled wagons.

"I should have been horrible to you, too," Jason said. As if he could be horrible to Megan. "You were in real danger. Those two braves were eyeing you. Tonight, by rights, Matt would be dead and you and Jenny would be Mrs. Kills-with-a-Spear or something."

Megan snorted out a little laugh. They spoke quietly, for most of the camp was asleep. The sound of Salmon Kendall's snores made a steady, rhythmic bass note in the background, overridden by the calls of night birds and the rustle of soft wind that played the brush and scrub like a harp.

Well, a very dry and brittle harp.

"Well, I'm glad you came and saved us. I don't want to be Mrs. Kills-with-a-Spear."

He looked down at her, this setter-haired, elfin thing who had stolen his heart, and he was tempted, so tempted to just throw his future aside, just chuck it all and promise to stay with her, ask her to marry him, to be with him always.

But he fought off the temptation.

He walked her back to the wagon, then relieved Wash of sentry duty.

He had a lot of thinking to do.

Chapter 30

Summer came, and under the blistering heat, the pioneers built homes and businesses from the adobe bricks Jason showed them how to make from dirt, water, and straw. Saul dug his well deeper and deeper and deeper, and eventually the stream dried up.

Matt MacDonald began construction of his new ranch house, several miles south of Fury. He had grand dreams, all right, and he labored out there night and day with no one but Gil Collins, whom he had hired away from Jason, to help him.

Jason oversaw the town proper. He and Ward and Salmon and several other men helped Saul build his hardware store, with living quarters on a second floor. They used the beds and side timbers of both Saul's wagons to floor the second story, and chopped down ten enormous cottonwoods to make the exposed beams of the ceilings.

Somewhere along the line, they had mutually decided to all work on one man's home or business until it was finished, and then move on, as a gang, to the next. It worked fine, and in this way they also built the Nordstroms' mercantile and a livery and got started on a house for Salmon Kendall, who had recently wed Carrie English and taken on Chrissy and Rags as his own, too. Chrissy seemed to be getting along famously with Sammy and Peony, who enjoyed having a little sister. They had taken to Carrie, too, although it was obvious that the loss of their mother still cut deep.

Around Saul's well they built a low wall, put an A-frame over it for reeling buckets up and down, and it sat in the center of a large patio in the very center of what was becoming the town of Fury.

Around the perimeter of this "town square," the buildings slowly rose here and there, like the scattered teeth of an old man. In between, there sat wagons not yet evacuated or abandoned, their canvases spread and staked like open-air tents.

"It's really turning into something," Jason said to Jenny, one night after the work was done and they finished their supper.

"You didn't think it would?" Jenny asked him. "I always knew they'd make something wonderful."

Jenny, now sixteen, had bloomed over these last few months. Her blond hair was streaked quite fetchingly by the sun, her complexion glowed, and she had grown a half inch taller and filled out. She was no longer the gawky colt of a girl he remembered, but a beautiful young woman. The realization came as something of a shock to him.

"You always had more faith than anybody I ever knew, baby sister," he said.

"Papa used to call me that, too."

"I know." He put an arm around her shoulders and gave her a little hug.

"You're thinking about leaving, aren't you?"

Once again, he was surprised. He hadn't known it was that obvious. "Yes, I guess I am."

"Then you'll go alone, Jason. I'm not going with you."

He stared at her, lost for words.

"I'm going to marry Matt MacDonald and stay here and raise babies, horses, and cattle, in that order."

This time, he found the words. "No! No, you're not! You're

coming with me. You're going to live where there are no Indians, no bandits, where people can act like people and not animals, Jenny. And you're going to marry some nice, civilized, educated man, not a fool like Matt MacDonald!"

She slapped his face so hard it rattled his teeth. "I am too going to marry Matt!"

"Jenny, has he even asked?"

"He's not a fool!" She turned and ran to the wagon before he could think to say anything. She was probably hurrying to repeat everything he'd said to Megan.

Great, just great.

And he stood there, rubbing his cheek and wondering what in the world had possessed him to choose those particular words. He probably shouldn't have called Matt a fool, for one thing, although that was the nicest tag he could think of to hang on him. Stupid, dumb son of a bitch would have been closer to it.

And then he began to think about what she'd said. Raise babies and horses and cattle.

In that order?

He marched after her, hands and jaw clenched. If that bastard had been at her, he'd kill him.

He reached the wagon and climbed up onto the seat. Turning backward to face the cargo area, he shouted, "Jenny!"

Two faces popped up from beneath the quilts: Megan's and Jenny's. Megan looked surprised, but Jenny just looked mad.

"Jenny, has Matt MacDonald . . . has he . . . ?"

Megan cried, "Jason Fury!"

But Jason only had eyes for his sister. He forced himself to spit out the words. "Has he got you in a family way, Jenny?"

Jenny looked completely shocked. "Jason! Of course not! How dare you even *think* that I—"

Jason closed his eyes. "Thank God," he whispered, and slipped away.

* * *

The next morning, after talking to Jenny again and making something of a peace with her, Jason made ready to leave. He'd resigned himself to follow Jenny's wishes. After all, she was grown, and he couldn't exactly kidnap her to bring her along, could he? He had decided to go up to San Francisco instead of back East. It was a big town, and a rich one. Surely they had colleges up there, too, and plenty of opportunities for an enterprising young man to work his way through school.

Also, it meant that he'd be closer to Jenny.

And Megan.

Maybe, after he got settled and got some education under his belt, he could come back for Megan. If she'd have him. If she hadn't already married.

"Stop it, you peckerwood," he muttered as he saddled up Cleo. If he didn't, he'd talk himself into staying. That was the last thing he wanted to do.

So he managed to pull his mind away from Megan and set it on a more useful purpose—plotting his course to San Francisco.

He figured to head due west, to the coast, and then ride straight north. He'd never exactly taken that route before—his total experience of the road west was one trip over the southern route when he was fourteen and one trip over the Oregon Trail when he was twelve, both of which had been overseen by his father. But he figured that if he did as he had planned, he couldn't miss San Francisco.

He heard footsteps behind him. "Jason?" It was Megan. She said, "You're really going, then. Jenny told me, but I didn't believe her. I thought you'd stay until the whole town was built, anyway."

"You've got a good enough start on everything," he replied. "And you know towns. It'll never be finished." They had picked up four more wagonloads of folks just last week. He tried not to look at her, but then she put her hand on his arm, and he turned toward her as if her touch had magnetized him.

"Jason," she whispered, her eyes brimming with tears.

He kissed her. He kissed her hard and long, knowing that he might never be allowed this privilege again.

And then abruptly, he let go of her, leaving her swaying, and mounted his mare. His throat was so thick that he had no words to say good-bye. He simply nodded, his heart full, then rode away.

Roughly twenty minutes after Jason bade good-bye to Megan and rode west, Matthew was awakened from his siesta by Gil Collins, whom he'd hired to help him build his house.

"What?" he said, cranky with the heat and tired from the work.

Gil hurried down from the ladder, which leaned against the partially finished second story, and started running for the horses. "Riders!" he shouted as Matt climbed to his feet. "Comin' fast from the south."

Matt stopped and cocked his fists on his hips. "I suppose these are more of Fury's imaginary Apache?"

Gil leapt into the saddle, grabbed Matt's pinto by the reins, and brought him to Matt at a hard trot. "Not imaginary. Look." Then he tossed Matt the pinto's reins and lit out toward Fury at a dead gallop.

"Coward," Matt grumbled under his breath, but he swung up on the horse, just to get a higher vantage point.

He looked toward the south.

Through clenched teeth, he said, "Damn it!" then lashed the pinto.

He had only loped about thirty yards before the first arrow sank into his arm like a hot branding iron. He didn't look back. He was afraid to see what was chasing him, although the first whoops were just now reaching his ears.

He hunkered lower in the saddle and dug his spurs into the pinto's flanks.

His pinto was fast, faster even than Jason's Cleo or any of

his father's Morgans. He slowly gained on Gil, who was racing for town, and then drew even with him. He glimpsed the fear on Gil's face and saw him draw his revolver.

Gil began to fire just after Matt passed him.

In Fury, Saul was the first one to hear the shots. "Listen!" he said to the others. "Do you hear?"

Randall Nordstrom furrowed his brow. "That's out Matt's way. You think they're hunting rabbits?"

"Too close," said Salmon. He scurried up the ladder to the window of Nordstrom's second floor, then stood up in the window casing to get a better look.

"What?" asked Saul.

Salmon came halfway down the ladder, then jumped the rest of the way. "Apache! And Matt and Gil are ridin' in, hell-bent for leather!"

Saul started to yell, "Circle the wagons!" then remembered that half their wagons were broken up or staked out. Thank God the Mortons had taken most of the livestock up north with them, to where they were building their houses.

Salmon was yelling, "Apache! Get your arms! Apache!" and Randall Nordstrom was already upstairs, in his store, pointing a rifle out the glassless window.

Saul ran to the northwest edge of the square and the ammunition wagon, which hadn't yet been unloaded, and grabbed a couple handfuls of cartridge boxes. One, he tossed up to Randall. The others, he passed out to the men who were already running to Fury's southern perimeter.

To his side, Rachael ran out the front door of his store. He saw her and he called, "Rachael, the children?"

"Under their beds. Saul, come now!"

He ran for her just as Matt MacDonald thundered between them. Saul didn't have to think twice. "Matt!" he cried as the boy leapt off his horse.

Saul could see he was wounded. "Come!" He waved frantically. He could hear the Indians now, hear them growing close with every second. Already, the men on the southern side of the square were firing. "Matt, come here! Come inside!"

Gil Collins came into town just as Saul helped Matt through the door. Gil had taken an arrow deep in his back, and was slumped over his horse's neck.

Saul flagged down the tired horse, slid Gil's limp body to the ground, and slapped the horse on the rump before he dragged Gil inside and bolted the door behind them.

Catty-corner across the town square, to the south, the men opened fire.

Chapter 31

Jason turned to take one last look at the distant horizon, one last look at the land in which he'd left his sister and his love and, he admitted, his friends.

But something was wrong with the horizon. Above the line of trees that followed the creek there rose a thin, moving line of dust. And it was moving toward Fury.

His first thought was Apache, but then he got a grip, telling himself that it was likely another false alarm. Probably just another federal marshal, out on another fool's errand.

But he turned around anyway, and headed back where he'd come from. He urged the palomino into a soft lope. You couldn't be too careful, he supposed, and he could always leave again in the morning.

Maybe he could get Jenny to make him up some beef sandwiches for the road, if they slaughtered a steer tonight.

The sound of the battle came to Ezekial Morton, two miles north of Fury. "Zachary!" he called to his older brother. "There's trouble in town!"

Ezekial's daughters, Europa and Electa, both big, strapping girls, looked up from their chore of mixing adobe and making bricks, glad for the distraction, and joined their father and uncle.

"Mama!" Europa called to the house, or anyway, what there was of it at this point. "Mama, bring Aunt Suzannah!"

Suzannah and Eliza came from the house, and the whole family stood there, listening to the distant gunfire. Ezekial thought it sounded like Independence Day. If you were British.

He suddenly felt cold all over, despite the heat.

"Should we go back?" Electa asked. She was always the optimist, his Electa.

"And do what?" her uncle Zachary said, stroking his beard. "We are best to stay here. Suzannah, put out that cook fire. Now. It makes too much smoke."

Suzannah obeyed as fast as her aged legs would move her.

"Eliza, darlin', you and the girls go inside, too," Ezekial said. "Arm yourselves. Zachary and I will keep watch."

Zachary cocked a grizzled brow. "We will?"

"Yes, Zach. We will."

"Well, I think I'll have a pipe, then." He held out his tobacco pouch. "Care to try my blend?"

"Don't mind if I do."

Jason slowed up on the far side of the creek and made his way through the trees on foot, leading his horse. The sounds and cries were unmistakable, now. This was not an errant marshal. These were Apache on a raid. It sounded like a passel of them, too.

Still on the other side of the creek, hidden from the attackers, he made his way upstream—or what would have been upstream, if there'd been any water flowing—until he was at the far north edge of the town.

Then he mounted his horse, wove through the cottonwoods, and at their edge, suddenly raced forward toward the ammo wagon. He knew the men had to be running low by now.

The Apache were so preoccupied by the settlers, who seemed to have primarily grouped at the south end of town, that they didn't notice him, and he grabbed up all the ammunition he could carry in a gunnysack, left Cleo behind the wagon, and hurried along the fronts of the buildings on the east side of the square, the sack of ammo in one hand and his gun in the other.

Still, no one saw him until a door suddenly opened and he found himself yanked inside. He turned his gun on the person that had dragged him in, then saw it was Saul.

"You came back?" Saul asked, surprised.

"Looks like," Jason answered, then handed the ammunition bag over. While Saul dug through it, Jason spied Gil in the corner, hurt bad. He didn't need to ask what had happened. Instead, he asked, "Where's Morelli?"

Saul motioned with his head. "South wall. Matt MacDonald's upstairs. He galloped in about two shakes before the Apache."

Muttering, "It figures," he snatched back the sack. "Got everything you need?"

"Yes."

"Then get back to it. I've got to get down to the men." He stood up, staying well back from the windows, and turned for the door, then hesitated. "Where are your boys?"

"Upstairs. Rachel put them under their beds."

"Bring them down. The first thing the Apache will do, if we can't turn 'em back, is set fire to the roofs."

"What? But how?"

"Flaming arrows." Jason shut the door between them.

What he saw didn't hearten him much. The new livery was already on fire. Flames licked at the cottonwood roof, bellowed from the windows, and ran the length of the new cottonwood fence. It billowed black smoke.

"Well, I suppose that'll keep 'em from sprouting," he muttered as, hunkered low, he made his way toward the battle.

Above him, in front of Nordstrom's, he heard a shot ring out and looked up just in time to see the muzzle of a rifle withdraw.

"That you, Randall?" he called.

"Yah!" came the shouted answer. Jason dug through the bag until he found .44 rimfire cartridges, then hollered, "Catch! Ammo!"

Nordstrom's head and one arm popped through the opening, and he snatched up the box of cartridges Jason threw.

Jason heard his muted "Thank you!" as he scuttled down the street.

But somebody had seen him, for just then three Apache arrows buried themselves in the dirt at his feet.

He pulled his gun and fired back, although he didn't know exactly who to fire at. Any Indian would do at this point.

They had come around, between, and over the southern buildings now, and were attacking from both sides of them. Jason shot two braves that were hacking at the roof of Milcher's new church. He didn't know who shot the other one, but all three tumbled to the ground like rag dolls.

He was rewarded for this by an Apache arrow that sank into his thigh. It stung like hell, but all he could do for the time being was break off the shaft. Morelli would have to cut it out. He already knew he couldn't push it through because he could feel it scraping the bone.

Some of the Apache had guns, but as far as he could tell, they didn't have any repeaters. Yet.

Limping, he slid around the corner of the building, into an alley, and across it to peek around the corner of the wagon parked at its side.

The savages were swarming over the buildings now. He knew he'd never get any ammunition through to his people. And then he suddenly remembered Salmon Kendall. Salmon Kendall was the only one with an old rifle, one that took powder and ball. And in that sack, he'd put balls and powder for Salmon.

He had an idea. It was dangerous, and it might not work at all, but it was all he had at the moment.

He ducked back into the shadows of the wagon's under-carriage and quickly unraveled three burlap strings from the bag, which he proceeded to braid together, just as he had braided his sister's hair when she was younger.

He affixed one end of the braid to the bag, and then pulled out the small keg of powder, the smallest one he'd been able to find in the ammo wagon. He opened it and shook half its contents out over everything else in the sack, and also over the length of his makeshift fuse.

He hoped it would work. He'd never done it before, never even seen it done. He said a brief prayer, reclosed the half-full keg and stuck it back inside the bag, then lit the fuse.

It burned faster than he'd expected, and he had to toss it in a hurry. Even so, in that brief moment he was exposed, he took another arrow to the shoulder, and thought, *What am I? A pincushion?*

He jumped back into the shadow of the wagon again and waited. Nothing happened. *Damn it!* Either the quickness of the throw had blown out the fuse, or the concussion when it hit had knocked the fuse free of the sack. Either way, his makeshift bomb hadn't gone off.

He crawled underneath the wagon, and on his belly, he took aim and shouted, "Take cover, men!" He fired. And missed.

He hit it with the second shot.

The bag exploded in a thick haze of black smoke, and bullets zinged every which way. Since the Indians were out in the open, it did them, by far, the most damage. Bodies fell right and left, scattered in piles like autumn leaves, and the wood over Jason's head was splintered by three wild slugs.

Fortunately, most of the townsmen had heard and heeded his warning, and jumped back inside what few buildings there were. He still heard shots being fired inside the buildings, their sound muffled as opposed to the bright zings of the ordnance from the bag.

Blood flowed in a river from Jason's leg. He felt weak, and with the last of his strength, he attempted to tie off the leg with his bandanna. That was the last thing he remembered, anyway. Trying to put the bandanna around his thigh, and it being incredibly difficult.

When he woke, he was in Nordstrom's mercantile, laid out on a wide plank, held up by two sawhorses. And the first notion that entered his mind was that they were readying him for burial.

But then Dr. Morelli appeared at his side and said, "How do you feel, Jason?"

"Like I've been on a three-day drunk."

"That's the laudanum," Morelli replied curtly, though with a smile. "And the blood loss. That arrow you took to the leg nearly killed you. Be more careful next time, son. And now, if you'll pardon me, I have other patients. Lie still. Try to sleep."

Try to sleep? There were so many questions he wanted to ask, so many faces that he wanted to see, alive and well.

"Doc?" he asked as Morelli opened the door. "Can I see my sister? And . . . and Megan MacDonald?"

"They're toting water to the men putting out the fire at the livery. They'll be along soon enough."

Jason sighed with relief. They were both all right and unscathed if they were well enough to carry water. He fell into a deep and dreamless sleep.

When he woke again, it was night, and Jenny was sitting by his side.

"It's about time," she said, and smiled at him.

"And what time would that be?" He was feeling less well than he had before, but the wooziness was gone. Now he was sort of wishing it would came back.

"It's nine. I saved you some supper, if you're interested."

He was, and sat up to take his food. His arm was sore, but he knew it would pass. He'd checked under the bandage, and from the burns surrounding it had seen that Morelli had resorted to a little bit of old-time frontier medicine—he'd cut off most of the shaft, cut a groove in what remained, filled it with gunpowder, and shoved it out the other side of Jason's shoulder while it was burning, removing the arrow and cauterizing the wound all at once.

Smart.

He scraped the plate clean in five minutes.

"Didn't know you were that hungry, or I would have brought more," said Jenny.

"I didn't know I was that hungry, either," he said, then changed the subject abruptly. "Who lived and who died, and what happened to the rest of the Apache?"

"The Apache ran off." Jenny looked at her lap.

"Jenny?"

"Dead will be quicker."

"Thank God for that."

"Yes, I suppose so."

"Who'd we lose?"

"Gil Collins. He was dead halfway through the battle. He was dead when Dr. Morelli got to him. Elmer Jameson. He was freeing the horses from the livery when the Indians set it on fire. He never came out. Mr. Nordstrom got hit with an arrow, but he'll be all right, Dr. Morelli says. Same thing for Matt MacDonald and Ward Wanamaker."

"And that's it?"

"One of the new people, too, the ones that stayed from the last train that came through. I don't know his name, but he took an arrow to the neck and a lance to his side, and the doctor said he must have had an angel sitting on his shoulder. Both of them missed anything vital."

"The Mortons?"

"Ward and Salmon rode up to see to them. They were fine." She grinned. "I guess that when your little powder keg thing went off, Miss Europa fainted. That's what Zachary said, anyway."

"Mr. Morton," Jason corrected out of habit.

"Mr. Zachary Morton," Jenny repeated, playing along.

He paused before he said, "And Megan?"

"We've been taking turns sitting with you. She left to stretch her legs about five minutes before you woke up, you ravenous beast, you."

He grinned, then flinched.

"Lay back down. The doctor said you were to stay flat on your back for at least two days."

"Easy for him to say. He doesn't have to lie on a couple of wooden planks with no mattress and no pillow."

"Oh, don't worry. Megan's bringing quilts and a pillow from our wagon." She was talking to him like a fussy child now, and he wasn't sure he liked it.

The door opened, and instead of Megan, there stood a contingent of townspeople, Salmon Kendall in the lead. "We've had us a meeting," Salmon said as he took off his hat. The other members of his party followed suit as they filed in.

"What sort of meeting?" Jason asked, somewhat leerily.

"Well, first off, we wanna thank you for some mighty fast thinking this afternoon. We thought you had gone off to California."

"I came back."

Salmon nodded knowingly, and so did Saul, behind him. "And why'd you do that?" Salmon went on.

"I saw the dust cloud. Didn't know if it was another marshal or Apache, but didn't figure it was worth taking the chance."

"You see?" Saul piped up. "Loyal, he is."

"And brave," added Megan, who had just stepped in, her arms full of bedding.

"Salmon, you heard me say it, Jason Fury would not let us down."

"I heard," said Salmon.

"Isn't our town named for his papa?" Saul went on. "Is not Fury a name to be reckoned with in the West?"

As a man, the crowd nodded and murmured, "Yes."

But Jason wasn't in the mood for flattery. He said, "Get to the point, Salmon."

"And he sees to the heart of the matter!" said Saul.

"The point is, Jason, we had us a little meeting. And we elected you sheriff of Fury."

"You did *what*?" Jason shouted, and was immediately sorry. His head echoed with his own words, and he put a hand to his forehead.

"For a term of two years," Saul added. "Effective immediately."

"God bless you, son," said the Reverend Milcher, who had managed to find the farthest corner from Saul to stand in.

"I won't do it." Jason spoke more softly this time,

"I believe you will," said Saul, a half grin curving his lips. "Why?"

"Because you can't quit 'less the mayor accepts your resignation," Wash piped up from the rear of the crowd.

"And I'm the mayor," said Salmon, leaving Jason thunderstruck.

Salmon turned to the throng and said, "I believe our own Sheriff Fury needs his rest now, folks. Shall we let him have it, or should we stay and argue some more"—he turned his head back toward Jason—"about things that can't be changed?"

The crowd began to funnel out through the door.

Jason closed his eyes in resignation and muttered, "Aw, crud."

BOOK TWO

Hard Country

Chapter 1

With only a slight limp as a reminder that he had taken an Apache arrow in his left thigh only a few weeks earlier, Jason Fury walked to the door of his newly constructed office and leaned a shoulder against the jamb. He thumbed his hat back on his thick blond hair, then stood there and looked out at the town.

His town.

Whether he wanted it or not.

Pinned to the breast of the buckskin shirt over Jason's broad chest was a badge that his friend Saul Cohen had fashioned out of tin. The word MARSHAL had been etched into the metal, the letters running in a slight arch across the top half of the badge. Below it, in smaller letters, were the words FURY, ARIZONA TERRITORY.

Jason hadn't asked for the badge. He hadn't asked for the job either, but like the tin star, it had been sort of forced on him by his friends. Right after the battle with the Apaches that had left him skewered by a couple of arrows, one in his right thigh and the other in his left shoulder, Saul, Salmon Kendall, Dr. Morelli, and some of the other townspeople had come to the room in Nordstrom's Mercantile where Jason was recuperating and announced that if Fury was going to be a proper town, it had to have law and order. They had elected Jason to be the sheriff and Salmon as the mayor. And they wouldn't take no for an answer, even though they knew that Jason's plan called for him to ride on to California, where he hoped to seek higher education and his fortune in San Francisco.

It had taken a lot of resolve on Jason's part to leave the settlement, because beautiful, redheaded Megan MacDonald, the girl he had fallen in love with during the wagon train journey, was here and riding out meant never seeing her again. But he had managed to do it, giving her a last kiss and saying good-bye to her forever.

Then fate had intervened, in the form of a band of bloodthirsty Apaches, and Jason had found himself racing back to help defend the town. He had been wounded, laid up, and then elected sheriff before he could do anything about it.

Somebody had realized sheriff was a countywide office, and since they didn't know what county they were in, or if Arizona Territory even had counties yet, Jason's job title had been changed to that of Marshal of Fury. The words didn't mean all that much, he thought now as he looked down at the badge pinned to his shirt.

Whatever you called it, he was still stuck here where he didn't really want to be.

But if you want to leave that bad, nobody's stopping you, he reminded himself. He could go down to the livery stable, saddle up Cleo, his palomino mare, and ride out of Fury once and for all. Some folks, like Matt MacDonald, would even be glad to see him go—despite the fact that Jason had saved the ungrateful Matt's life more than once on the trip out here.

"Morning, Marshal," a voice said from his right. "How are you this fine day?"

Jason looked around to see Saul Cohen walking toward him. The wiry man in his thirties was probably Jason's best friend in Fury. Saul was smart and had exhibited plenty of courage during the wagon train journey. He and his wife ran the local hardware store and were raising three fine boys. As far as Jason was concerned, Saul was one of Fury's leading citizens, and he didn't give a damn how the Reverend Mr. Milcher felt about Jews.

Jason nodded a friendly hello, then twisting his torso slightly as if testing it, said, "Still a mite stiff from that arrow wound, but it's getting better. I reckon I'm fine."

"Another wagonload of settlers rolled in a little while ago," Saul said. "This new family brings the population of Fury to one hundred and twelve souls. Your father would be proud, Jason."

Jason supposed Saul was right. Jedediah Fury had taken pride in the number of immigrants he had taken west during a two-decade-long career as a wagon master. Chances are that Jedediah would have advised against settling here in Arizona, and told Saul and the others that they ought to go on to California as they had planned when they left Kansas City, but none of them would ever know for sure.

Jedediah Fury had been killed by the Comanches back in Indian Territory and was laid to rest there, only partway through his final trip as wagon master. The task of leading the wagon train on to its destination had fallen to Jedediah's son Jason.

The settlers had made it this far, to the broad, somewhat fertile valley known as El Despoblado—Spanish for "the uninhabited place"—with its cottonwood-lined creeks and arable soil, before deciding to change their plans and stop to build a new town . . . a town they would name in honor of Jedediah Fury.

And whether Jason liked it or not, he had to admit that in the weeks since the Indian attack, this town called Fury had been growing by leaps and bounds. The settlers all banded together to put up each building in turn. One of the structures that had risen in a hurry was the adobe building that housed the marshal's office. Directly behind it, and connected to it, was a small jail constructed of thick, heavy cottonwood beams. It would be more difficult to break out of than an adobe jail would have been. So far, the lockup hadn't been used, but Jason knew it was only a matter of time before he had to arrest somebody.

One of the first things Saul had done, even before getting his hardware store open, was to dig a well for the town. The creeks were flowing right now, but that wouldn't always be the case. Arizona Territory was known for its arid weather. The hope was that the well put in by Saul and several of the other men would never run dry. It sat in the very center of the settlement, its location proclaiming its importance to these hardy pioneers. A covered patio had been erected around and above it, to give shade from the merciless sun and to provide a framework for the mechanism by which water could be lifted from underground.

Surrounding that central plaza were several dozen buildings. Fury already had a look of permanence about it. The town was here to stay.

And so, Jason reckoned, was he. His feelings for Megan MacDonald would see to that, not to mention the responsibility he felt for Saul, Salmon Kendall, and the other settlers. Also, his younger sister Jenny was here and wasn't likely to be leaving any time soon. She had fallen hard for Matt MacDonald, Megan's older brother.

Jason just wished that Matt was more like Megan. Instead, Matt was an arrogant, headstrong bully, and he and Jason had disliked each other ever since they met in Kansas City, when Jason stepped in to stop Matt from beating up on a younger, smaller boy. Jenny was normally a smart girl—shoot, she had even made it all the way through eighth grade and liked to read—and what she saw in Matt MacDonald was just flat out beyond Jason's comprehension.

"You brood too much, my friend," Saul said, breaking into Jason's reverie. "It's enjoying life you should be doing. The town is booming, the Apaches have not returned, and your wounds are almost healed."

"Something else will come along," Jason said. "Some sort of trouble."

Saul shrugged. "More than likely. Man is born to trouble, as your Scriptures say. But we persevere."

Jason nodded, hoping that his friend was right.

Saul took a turnip watch from his vest pocket, flipped it open, and checked the time. "I'd best get back and open up," he said, referring to his hardware store. It occupied the first floor of one of the buildings, and the living quarters for Saul, his wife Rachael, and their sons David, Jacob, and Abraham were on the second floor above it. Saul lifted a hand in a farewell wave as he turned and walked back along the street.

Might as well make his morning rounds, Jason decided. Not that much was going on early in the day like this. The handful of businesses were just opening for the day. Not many people were on the street.

Jason tried not to limp as he walked. His leg was getting stronger every day, and he didn't like to give in to any weakness. As he strolled along, he looked past the end of town toward the cottonwood-lined creek, and paused as he noticed that three men on horseback had stopped beside the stream to let their mounts drink. At this distance it was difficult to be sure, but Jason didn't think that he recognized any of the men.

Well, it wasn't that unusual for strangers to pass through the area, he told himself. The wagon trail ran very near the settlement, and not only wagons used it. Men who were headed for California also rode through. Maybe those three were just drifters on their way somewhere else. They might water their horses and move on.

Instead, pulling back on the reins before the horses drank too much, the men turned their mounts and rode into Fury at a slow, deliberate pace.

Jason's eyes narrowed as he watched them. A family of settlers in a wagon was one thing; men on horseback were another. It could be assumed that most immigrants weren't looking for trouble. Jason had no way of knowing why this trio of strangers had come to Fury, though.

The men reined to a halt in front of an adobe building at the edge of town. They seemed to know where they were going. Jason wasn't surprised by that. Word got around. Even though there was no sign in front of the building, those men knew where to go to get a drink.

Abigail Krimp owned the place. She had been working as a saloon girl in Kansas City when she and her paramour, gambler Rome Lefebrve, had decided to join the wagon train heading west. Jedediah hadn't wanted them along and had said so in no uncertain terms. But the two of them had followed along anyway in their buggy, and eventually Jedediah had relented and let them join up.

Rome had been killed in the same clash with the Comanches that had taken Jedediah's life. Abigail hadn't seemed too broken up about losing him. Jason had a feeling that Rome hadn't treated Abigail very well. From there on out Abigail had been a fairly dependable member of the party and hadn't caused any trouble, although the womenfolk disapproved of her because of her former profession and she made Jason a mite uncomfortable with her open admiration of him. She was around thirty, with a lot of red hair piled high on her head, and was still attractive in a shopworn way.

Abigail hadn't talked about her plans. Jason had hoped she intended to open a dressmaking shop or something like that. But once her building was constructed, she had set up a bar and opened for business. Jason hadn't even known she had any liquor along. She must have bought it while the wagon train was stopped in Tucson, he decided, and hidden the kegs in the spare wagon she'd been driving since abandoning the buggy.

Reverend Milcher and his wife Lavinia were scandalized by this development, of course. Since Milcher was the one who had put the wagon train together in the first place, in some ways he regarded Fury as *his* town. Some of the other folks didn't like the idea of having a saloon in the settlement either. Jason wasn't sure what else went on at Abigail's place, especially in the back room, and to tell the truth, he didn't want to know.

Even though it was mighty early in the day, that didn't matter to some people, Jason thought as he watched the men disappear through the open door of the adobe building. Somebody always wanted a drink no matter what time it was.

With a shake of his head, he turned and walked back toward his office.

He hadn't quite gotten there when a shot rang out somewhere behind him.

Chapter 2

Matt MacDonald cuffed his hat back and sleeved sweat from his forehead. Once the sun was up, it got hot in a hurry here in Arizona Territory. He had already taken his shirt off, revealing a powerful, well-muscled torso, but he kept his hat on to shade his head as he and Ward Wanamaker used a two-handed saw to cut rough planks from the felled trunks of cottonwood trees.

Wash Keough, an old friend of Jedediah Fury who had spent time as a mountain man and had joined the wagon train in Santa Fe, had warned them that cottonwood had a habit of sprouting new growth, even when it was cut down and worked into fence posts or planks. But what the hell else were they going to use for lumber out here where no other trees were visible for miles around? Even the cottonwoods were found only along creek banks. Other than that, the vegetation in the area consisted of grass and low, scrubby bushes.

"We can take a break if you want to, Matt," Ward said. He was one of the men Jedediah had hired back in Kansas City to come along on the journey as workers, and he had decided to stay and settle in Fury. One of his fellow hired men, Gil Collins, had been the first one to sign on with Matt as a ranch hand, but Gil had been killed by an Apache arrow. Ward had taken his place, but only until Matt got the new spread going. He hadn't committed to staying on full time. In fact, Matt suspected that Ward didn't like him much.

That was all right. Matt didn't care about having friends, as long as he had workers he could depend on.

Anyway, Jenny Fury liked him. Jenny liked him a lot. Enough so that she hadn't put up a fuss when Matt kissed her.

He planned to do more than that with Jenny, who was built mighty nice for a girl of sixteen. He knew that because he had seen her climb out of a rain-swollen creek in only her underwear, after she had jumped in to rescue a mutt that had gotten washed away by the flood. The thin garments had been next to invisible once they were soaked, and the image of Jenny standing there like that with every curve of her body revealed and her long blond hair plastered to her head by the water was burned into Matt's brain.

He had decided, right then and there, that he was going to marry up with Jenny Fury one of these days, and nothing had happened since then to change his mind. The only thing that gave him pause was the fact that Jenny's brother was that high-and-mighty bastard Jason Fury, who thought he was better than everybody else just because his pa had been the wagon master. Now those fools in the settlement had gone and made Jason their lawman. They would come to regret that decision, Matt was sure of it. They should have let him go on to California like he wanted.

With his jaw tightening as he thought about Jason Fury, Matt shook his head and said to Ward, "No, let's get this lumber cut. I want to get that barn up as soon as I can."

The house Matt had started building with Gil Collins's help was pretty much finished now, although some work remained to do on the inside. But it was snug enough for Matt and Ward to sleep in at night, so they had moved on to building the barn where Matt's cattle and the fine Morgan horses that had belonged to his father would be housed. Hamish MacDonald had valued those horses over almost everything else. More than once, Matt had felt like his father loved the Morgans more than he did his own son.

Hamish was gone now, killed when his wagon toppled over the edge of a high mountain trail in the Sangre de Cristos, over in New Mexico Territory. Matt blamed Jason Fury for his father's death. Jason hadn't wanted to take that upper trail, but he had maneuvered things so that Hamish practically had to if he wanted to maintain any shred of his pride and dignity. Because of that, Hamish had died.

Matt had made another vow to himself where the Fury family was concerned, besides planning to marry Jenny.

One of these days he was going to kill her older brother.

If it had been up to Ward Wanamaker, he would have built the barn before the house, so that the stock would be protected. Seemed like the animals ought to come first over Matt's comfort.

But of course it wasn't up to him. They were Matt's horses and cattle, and this was Matt's place. Ward was just a hired hand, as he had been all his life. He took orders, worked hard, and stayed out of trouble.

Trouble was his first thought as he glanced past Matt while they worked the two-handed saw back and forth. Ward saw a plume of dust rising in the distance. He stopped sawing so suddenly that Matt was thrown off balance for a second.

"What the hell did you do that for?" Matt complained.

Ward nodded toward the dust. "Riders comin'."

Matt turned to look, his body stiffening with tension as he did so. Out here, a cloud of dust like that could mean several different things, but few of them were good. Matt reached for his shirt and began tugging it on in a hurry. Ward picked up the Henry rifle he had leaned against the wall of the house when they started sawing.

"Reckon we should go in the house?" Matt asked as he finished buttoning his shirt.

"Time enough for that when we see who they are," Ward answered. "Might not be Apaches."

A few minutes later, it became apparent that the approaching riders weren't Indians. The broad-brimmed hats they wore identified them as white men. Ward relaxed a little, but the nervousness he felt didn't go away completely. These strangers could still be up to no good, even if they weren't Apaches.

The four men brought their horses to a stop about twenty feet away. The cloud of dust kicked up by the animals' hooves swirled around them for a moment before it began to clear. As it did so, Ward saw that one of the men sat his horse a little in front of the others, as if he were the leader of the group.

This man was the oldest of the four, no doubt about that. His hatchetlike face was lined and weathered by years of exposure to sun and wind, and it had been burned to the color of old saddle leather. That made the white of his drooping mustaches stand out starkly. His bushy eyebrows were white as well and crowded down over deep-set eyes. The brim of the battered old hat he wore was pushed up in front. A pair of gunbelts was crisscrossed around his hips.

The other three men had the same sort of hard, rugged look about them, if not quite to the extent that the white-haired man did. Ward had a bad feeling in his gut as he studied all four of them.

The old man jerked a hand toward the house. "Who does this here shanty belong to?" he demanded.

"This is my house," Matt said with a quick flash of anger that came as no surprise to Ward. In the time Ward had known him, the younger man had never demonstrated an overabundance of good sense. "And it's no shanty," Matt went on. "Who the hell are you to come in here asking questions?"

The old man leaned back and drew in a deep breath, as if

he couldn't believe that Matt had just spoken to him in that tone. "I'm Ezra Dixon," he declared. His voice was like ten miles of bad road. "This is my range."

Matt gave a stubborn shake of his head. "No, sir. It's open range, and I've claimed it. This is going to be my ranch. I plan to raise the finest horses in the whole territory."

Ezra Dixon's eyes were set in what looked like a perpetual squint. They narrowed even more as he frowned at Matt. He grated, "You damn little pissant. You got any idea who you're talkin' to?"

"An old man who's too big for his damn britches," Matt responded before Ward even had a chance to give him a warning look. Not that Matt would have paid any attention to it anyway.

Dixon's glower became even darker. For a long moment he didn't say anything.

Then he glanced over his shoulder at the three men with him and ordered, "Kill 'em."

Ward had been edging toward the open door of the house while Matt and Dixon were busy trying to out-arrogant each other. Now, as Dixon snapped the command, Ward grabbed Matt's collar with his left hand and dived toward the doorway, hauling the younger man with him. He hoped Matt's shirt wouldn't rip, because if it did, Matt was about to get riddled with lead. At the same time, Ward jerked the Henry up with his other hand and fired, not really aiming, just thrusting the gun in the general direction of Dixon and the other men. The whipcrack of the rifle was followed instantly by the heavier booming reports of revolvers.

Ward was already through the door as slugs began to thud into the wall of the house. Matt yelped in pain. Ward hoped he wasn't hit too bad. Matt sprawled on the floor. Ward almost fell, but caught his balance, kicked the door shut, and dropped the bar that held it closed. The door and the walls were thick enough to stop the bullets from penetrating.

Ward supposed it was a good thing the house was almost finished after all.

Matt scrambled to his feet as Ward knelt at one of the rifle slits they had left in the wall. "They're shooting at us!" he said as if he couldn't believe it.

"Yeah, they appear to be," Ward agreed. "How bad are you hit?"

"What? I'm not hit."

"What'd you yell for, then?"

"I twisted my ankle when you jerked me like that. You should have been more careful."

"Yeah, you're welcome for savin' your sorry hide," Ward muttered.

"What did you say?"

"Nothin'." Ward saw one of the men pass through his field of view from the rifle slit and squeezed the Henry's trigger, but he didn't think his shot hit its target. "Take one of those other slits and give me a hand here. Maybe we can run those boys off."

Matt knelt at a slit on the other side of the door and poked the barrel of his Colt in the opening. "Why are they trying to kill us?"

"Because you mouthed off at that fella Dixon. I reckon he must think he's the big-skookum he-wolf around here. There's not much law in this territory yet, so the only way a man like Dixon can feel safe is by killing anybody he thinks of as a threat." Ward fired again. "Which now includes us, I'm afraid."

Matt's revolver blasted. "But he's got no right! This is my range now!"

"Range belongs to whoever can hold it and use it. Right now that looks like Dixon."

"He can't get away with this. I'll have the army on him if I have to."

Ward didn't pay much attention to Matt's ranting. He

sniffed the air instead and shook his head as a grim look appeared on his face.

"I was afraid of that," he said.

"Afraid of what?"

"Smell that smoke? They've set something on fire." Ward drew in a deep breath and let it out in a resigned sigh. "I reckon they figure on burnin' us out."

Chapter 3

At the sound of the shot, Jason wheeled around. While he wasn't sure exactly where it had come from, he knew the sound had originated somewhere down on the end of town where Abigail's place was located. He trotted toward the adobe building, loosening his gun in its holster as he hurried along the street.

Other people had heard the shot, too. Saul Cohen and Randall Nordstrom both appeared in the doorways of their stores, across the street from each other. Dr. Morelli stepped out the front door of his house, as did Reverend Milcher.

"Need a hand, Jason?" Saul called. "I'll get my shotgun."

"Stay put," Jason said. Like it or not, protecting the citizens of Fury was his job now. He didn't want them to endanger themselves by helping him perform that job.

No more shots had sounded. Jason tried to tell himself that was a good sign. Unless, of course, somebody was already dead.

He drew his gun as he reached the door of Abigail's. Although he could handle a Colt with considerable speed and accuracy, he was no gunslinger. If he was going to be involved in a shootout, he wanted every advantage he could get.

The acrid smell of gun smoke still lingered in the air,

telling him that this was where the shot had originated, all right. Several tables were scattered around the room, with empty kegs serving as makeshift chairs. Abigail had placed several planks across barrels to form a bar on one side of the room. The tables were all empty at this hour. The three strangers stood at the bar with glasses of whiskey in front of them. Abigail was behind the bar, clutching the bottle she had used to splash liquor into those glasses. Her face was pale and strained.

Wash Keough sat on the floor across the room, his back propped against the wall. His right hand clutched his upper left arm. Blood trickled between the tightly gripping fingers. Wash was pale too under his tan.

"What's going on here?" Jason demanded.

One of the men looked over his shoulder. He was a Mexican, with a broad-brimmed sombrero canted back on his head. His charro jacket and tight trousers were covered with trail dust, and dust also made his black beard look gray. He nudged one of his companions, both of whom were white and just as dusty and rugged-looking as the Mexican.

The man who had been nudged turned toward Jason and raised his glass as if saluting him. "Morning, Marshal," he said.

Jason ignored him and stepped over to Wash. "Are you all right?" he asked the old mountain man.

"Yeah, it ain't nothin' but a scratch," Wash replied. "Hurts like hell, but that's all."

Jason reached down with his left hand, gripped Wash's right arm, and helped the older man to his feet. "Go on down and get Dr. Morelli to patch you up."

"Shoot, this ain't hardly bad enough to bother the doc—"

"Go on, Wash," Jason said. If he was going to have trouble with these strangers, he didn't want to have to worry about the wounded old-timer's welfare while lead was flying.

Grumbling, Wash did as Jason told him. He stumbled out of the adobe with the long gray horsetail of his hair swinging down his back. Wash hadn't cut his hair in nigh on to twenty years.

Jason faced the three strangers again. "Who shot him?" he asked in a flat, hard voice.

"How do you know he didn't shoot himself by accident, Marshal?" asked the man who had lifted a glass to him earlier. "The old man was packing iron."

"His gun was still in its holster, and anyway, Wash Keough is too savvy a man to ever shoot himself."

"Keough," the Mexican said. "I have heard of him. I did not know I was shooting such a man."

"So you admit you're the one who gunned him?"

The other man said, "I didn't hear Flores or either of us denying that, did you, Marshal?"

Jason wished the man would stop calling him *Marshal* like that, with such a mocking tone in his voice. He said, "Who are you?"

"You know Flores's name. I'm Trumbull, and this is Yates."

"Howdy," the third man said with an ugly, gap-toothed grin.

"Why'd you shoot him?"

Flores shrugged. "My boots, Señor. When the old gringo was coming out of the back room, he hit a spittoon with his foot, and it splashed on my boots. I could not allow such an insult to pass."

Abigail spoke up for the first time since Jason had entered the room. "It was an accident," she said. "Wash had had too much to drink. He didn't mean to do it."

Even though Wash had seemed fairly sober, Jason had been able to smell the booze on the old man. Wash was fond of liquor, all right. Too fond. But the shock of getting shot must have driven most of the drunkenness right out of him.

"You didn't have to shoot him," Jason said to Flores, feeling anger well up inside him. He had seen men like these before, hardcases who thought they were a law unto themselves.

They were about to find out different.

Flores shook his head and chuckled. "Señor Marshal, you do not understand. My honor was offended. I had to satisfy it, or I would not be able to live with myself. Consider the old man lucky. I could have killed him."

"He could'a done it too," Yates said. "I seen him kill men for less."

"So I shot him"—Flores drew his gun with such speed that Jason's eyes couldn't follow the movement, then twirled it and slid it back into leather with equal swiftness—"and thus it was done. There is nothing more to say."

Jason hated the smirks on their faces, hated even more the fear he felt gnawing at his guts. Flores was too fast to go up against. Even though Jason already had his gun in his hand, if he tried to shoot the Mexican, Flores would probably get lead in him before Jason could ever pull the trigger.

But what else could he do? If Fury was going to be a real town, it had to have laws, and somebody to enforce them. For now, Jason was that somebody.

Until Flores or one of the others killed him in a few minutes anyway.

Jason took a deep breath. "You're under arrest."

Flores shook his head again, and this time his expression was sad. "Oh, Señor, you do not want to do that."

"Don't have any choice. Put your gun on the bar and come with me." Jason glanced at Trumbull and Yates. "You two just stay out of this. It's none of your concern. You didn't shoot anybody, so you're not under arrest."

"You've got that wrong, Marshal," Trumbull said. "You're not taking Flores to jail. If you try . . . you die."

Jason summoned up all the boldness he could, hoping against hope that he could bluff his way through this. "Who's going to kill me?" he asked. "You?" His tone made it clear he didn't think that was going to happen.

For a second he thought he saw a flicker of doubt in Trumbull's eyes. They didn't know who he was. They couldn't be sure of who they were dealing with. Maybe he really was fast enough to take them all. Did they really want to risk it over something like this?

Then Jason saw the resolve firm up in Trumbull's eyes and knew he was about to die here. He thought about Megan and wished he could have seen her, held her, kissed her, one last time.

A man stepped out of the back room and aimed a shotgun along the bar. At the same time another man appeared in the front door with a rifle in his hands. Jason barely had time to recognize Saul Cohen and Salmon Kendall before Saul said to Abigail, "Miss Krimp, you had better get down behind those barrels, so when I pull these triggers you won't get hit by the buckshot."

Salmon pointed his rifle at Yates and said, "I got a bead on the ugly one on the end, Jason. You can have either of the other two, that is, if Saul's Greener leaves anything of 'em."

Now the odds were even. More than even, when you considered that Jason, Saul, and Salmon already had their guns in their hands. And that double-barreled shotgun of Saul's was a fearsome weapon. At this range, it might put down all three of the hardcases by itself.

"All right," Trumbull said, the words coming out flat between clenched teeth. "Looks like you settlers have got the drop on us. But don't think this is over."

"It's over, all right," Jason said, feeling relief go through him. "All three of you this time. Put your guns on the bar and step away from them."

Within a few minutes, the hardcases were disarmed, including the knife that Yates had in his boot and the long blade that Flores carried in a sheath worn down his back that was attached to a rawhide thong around his neck. Keeping the scattergun trained on the prisoners, Saul grinned and said, "Looks like you're going to get some use out of that nice new jail, Jason."

"And it's about time," Salmon added. "I was about to decide we'd wasted all that lumber and energy."

The three of them marched the prisoners down the street at gunpoint, which attracted quite a crowd. It seemed to Jason that all 112 citizens of Fury had turned out to watch, even though he knew that wasn't really the case. He saw Megan and Jenny, who were best friends, standing in front of Nord-strom's. The girls looked proud of him.

They didn't have anything to be proud of, Jason thought bitterly. If Saul and Salmon hadn't stepped in to help him—even though he had said for everybody else to stay out of it—he would be lying on the floor of Abigail's place right now, either bleeding his life away or already dead. He knew that as well as he knew his own name.

The jail had two cells that faced each other across a narrow hallway. Each cell was enclosed by solid timbers, with no windows to the outside and only a small window in each heavy door. They didn't sport iron bars like a typical jail cell, but the purpose was to keep prisoners locked up, so it didn't really matter what they looked like as long as they did the job.

Jason and his unofficial deputies herded Trumbull and Yates into one cell and Flores into the other. When the doors were closed, Jason snapped heavy padlocks that had come from Saul's store on them. Flores began cursing him in Span-ish. At least, Jason thought the words were curses; he wasn't fluent enough yet in that lingo to be sure.

"That was mighty close," Salmon said as he and Jason and Saul walked back into the marshal's office. "I'm glad Saul and me got there when we did. You might've had a hard time arresting all three of those fellas, Jason."

"You mean they would have killed me," Jason said.

"Oh, no, I'm sure you would've handled them just fine without us—"

Jason shook his head, cutting off Salmon's protest. The mayor, who had a farm just outside town with his wife Carrie, was a good friend, but Jason knew Salmon was just trying to make him feel better about what had happened.

"If I'm going to be the marshal of this town," he said, "I have to make sure that something like this never happens again."

The problem was, he thought as he dropped his hand to the butt of his gun and brushed his fingers over the walnut grips, right now he didn't know how he was going to do that.

Chapter 4

One of the men laying siege to the MacDonald ranch house darted into view, holding a makeshift torch that had been fashioned from a scrap piece of lumber with some strips of cloth torn from a shirt wrapped around one end. Ward recalled seeing a coal-oil lantern outside, sitting on a cottonwood stump. Dixon's men must have gotten that lantern and used the coal oil to soak the cloth, because it was burning real good.

Those thoughts went through Ward's brain in an instant. At the same time, he was drawing a bead and squeezing the Henry's trigger. The rifle cracked and kicked against his shoulder. He saw the man with the torch go over backward just as he drew back his arm to throw the blazing brand toward the house. The torch fell harmlessly into the dirt.

But where there was one torch, there could be others, and Ward couldn't hope to shoot all the men before they set fire to the house.

"Sorry, Matt," he said, "but I'm not gonna sit in here and burn to death. I'm just not."

"What are you going to do?" Matt asked with an edge of panic in his voice. "Surrender?"

"I'm going out there, all right, but I'm going out shooting. I'd rather die with a bullet in me."

Ward glanced up as he heard something hit the roof. That would be another torch, he thought, and sure enough, a second later the smell of smoke began to get stronger. He stood up, his hands tight around the Henry.

"Do what you want to, Matt," he said. He would have added something about it being nice to have known him, but that would have been a lie. It hadn't been all that nice knowing Matt MacDonald. And at this moment, with the time remaining to him numbered in minutes or even seconds, Ward didn't see any point in lying.

He lifted the bar on the door, grabbed the latch, and threw it open. With a yell, he charged outside and flung himself to the ground, ready to spray as much lead as he could from the rifle before they killed him.

Instead of shots, he heard hoofbeats. He lifted his head and looked around in confusion. The crackle of flames came from behind him. Twisting his neck, he looked back to see that the roof of the house was on fire. But he didn't see Dixon or any of the rancher's men, and nobody was shooting at him.

Dixon and his men were gone. They'd lit a shuck out of there for some reason. That was the only explanation that made any sense.

The hoofbeats were louder now. Quite a few riders were approaching the place. They had caused Dixon to flee, Ward thought as he climbed to his feet. Who could they be? Apaches?

That was the most likely answer. Dixon and his men would have run from a war party.

"Matt!" Ward called. "Matt, get out here! Quick!"

If they worked together, they might be able to put out that fire on the roof before it spread too far. But if they were going to do that, they had to get it done before the Indians attacked. Then they could take shelter in the house and try to drive off the Apaches. They'd probably die anyway, but at least they could put up a fight.

Matt appeared in the doorway as Ward hurried over to lean a ladder against the wall. "What is it? What's happened?"

"Dixon's gone," Ward said as he propped his rifle against the wall and grabbed an empty tow sack that had held grain for Matt's fine Morgan horses. "We've got to get that fire put out before it takes the house."

He scrambled up the ladder to the roof and started slapping at the flames with the tow sack. Matt followed his example, and since the fire was slow to spread, they were able to extinguish the blaze in a few minutes' time.

But even that was too long. The hoofbeats were loud now, and the cloud of dust raised by the horses blew over the house, blinding both Ward and Matt for a moment.

As Ward coughed and blinked his eyes against the choking dust, he heard something he had never expected to hear. A deep voice bawled in English, "Company . . . *halt!*"

As his vision cleared, Ward saw a couple of dozen cavalry troopers reining their mounts to a stop in the yard in front of the house. A stiff-necked young lieutenant and a grizzled old sergeant were at the head of the patrol. The officer looked up at Ward and Matt standing on the charred roof and said, "You men! What's going on here?"

Ward breathed a sigh of relief. Dixon had probably taken the approaching cavalry patrol for Indians too. Or maybe he had known they were soldiers; either way, the rancher and his men had fled, and that had saved the lives of the two men holed up in the house.

"Mighty glad to see you, Lieutenant," Ward said. "As you can see for yourself, some fellas were tryin' to burn us out."

"Apaches?" the sergeant asked. He was a short, wiry man with a bristly gray mustache. His battered old campaign cap showed as much wear as the sergeant himself did.

"I'll ask the questions, Sergeant," the lieutenant snapped.

"Yes, sir."

The officer turned back to Ward and Matt. "Was it Apaches? And come down from there, you two. I don't like having to tilt my head back to talk to you."

No, with such a stiff neck, he wouldn't like that, Ward thought. But he kept the comment to himself as he climbed down the ladder to the ground, followed by Matt.

Matt answered the lieutenant's question. "It wasn't Apaches," he said. "It was a son of a bitch named Ezra Dixon and some men who work for him. I want them arrested and thrown in jail, Lieutenant. They tried to murder us, and when that didn't work, they attempted to burn the house down around us. You can see the evidence of that for yourself." Matt waved a hand toward the roof.

The lieutenant frowned. "So this was . . . a civilian dispute?"

"It was attempted murder! Surely the army doesn't condone such violence!"

"What the army condones or doesn't condone is irrelevant here. Trouble between civilians is none of the military's business. If you have a complaint against this man Dixon, you'll have to lodge it with the civilian authorities."

"But . . . but . . ." Matt was so mad and frustrated all he could do was sputter.

"You've heard of Dixon?" Ward asked.

The sergeant spat and said, "We've heard of him. Highhanded varmint. Thinks he runs things around here because he's been in the territory longer'n pert' near anybody else. Reckon in a way he's right."

The lieutenant glared at his subordinate. The sergeant muttered an apology for butting in, but didn't look like he really meant it.

"I'm glad we heard the shooting and came to investigate," the lieutenant said to Ward and Matt. "But since there's nothing we can do, we'll have to continue our patrol."

"What's your name?" Matt demanded. His face was so flushed with anger it looked sunburned.

"I'm Lieutenant Wilfred Carter, from Camp Grant. This is Sergeant Halligan."

The sergeant ticked a finger against the bill of his campaign cap. "Howdy."

"I'm going to lodge a complaint, all right, Lieutenant," Matt went on, "but it'll be with your superior officer. I intend to tell him how you refused to pursue those men who tried to kill us."

"Do whatever you want, mister," Carter snapped. "The captain will tell you the same thing I just told you. This isn't a military problem. It's a matter for the local law."

"Damn it!" Matt exploded. "There isn't any law in these parts except that blasted Jason Fury, and he's not even a real marshal!"

"Fury?" Sergeant Halligan said. "Any relation to Jedediah Fury?"

"His boy," Ward said. "You knew Jedediah?"

Halligan nodded. "Run into him a few times when he was leadin' wagon trains west. How is the old boy?"

"Dead," Ward said. "Killed in a run-in with Comanch' on the way out here."

Halligan shook his head. "That's a damned shame, and I'm sorry to hear it. Jedediah Fury would do to ride the river with."

"Jason's the same way," said Ward. "Or he's getting there anyway."

Matt didn't like hearing anything good said about Jason, but Ward didn't care. After Jedediah's death, Jason had handled himself, and the wagon train, about as well as anybody could have. He had gotten most of the pilgrims safely to Arizona Territory, and had taken on the job of bringing law and order to the settlement that was named after his father. Maybe Jason had been railroaded a little bit into becoming marshal, but in the end he had accepted the responsibility.

"Take it up with this Marshal Fury, whoever he is," Carter said. He turned his horse around. "Sergeant, resume patrol."

"Yes, sir." Halligan lifted his hand and waved it forward. "Move out!"

As the troopers urged their horses into a brisk walk after Lieutenant Carter, Halligan paused to add one more comment to Ward and Matt.

"Like I said, we've heard of Ezra Dixon. He's a dangerous hombre when he's crossed. I reckon you fellas have figured that out already, but you'd better remember it."

Halligan gave them a curt nod, then heeled his horse into a trot and rode after the rest of the patrol, catching up quickly to take his place with the lieutenant at the head of the troopers.

"Do you believe that?" Matt asked. "That damn lieutenant's just going to ignore the fact that Dixon tried to kill us!"

"He's right. You need to talk to the local law about it. That means Jason, whether you like it or not, Matt."

Matt glared at him. "Whose side are you on anyway, Wanamaker?"

Ward shook his head. "I hired on to help you finish your house and build a barn, Matt. That doesn't mean I'm on your side, or anybody's side, for that matter."

"Then get the hell out," Matt grated. "I expect loyalty from my men, damn it!"

Ward gave a grim nod and said, "Well, there's your mistake. I ain't your man, Matt. I ain't anybody's man but my own. And here's a funny thing . . . I don't feel much like riskin' my life for you anymore."

Ward didn't look back as he went to saddle up his horse and get out of there. He ignored Matt when the younger man yelled, "Go to hell!" at his back.

As far as Ward was concerned, he had already been to hell—and it was called working for Matt MacDonald.

Chapter 5

With Flores, Trumbull, and Yates safely locked up in the new jail, Jason walked down to the house where Dr. Michael Morelli had his office, as well as the living quarters for the physician, his wife Olympia, and their three children. Olympia greeted Jason at the door with a smile and ushered him into the front room that served as an examination and treatment room.

Wash Keough sat on the long, narrow table. His buckskin shirt was off, and Dr. Morelli was just finishing the job of bandaging the old-timer's wounded arm.

"How does it look, Doctor?" Jason asked. "Will this old pelican live?"

"Mind your manners, boy!" Wash said. "Jedediah should'a beat you more when you was young, so's you'd respect your elders."

"He'll be fine," Morelli said. "The bullet just dug a shallow groove in his arm. I've cleaned and bandaged the wound, and it should heal without much trouble. The arm's going to be pretty stiff and sore for a few days, though."

"Good thing it ain't my drinkin' arm," Wash said.

"Speaking of that, maybe you shouldn't be putting away

quite so much of that who-hit-John," Jason said. "It can't be good for you. Tell him, Doctor."

Morelli shrugged. "Unfortunately, I'd say that Wash's insides are already as pickled as they're going to get."

"See?" Wash said with a look of triumph. "What do you expect me to drink? Water? Hell's bells, next thing you know, you'll be tellin' me I ought to bathe in it!"

"Now that you mention it . . ." Jason began.

"Gentlemen, why don't you take this discussion outside?" Morelli suggested. "I might have other patients to tend to."

Wash put on his bullet-torn, bloodstained shirt, grimacing as he lifted his injured arm to push it through the sleeve. "How much I owe you?" he asked the doctor.

"Fifty cents."

Wash squinted at Jason. "You mind, boy? I'm a mite short on funds at the moment."

"Abigail Krimp got the last of your money, that's what you mean," Jason said as he reached in his pocket for a coin.

Wash cackled as he dug the elbow of his good arm into Jason's ribs. "And she was worth ever' cent of it, boy, if'n you know what I mean!"

Jason knew, all right, although he would have just as soon not have. He paid Morelli and steered Wash out of the doctor's office.

When they reached the street, Jason said, "I've got a serious question to ask you, Wash, if you're sober enough to answer it."

"If this is about how come me to knock over that spittoon, it was a accident, I tell you—"

"I don't care about that," Jason broke in. "I know you were too drunk to know what you were doing. We all lived through it somehow, thanks to good luck and good friends. But I'd rather not have to depend on those things in the future."

Wash stopped in his tracks and gave Jason a squint-eyed look. "What are you gettin' at, boy?"

Jason patted the butt of his Colt and asked, "Have you ever known anybody who was really good with one of these?"

"A gun, you mean?" Wash gripped the handle of the old cap-and-ball pistol holstered at his waist. "Why, I can handle a smokepole 'bout as good as anybody you'll ever—"

"No, I don't want a bunch of bragging," Jason said. "I want the truth. I've seen you use a gun, remember? You're not bad. Neither am I. But neither of us are what you'd call greased lightning with a Colt either."

Wash shrugged. "Yeah, I reckon you're right. You ever hear tell of a fella called Preacher?"

Jason frowned as he tried to remember. "I think I heard my pa mention him a time or two."

"Preacher's a mountain man. He's gettin' on in years a mite now, but when these here repeatin' revolvers come along, he weren't too old to learn how to use one of 'em. Turned out he was natural-born slick on the draw, son. Fastest I ever saw, leastways until the last time I run into Preacher. He was travelin' then with a young buck he called Smoke, and accordin' to Preacher, this here Smoke's even faster'n him. If that's true, then those two are a pair you'll never see the likes of again." Wash tugged at one of his drooping mustaches. "What're you gettin' at, Jason? You ain't got me reminiscin' for no good reason."

"I have to get better with a gun," Jason said. "If I'm going to be the marshal of this settlement, there'll be times like today when I need to be fast on the draw."

"The odds was three agin one," Wash pointed out. "If you'd tried to shoot it out with them fellas, chances are you'd'a wound up dead no matter how good you were."

"What about Preacher and Smoke? Could they handle odds like that?"

"Well, yeah, I reckon so. But they's different."

"I have to learn to be that good. And I need somebody to teach me."

Wash shook his head. "Son, ain't nobody can teach you what Preacher and Smoke got. They was borned with it."

"But I can get better," Jason insisted. "I'm already a good shot, an accurate shot. I just have to get faster."

"Practice is the only way to do that. You draw that hogleg a hundred times a day. No, a thousand. Do that for long enough, and you'll get faster." Wash rubbed his jaw and frowned in thought. "I might be able to give you a few pointers, things that I seen Preacher do over the years. But I ain't promisin' nothin', mind you."

"Thanks, Wash." Jason gripped the old-timer's right shoulder. "I'm obliged to you."

"Best save your thanks until you figure out whether I'm really helpin' you . . . or just makin' it easier for you to get yourself killed faster."

Jason didn't want the townspeople to see what he was doing, so he and Wash went behind the jail. Once they got there, the old-timer said, "Let me see your draw."

Jason stood with his hands hanging at his sides. His right arm moved, coming up fast in a smooth, efficient motion. His fingers wrapped around the butt of the Colt and pulled it from the holster. When the barrel was clear of leather, he brought the gun up with his arm extended straight out in front of him.

Wash shook his head and sighed. "That weren't too bad until you stuck your arm out like that. That takes so long you'd be ventilated 'fore you ever got a shot off."

"My pa taught me to aim a gun like I was pointing my finger," Jason said.

"Yeah, that's true, but you got to learn to shoot from the hip. Point down there, not way up here." Wash demonstrated by making a gun out of his hand, pointing the index finger, and sticking the thumb straight up. He pantomimed drawing several times, leaving his old pistol in the holster and using his hand instead. "Bam! Like that. Bam! Bam!"

"Can I play too?"

The new voice took both Jason and Wash by surprise. They whirled around, and Jason's hand flew to the butt of his Colt.

David Cohen, Saul's oldest boy, jumped back, his eyes widening in fear. He held his hands out and said, "Don't shoot me, Marshal! Please don't shoot me!"

Jason was mortified. He realized he was still grasping the gun, and let go of it like it was a rattlesnake or a hot coal.

"Settle down, younker," Wash said. "Nobody's gonna hurt you. You just spooked us a mite, that's all."

"I didn't mean to," David said, with a look on his face like he was fighting back tears. "I . . . I saw somebody back here, and when I realized you were playing guns, like my brothers and I sometimes do, I . . . I thought maybe I could play too. . . ."

The incident had frightened him too much for him to hold it in any longer. He started to cry.

"I didn't m-mean to cause trouble," he said between sobs.

"It's all right, David," Jason said. "You didn't do anything wrong, and nobody's mad at you." He went over to the boy and gave him a clumsy pat on the shoulder. "Just settle down now, all right? There's no reason for you to cry."

David sniffled a few times and wiped his eyes with the back of his hand. "Y-you're sure?"

"Certain sure," Wash told him.

David blinked away the last of the tears and looked at the two adults. "If you weren't playing," he said, "what *were* you doing?"

"Mr. Keough was just, uh, showing me some things," Jason said. "About how to draw and fire a gun faster."

"Why would you need to know how to do that, Marshal? You're already better with a gun than anybody I ever saw. My pa says the same thing."

Jason didn't point out that neither Saul nor David had seen

all that many gunmen. They hadn't lived on the frontier long enough for that.

To tell the truth, neither had Jason. He had made several trips west with his father, when Jedediah was guiding wagon trains on the Santa Fe Trail and the Oregon Trail. But most of his life had been spent back east in Maryland, where the family had lived for most of Jason's childhood.

And until he had wound up here in Fury, Jason's plan had been to return to the East, attend the best university he could afford, and make something of himself. Something more than a lawman in a pioneer town. He had modified that plan and started to San Francisco, but that hadn't worked out either.

"Don't say anything to your pa about what happened here," he said now to David Cohen. He didn't want Saul knowing about the fast-draw practice—or the fact that he'd come close to pulling iron on the boy.

"I won't tell him," David said as a shrewd gleam appeared in his eyes, "if you'll let me come and watch you practice."

Jason frowned. "Well, I don't know. . . ."

"Don't see as how it'd hurt anything," Wash put in. "I reckon we can trust this young fella to keep his word."

David bobbed his head. "Yes, sir, Mr. Keough, you sure can! I swear!"

"All right," Jason agreed, even though he didn't much like it.

"And when you get to be a fast draw, then you can teach me!"

Jason was about to draw the line there when he heard the sound of rapid hoofbeats coming from Fury's main street. When somebody was in a hurry, it usually meant there was trouble. He said to David, "We'll talk about that later," then started toward the street to see what was going on. Wash and the boy followed him.

When Jason reached the front of the building housing the marshal's office, he saw Matt MacDonald reining his lathered mount to a halt. Matt was hard on that pinto of his. From the looks of it, he had nearly run the horse into the ground.

"There you are, Fury!" Matt said.

"You been looking for me, Matt?" Jason asked, knowing full well that Matt had just arrived in town.

"Never mind about that. I've got a crime to report."

"What sort of crime?"

"Somebody just tried to kill me!" Matt glared at Jason. "And I damn well expect you to do something about it!"

Chapter 6

Jason Fury and Matt MacDonald were the same age and built along the same lines—muscular, broad-shouldered, powerful young men. Both had a rugged handsomeness about them that attracted admiring gazes from women—open admiration on the part of the younger females, more discreet but no less appreciative glances from the older ones.

But that was where the similarities between them ended. Matt was arrogant, domineering, even cruel. A born bully. He had been beating up a younger, smaller boy when he and Jason first met, back in Kansas City. They had wound up slugging away at each other, with Jason emerging from the ruckus victorious.

The young man Jason had rescued, Thomas Milcher, was one of the Reverend Milcher's children. Tragically, Thomas hadn't lived to reach the new settlement. He had died in the same Comanche attack that had taken Jedediah Fury's life, part of the toll in human lives that the expansion of civilization always extracted.

Jason thought for a second about Tommy Milcher as Matt glowered at him, but then he shoved the memory aside and said, "What are you talking about? Who tried to kill you?" A thought occurred to Jason, and he added, "Where's Ward? He was out at your place, wasn't he?"

Matt grunted as he swung down from the saddle. "Don't worry about that coward," he said. "Wanamaker's fine. Probably down at the Krimp woman's place guzzling whiskey by now."

Jason's jaw tightened in anger. Ward Wanamaker was a good man and no coward. Jason knew that from experience, having fought alongside Ward on more than one occasion.

"You still haven't told me what happened."

"It was a man named Ezra Dixon." Matt grimaced as if the name tasted bad in his mouth. "Claims he's a rancher. He and some of his men rode up to my place while Wanamaker and I were working. Dixon said that was his range and warned me to get off."

Jason had warned the settlers of that very possibility, so he wasn't surprised by what Matt had just told him.

"Let me guess," he said. "You told Dixon to go to hell."

"Damn right I did! Nobody's gonna come along and run me off my own land."

Jason didn't bother pointing out that the land hadn't been Matt's until he came along and said it was. And that didn't make it so.

"So then they started shooting at you."

"That's right. Wanamaker and I had to fort up inside the house and hold them off. Then they tried to burn us out."

Jason was going to have to ask Ward about this. It would be interesting to get Ward's version of the story and compare it to Matt's.

"What happened then? I can see you didn't get burned up."

"A cavalry patrol came along and scared off Dixon and his men. If they hadn't, I reckon Wanamaker and I would be dead by now."

That was the first Jason had heard of cavalry patrolling in the area, but it was to be expected, considering the continuing threat from the Apaches. He nodded and said, "All this is interesting, Matt, but what do you expect me to do about it?"

Matt stared at him. "What do I expect you to do about it?" he repeated. "I expect you to arrest Dixon and his men and charge them with attempted murder and arson! Wanamaker and I were nearly killed, and I'm going to have to replace the part of my roof that burned."

Jason thought about it, but only for a second. "There's a problem there," he said. "Dixon didn't do any of that in town. My authority is only good here in the settlement."

Matt was so red-faced with anger that he looked like he was about to pop a blood vessel. "Damn it, that son of a bitch lieutenant said he couldn't do anything about it either, and told me to report Dixon to the local authorities. That's you, Fury."

Wash nudged Jason's arm and cleared his throat. Jason looked around at the old-timer, who nodded toward David Cohen, still standing there and taking in everything with avid interest, including Matt's curses.

"David, you run on back to your pa's store," Jason told the boy.

"But Marshal—" David began.

"No arguing now. We made a deal, remember?"

"Yeah, I guess. I'll see you later?"

Jason nodded. "You bet."

David loped off toward the hardware store. Jason turned back to Matt, who said, "You really mean to tell me that you're not going to do anything about what happened to me?"

"I can't, Matt. I don't know how to make it any clearer than that. What you need to do is figure out what county we're in and where the county seat is, and report Dixon to the sheriff. He's the only one who had any authority to do anything."

"Maybe you're just too scared to go up against Dixon."

Jason fought down the urge to plant his fist smack-dab in the middle of Matt's face. He said, "I've told you all I know to tell you. If Dixon or his men come to town and cause trouble, I'll arrest them. Otherwise, there's nothing I can do."

Muttering curses, Matt grabbed his horse's reins and stalked away, jerking the animal's head to make it come along with him. He stomped off toward Abigail's place, no doubt intending to fuel his anger even more with some whiskey.

"That fella just don't like you, Jason," Wash said. "Even a blind man could see that."

"The feeling's mutual," Jason said.

But despite what he had just told Matt, he had the uneasy feeling that he was going to be drawn into this trouble between Matt and Ezra Dixon. From the sound of it, it was already a shooting war.

And knowing Matt, Jason figured things would get worse before they got better.

Jenny Fury had been shopping with Megan MacDonald when the trouble broke out down at Abigail Krimp's. She had seen Jason go in there and had worried that more shots would ring out and her brother would never come out of the place alive. The relief she'd felt when she saw Jason emerge from the building, along with Mr. Cohen and Mayor Kendall and the three prisoners, had made Jenny's knees weak for a few seconds.

She loved her brother. Even though she was going to marry Matt MacDonald—as soon as he got around to asking her—she didn't want anything to happen to Jason. Jenny figured that in time, she could get Jason to understand just what a fine man Matt really was.

Like all big brothers, Jason thought he knew what was best for his little sister. But he was wrong. Jenny was sure of it.

A while later, she spotted Matt riding into town, and her heart jumped as it always did when she saw him. He was hurrying, though, like something was wrong, and he rode straight to the marshal's office. Jason and Mr. Keough and one of the Cohen boys came from around in back, and Jason and Matt started talking. Jenny couldn't hear what they were saying, but she could tell that Matt was upset.

Jason just had to learn how to get along with Matt. She would give him a talking to, Jenny vowed.

For now, though, she bided her time, lingering across the street until Matt finished talking with her brother. Matt turned and started down the street, leading his horse. Jenny waited until Jason and Mr. Keough had gone inside the marshal's office before she hurried to intercept Matt.

"Hello," she said as she came trotting up to him. She knew it would have been more ladylike if she had pretended to meet up with him by accident, but she didn't have the patience for that.

Besides, Matt was heading in the general direction of Abigail Krimp's place, and Jenny didn't want him indulging in any of the . . . diversions . . . that Abigail's offered.

"What are you doing in town?" she went on.

"I came to talk to that brother of yours," Matt replied with a scowl. Jenny knew that Matt didn't like Jason either, but she figured that was Jason's fault. "There was some trouble out at my ranch."

"What happened?"

"Some fellas tried to kill me."

Jenny's hand went to her mouth in shock. "Oh, no! Are you all right?"

"Yeah, I'm fine," Matt answered in surly tones. "My ankle's a little twisted, but that's all. My new roof's got a hole burned in it, though."

"Those men tried to burn your house down?"

"With me and Ward Wanamaker inside it."

Anger filled Jenny at the thought of somebody trying to do that to Matt. "Did you tell Jason about it?" she wanted to know. "He's the marshal now. He can arrest them."

Matt gave a disgusted snort. "Yeah, I told him. But he refused to do anything about it. Said it didn't happen in his jurisdiction, or something like that."

Now part of Jenny's anger was directed toward her brother. "How can he be that way? He's the marshal! He's supposed to arrest anybody who breaks the law!"

"Only if they do it here in town, according to him."

Jenny's nostrils flared as she drew in a deep breath. "We'll just see about that."

Matt looked at her. "You'll talk to him for me?"

"Of course I will." She stopped just short of saying she would do anything for him. "I'll convince him to help you."

"I don't need Jason Fury's help," Matt said with a frown. "I just think he should do his job, that's all."

"That's what I meant," Jenny said quickly, not wanting to offend him. "You wait right here—"

Matt shook his head. "No, I'd better get back out to my ranch. By now, Dixon and his men might have come back and burned everything to the ground."

She put a hand on his arm and said, "You be careful, Matt. I . . . I'd hate to see anything happen to you."

"Don't worry about me. Just tell that brother of yours to stop shirking his duty, that's all."

Then he leaned over, bold as brass, and kissed her on the mouth. It was a quick kiss, but it thrilled Jenny all the way down to her toes, which curled in her shoes in response to the feelings he aroused in her.

Matt grinned that cocky grin of his as he mounted up and turned his horse toward the edge of town. Jenny stood there looking after him as he rode out of the settlement.

Then she turned and clenched her fists in determination as she stalked toward the marshal's office.

Jason was sitting behind his desk and Wash Keough was at the black cast-iron stove in the corner, pouring himself a cup of coffee, when Jenny came into the office, glared at her brother, and said, "Jason Fury, I want to talk to you!"

Chapter 7

Jason looked at his sister and thought, *Oh, hell*. Jenny had the bit in her teeth about something.

"It's about Matt," she went on.

He grunted. "I'm not surprised. He seems to be just about the only thing you think about these days."

"He told me what happened earlier out at his place. He also told me you said you couldn't do anything about it."

"I can't." Jason shrugged. "I don't have a lick of authority except here in town."

"Well, that's just crazy! You're the marshal."

"*Town* marshal. Matt's going to have to report Dixon to the county sheriff if he wants the law to do anything about it."

She crossed her arms and glared at him. "You're only saying that because you don't like him. You're not being fair to Matt. You've never been fair to him."

"I fished him out of that flooded creek and kept him from drowning, didn't I?" Jason snapped.

Jenny gave a disdainful sniff. "I'm surprised you did that. It was out of your jurisdiction, wasn't it?"

Jason gritted his teeth and didn't point out that he hadn't even been a lawman at the time. He had rescued Matt because he couldn't stand by and let anybody drown, even somebody he didn't like. And if he had been out at Matt's ranch when Ezra Dixon attacked the place, he would have pitched in to help defend it, not as a star-packer but just as a fellow human being.

This situation was different. Dixon had already committed the crime—assuming that everything Matt said was true. If Jason took action against him now, it wouldn't be in self-defense. It would be as a representative of the law, which changed everything.

Making Jenny understand that was going to be next thing to impossible, though, he realized as he looked at his sister. She was so blinded by her feelings for Matt that she couldn't see the truth. Jason might not be able to understand why she felt that way about Matt, but he acknowledged that Jenny's emotions were real.

"If Dixon comes into town, I'll have a talk with him. That's all I can do."

Jenny blew her breath out, glared at Jason some more, and shook her head. She turned on her heel and stalked out of the office, slamming the door behind her.

Wash took a sip of his coffee and commented, "Your little sis sure has a burr under her saddle."

"Jenny's always been that way. You can't argue with her. She's so convinced she's right that it's like butting your head against a stone wall."

"Maybe you ought to go see this fella Dixon not as a lawman, but as Jenny's big brother. After all, Matt MacDonald's gonna be your brother-in-law 'fore too much longer."

Jason turned a sharp look toward the old-timer. "You know something I don't, Wash?"

"Hell, I got eyes, don't I?" Wash said with a shrug. "I seen the way them two look at each other. It's just a matter of time, and I don't think it'll be very long neither."

Jason sighed. "I'm afraid you're right about that."

"For what it's worth, even though I ain't got much use for Matt, he seems to really care for your sister."

Jason pushed himself to his feet. "What would I say to Dixon?" he asked. "I can't tell him to leave Matt alone or the law will be after him."

"Why not? You can tell him that if he attacks Matt's place again, *you'll* contact the sheriff. Chances are the fella would be more likely to respond to a yell for help from a fellow badge-toter. Maybe Dixon would see it the same way and decide to leave Matt alone."

Jason rubbed his jaw and frowned in thought. Wash might be right about that, he decided. He might be able to bring the power of the law to bear against Dixon, or at least threaten to, without exceeding his own authority.

"I guess it's worth a try," he said after a moment. "Since it's your idea, though, how about riding out there with me?"

Wash grinned. "You mean ride up to a place owned by a high-handed son of a bitch who's in the habit o' shootin' at anybody who gets in his way? Sure, why not? Sounds like it might be entertainin'."

Jason didn't think so, but at least if he made the effort, it would get Jenny off his back.

And he didn't think that even a man like Ezra Dixon would gun down a lawman in broad daylight for no good reason.

The first thing Jason did was to go looking for Ward Wanamaker, just to make sure that the story Matt had told him was really what had happened. Jason didn't think Matt had been lying about the fight, but Matt had a habit of telling every story so that he came off as either the hero or the victim, depending on the circumstances.

Jason and Wash found the lean, sandy-haired Ward at Abigail's place, leaning on the plank bar and downing a shot of whiskey. He greeted them with a smile and a friendly "Howdy, fellas."

From the other side of the bar, Abigail asked, "Did you get those troublemakers locked up all right, Marshal?"

"Sure did," Jason replied with a nod. "I haven't decided what to do with them yet, but they're locked up where they can't get out."

Abigail gave Wash a pointed look. "You missed one of them, I'd say."

"Aw, now, Abby," Wash protested. "You know that ruckus weren't my fault. I never meant to knock that spittoon over on Flores's boots."

"You might not have if you hadn't been so drunk you didn't know what you were doing. And my name's Abigail, not Abby, thank you very much."

"You didn't seem to mind how much booze I was drinkin' when you was collectin' from me for it," Wash pointed out.

"We came to talk to Ward, remember?" Jason reminded him. "Not to wrangle with Miss Krimp."

She smiled at him. "You should call me Abigail, Jason. We've known each other long enough for that."

They had known each other since Kansas City, in fact, where Abigail had made it plain that she found Jason very attractive and wouldn't mind if he felt the same way about her. She knew that Jason was interested in Megan MacDonald, but she hadn't quite given up her designs on him.

Jason was glad that Ward changed the subject by saying, "You want to talk to me, Jason? What about?"

"I hear you had some trouble out at Matt's ranch today."

Ward nodded. "Yeah, and it sounds like there was a ruckus here too."

Jason waved that away. "Never mind about that. What happened to you and Matt?"

"Fella who called himself Dixon rode up with some tough hombres backing him and tried to run us off. Said he was a rancher and that was his range. Matt pretty much called him a liar."

"So Dixon and his men started shooting."

Ward pushed his empty glass across the bar to Abigail and nodded. "Yeah. We got in the house before they ventilated us, and damned lucky we were to make it too."

"That's when they tried to burn you out?"

"Matt's been talking to you, I see. Yeah, they managed to throw a torch onto the roof. I was about to go out shootin', rather than sit there and let the place burn down around my ears, but then Dixon and his men took off for the tall and uncut. A cavalry patrol came riding up a minute later. I reckon Dixon and the others heard the horses coming and took those troopers for Apaches. Good luck for us again."

Wash asked, "Them soldier boys come from Camp Grant?"

"That's what they said. And Matt was madder than a wet cat when the lieutenant in charge of the patrol said he wasn't gonna go chasing after Dixon."

"A dispute between civilians is none of the army's business," Jason said.

"Yep. That's what the shavetail said. But Matt sure didn't like it."

A faint smile touched Jason's mouth. "He wasn't happy when I told him that I didn't have any jurisdiction over Dixon's activities either as long as they didn't happen in town."

"So you're not planning to do anything about it either?"

"I didn't say that. Wash and I are going to ride out and have a talk with Dixon. I can't arrest the man, but I can tell him that I'll call in the county sheriff if he continues to make trouble."

"That won't sit well with Dixon, I'm guessing," Ward said.

Jason shrugged. "I don't care if it sits well with him or not. Matt was a member of that wagon train, and I reckon I still feel a little responsibility for him. And you're my friend, Ward. I don't like it when folks try to kill you."

"Me neither," Ward said with a chuckle. "Well, good luck with Dixon. You want me to ride out there with you fellas?"

Jason shook his head. "No, I was thinking maybe I'd ask you to keep an eye on things here in town for me while we're gone."

"Like a deputy?"

"I can't make that official, and I sure as hell can't pay you for it. But I've been thinking about talking to Mayor Kendall and the rest of the town leaders about hiring a deputy, at least part-time. If the settlement keeps growing like it has been, it's going to need more than one lawman."

"That sounds like something I'd be interested in doing. For now, I'll be glad to keep an eye out for trouble, just as a favor to you, Jason."

"I'm obliged," Jason said as he slapped Ward on the shoulder. "Come on, Wash."

They went to the livery stable down the street, saddled their horses, and rode out, heading south toward the MacDonald ranch. Jason didn't look for either Matt or Jenny before leaving to tell them what his plans were. If his visit to Dixon's ranch worked out and accomplished something, that would be fine. If it didn't . . . well, best not to get Jenny's hopes up.

"How do you plan on findin' Dixon's spread?" Wash asked. "I never even heard o' the varmint until today."

"Neither did I," Jason said, "but if he claims that Matt's place is on his range, it's got to be somewhere in the same direction, doesn't it?"

"Yeah, but this is a mighty big country. Dixon's headquarters might be ten or twenty miles from Matt's place."

Jason frowned. He hadn't thought of that. He had been west enough times to know just how vast the frontier really was, but sometimes he forgot. Back East, finding someone was never really that difficult. There weren't miles and miles of empty range for them to disappear into.

Jason was confident he could locate Dixon's ranch. He rode

toward Matt's place, intending to swing wide around it when they got there. At the same time, he could make sure that Dixon and his men hadn't returned to cause more trouble.

That was the plan anyway. But they hadn't reached Matt's new spread when a rifle suddenly cracked and a bullet whined over their heads.

Chapter 8

Jason and Wash both reined in and reached for their guns, but before they could draw the weapons, half-a-dozen men on horseback boiled up out of a nearby draw. Two of them carried rifles, and the other four already had revolvers pulled and leveled.

"Hold on, son," Wash said in a low but urgent voice. "Best take your hand away from that hogleg 'fore you get holes blasted in you."

Jason had come to the same conclusion. He lifted both hands to shoulder level, still gripping Cleo's reins in the left one. Wash did likewise. Neither of them moved as the men rode up to them.

One of the riders holding a rifle scowled at them and demanded, "Who the hell are you two rannies?"

Jason's voice was angry as he replied, "I'm Jason Fury, the marshal of Fury."

One of the other men cackled and said, "What's that? Sounds like you're repeatin' yourself!"

Jason's jaw tightened. "I said—"

The man who had spoken first interrupted him. "We know what you said. We've heard about that so-called settlement of yours. You're a mite young to have a town named after you, mister."

"It was named after my father, not me," Jason explained, keeping a tight rein on his temper. "And there's nothing so-called about it. Fury is a real town."

The spokesman for the group spat off to the side of his horse. "An outlaw town, if you ask me. Those pilgrims had no right to settle there. El Despoblado is Mr. Dixon's range."

The men were all dressed like cowboys, and Jason had already figured out they had to be some of Ezra Dixon's crew. He said, "The area called El Despoblado is mighty big. It can't all belong to Dixon. In fact, I'm betting that only a little piece of it is legally his."

"Legal don't matter. He's been runnin' his stock on it for more'n ten years. It's his."

"Legal matters to me," Jason shot back. He nodded toward the badge pinned to his shirt. "Like I told you, I'm a marshal."

"Fake town, fake lawman. And you still ain't told me what you're doin' out here."

"Looking for Dixon's ranch, as a matter of fact."

The man snorted. "You're on it. Have been ever since you left town."

Jason realized he would be wasting his time arguing that point with the man. He said instead, "What about Dixon's ranch house? Can you take us there? You work for him, don't you?"

"Damn right we do. I'm Ord Kerby, segundo o' the Slash D."

"Marshal Jason Fury," Jason said, introducing himself again. "This fella with me is Wash Keough. All right if we put our hands down now?"

"Not until we've taken your guns," Kerby snapped.

Wash's mustaches fairly quivered with indignation. In a low voice, he said, "I ain't much of a mind to be givin' up my guns, Jason. Always felt a mite naked when I weren't packin' iron."

Jason sensed the tension growing tighter among the ranch

hands. They were spoiling for a fight, and Wash might give them one.

One of the cowboys asked, "Did you say that old man's name is Keough?"

Jason nodded. "That's right."

"I've heard of him, Ord," the man said to the Slash D segundo. "He may not look like much, but he's supposed to be a ring-tailed terror when you get him goin'."

One of the other men said, "And I reckon the boy must be ol' Jedediah Fury's son."

That brought a newfound respect—or at least wariness—to the eyes of several of the cowboys. Jason knew that his father's long career as a wagon master had made him known across the West. It came as no surprise that some of these men had heard of Jedediah Fury.

Ord Kerby chewed over what he had just heard, and said after a moment, "You say you're just lookin' for the boss?"

"That's right."

"What for?"

"I want to talk to him, that's all," Jason answered.

"What's this about?"

Jason took a chance and said, "It's about the man Dixon tried to kill earlier today."

"That son of a bitch had it comin'!" one of the cowboys called. "He claimed he had a right to be on Slash D range!"

Jason didn't argue about that either. He said, "That's why I want to talk to Dixon. I hope we can clear all this up without any bloodshed."

Kerby grunted. "Tell that to Ben Ellsworth. He's got a hole in his shoulder where one of those bastards plugged him."

"What was he doing at the time?" Jason took a guess. "Trying to throw a torch on the roof of Matt MacDonald's house?"

"A house that don't belong there!" Kerby said. But he didn't try to deny that the wounded man had been trying to set it on fire. The segundo gave a curt nod and went on. "I reckon the boss is gonna want to talk to you varmints anyway, so we'll take you to the house."

"And leave us our guns," Jason said.

"And leave you your guns . . . for now," Kerby agreed. "But we'll be watchin' you mighty close, and if you try anything, you'll be full of lead before you can draw another breath."

"Fair enough." Jason went ahead and lowered his arms without asking again for permission to do so. "Lead the way."

The riders formed a loose circle around Jason and Wash and set out toward the south at a brisk trot. Jason spotted a low range of brown, rocky hills in that direction, forming the southern edge of the vast plain known as El Despoblado. As they came closer, he saw that the hills were dotted here and there with the green of pine and juniper, but for the most part they were barren and arid.

Ezra Dixon's home was located on the northernmost of those hills. Jason spotted it as they approached. A sprawling log structure with two stories, it perched atop the rise, reminding Jason of medieval castles he had seen pictured in books. A much more rustic castle than those European ones, to be sure, but it was an impressive sight anyway.

Kerby must have seen the expression on Jason's face, because he said, "The place wasn't always so big and fancy. When the boss built it, it wasn't much bigger'n a line shack. He added on to it, though, bit by bit, until it was what it is now. Sort of like the whole Slash D. Best ranch in the territory."

Jason thought that judgment was probably sound. He had spotted quite a few cattle already, and they looked like fine animals. Back East, the beef market was booming following the end of the Civil War, Jason had heard, and demand was so high that ranchers in Texas had started gathering their stock into large herds and driving them north to the railroad in Kansas. Jason wondered if cattlemen here in Arizona Territory would do the same thing, or perhaps drive their herds farther west, to California. The way people were flooding into the territory, it might not be necessary to do either of those things. Miners were flocking to certain areas, so there might be enough of a demand to support the ranchers without them having to make a long trail drive.

An image entered his mind unbidden. He saw the settlement of Fury as it might one day be—a cattle town, a supply center for the ranches and farms around it, maybe even a stop on the railroad. There was no limit to how much the place might grow and prosper. And if it did, that would be good for the original settlers, the people like Salmon Kendall and Saul Cohen and Michael Morelli, who had been courageous enough to look around and say, *This is it. This is where we will make our homes.*

As those thoughts went through Jason's mind, he realized he wanted to be part of that. He wanted to see his friends grow rich and successful, to raise their families and be happy. If that meant putting off his own plans and dreams for a while, then so be it. The gamble was worthwhile.

Legally, his jurisdiction might not stretch out here, he told himself, but it didn't matter. What Ezra Dixon did affected the town, and Jason wasn't going to stand by and let the rancher run roughshod over any of its citizens, even Matt MacDonald. Matt might not live in the settlement anymore, but since he had been a part of the original wagon train, Jason regarded him as one of them.

A creek emerged from the hills at the base of the hill where the ranch house was located. The outbuildings were all down there, including a bunkhouse, a large barn, and a blacksmith shop. Several sprawling corrals were near the barn. As the riders approached, Jason saw a man breaking horses in one of those corrals. The bronc being ridden at the moment was a big black, and it leaped and sunfished and twisted like mad in a frantic attempt to dislodge the unwelcome human on its back.

As the group of riders drew even with the corral, the bronc

finally won its battle. The horse-breaker went sailing off its back to land on the ground with a thud and a cloud of dust. One of the cowboys escorting Jason and Wash grimaced and said, "Ouch." Several of the others laughed.

Kerby turned his head and glared at them. "I don't see any o' you rannies doin' any better. If you think you can ride that damn devil horse, why don't you climb in there and give it a try?"

"Take it easy, Ord," one of the men said. "We didn't mean nothin' by it. Just that it must've hurt to land like that."

"Yeah, well, take these two on up to see the boss," Kerby said, jerking a thumb toward the big log house on top of the hill. "I'm gonna go see if Will's hurt."

The cowboy who had been bucked off hadn't gotten up yet. He was moving around a little, so Jason thought he was probably just stunned by the fall, but it was possible he could have been injured more seriously than that. Kerby peeled off from the group and rode over to the corral, while the other five men kept Jason and Wash moving toward the house.

A path led up the hundred yards or so to the top of the hill. By the time the group of riders reached the end of it, a couple of big dogs standing on the porch of the house were barking. Their fur bristled as they greeted the newcomers, and drool dripped from their mouths. They looked as if they'd like nothing better than to gnaw on Jason and Wash for a while.

The dogs sat down and shut up right away, though, when a man stepped out of the house and spoke to them in a sharp tone of voice. His white hair and weathered face were indicators of his age, but the movements of his lithe, wiry body were those of a younger man. Jason guessed from the man's arrogant bearing and defiant gaze that he was looking at Ezra Dixon.

"What now?" the man asked when the group of riders had reined to a halt in front of the house. "Who are these two yahoos?"

"They say they want to talk to you, Boss," one of the cowboys replied. "The kid claims to be the marshal of that settlement that sprung up about ten miles north o' here."

"It's no claim," Jason snapped. He didn't like being referred to as a kid. "I'm the legally appointed marshal of Fury."

Dixon spat off the porch. "That's what I think o' your legal appointment, boy. Town's got no right to be there, and neither have you. Now speak your piece and get the hell off my range, 'fore I send you back to that settlement covered with tar an' feathers!"

Chapter 9

With an effort, Jason kept his temper under control. He didn't like being spoken to that way, and he didn't like Ezra Dixon. The reaction was instinctive and immediate.

"Earlier today, you tried to kill a couple of men working on a ranch west of here," Jason said in a flat, hard voice.

"A couple o' trespassers who had no right to be there, puttin' up a house and barn on my range and callin' it theirs!"

One of the dogs growled. Dixon shushed it.

"What'd they do?" the rancher went on. "Come cryin' to the law?"

"I was asked to look into the matter," Jason said. "That's why I'm here. If what you're saying is true, then they *didn't* have a right to be there. That still doesn't give *you* the right to try to kill them and burn the place down."

Dixon snorted. "I ain't in the habit o' lyin'. Of course it's true! That's my range! Has been for more'n ten years. I come out here before the war, almost before there were any other white men in this part o' the territory. Fought Apaches, bandits from below the border, and bad weather. Buried a wife and two sons here. Don't you ever go to sayin' this ain't my range!"

A part of Jason sympathized with the man. He was sure it

hadn't been easy establishing a foothold in this hard, savage country. Dixon had sacrificed to start his ranch, no doubt about that.

But it didn't have anything to do with the law. Jason said, "My understanding is that most of this area is open range, that it belongs to whoever claims it. If you filed a legal claim to the place where Matt MacDonald is building his ranch, then I'll tell him he's out of luck and that he has to get off of it. But if you didn't, then he's got as much right to it as anybody else, including you."

Dixon's deep-set eyes narrowed. "You're talkin' about a damn piece of paper, ain't you, boy?"

"Pieces of paper are what civilization depends on, Mr. Dixon," Jason said.

"Yeah, well, maybe that's what wrong with it! Nobody gives a damn anymore about anything except what some blasted paper-pushers say!" Dixon swept a gnarled hand around in a curt gesture, taking in their surroundings. "Nobody cares that I watered this ground with my blood! And I ain't ashamed to say it, with my tears too! All they want is a damn piece of paper!"

"Ain't it the truth," Wash muttered.

Jason glanced over at him. "Whose side are you on?" he asked under his breath.

Wash didn't have to answer, because Dixon said, "If it's any o' your business, mister—which it ain't, to my way o' thinkin'—I *don't* have that paper you're talkin' about. Never needed it before, and I don't need it now."

"Then you *don't* have legal title to the land that MacDonald claimed?"

"Didn't I just say that? You deaf as well as stupid?"

Jason bit back an angry curse. Forcing himself to stay calm, he said, "In that case, I have to tell you that if you or your men bother Matt MacDonald again, I'll report it to the county sheriff and get some deputies in here to force you to comply with the law."

A harsh laugh came from Dixon. "That's supposed to scare me? Boy, you got a lot to learn about the sort o' man you're dealin' with here. You tell that fella—MacDonald, you say his name is?—you tell him that unless he gets off my range, I'm gonna kill him, and it won't matter none to him what the law does about it, 'cause he'll already be buzzard bait!"

The sheer ferocity and hatred in Dixon's voice made Jason's jaw clench. He wanted to lash out at the old rancher, but instead he said, "You can be arrested for threatening to kill somebody, you know."

"Not by you. Not unless I do it in that town o' yours." Dixon laughed. "I know *that* much law, sonny. Your badge don't mean shit out here."

The trip to the Slash D had been wasted. Jason knew that now. Dixon wasn't going to give an inch. Jason figured Matt wouldn't either. That meant sooner or later there would be more gunplay, more violence, maybe a full-fledged range war.

And right now, Jason didn't see any way in hell he could head it off before it got started.

"Are we free to go?"

Dixon waved a hand again. "Sure, go on. I'm sick o' lookin at you anyway."

Something else occurred to Jason. "What about the town itself? Do you want everybody there to pack up and leave too?"

The speed with which Dixon answered told Jason that the rancher had already considered that very question. "No, I reckon the settlement can stay. It's right there close to that trail the wagon trains use on their way to California. Not really good grazin' land thereabouts."

"What about the people who are putting in farms outside of town?"

"Long as they don't come too far in this direction, I got no problem with that, even though I don't have much use for farmers in general, you understand. Can't see how anybody'd want to make a livin' grubbin' around in the dirt."

Before Jason could say anything in response to that, the sound of hoofbeats made him look around. Kerby and the cowboy who had been trying to ride the big black horse in the corral had walked up the path to the house, the segundo leading his mount. The cowboy with him was limping.

Dixon saw that too, and looked worried as he exclaimed, "Will? Will, honey, are you all right?"

Honey? Jason thought.

A strong brown hand reached up and tugged the cowboy's hat off, letting long, dark brown hair spill out from under it. Without the broad brim of the hat shading the face, Jason saw that it belonged to a woman, and a mighty good-looking one at that. Even smudged with dust and dirt, she was pretty enough to take a fella's breath away.

"I'm fine, Pa," she said. "Just twisted my leg a little when that devil horse threw me."

"Damn it, I've told you that you don't have to ride him!" Dixon said. "Let somebody else do it."

"I'm the best hand you've got when it comes to busting horses," she argued. "It's my job."

Wash leaned toward Jason and hissed, "You're starin', son."

Jason supposed he was. It was hard not to stare. The woman was young, probably a year or two younger than Jason, tall and slender but not skinny. The man's shirt and denim trousers she wore did a pretty good job of concealing her shape, but Jason could see enough to know that she was built like a woman was supposed to be built, with all the right curves in all the right places.

Wash wasn't the only one who had noticed Jason looking at her. She turned her head, and her brown eyes met Jason's gaze squarely. "What are you looking at, mister?"

"I'm sorry," he said. "I don't mean to be rude. It's just that when I saw somebody trying to ride that horse, I figured it was a man."

"Yeah, well, I could sit a saddle before I could walk. Isn't that right, Pa?"

"It is for a fact," Dixon said, and for the first time, Jason heard something besides anger, resentment, and arrogance in the old man's voice. He heard pride. "I never saw nobody who took to ridin' like you did, girl, not even your brothers, God rest their poor souls."

She stepped closer to Jason and stuck her hand up. "I'm Will Dixon," she introduced herself. "Short for Wilhemina. But don't you call me that, or I'll have to whip you."

"Will! Step away from those men! They ain't here on no friendly visit." Dixon sneered. "The young one's a lawman. Says I got no right to range that's always been mine, ever since we come here."

Will Dixon lowered her hand and took a step back. "Is that true?"

"I was just trying to get your father to understand—"

"Oh, he understands, all right. He's forgotten more about this land than a fella like you will ever know. I reckon he told you to git?"

"As a matter of fact . . ."

"I thought so. Now I'm telling you. Get off the Slash D, and stay off!"

Somehow, the words stung even more coming from her than they had from Dixon. With his face set grimly, Jason nodded and lifted the palomino's reins. He and Wash turned their horses and heeled them into a trot, heading back down the hill.

But when they reached the bottom, Jason couldn't resist the impulse to look back. He saw that Will had stepped up onto the porch with her father and stood there beside Dixon now, just as straight and unyielding as he was.

"Whatever you're thinkin', son," Wash said, "you best forget it. That gal is all whang leather and just as tough as her old man."

"Yeah, you're probably right." Jason forced his thoughts back onto the problem at hand as they rode away from the Dixon ranch. "What do you think Matt's going to do when he hears about this?"

"I reckon he'll get his back up and dig in his heels and start gettin' ready for a fight."

"He can't put up a fight. Ward's quit him. He doesn't even have anybody working for him. Dixon probably has twenty or thirty ranch hands on his spread."

"Matt's got nobody right now," Wash pointed out. "That don't mean he won't hire some men to help him. Folks are movin' into Fury all the time now."

And some of the men who drifted into town were pretty unsavory types, Jason thought. Matt had some of the money from his father's stake left. Did he have enough to pay fighting wages?

If he did, things were liable to get a lot worse before they got better.

Regardless of that, Jason knew he had to let Matt know what the outcome of his visit to the Slash D had been. He and Wash swung toward the west, and soon came in sight of the MacDonald ranch house and the skeletal framework of the partially built barn.

Matt heard them coming and stepped out of the house to meet them, a rifle clutched in his hands. "What do you want, Fury?" he demanded.

"I rode out to Dixon's ranch and had a talk with him, like you wanted," Jason said.

"I didn't want you to talk to the bastard. I wanted you to arrest him."

"I told you, I can't do that. But Jenny convinced me I ought to try to talk some sense into Dixon's head."

That brought a smirk to Matt's face. "She did, did she? That little sister of yours is a smart girl. You ought to listen to her more often."

Jason didn't want to think about Matt considering Jenny pretty. It was bad enough knowing that Jenny wanted to marry Matt and have his babies. She had said as much to Jason in a fit of anger.

"Look, Dixon's still threatening to kill you if you don't get off this land. Why don't you think about moving? There's some good range north of the settlement too, and maybe that would be far enough away from Dixon that he wouldn't mind."

"What the hell are you talking about? He's got no legal claim to this land! You know that."

Jason shrugged. "He admitted as much. But that doesn't mean anything to an old-timer like him. He'll fight for what he considers his."

"So will I," Matt said. "You'd do well to remember that." He tucked his rifle under his arm. "If there's nothing else, I've got work to do."

"Suit yourself," Jason said. "But I'd be mighty careful if I was you. Dixon's liable to come calling again."

"I'll give him a hot-lead welcome if he does."

Jason just shook his head and turned his horse around. As he and Wash rode away, the old-timer said, "That boy's stubborn streak is gonna get him killed."

"Yeah," Jason agreed with a bleak look on his face. "I just hope a lot of other people don't wind up dead along with him."

Chapter 10

It was early evening by the time they rode back into Fury, and another problem had occurred to Jason.

"I've got to do something with those fellas I locked up earlier," he said to Wash. "The one who plugged you in the arm, and his friends."

"I ain't one to hold grudges. You can let 'em go as far as I'm concerned."

"Not until I talk to Salmon about it." Jason grinned. "There ought to be a little fine or something for winging an old pelican."

Wash snorted.

Luck was with Jason. He spotted the mayor of Fury standing in front of Cohen's Hardware, talking with Saul. Salmon lifted a hand in greeting as Jason and Wash reined their mounts toward him.

"Hello, fellas. I was just down at the marshal's office, and Ward Wanamaker told me you'd ridden out to see Ezra Dixon, Jason."

Jason swung down from the saddle and nodded. "That's right. I wanted to see if I could talk some sense into his head about Matt MacDonald."

"Now there's a couple of things you don't put together too often—sense and Matt MacDonald," Salmon said with a smile.

"Dixon's the same way. Hardheaded as the day is long. And he still says that he'll kill Matt if he doesn't get off what Dixon considers his range."

Salmon's smile turned into a frown. "I'm not all that fond of Matt," he said, "but I'd hate to see him gunned down or burned out. Maybe he's the one you ought to be talking to."

Jason shook his head. "Wash and I just tried that. Matt won't budge. It's like the old saying about the irresistible force and the immovable object."

"Don't reckon I've heard that one, but I can figure out what you mean. I guess the best we can hope for is that the trouble won't spill over into town."

That was a worry, all right, Jason thought, but it wasn't his only one. If anything happened to Matt, Jenny would be heartbroken. Whether Jason liked Matt or not, he didn't want his sister to have to go through the pain of losing him.

Right at the moment, though, there was nothing else he could do, and Salmon changed the subject by saying, "Ward told me you were talking to him about making him a deputy."

"That's right," Jason said. "I hope I didn't overstep my bounds. I didn't promise him any wages, or anything like that."

Salmon shook his head. "No, no, that's fine. Saul and I were just talking about the fact that you're going to need some help keeping order around here. Ward's a good man for the job."

"We're going to talk to all the businessmen in the settlement," Saul put in. "They're already chipping in to pay your salary, Jason. It wouldn't cost much more for them to come up with some wages for Ward too." Saul looked at Wash. "Unless *you'd* be interested in the job?"

"Me?" Wash poked himself in the chest with a thumb. "A deputy? Lord, no! I don't mind helpin' Jason out ever' now and then, but it's 'cause me and his pa was friends. Don't give me no badge."

Jason was glad to hear the old-timer say that. He liked Wash and knew that he was a good man in a fight, but Wash was a mite too fond of his liquor to make a dependable deputy. Jason was happy just to have him as a friend.

"All right, it's settled then," Salmon said. "Ward will be Fury's deputy marshal. Better warn him the pay won't be much, though. It's all right with me if he works at some other jobs, as long as he's able to handle whatever you need him to do too. Like guarding those prisoners, the way he's doing now."

"I'm glad you mentioned them, Salmon," Jason said. "What am I supposed to do with them?"

Salmon and Saul looked at each other, and both men frowned. "Hell, I don't know," Salmon said. "Saul, what do you think?"

"We haven't enacted any town ordinances yet," Saul said, "but surely it's got to be against the law to shoot at somebody, right?"

Wash put his other hand on his wounded arm and gave a dramatic sigh. "Seems that way to me. A fella ought to have to pay a fine for that. And maybe the money should go to the gent who got shot. Seems fair enough to me."

"We need to put together an actual town council so we can pass some laws," Salmon said. "But until then, why don't you just fine that Mexican for disturbin' the peace and let it go at that?"

Jason nodded. "That's what I was thinking too. He ought to be charged with attempted murder, but with no judge or court here, we'd have to take him to Tucson or Phoenix to do it."

"More trouble than it's worth," Saul said. "I agree with Salmon. Fine the man, and tell him and his friends to get out of Fury and not come back."

"All right," Jason said. "Come on, Wash."

They led their horses to the livery stable, unsaddled them, then turned them over to the hostler for a rubdown and some grain. When they reached the marshal's office, they found

Ward Wanamaker in Jason's chair, leaned back with his feet propped on the desk.

Ward sat up in a hurry, but Jason motioned for him to take it easy. "We don't stand on ceremony around here . . . Deputy Wanamaker," he added.

Ward grinned. "I've got the job?"

"That's right. Mayor Kendall and Saul Cohen thought it was a good idea. They're going to try to drum up some money to pay you, but Salmon said to warn you it may not be much."

"I don't care about that," Ward said. "I can pick up some cash working odd jobs around town. And I don't need much to get by on."

Jason stuck out his hand, and Ward stood up and gripped it. "It's a deal then," Jason said. "And for your first official job, Deputy, why don't you bring those prisoners out here?"

"You're gonna let 'em go?" Ward asked.

"If we keep them much longer, the town's going to have to feed them supper. We don't want that."

Ward chuckled and went to the door into the cell block. He unlocked it and swung it open, then disappeared into the short hallway. He came back a minute later, herding Flores, Trumbull, and Yates ahead of him. He had his pistol in his hand, trained on their backs in case they tried anything.

The three hardcases, while still angry about being locked up, cooperated. Jason sat down behind the desk, looked at them, and said, "Flores, you're being fined twenty-five dollars for disturbing the peace and injuring one of Fury's citizens. You're lucky to be getting off so easy. By all rights, I could lock you up for the next couple of months."

Flores sneered at him. "And if I refuse to pay this fine?"

Jason inclined his head toward the cells. "Then you go back in there . . . and I'll let you out when I'm damned good and ready."

"This is not legal!"

"I'm the law in Fury," Jason said, his voice hardening. "If I say it's legal, then it is. And the town will back me up on it too."

"What about us?" Trumbull asked.

Jason shrugged. "You and Yates are free to go. You didn't do anything you could be charged for. But I'll tell you the same thing I was about to tell your friend. Get out of Fury, and stay out. You're not welcome here, and if you come back, you'll wind up in jail again . . . or worse."

"That sounds mighty like a threat," Yates grated.

Jason shook his head. "No threat, just some good advice. You'd be wise to follow it."

Trumbull glared at him for a couple more seconds, then turned to Flores and said, "Pay the damn fine and let's get out of here."

"But it is not fair!" Flores jerked a hand toward Wash. "You saw what the old *borrochon* did to my boots!"

"I don't care. We're done with this damn place. We got things to do, remember?"

"Sí, sí," Flores muttered. He dug around in the pocket of his charro jacket and came out with several coins. Contemptuously, he tossed them onto Jason's desk. "There is your fine . . . *Marshal.*"

He made the word sound like an obscenity.

"What about our guns?" Trumbull asked.

Jason stood up, went to a cabinet with a lock on the door, and retrieved the weapons that had been taken from the men earlier. "They're unloaded," he said as he returned them to their owners. "Don't stop to load them until you're out of town. I'll be watching, and if you do, it'll mean more trouble."

They gave him go-to-hell looks as they buckled on their gunbelts, but they didn't argue with the order. With some final cold, hostile stares, the three hardcases trooped out of the office.

Jason, Wash, and Ward stepped outside to watch them leave town. All three men carried rifles now, and were ready to use them if the hardcases tried anything else. But Flores, Trumbull, and Yates just retrieved their horses from the hitch rack in front of Abigail's place, mounted up, and rode out.

A sigh of relief came from Jason. "I'm glad to see those three gone."

"You think they'll stay away, like you told them to?" Ward asked.

"I hope so. If they don't . . ." Jason shrugged. "I reckon we'll deal with that when the time comes."

Ward nodded and said, "You need me for anything else tonight, Marshal?"

"Nope, not unless some more trouble crops up. Which I'm hoping it won't."

"Well, I'll be around town if it does." Ward lifted a hand in farewell as he moved off down the street. "So long."

"He's a good fella," Wash said. "Make you a fine deputy."

"I think so too."

The old-timer tugged at his mustache and got a shrewd look on his face. "Now, about that twenty-five-dollar fine Flores paid . . ."

"That goes in the town coffers," Jason said.

"Has the town *got* coffers?"

"It does now."

"Don't hardly seem right." Wash clutched his injured arm again and winced in pain. "I'm the one who got shot, after all. And it sure does pain me."

"If you'd leave it alone, maybe it'd stop hurting so much." Jason smiled. "Sorry, Wash. That money goes to the town. I'm going to take it over to Saul's and let him lock it up in his safe. For the time being, he'll be Fury's treasurer."

"All right, all right. I'll go see Abigail. She don't mind extendin' a little credit to a poor ol' man."

"Don't drink too much," Jason said, although he suspected that the words fell on deaf ears.

Wash shambled off, and Jason turned back to the marshal's

office. He stopped just outside the door, though, because he spotted someone walking toward him through the early evening gloom. As the figure came closer, he recognized Megan MacDonald.

"Jason," she said, "I'd like to talk to you."

Chapter 11

Jason wasn't going to turn down a chance to spend some time with Megan, although from the sound of her voice he judged that something was troubling her.

He could make a pretty good guess what it was too. It had to be something to do with her brother.

Megan looked as pretty as ever as she stepped into the light that spilled through the open doorway of the marshal's office. Her long auburn hair was pulled into a ponytail that hung down her back. Her green eyes were compelling. As Jason looked at her, he felt a twinge of guilt for being so impressed with Will Dixon's looks during his visit to the Slash D earlier in the day. He was so fond of Megan that he shouldn't even be looking at any other women, let alone thinking about how pretty they were.

"What can I do for you, Megan?" he asked.

"Can we go inside?"

"Sure." He held out a hand to usher her in ahead of him. As he followed her into the office, he asked, "Would you like a cup of coffee? It's been sitting in the pot so long it's probably strong enough by now to get up and walk off on its own two legs, but—"

"No, that's fine." Megan turned to face him as he eased the

door closed. "Jenny told me what happened between Matt and that man Dixon. She said Matt was all right, but I didn't get a chance to talk to him myself while he was in town."

Jason nodded. "He wasn't hurt, other than a twisted ankle. It's nothing to worry about."

"What about Dixon? Is *he* something to worry about?"

Jason wanted to lie to her. He didn't want her troubling herself over Matt. But he respected her too much to do that, and sooner or later—probably sooner—she would just find out the truth anyway.

"Dixon's stubborn as a mule. He thinks that the land Matt has claimed is part of his range. If Matt doesn't get off of it . . ." Jason shrugged. "There'll be trouble, all right."

"Shooting trouble?"

"Maybe."

Megan drew in a deep breath. "I was afraid of that. Jenny said you were going to talk to Dixon."

"I did," Jason said. "It didn't do a bit of good. I had another talk with your brother too, but it didn't change anything. They're like a couple of bulls, Megan, one young and one old but equally determined to butt heads. Problem is, Matt's alone, while Dixon's got a tough, salty crew to help him out."

"But you can help Matt . . . can't you?" She came a step closer to him, close enough to lay a hand on his arm. "I know you and Matt don't get along. Lord knows, sometimes he's such a fool that he drives *me* to distraction. But he's my brother, Jason."

"I know," he said, feeling the same sort of emotional tug-of-war that she did. He didn't love Matt MacDonald like a brother, of course; in fact he could barely stand the man. But if anything happened to Matt, Jenny wasn't the only one who would be heartbroken.

Like it or not, Jason was trapped. Because of the women in his life, he couldn't ignore the danger to Matt.

"I'll try to think of something," he said. "There's got to be some way to work this out."

"Thank you, Jason." Megan moved closer still, and he just sort of naturally put his hands on her shoulders. As she closed her eyes, he bent to kiss her. Megan slipped her arms around him and held him tight.

The kiss lasted only a moment before she slipped out of his embrace. With a shy smile, she looked down at the floor and said, "Good night, Jason."

"Wait a minute. I'll walk you home."

"That's not necessary. I'll be fine."

She left the office, and he sat down behind the desk to wrack his brain and search for solutions to the problems facing him.

Unfortunately, memories kept crowding in on his brain. Memories of the way Megan had just felt in his arms and the sweetness of her lips . . .

And of the bold, challenging look in the eyes of Will Dixon.

Much to Jason's surprise, things were pretty quiet in Fury for the next couple of weeks. The three hardcases he had run out of town didn't come back, and the simmering feud between Matt MacDonald and Ezra Dixon stayed in the background, not boiling over into violence. Matt hired some men to help him finish building his barn and corrals. They were newcomers to Fury and didn't know the potential trouble they were getting into, but even when they heard about the threat from Dixon, they stayed on. Matt always had at least two men standing guard with rifles at the ready while he and the others worked.

The settlement continued to grow. Fury's population was nearly two hundred now, and several new businesses opened each week. A café, known as the Red Top because of the

Spanish tiles that formed its roof, was a welcome addition to the town. A couple of saloons opened, giving Abigail Krimp some competition. Several wagon trains rolled along the nearby trail, stopping to stock up on provisions and other supplies before they continued on to California. Saul Cohen and Randall Nordstrom did a booming business from the immigrant trade.

A town council was formed to go along with the mayor, giving Fury a governing body. They passed several ordinances, including one that said no firearms were to be discharged in town, and levied a small tax on the businesses to pay for Jason's and Ward's wages. The mayor and council members served as volunteers, working for free, so the wages for the lawmen were the town's only real expense so far.

Wash shook his head ruefully after attending the first council meeting. "This town's done taken its first steps on the road to ruin, boy," he said to Jason as they walked along the street toward the marshal's office. "A bunch o' laws and taxes are the plumb ruination of everything good about a place."

"That's just part of civilization, Wash."

"You done made my point. Civilization ain't natural. It always gets so big and fat that sooner or later it comes crashin' down because of its own weight. Might not be in our lifetimes, mind you, but it'll happen. Mark my words."

Jason hoped the old pelican was wrong. But only time would tell, he supposed.

Wash was still ranting. "Hell, if Fury gets much bigger, I'm gonna have to leave. It's already gettin' too crowded around— Who the hell's that?"

Wash came to an abrupt halt, and Jason stopped walking beside him. Jason saw what Wash had just seen. Four men were riding along Fury's main street toward them. Strangers who held themselves loose and easy in their saddles. Their heads didn't move much, but their eyes did, always alert and watchful.

That was a sure sign of men who were accustomed to trouble.

The strangers bristled with guns too. A couple of them sported two Colts apiece, and rifle butts stuck up from saddle boots on all four horses. The men's jaws were beard-stubbled, and their rough clothes were covered with dust. From the looks of them, they had been on the trail for quite a while.

Jason veered toward the strangers. Wash's shorter legs hurried to keep up with him. "Best be careful, son," the old-timer said. "Those hombres look like they been to see the elephant . . . and shot it when they got there."

The strangers had a hard-bitten, dangerous look about them, no doubt about that. The man in the lead had a black hat thumbed back on a thatch of curly, sand-colored hair, and even though he smiled as Jason approached, his pale blue eyes remained cold and hard as flint. Jason knew the man had spotted the badge on his shirt.

"Howdy, Sheriff," the stranger said as he pulled back on the reins and brought his mount to a halt.

"It's Marshal," Jason said. "Marshal Jason Fury."

"Pleased to meet you," the man said, even though Jason could tell that he wasn't. "Name's Bill Rye." He nodded toward the other three, who had reined in beside him. "This is Jack Dupree—they call him Three-Finger Jack—Ned Potter, and Nib Sloan."

"What brings you to Fury?"

Bill Rye didn't answer right away. Instead, he grinned and said, "Town's got the same name as you, eh, Marshal? They must think highly of you around here."

"It was named after my father," Jason said, wondering if he was going to have to explain that to every newcomer who rode into town from now on. "And you didn't answer my question, Mr. Rye."

"That's right, I didn't." For a second Jason thought Rye was going to refuse to, but then the man went on. "We're looking for somebody. Man name of Matt MacDonald."

A chill went through Jason at those words. He had seen men like Rye and the others before. Gun-hung, hard-faced men whose stock in trade was killing. They dealt in hot lead. Every so often, the wagon trains being led by Jason's father had crossed trails with such men, and Jason recalled Jedediah talking about them.

"They got eyes like snakes," Jedediah had said. "They're ain't nothin' human in 'em. And like a snake, their bite is fast and deadly. Best to steer clear of them if you can, but if you can't . . . well, make sure you chop the head off with your first blow, because if you don't, you won't get a second chance."

Bill Rye continued to smile at Jason. "You know this fella MacDonald, Marshal?"

"What's your business with him?" Jason thought he knew the answer to that question already. Rye, Dupree, Potter, and Sloan had come to Fury to kill Matt. Instead of dealing himself with the man he considered an interloper, Ezra Dixon had hired these killers to get rid of Matt.

"Some might say that what we want with MacDonald is our business, Marshal, not yours," Rye said. "But I'm feeling friendly today, so I'll tell you . . . MacDonald sent for us. We're going to work for him."

That news threw Jason for a loop. It was just the opposite of what he had expected. *Matt* was the one who had sent for help, not Dixon.

Assuming, of course, that Rye was telling the truth. Jason decided that he couldn't take a chance that the man was lying to him.

"MacDonald's out at his ranch," he said. "I'll show you where it is."

"Much obliged, but you don't have to trouble yourself. Just tell us where to find it."

"I'll show you," Jason repeated. "It's no trouble."

Rye shrugged. "Suit yourself. It don't make no nevermind to us."

"Wait here. I'll get my horse."

As Jason turned and walked toward the livery stable, Wash hurried alongside him and said in a low voice, "Them fellas is gunfighters, Jason. Matt's gone and hired himself some shootists."

"I know," Jason said with a grim nod. "Find Ward and tell him to keep an eye on things here in town while I'm gone."

"Sure. But you know what's gonna happen once Dixon hears about this, don't you?"

"I know," Jason said. "Matt just raised the stakes in this game."

And with that raise, the next hand was more likely than ever to turn deadly.

Chapter 12

Cleo had been favoring one leg the past few days, so Jason left the palomino mare in her stall at the stable and saddled up Gumption, his father's old blue roan, instead. Gumption was something of a plodder but still strong, and Jason didn't figure he would need Cleo's speed on this trip out to Matt's ranch and back.

Wash insisted on coming with him. "It's possible that fella was lyin', and what they're really after is killin' Matt," he said to Jason while they were in the stable, after Wash had passed along Jason's message to Ward Wanamaker. "You might need a hand stoppin' 'em."

Jason wasn't sure that he and Wash and Matt could stop the strangers from doing whatever they wanted to. None of them were gunslingers, although Jason had practiced his draw a great deal over the past couple of weeks. He thought that he was quite a bit faster than he had been, without sacrificing any of his accuracy. But he was nowhere near in the same league as hired guns were.

He tried to persuade Wash to stay in town, but the argument did no good. In the end, the old-timer was beside him as they rode back to join Rye, Dupree, Potter, and Sloan.

"I still say you don't have to go out there with us, Marshal," Rye commented.

"I'm going," Jason said.

Rye shrugged. "Lead the way then."

They rode out. On the way, Jason spotted Megan and Jenny, together as they usually were. The two young women looked puzzled and more than a little worried at the sight of Jason and Wash leaving town with four hard-looking strangers.

The girls might have a right to be worried, Jason thought. He had no idea what was going to happen when they reached Matt's ranch.

Bill Rye was a friendly sort, at least on the surface, talking and asking questions about the country hereabouts and making jokes. His eyes never warmed up, though. The other men remained as sullen and taciturn as they had been when they rode into Fury.

The riders were about halfway to Matt MacDonald's place when Rye said, "There are some fellas doggin' our trail, Marshal. You know anything about that? Ask somebody to follow along and keep an eye on us, did you?"

The gunman's jovial voice had turned almost as chilly as his gaze. Jason looked around and didn't spot anybody. He said, "Are you sure?"

"Sure enough. They're stayin' out of sight most of the time, bein' careful not to get skylighted. The boys and I don't take kindly to bein' double-crossed."

"I don't know anything about any double cross," Jason snapped. "And whoever's back there, I didn't have anything to do with it." An idea occurred to him. "They're probably Ezra Dixon's men. They spotted us and want to know who we are. Dixon doesn't like people riding on what he considers his range."

Rye thought it over and then nodded. "Seems like I heard something about that," he said. "I'll take your word for it, Marshal . . . for now."

They rode on, and by the time they reached Matt's ranch,

Jason had spotted the men trailing them too. He was more convinced that ever that they were some of Dixon's men, the way they hung back, spying, but never approaching too close.

Someone at the ranch must have seen them coming, because Matt and his hired hands were ready for them. No one was in sight when Jason, Wash, and the four strangers rode in. As they reined to a halt, however, a voice called out, "Nobody move! You're covered!"

Jason recognized the voice as Matt's. He looked around and spotted the barrel of a rifle protruding from the hayloft door in the barn. More rifle barrels poked from open windows in the house, and a man leaned into view from behind a corner of the building, also peering at them over the barrel of a rifle.

"Are folks around here always this glad to see strangers?" Rye asked with a grin.

Jason ignored him. "Matt!" he called. "Matt MacDonald! Show yourself!"

The front door swung back. Jason saw movement inside, but Matt hung back in the shadows, inside the house. The barrel of the rifle he held was the only thing readily visible.

"What do you want, Fury?" Matt asked. "Who are those men with you?"

"You tell me," Jason said. "According to them, you're the one they're looking for."

Jason watched Rye and the other gunmen from the corner of his eye. If they wanted to kill Matt, they sure weren't acting like it. In fact, they seemed relaxed now.

"MacDonald," Rye said. "I'm Bill Rye. This is Three-Finger Jack Dupree, Nib Sloan, and Ned Potter with me. You wrote me a letter. It caught up to me in Denver."

Matt finally stepped out onto the porch of his house. "Rye?" he asked. "You got proof of that?"

"I've got that letter you wrote." The gunman took a folded

piece of paper from his shirt pocket and tossed it onto the porch at Matt's feet. "Take a look at it if you don't believe me."

Matt pointed the rifle at Rye with his right hand while he bent and picked up the paper with his left. He flapped it back and forth until it opened, and finally took his eyes off the gunman to look at the words written on it. Jason could see the tension ease in Matt's body as he recognized the letter.

"It's the one I sent you, all right," Matt said. He lowered the rifle and called to the other men hidden around the place, "They're all right! I hired them!"

"You haven't hired us yet," Rye pointed out. "We came to talk business, sure, but we don't have a deal yet."

"Come on inside then. We'll discuss it." Matt looked at Jason and Wash. "What are you doing here, Fury?"

"These fellas rode into town looking for you," Jason said. "They didn't say what for, so I thought I ought to come along."

Rye grinned and said, "I don't think your friend the marshal trusted us, MacDonald. Reckon he thought we might mean you some harm."

"So you were looking out for my best interests, eh?" Matt said to Jason. "Well, that's a welcome change, seein' as how you turned your back on me when Dixon attacked me the first time."

Jason reined in the anger he felt. "I explained to you why I couldn't do anything about that. And I went to talk to Dixon. That was more meddling than I should have done."

"Take your so-called meddling and go to hell. I don't need your help anymore, Fury."

"Because you're planning to hire these gunslingers?"

Matt smiled, but it wasn't a pleasant expression. "Next time Dixon tries to give me trouble, he'll get a mighty warm welcome."

"Maybe we better settle our business first," Rye suggested. He and the other men dismounted, looped their reins around a hitching post Matt had put up in front of the porch, and climbed the steps.

"I guess we're not needed here anymore, Wash," Jason said.

"You never were," Matt told him with a sneer.

Tight-lipped, Jason turned Gumption around and heeled the blue roan into an easy lope. Wash followed, moving up alongside as they left the ranch.

"Ain't no good gonna come from this," Wash predicted. "When Dixon finds out the boy's hired him some gunslingers, it'll just start the ball that much sooner."

"I'm afraid you're right," Jason said with a nod. War was almost inevitable now.

He just hoped it wouldn't spill over into the streets of Fury.

Megan was waiting for him in the marshal's office when he got back to town.

"Thank God you're all right, Jason," she said as she hugged him. Jason felt a little embarrassed because Wash had followed him into the office and witnessed that display of affection, but the old man was whistling a tune between his teeth and pretending not to notice.

Megan stepped back and went on. "Who were those men I saw you with earlier? They looked like outlaws."

"Next thing to it," Jason said as he hung his hat on a nail beside the door. "They're hired guns . . . hired by your brother to fight Ezra Dixon, unless I miss my guess."

Megan's hand went to her mouth. "Oh, no. That's just going to make things worse, isn't it?"

"Hard to say, but chances are it's not going to make things any better."

Considering that a couple of weeks had passed with Dixon leaving Matt MacDonald alone, Jason had begun to hope that the old cattleman had decided not to try to push Matt off that range. Maybe his daughter had talked some sense to him—although to tell the truth, Will Dixon had struck Jason as being almost as hotheaded as her father.

Now, even if Dixon had decided that the range wasn't worth any more bloodshed, once he heard about Rye and the other gunslingers Matt had hired, the old man would be insulted. He would take it as a direct challenge to his authority, which had ruled unquestioned around here for more than a decade, and his pride wouldn't allow him to let things rest.

The presence of those gunmen was like throwing coal oil on a fire. It was just going to blaze up higher and hotter than ever.

Jason clung to one shred of hope. Maybe Matt wouldn't be able to come to an agreement with those hired guns. The services of men like that didn't come cheap. Matt might not have enough money left to hire them. He had already spent quite a bit of what he had left from his father's stake on setting up the ranch.

"What can we do?" Megan asked.

"Nothing," Jason told her. "Wait to see what happens." He didn't like the idea of sitting back and letting events dictate the course of his own actions, but he didn't see what other option he had.

"Maybe I should go out there and try to talk to Matt," she suggested.

Jason shook his head. "I'd feel better about things if you'd stay here in town, Megan. You don't need to go to the ranch."

"He's my brother! I can't just abandon him to whatever fate is waiting for him, even if he *is* bringing it down on his own head!"

"I understand that. Just give it a few days, that's all I'm asking."

Megan frowned, but after a moment she nodded. "All right. But the next time Matt comes into town, I'm going to corner him and give him a piece of my mind."

"You do that," Jason said. No matter what Megan might

say to her brother, though, Jason didn't think it was going to do any good. Events had already been set in motion. Like an avalanche rolling down a hill, they couldn't be stopped.

And like an avalanche, they would wipe out whoever was unlucky enough to be in their way.

Chapter 13

When the explosion came, it wasn't out on the range, either at Matt's place or at Ezra Dixon's Slash D.

It was in town, just as Jason had feared it might be.

A man from Tucson named Alf Blodgett had driven into Fury a few days earlier in a big wagon loaded with barrels of beer and whiskey. A couple of smaller wagons followed him, one full of tables and chairs, the other one packed with women who leaned out, smiled, waved, and called to the men in the streets, promising them all manner of delights. The ample flesh that was displayed in their low-cut gowns made its own promises.

Blodgett had operated a saloon in Tucson for several years before deciding to move to Fury. From England originally, he was a burly man almost as wide as he was tall, with a head as bald as an egg except for handlebar mustaches that curled up on the ends. He called his establishment the Crown and Garter and referred to it as a pub, but it was a frontier saloon, pure and simple, dedicated to the simple proposition that the quickest way to separate a customer from his money was to get him drunk, get him laid, and get him out.

Reverend Milcher and his wife Lavinia and some of the other respectable folks in Fury weren't happy about the arrival of Alf Blodgett. But they hadn't been happy about Abigail Krimp either, and to tell the truth, Reverend Milcher could have done without the Cohen family too, despite the fact that Saul was a member of the town council and one of the most tireless workers on behalf of the settlement. To the reverend, a Hebrew was a Hebrew no matter what else he might do, and as such deserved to be driven out from civilized society like the Christ-killer he was.

Luckily for all concerned, especially anybody who used the water from the well that Saul had helped to dig, the Reverend Mr. Milcher was mostly bluster. Only a few people took him seriously, even though he had been the one who put the original wagon train together.

It took Blodgett about a day to get his saloon set up and open for business. After that, he had a steady stream of customers in and out of the place.

Jason was sitting in a straight-backed chair just outside the door of the marshal's office when he saw several cowboys ride into town. He recognized them as some of Dixon's men, recalling them from his visit to the Slash D. One of them was Ord Kerby, Dixon's segundo. They stopped in front of Blodgett's place, dismounted and tied their horses to a hitch rack, and went into the Crown and Garter.

It was possible that some of the Slash D hands had been in Fury before, since Jason didn't know all of them. This was the first time he was sure that some of Dixon's men were in town. He put his hands on his knees and pushed himself to his feet, intending to walk down to Blodgett's and step inside just to keep an eye on Kerby and the other cowboys.

Before he could get there, four more men trotted their horses into the settlement and reined to a halt in front of the new saloon. Jason's heart pounded a little harder when he recognized Bill Rye, Jack Dupree, Ned Potter, and Nib Sloan. Since he hadn't seen the gunmen around since leaving them at Matt's house several days earlier, he hoped that they hadn't been able to make a deal with Matt and had drifted on out of the area.

Obviously, they were still here, and that wasn't good. Even worse was the fact that they strode into the Crown and Garter, where Dixon's men were.

Matt wondered where Ward Wanamaker was. He might need Ward's help if trouble broke out. Unfortunately, there was no time to go looking for the part-time deputy. Jason felt urgency dogging him as he hurried down to Blodgett's. The Englishman had put up some batwings in the door of his place. Jason pushed them aside and stepped into the saloon.

He hadn't been in here before, and the first thing he noticed was the big flag hanging up behind the bar. It was the British flag—the Union Jack, he thought it was called. And while it was impressive, it held his attention for only a second, because something much more urgent was going on.

Folks were scrambling up from the tables and getting out of the line of fire as Ord Kerby and Bill Rye stood in front of the bar facing each other about fifteen feet apart.

The front of Kerby's shirt was wet, as if something had been splattered on it, and Jason knew right away without asking what had happened. Rye had come up beside the Slash D segundo and jostled his arm "accidentally," making Kerby spill his drink. Kerby had taken offense at that, just as Rye had known he would, and now the two men were facing each other on the verge of a gunfight.

"I said it was an accident," Rye was saying, his voice cold and flat. "I won't say any more than that."

"You'll apologize for bein' such a clumsy damn bastard!" Kerby blazed back at him. "Nobody spills a drink on me and gets away with it!"

Rye's left shoulder rose and fell in a minuscule shrug. His right didn't budge. The hand on that side hung beside the butt of his holstered gun, ready to hook and draw.

"If you're offended," Rye drawled, "there's one way to settle this. You're packin' iron, and so am I."

"Don't think I won't draw, because I will, by God! I know you're one o' those fancy gunslingers workin' for MacDonald, but I don't give a damn. I'm pretty slick with a gun myself!"

"If you want to prove that, you've got it to do," Rye goaded.

Jason raised his voice and said, "Nobody's doing anything! Both of you settle down. I mean it!"

Rye had his back to Jason. He didn't turn around to look at him as he said, "That must be the marshal. No law against a man defending himself if he's drawed on, is there, Marshal?"

"Nobody's drawing a gun," Jason said. "There's an ordinance against shooting off firearms in town."

"With an exception for self-defense, I imagine," Rye persisted. "I can't imagine any jury finding a man guilty who was just trying to keep himself from gettin' shot when the other fella drew first. Can you imagine that, Marshal?"

Jason knew that wasn't going to happen. No matter what laws or ordinances were passed, folks weren't going to sit by and let a man be convicted for defending himself or his family or his property. Anything else was sheer insanity.

But in this case, no matter what it looked like, if Rye pushed Kerby into drawing on him, it would be the next thing to murder. Jason didn't know how fast Kerby really was, but he doubted if the segundo would stand a chance against a professional like Rye.

"Back off, Fury," Kerby snapped. "I can take care o' myself. I don't need your help."

"The only one you'll need if you don't forget about this is the undertaker," Jason told him. "Rye said it was an accident. Let it go at that."

"No, sir! He's got to apologize like the boot-lickin' scum he is!"

The saloon was utterly silent following Kerby's insult, so

Rye's soft voice could be heard without any trouble as he asked, "How much more of this do I have to take, Marshal?"

"You started it," Jason grated.

"No, but I'll finish it if that gutless coward ever stops flapping his gums."

"By God, that's enough!" Kerby howled. Being called a coward had pushed him over the edge. He clawed at the butt of his gun and yanked the weapon from its holster.

The Colt in Kerby's hand wasn't even halfway level before Rye's gun spoke. Smoke and flame gouted from the muzzle of the weapon. Kerby rocked back as the bullet smashed into his chest. His face twisted in a grimace of agony. But he managed to reach out with his left hand and grab hold of the bar, keeping himself on his feet as he struggled to lift his gun and get at least one shot off.

Bill Rye didn't give him that chance. The gunfighter's revolver roared again, and this time Kerby's head jerked as the bullet caught him in the forehead, leaving a black-rimmed hole like a third eye as it bored on through the segundo's brain and burst out the back of his skull in a grisly shower of blood and bone fragments.

Kerby still didn't fall right away. The fingers of his left hand were still clamped on the edge of the bar. A sharp stink filled the air and mixed with the acrid tang of gun smoke as the dead man's bowels emptied. His knees finally unhinged and dropped him to the floor. His gun slid out of his hand, unfired.

If the rest of the Slash D hands had any thoughts about avenging their segundo, they had to abandon them as they looked across the saloon. Guns had appeared as if by magic in the hands of Rye's companions. Dupree, Sloan, and Potter looked like they would enjoy nothing better than starting a massacre.

In the hushed, horrified silence that followed the two booming gunshots, Jason said in a choked voice, "For God's sake, everybody hold your fire!"

He heard the batwings open behind him. Unwilling to take his eyes off the tense scene in front of him, Jason hoped that wasn't more trouble coming up behind him.

"It's me, Jason," Ward Wanamaker announced. "I got here as fast as I could after somebody told me there was about to be a shootout in here." An ominous double click sounded. "I've got a Greener here if I need it."

Behind the bar, Alf Blodgett was pale with fear. So were the girls who worked for him and the customers who had come in here to get a drink. If more shots were fired, and especially if Ward touched off both barrels of that scattergun, innocent folks were bound to get hurt, maybe even killed.

"Hold on, Ward," Jason said. Slowly and deliberately, he drew his pistol. "Rye, give me your gun. You're under arrest."

Rye shook his head. "I don't think so. Everybody in here saw that hombre draw first."

"Ord never had a chance against you, mister!" one of the Slash D men said in an angry, anguished voice. "You pushed him into drawing! It was murder, plain and simple!"

Mutters of agreement came from the other Dixon men.

"Not in the eyes of the law," Rye said. "And to show you how confident I am of that . . ." He lowered his gun, turned, and held the weapon out toward Jason, butt first. "I changed my mind, Marshal. I'll take my chances on being arrested."

Jason knew he couldn't make the charges stick against the gunman. The doctrine of self-defense was too deeply ingrained on the frontier, and rightly so. From time to time, somebody like Rye took advantage of it, but that couldn't be helped. Right now, the main thing Jason wanted was to get Rye and the other gunslingers out of here, so the situation would be defused and nobody else would have to die.

He took Rye's gun and said, "Come on. We'll go down to the marshal's office." Looking at Dupree, Sloan, and Potter, he added, "You men come along too."

"Don't you worry about that," Dupree said. "We ain't

lettin' Bill out of our sight. We know how folks in these little towns like to likker themselves up and start a lynch mob."

"There'll be no lynchings in Fury," Jason declared. "Not while I'm alive."

Unfortunately, all it would take to change that situation was one bullet.

Chapter 14

Jason and Ward were able to get Rye and the other gunmen out of the Crown and Garter and march them down to the marshal's office and jail without any more shots ringing out, although bitter curses from the Slash D hands followed them. Once they were inside the office with the door closed behind them, Rye held out his hand and said, "I'll take my gun back now, Marshal."

"Not just yet," Jason said.

Rye's face hardened. "Don't even think about trying to lock us up, Marshal. The boys and me don't cotton to being behind bars."

"Our cells don't *have* any bars," Jason said. "But I'm not going to lock you up. I just want you to sit down in here and wait a while, until things in town cool down a little."

"Until those cowboys leave, you mean."

Jason nodded. "That's right. Once they've headed back to the Slash D, then you and your friends can get out of town and go back to MacDonald's place. I assume you're still working for him?"

"That's right."

Jason sighed. "I had hoped that you didn't reach a deal with him and left this part of the country."

Rye smirked. "No such luck for me, Marshal. MacDonald's gonna have a nice spread out there. I reckon we'll stick with him for a while."

In hopes of making even more money later, Jason thought. Matt had to be fully aware of the sort of men he had hired, but the thought might not have occurred to him that one of these days they could turn on *him*.

"Ward, you mind staying here and keeping an eye on these men?" Jason asked the deputy. "I'm going back down to the Crown and Garter to see what's going on there."

Ward nodded, but he looked a little nervous at the idea of being left in charge of four hired guns who hadn't been disarmed. Jason couldn't blame him for feeling that way. But Ward said, "Go ahead, Marshal, I'll be fine."

Rye picked up one of the ladder-back chairs, turned it around, and straddled it. With his usual cocky grin, he asked, "You gonna head off any lynch talk, Marshal?"

"I told you, there won't be any lynchings in Fury."

"We'll hold you to that."

While the other gunslingers were chuckling over Rye's grim humor, Jason left the office. He paused just outside to take a deep breath. Quite a few people were still on the street. The shooting had drawn them out, and they hadn't gone about their business yet. Knots of townspeople gathered together talking, and Jason didn't have to guess what the subjects of the discussions were. The citizens were talking about the killing in Alf Blodgett's new saloon.

Jason saw Cyrus Valentine's wagon parked in front of the Crown and Garter. Valentine had been there a week, having moved down from Phoenix to set up an undertaking parlor. Before that, bodies had been prepared for burial by Dr. Morelli, and Salmon Kendall, Saul Cohen, and Randall Nordstrom had knocked together the coffins. All of them were more than happy to turn those chores over to Cyrus Valentine.

While Jason watched, Cyrus came out of the saloon along with his helper, each of them at one end of a blanket-wrapped bundle. Jason knew that inside that blanket was the body of Ord Kerby. Carefully, the men placed the body in the back of the wagon and drew a canvas cover over it. Then they climbed onto the driver's seat, Cyrus took up the reins, and flapped them to get the two mules hitched to the wagon moving. He drove at a slow, dignified pace toward the undertaking parlor. Eventually Cyrus would have an actual hearse, Jason thought—but not until enough people had died in Fury for him to be able to afford it. That wasn't a comforting thought.

The four Slash D cowboys who had been with Kerby emerged from the saloon. One of them went to the hitch rack, untied his horse, swung up into the saddle, and raced out of town at a gallop. Jason had no doubts about where the man was going—he was headed for the Slash D to tell Ezra Dixon what had happened to his segundo.

Two of the remaining men followed Cyrus Valentine's wagon down the street, while the fourth man angled toward Jason. His face was still flushed with anger.

"Did you lock up that murderin' gunslinger?" he demanded as he stalked up to Jason.

"He's in the marshal's office," Jason replied as he jerked his head toward the building. "So are the others."

"But I'll bet they ain't behind bars, are they?"

"We don't *have* any bars on the cells," Jason said again. "But they're not locked up, no. Kerby drew first. There's no getting around that."

"What're you gonna do?" the cowboy asked with a sneer. "Fine that bastard five dollars for firin' off a gun in town and let him go?"

Jason hated to admit it, even to himself, but that was about all he *could* do legally. He said, "You just let me and the mayor and the town council take care of that. That's how things are going to be handled in this town. We'll do everything the law allows."

The cowboy just glared and shook his head. "You must come from back East or somewhere, mister. If you'd lived out here on the frontier for very long, you'd know that law ain't always the same thing as justice."

Jason was beginning to understand that. He didn't like it, but it was becoming clearer and clearer to him.

"We'll just see what happens once the boss and the rest of the crew get here," the cowboy went on. "Then you'll see some justice."

"I told you, there won't be any lynchings in my town."

The cowboy just smirked at him, and the expression was as annoying on his face as it was on Bill Rye's.

"Why don't you move along?" Jason suggested.

"Public street, ain't it?"

Jason was forced to admit that it was.

"Then I reckon I'll just wait right here until the boss gets to town," the man said.

Jason knew what the Slash D hand was doing. He was keeping an eye on the marshal's office to make sure that Rye and the other hired guns didn't leave before Dixon arrived. Jason was sure that if the gunslingers left the office and started for their horses, the cowboy would summon his friends from the undertaking parlor, and then there would be a gun battle right here on Fury's main street. Jason couldn't allow that.

"Suit yourself," he told the man, then turned on his heel and went back into the office.

Ward was watching through the window. As Jason closed the door, the deputy asked, "What's goin' on out there, Jason? Why's that fella from the Slash D just standin' there?"

Before Jason could answer, Rye said, "I can tell you that, Deputy. He's watching to make sure we don't get away."

Ward looked concerned, especially when Jason nodded. "Rye's right. One of them rode hell-for-leather out of town. I'm sure he's headed for the Slash D. The other two are down at the undertaker's, but that's not far enough away. They'll come running if there's trouble."

"Let us go, Marshal," Rye suggested. "Those three cowboys

are no match for us. Your new undertaker will be mighty pleased with the amount of work he's getting."

"Stay right there, damn it," Jason snapped. "I'll figure out something."

At the moment, though, he had no idea what it was going to be.

A few minutes later, footsteps sounded just outside the office. Jason put his hand on the butt of his Colt and Ward tightened his grip on the rifle in his hands. A knock sounded on the door, and Saul Cohen's voice called, "It's your friends, Jason. Let us in."

Trying not to sigh in relief, Jason went to the door and swung it open. Saul stood there along with Salmon, Nordstrom, and the other members of the town council. Wash Keough was with the group as well. Each one of the men carried either a rifle or a shotgun.

"We've heard what's going on," Saul said, "and we've come to help."

Jason felt a surge of gratitude toward these men, but at the same time, he knew he couldn't accept what they were offering.

"I appreciate it, Saul, but you fellas need to go back to your homes and businesses. Taking care of trouble like this is my job, not yours."

"And mine," Ward added.

"But there are only two of you," Saul argued. "God knows how many men Dixon will bring to town with him."

"However many, we'll deal with them," Jason insisted. "Dixon will back down quickly enough when he realizes that I won't stand for any lawlessness."

Rye laughed, and the other gunslingers chuckled.

Jason spun toward them, his anger getting the better of him for a second. "You don't seem to understand what you're looking at here, Rye," he said. "Dixon may have twenty or thirty men with him. If he doesn't want to be stopped, I can't stop him. None of us can."

"Twenty or thirty cowhands don't amount to much," Rye

said. "Even the toughest of them won't be as good with a gun as all of us are. If there's any shootin', Dixon will die first, and when half a dozen more of them have gone down with our lead in them, the rest will quit. You just wait and see."

"What if you're wrong?"

Rye shrugged. "Then I reckon we'll die, but that won't matter to Dixon, because he'll be in hell before us. And it's not like all four of us haven't gambled our lives before now."

Jason knew the gunman was right. The Slash D crew might be a tough, salty bunch, but they were no match for professional killers. Rye probably hadn't had in mind provoking a showdown quite so soon when he killed Kerby, but now that it was shaping up that way, the hired guns would try to turn that to their advantage. Matt MacDonald hadn't mentioned anything about wanting Dixon dead; according to everything Matt had said, he just wanted Dixon to leave him alone.

But Dixon's death would put an abrupt end to any potential range war, wouldn't it?

A memory suddenly entered Jason's mind, the mental image of Will Dixon. Her father's death might not end things at all. Will had seemed capable of picking up the gauntlet and continuing the war herself, if the men from the Slash D would follow her. And Jason had a feeling that they would.

He had a feeling too that the bloodshed had just started.

The sudden pounding of hoofbeats in the street outside made Jason's head jerk up. A lot of riders came down the street and stopped in front of the marshal's office. Ward heard them too, and muttered, "Can't be the Slash D. Ain't been time for them to get here."

But it was indeed Ezra Dixon's gravelly voice that bellowed, "Marshal! You in there with them damn killers? Come on out! I'm here to see justice done!"

Chapter 15

"At least that settles the question of whether or not we'll be leaving you and Ward here on your own, Jason," Saul said with a faint smile. "We're part of this now."

Jason had no choice but to agree with that. He nodded and said, "Be ready for trouble, but nobody starts shooting unless and until I do."

"You're the marshal," Salmon said.

That's right, he was, Jason thought, and it was times like this when he told himself he should have lit that shuck for California when he had the chance!

But something would have drawn him back here to Fury no matter what he tried to do, he sensed. His destiny and that of this settlement seemed to be inextricably bound up together.

He started to draw his gun, then decided not to. No point in forcing Dixon to a confrontation any sooner than necessary. Jason took a deep breath, opened the door, and stepped out of the office, forcing his face to remain set in calm lines.

Ezra Dixon sat there on a long-legged, rawboned roan horse, leaning forward with an outraged expression on his flushed, hatchetlike face. Jason was expecting that, but he was a little surprised to see Will mounted beside her father on the black stallion he had seen her breaking that day on the

Slash D. She rode astride like a man, of course—Jason couldn't imagine her riding any other way—and wore denim trousers and a denim jacket over a homespun shirt. The neck strap of her flat-crowned brown hat was taut under her chin. Her dark hair hung down her back in a long braid.

And like her father, she wore a holstered revolver and seemed itching to use it.

Unlike Dixon, though, tears shone in Will's eyes. They were the only feminine touch about her at the moment.

Jason didn't see the cowboy who had gone galloping out of the settlement after the shootout between Rye and Kerby, but half-a-dozen other Slash D hands were with Dixon and Will. They must have been on their way to town when they ran into the messenger bearing news of Kerby's death. Dixon had probably sent that cowboy galloping on to the ranch to fetch reinforcements.

Dixon jerked his head in a grim nod and said, "Marshal." He was holding his temper in check with a visible effort.

"Mr. Dixon, I won't beat around the bush," Jason said. "I know why you're here. You've heard that Ord Kerby was killed in a gunfight—"

Dixon's disdainful snort interrupted him. "You call it a gunfight. I call it plain murder. That fella who killed Ord is one of MacDonald's hired gunhands. Ord was never no match for a snake-blooded skunk like that."

"No, he wasn't," Jason agreed. "That's why he shouldn't have drawn on Rye."

"The bastard didn't give him no choice!"

"People *always* have a choice."

Dixon let out another contemptuous snort. "If you believe that, boy, you're even dumber than I thought you were."

Jason felt his face growing warm. He told himself it was from anger, not embarrassment. But he didn't like the way Will was looking at him, like he was the lowliest worm on the face of the earth.

Of course, he reminded himself, he didn't have any reason to give a damn what opinion Will Dixon held of him.

He decided to be blunt. "What is it you want?" he asked Dixon.

"You know good and well what I want. If you ain't gonna see that justice is done, I'll handle it myself."

"By stringing up Rye from one of those cottonwoods beside the creek?"

Dixon sneered. "That's what a killer like him deserves."

"You ordered your men to kill Matt MacDonald and Ward Wanamaker that day you tried to burn down Matt's house," Jason pointed out.

"That's different, blast it!" Dixon barked. "They was squattin' on my range. They had it comin'!"

"In other words, you're a law unto yourself." Jason's tone was scathing now. "Well, not in this settlement, Dixon! You might as well get used to the idea that there's *real* law and order in Fury! And there'll be no lynch mobs here as long as I'm the marshal!"

Dixon was breathing so hard with rage that his mustaches fluttered a little. His hand edged toward the butt of his gun. "Then maybe it's time you ain't the marshal anymore, you high-an'-mighty little—"

Whatever he was going to call Jason went unvoiced, because at that moment Salmon Kendall stepped out of the building, leveled the rifle in his hands at Dixon, and said in a loud, clear voice, "The only ones who can remove Jason Fury from the job of marshal are me and the town council. In case you didn't know it, Mr. Dixon, I'm Salmon Kendall, the mayor of this settlement, and I don't appreciate you comin' in here and tryin' to run roughshod over us."

"Nor do I," Saul added as he emerged from the marshal's office with his shotgun. He introduced himself. "Saul Cohen, owner of the hardware store over there. I could use your business, Mr. Dixon." He allowed himself a smile. "That's why I'd hate to have to shoot you."

One by one, the other citizens who had come to the marshal's office to help Jason stepped out of the building, leaving only Ward Wanamaker inside to watch over Rye and the other gunmen. The citizens' faces were grim and set with determination. Dixon looked from man to man and finally burst out, "Damn it, can't you see there's a girl here? She's liable to get hurt!"

"You're the one who brought her with you," Jason said.

"Don't talk about me like I'm a child," Will snapped. "My father didn't *bring* me here. When we heard what had happened to Ord, I wouldn't let him leave me behind."

"That's right," Jason recalled. "You and Kerby were sweet on each other. I'm sorry for your loss, Miss Dixon."

"Oh, for God's sake! Ord Kerby may have had a crush on me, but I wasn't sweet on him. But he was a friend, and more than that, he rode for the Slash D! That's all that really matters!"

Jason knew what she meant. Among men who worked with cattle, loyalty to the boss—riding for the brand—was the most important thing of all. A man's pride and honor were tied up with how he did that. And the boss—and in this case, the boss's daughter—returned that loyalty.

Jason looked at Dixon again and said, "We've got a standoff here. Maybe you can get past us and get to Rye and the others, but even if you do, then you'll have them to deal with. There's a good chance none of you will make it out of here alive, Dixon . . . including your daughter." He paused, then said, "I don't want that. I don't want anybody else to die. One killing is enough for today."

"It ain't right," Dixon said. "It just ain't right."

"Maybe not, but that's the way it is. Turn around and ride out of here. Let the law handle this situation."

"The law!" Dixon scoffed. "You ain't gonna do anything to that killer!"

"Kerby drew first. I hate to be stubborn about it, but those are the plain, simple facts of the matter."

"Ain't nothin' plain and simple about this." Dixon chewed on his mustache for a moment, then gave an abrupt nod. "All right," he said. "If that's the way it is, then I reckon I know what to do."

Jason waited, and when Dixon didn't say anything else, he blurted out, "What?"

The rancher narrowed his eyes and said, "Since it's all right with the law for MacDonald to hire himself some killers, I figure it'll be all right for me to do the same thing."

Jason felt his heart start to pound a little faster. "You don't want to do that," he warned. "It'll just make things worse."

"No, I'll make sure it's done all legal-like." Dixon's laugh was cold as ice. "The fellas I hire won't draw first. That's all you care about, ain't it, Marshal?"

"This town doesn't need any more gunslingers—"

"Well, it's gonna get 'em! MacDonald wants a real war, I'll give him a real war, by God!"

And with that, Dixon wheeled his horse and put the spurs to the roan, sending it leaping ahead in a gallop. He rode out of town with his men following him, dust billowing up from the pounding hooves of their mounts.

The only one left behind was Will. She stayed where she was, glaring at a dumbfounded Jason. After a moment she said, "You don't realize what a big mistake you've made by protecting those killers, Marshal. I had talked my father into leaving MacDonald alone for the time being. I told him he should wait a while until we had a chance to see how things were going to play out." She shook her head and went on bitterly. "Well, we've seen, all right."

"Why would you do that?" Jason asked her. "Why would you get him to lay off MacDonald?"

"Because I didn't want to see him get hurt. I didn't want any of our men hurt. I wasn't sure MacDonald was worth it. But he's raised the stakes now, Marshal, and there won't be any turning back. When my pa says there'll be war, he means it."

Jason didn't doubt that. But he still thought there might be some way to avoid mass bloodshed, if only he had more time to think of something. . . .

"Miss Dixon—" he began.

Will just shook her head, jerked her horse around, and heeled the big black into a run. She galloped out of town, trailing her father and the hands from the Slash D.

Jason stared after her, and into the silence Saul said, "Well, that could have gone better, I suppose. But it could have gone worse too. At least nobody else is dead."

"Yet," Jason said. He turned and started toward the door of the marshal's office. Seeing the look on his face, Saul, Salmon, and the other men got out of his way.

Rye still straddled the chair. Dupree, Potter, and Sloan stood nearby, their stances casual. Jason stared hard at Rye and said, tight-lipped, "One-hundred-dollar fine for discharging a firearm in town."

"Kind of steep, ain't it?" Rye asked with a grin.

"The marshal sets the fines," Salmon said, swinging the barrel of his rifle meaningfully in Rye's direction, "and the town council backs him up on that. Ain't that right, boys?"

"Correct, Mr. Mayor," Saul said.

Rye shrugged, never losing his grin. "Sure, whatever you say." He took five twenty-dollar gold pieces from his pocket and made a neat stack of them on Jason's desk. "There you go, Marshal. Now I want a receipt saying that I paid in full."

Fighting to keep his hands from shaking in anger, Jason wrote out the paper and handed it to Rye. "There. There's your damn receipt."

Rye tucked it in his pocket and said mockingly, "Seems like I'm being a good citizen about this, Marshal. I'm not sure why you're mad at me."

"Stay out of Fury," Jason snapped. He looked at the other gunnies. "All of you. You're not welcome in this settlement."

"You can't do that," Three-Finger Jack Dupree said with a frown. "We got a right—"

"And the owners of every business in town have a right to refuse your trade," Saul said. "I can assure you, that's exactly what they'll do. So you see, there's no reason for you to visit this settlement."

"I'll arrest you if you set foot in town and figure out the charges later," Jason vowed. "Now get out, all of you."

Rye stood up. Even though Rye masked it with a look of affability, Jason saw the cold hatred in the gunman's eyes. "None of this is over," Rye said as he started toward the door. "Not the business with Dixon . . . and not our business with *you,* Marshal."

The four men filed out of the office. Jason said to Ward, "Watch them and make sure they actually leave town."

Ward nodded. "Sure. What if Dixon and his men ambush them after they ride out?"

"That's their problem," Jason said. He hung up his hat and went behind the desk. A feeling of utter weariness came over him, and he sank down into the chair. Waving a hand at the stack of double eagles, he added, "Saul, get that fine money and put it away in your safe."

"Sure, Jason." Saul picked up the coins, then said, "You did the best you could. It's a miracle there wasn't more bloodshed."

"That's right," Salmon added. "You've proven that we did the right thing by makin' you marshal."

Jason still wasn't sure he had done the right thing by accepting. The bloody massacre that had nearly taken place today might have been postponed, but it hadn't been prevented yet. Like a storm on the horizon, violence could still break out at any time. . . .

And if it was bad enough, it might wash away the town of Fury and everyone in it.

Chapter 16

For the next week, the town seemed to hold its breath, waiting for more trouble to break out. Nothing happened, though. The gunslingers Matt had hired must have stayed close to his ranch. They didn't come back to town anyway, and that was all Jason really cared about. At times he found himself musing that it would be better all around if Matt and Dixon just wiped each other out and were done with it.

But then he thought again and realized that if Matt died, both Jenny and Megan would be hurt by that, and somewhat surprisingly, he had the same sort of thought about Will Dixon. Will wouldn't want to lose her father any more than Jenny and Megan would want to lose Matt.

Of course, from what he had seen of Will Dixon, she probably would be right at the old buzzard's side in any gun battle.

Another wagon train came through, stopping in Fury to stock up on supplies. The wagon master was a burly, balding man with a short salt-and-pepper beard. His name was Jim Austin, and Jason remembered him as an old friend of his father.

Austin pumped Jason's hand in a bone-crushing grip and slapped him on the back as they stood in Nordstrom's Mercantile, where Jason had come in search of the wagon master.

"Jason Fury, by God! It's good to see you, son." Austin grew solemn as he went on. "I heard about what happened to Jedediah. Damn shame. He was a fine man. Why, I remember the high ol' times we had back when we were younkers, me and Jedediah and your uncle John. Whatever happened to that fiddlefooted uncle o' yours anyway?"

Jason didn't know and brushed the question aside. "Have you picked up any news along the trail, Mr. Austin?"

With a frown, Austin nodded. "The Comanch' are still raisin' hell over in Texas and New Mexico Territory. What do you hear about the Apaches?"

"Keep your eyes open and circle the wagons tight at night," Jason advised. "It's been less than two months since a band of them attacked the town here, right after it was established."

"Them bold devils! Attacked the town, you say?"

Jason nodded. "We were able to drive them off, and they haven't been back since. I'm hoping the settlement has grown enough by now that they'll steer clear of it from now on, but I don't reckon we can count on that."

"Can't count on much o' anything where Apaches are concerned, 'cept that they'll give you trouble sooner or later." Austin scratched at his beard. "Heard tell that Juan Alba's been raidin' north of the border again too. Just what we need to go along with Apaches . . . a gang o' desperadoes made up o' Mexican *bandidos* and every other kind o' border trash."

"I've heard about Alba," Jason said. "Thank goodness he's left us alone so far. Some of the things I hear about him make him sound worse than an Apache."

"That's 'cause he's half Mex and half 'Pache, and the worst o' both. Sort of like crossin' a rattlesnake and a scorpion, I reckon. Ugly as hell, and you sure don't want it bitin' you."

"Any other news?" Jason asked.

"Well . . . they've started buildin' a railroad that's gonna go clear across the country when they're done with it, or so they say." Austin sighed. "When they run rails from one side o' the country to the other, I reckon my day, and the days o' men like me, will be done. Won't be no more wagon trains, so there won't be no call for wagon masters anymore."

Jason shook his head. "It'll take years and years for them to accomplish such a thing. Maybe even decades."

"I wouldn't count on that," Austin said. "Once folks in this country get their minds set on doin' somethin', there ain't hardly any stoppin' 'em. Onliest thing that ever slows us Americans down is when we go to squabblin' amongst ourselves, like that there war we just finished up not all that long ago. Lord, I hope we don't never have to go through somethin' like that again."

Jason nodded in agreement. He had been in the army during the war, but he had spent his time in Washington, pushing papers, while his older brother had fallen on the field of battle. Jason was proud of Jeremy, but at the same time, he wished the country had never seen the need to tear itself apart that way. Then Jeremy would still be around, and so would millions of other young men who had marched off to the sound of distant drums and never returned.

"One other thing you might want to know about," Austin said. "Funny thing happened a couple o' nights ago. Some fellas rode up to our camp and helloed, asked if they could come in and share our supper. I told 'em to ride in nice and slowlike, so's we could look 'em over. Can't be too careful out on the trail, you know."

Jason nodded. He knew exactly what Austin meant. Every wagon master was leery of strangers, and considering how many drifters were up to no good, they had every right to be.

Austin went on. "I didn't much like the cut o' their jib, as an ol' sailor I knew used to say, but there was only six of 'em and we're well armed. Got men who know how to use their guns too. So I told those fellas they could share our supper but they'd have to find some other place to camp. They seemed to take that all right, and they didn't cause us a lick o' trouble while they was there."

Jason felt his impatience growing. It was sometimes difficult for older men like Austin to get to the point. Out of respect for his father's friendship with the man, Jason didn't try to hurry him.

"Now here's what might interest you," Austin went on. "The fella who seemed to be the ramrod o' the bunch asked me if I'd ever heard of a settlement called Fury. I said sure, I'd heard talk about the place whilst we was in Tucson. The fella said that's where they was headed and wanted to know if they were on the right trail."

Jason felt the stirrings of unease inside him. "Did these men tell you their names?" he asked Austin.

The wagon master shook his head. "Nope, and I couldn't very well ask."

Jason understood that. Westerners figured that if somebody wanted you to know something, they would volunteer the information.

"I recognized the hombre, though," Austin said. "Saw him a couple o' years ago in Santa Fe. Name of Gallister. Heard of him?"

"Flint Gallister?" Jason asked.

Austin nodded. "One an' the same. Once I realized who he was, some o' the other fellas looked a mite familiar too. Pretty sure one of 'em was Little Ben Williams, and another was Trapdoor Hargity. I see them names mean somethin' to you."

"They're gunfighters," Jason said. "Hired killers."

"Yep. They should've made better time gettin' here than we did. You seen hide nor hair of 'em?"

Jason shook his head and said, "No, but there are enough people in town now that I suppose they could be here and I just haven't noticed them."

"One more thing . . . Gallister asked me if I knew how to find a ranch belongin' to a gent named Dixon. I told him I didn't have no idea about that. You know this fella Dixon, Jason?"

"I'm afraid I do," Jason replied as he felt a hollow sensation in his stomach. There was only one explanation for what Austin had just told him.

Ezra Dixon had threatened to send for some gunfighters of his own, to counter the threat posed by Bill Rye and the other hired killers working for Matt MacDonald. Obviously, Dixon had succeeded in doing so. Flint Gallister, Little Ben Williams, Trapdoor Hargity, and the other gun-wolves who had stopped for supper with Austin's wagon train might already be out at the Slash D, plotting their strategy.

"What's goin' on here?" Austin asked with a frown. "You got all hell about to break loose around here, son?"

Jason knew the answer to that, and wished that he didn't.

"I'm going to have to ride out to the Slash D and warn Dixon again not to start any trouble," Jason said.

Ward Wanamaker and Wash Keough both looked at him like he had lost his mind, and maybe he had.

"I've crossed trails with Flint Gallister a few times," Wash said. "He pure-dee hates star-packers, Jason. He's liable to take one look at that badge on your chest and slap leather."

"I'll have to take that chance."

The three men were in the marshal's office, Jason behind the desk, Wash in a chair in front of it, and Ward on the old sofa that had been moved in, a donation from one of the families that had moved into town and found that they didn't have room for the piece of furniture in their new house.

"It won't do any good," Ward said. "I hate to say it, Jason, but maybe we ought to just let Matt and Dixon fight it out. They're both so stubborn and so convinced they're right, they'll never listen to reason."

Jason didn't admit that the same thought had occurred to him on more than one occasion.

"Maybe you should take a ride over to Camp Grant and talk to the commandin' officer there," Wash suggested. "Just because that shavetail lieutenant who rode by Matt's place said the army can't get involved in this trouble don't mean you couldn't convince the commander otherwise."

"Maybe," Jason said. "This was all government land to start with around here, so they've got a stake in what happens, I guess. I'll give it a try if I can't get anywhere with Matt and Dixon."

Ward grunted, as if that were a foregone conclusion.

"I've asked Jenny to talk to Matt," Jason went on, "but she thinks he hasn't done anything wrong. And she's right, I guess. Matt has just as much right to the land he's claimed as Dixon does. It's not like he's trying to take over the whole Slash D. Really, I'm not sure Dixon would ever miss that range if he let it go."

"He's just too mule-headed to do it," Wash said.

"Exactly. Too stubborn and too proud." Jason stood up and reached for his hat. "I'll go talk to Matt one last time."

"Good luck," Ward said, and from his tone of voice it was obvious he thought Jason's good intentions didn't stand a chance.

To tell the truth, Jason felt the same way. But *he* was too proud and too stubborn not to try.

Keeping his eyes open for Apaches, gunslingers, or any other form of trouble, Jason rode Cleo out to Matt's ranch. Now, in addition to the house and the barn, a bunkhouse and some corrals had gone up. Jason had to admit that the place looked good. Matt could probably make a go of it if he had the chance.

Bill Rye and Nib Sloan lounged on stools in front of the bunkhouse. Jason didn't see the other two gunmen. As he dismounted, Rye called over to him, "Howdy, Marshal. What are you doin' out here?"

"Looking for your boss," Jason replied, and the sound of a door opening made him look toward the house.

Matt strode out onto the porch, a hostile expression on his face. "What the hell do you want, Fury?" he demanded.

"I came to try to talk some sense into your head," Jason said. "There's still a lot of open range north of town, where the Mortons have settled. Dixon hasn't bothered them. Chances are he wouldn't bother you up there either."

Matt laughed and waved a hand at the buildings. "Take a look around. You want me to just walk away from all this work because of some crazy old man who thinks he owns the whole territory?"

"I just don't want you getting killed, Matt," Jason said. "I know we've had our problems, but my sister seems to think the world of you, and you've got a sister yourself. Think about them."

"I *am* thinking about Jenny. This is going to be her home someday, and that day's not long off either. Did you know I asked her to marry me the other day?"

Jason stiffened. Jenny hadn't said a word about that to him. Somehow, he wasn't surprised that she hadn't. She knew how he felt about Matt MacDonald.

"She said yes too," Matt went on. "I'm going to be your brother-in-law before much longer, Fury. What do you think about that?"

Jason had to force the word out, but he managed to say, "Congratulations."

"If you want to browbeat somebody, go see Dixon," Matt said. "He's the one causing all the trouble."

That was true in a way, but Matt might not know everything that was going on. Jason said, "Have you heard of a man named Flint Gallister?"

Matt frowned. "I don't think so. Why?"

Jason inclined his head toward the bunkhouse. "Ask Rye who Gallister is. He'll know. Then tell him that Gallister is working for Dixon, along with Little Ben Williams, Trapdoor

Hargity, and some others just like them." Jason reached for Cleo's reins. "See what he thinks about *that*."

Matt gave him a hostile but somewhat puzzled stare as Jason mounted up and rode away from the ranch house. Maybe he shouldn't have told Matt about Gallister and the other gunmen Dixon had hired, Jason thought. But Matt had been bound to find out about them sooner or later. Dixon wouldn't wait long to send his new weapons against the enemy. At least now Matt would have some warning.

Jason was mulling that over as he rode back toward Fury, thinking so deeply that he wasn't paying much attention to anything else. It took the distant popping of guns to pull him out of his reverie.

But as he realized at last what he was hearing, his head jerked up and his eyes widened as he saw several plumes of black smoke rising in the sky in front of him. In shock and horror, he realized that the smoke and gunshots were coming from the direction of the settlement.

"No!"

The choked yell came from Jason's throat. The next instant, he dug his heels into Cleo's flanks and sent the palomino mare racing toward Fury as hard and fast as she could gallop.

Chapter 17

The shots grew louder, loud enough for Jason to hear them easily over the pounding hooves of his mount. A cloud of dust began to rise ahead of him, competing with the smoke to mar the clear blue sky. A group of riders came into view at the base of that dust cloud, small black dots that quickly resolved themselves into men on madly galloping horses.

Jason hauled back on the reins as he realized that forty or fifty men were charging straight at him, and chances were they weren't friendly. As they came closer, he saw that some of them were twisting around in their saddles to fire behind them with revolvers. Under those conditions, such shots couldn't be very accurate, but the men didn't care about that. They were just throwing lead to discourage pursuit.

Jason pulled his rifle from the saddle boot and worked the lever to throw a cartridge into the chamber. That was a case of habit taking over as much as anything, though. He was one man. He couldn't fight four dozen enemies. With luck he could bring down a handful of them, but the rest would just stampede right over him.

When an avalanche was coming at you, there was only one thing to do.

Get the hell out of the way.

With a shout of encouragement, Jason wheeled the palomino to the left and put the horse into a hard run. He was galloping at right angles to the path of the gunslinging horde, and his destination was a cactus-dotted ridge about five hundred yards away. If he could reach it before the onrushing riders overwhelmed him, he thought he would have a good chance of escaping.

Some of the riders must have spotted him and considered him a threat, because he felt as much as heard the wind-rip of a bullet past his head, coming too close for comfort. Dirt and pebbles spurted from the ground ahead of him, miniature volcanoes kicked up by the slugs slamming into the earth. Jason twisted in the saddle and brought his rifle to his shoulder. Cleo continued running smoothly as Jason began to fire, cranking off round after round as fast as he could work the weapon's lever and pull the trigger.

With dust choking his throat and stinging his eyes and bullets whipping around his head, Jason had no chance of seeing whether or not any of his shots found their targets. More than anything else, he was hoping to buy a little time, the few precious moments he needed to get out of the way of that wild, gun-blazing charge.

He had no idea who the attackers were; all he could tell about them was that they weren't Apaches. Although Apaches used horses from time to time, they hardly ever attacked on them. They weren't "horse Indians," like the Comanche or the Sioux. In fact, an Apache was more likely to use a horse as a meal than he was to ride one.

So the men trying to kill him had to be white, or at least Mexican. Knowing that didn't make Jason feel one damned bit better. Dead was dead, no matter who pulled the trigger on you.

Cleo had speed and stamina, and even more important, the mare had sand. She never quit. She just kept running, giving Jason her all, until horse and rider reached the base of the ridge and swept up the slope. Jason let Cleo have her head.

She slowed to swerve around clumps of cactus. Jason hung on tight, not wanting to take a tumble and land in those spiny devil plants.

It took only a few moments for Jason to reach the crest of the ridge, but with so much lead flying around him, it seemed more like an hour. When he reached the top he swung down from the saddle in a hurry, taking the rifle with him. Snatching off his hat, he used it to slap the mare on the rump and send Cleo charging on down the far side of the ridge, well out of the line of fire.

Jason whirled around and threw himself down on the ground. He poked the rifle barrel over the crest and squinted down at the small army charging past on the flats below him.

It was still difficult to see the riders because of the dust, but Jason caught occasional glimpses of them through eddying rents in the ochre-colored cloud. He had been right about them not being Apaches. They were a mixed lot, though.

He saw men in curled-brim Stetsons, high-crowned sombreros, cavalry campaign caps, even a few derbies. A couple of riders wore white shirts and trousers, with colorful sashes around their waists and red bands around their heads so that their long black hair flew out behind them. They were Indians, but not Apaches. Jason figured they were Yaquis from the mountains below the border, members of a tribe that was reputed to be even more bloodthirsty than the Apaches. Those two had to be pretty sorry specimens, though, because the Yaquis were supposed to hate both whites and Mexicans too deeply to be riding with a gang of them.

And that was exactly what he was looking at, Jason thought—a gang. No one but outlaws would be traveling in a wolf pack like that, shooting at everyone they saw and leaving behind the smoke of burning buildings.

That thought made Jason's breath hiss between his clenched teeth. He lifted his head and looked toward Fury. Pillars of smoke that dark and thick could come only from buildings that were being consumed by flames.

Rage flooded through him and made him snarl curses as he nestled his cheek against the stock of his rifle and tried to draw a bead on some of the raiders charging past him. Near the front of the group was a huge man with a jutting black beard, a sombrero with silver balls dangling from its circular brim, and a blood-red serape that had been jerked around by the wind so that it flapped behind him like a cape.

Juan Alba. The name sprang into Jason's mind. He had heard about the bandit chieftain sometimes known as the Scourge of the Borderlands. If he had ever seen anyone deserving of such a title, it was this man. Jason fired, knowing that even though he couldn't fight all of them, maybe he could bring down the leader.

The big man galloped on, unscathed. Not far from him, though, a horse suddenly took a tumble, going down in a cloud of dust and a welter of flailing hooves. The fallen horse's rider sailed out of the saddle and slammed into the ground, rolling over a couple of times before he was trampled by a couple of the riders who had been following him. Unable to swerve in time, the men rode right over the unfortunate bandit who had fallen. The steel-shod hooves of their mounts chopped and pounded him into something that barely seemed human. Jason grimaced at the sight until the dust swirled again and hid it from view.

Once Jason was out of their way, the outlaw horde might have been willing to pass on by and leave him alone, but the impulsive shot that had knocked down one of their number drew their attention, and several of them peeled off from the main bunch and galloped toward the cactus-strewn slope. Heedless of the fact that Jason held the high ground, they charged him, the guns in their fists spouting flame and powder smoke.

Staying low to make himself as small a target as possible, Jason fired a couple of times, and was rewarded by the sight of one of the outlaws sailing backward out of the saddle like he had been punched by a giant fist. Jason levered the rifle and squeezed the trigger again, but this time there was only a hollow click. The weapon was empty.

And the rest of Jason's ammunition was in his saddlebags, on the palomino. He twisted his head and looked down the back of the ridge. After that swat on the rump, Cleo had dashed off a couple of hundred yards.

"Son of a bitch!" Jason muttered as he leaped to his feet and started running. He held the empty rifle in his left hand and used his right to hold his hat on as he dashed toward the mare. He tried to whistle for her, in hopes that she would come to him, but it was difficult to find the breath for that while running full tilt.

Behind him, the three remaining outlaws thundered over the top of the ridge. One of them let out an exultant whoop as they saw their quarry fleeing on foot. If they had reined in and used their rifles, they probably could have cut him down, but instead they galloped their horses after him, evidently eager for a little vicious fun.

Jason was glad they were cruel bastards. That gave him a chance, slim though it was.

He finally managed to let out a piercing whistle. Cleo's head came up. The palomino spun around and started toward him, then stopped uncertainly for a second as the outlaws opened fire with their pistols. Jason whistled again and Cleo came on, cutting the distance between them. Bullets whined past him. His heart pounded, both from exertion and from the knowledge that death flickered through the air scant inches from his head.

He might have made it if a rock hadn't rolled unexpectedly under his foot, throwing him off balance and sending him careening ahead out of control. He fell, rolling down the slope, scraping exposed hide on the rocky ground and brushing against a cactus that lanced its spines through his shirt sleeve into the flesh of his upper arm. Jason thought he yelled in pain, but he couldn't be sure because the thunder of hoofbeats was deafening now. The outlaws were almost on top of him.

He rolled over onto his back. He had dropped the rifle, but somehow his Colt had gotten into his right hand. He had drawn the gun without even being aware of it. Now instinct took over as he jerked the gun up, eared back the hammer, and fired.

The flame from the muzzle blast almost singed the face of one of the horses. The bullet went past its ear, angling up, and struck the rider under the chin. The heavy slug tore through the man's mouth and on into his brain, exploding out the top of his skull. He flew out of the saddle, dead well before he hit the ground.

Jason rolled again to avoid the slashing hooves of another horse. The ground dropped out from under him, and he found himself sliding into a shallow gully. It was deep enough to give him some much-needed cover as he twisted around and snapped a shot at one of the remaining raiders. The man jerked in the saddle and hunched over, pressing an arm to his belly. In one of those frozen moments of time that sometimes occurred in battle, Jason found himself staring into the wounded man's face. He was a white man, lean and ugly, with black gaps in his teeth and straw-colored hair sticking out from under a flat-crowned black hat. His thin-lipped mouth twisted in a snarl as he tried to bring his gun up for a shot at Jason.

Jason pressed the Colt's trigger again and saw the man's face disappear in a red smear as the bullet smashed into it. The dead outlaw toppled from the saddle and crashed to the ground.

That was enough for the fourth man. He yanked his horse around and fled back toward the top of the ridge. Jason let him go. He lay there in the gully, his mouth full of grit and his chest heaving as he tried to catch his breath. He was too stunned for the knowledge that he had killed three out of the four outlaws who came after him to have fully soaked in yet.

When it did, he was even more amazed. He pushed himself to his feet, took fresh cartridges from the loops on his shell belt, and thumbed them into the Colt's cylinder, reloading in case some of the outlaws came back. From the looks of things, though, they weren't going to. The dust cloud was moving off to the south now.

Jason spotted his hat on the ground, picked it up, and whistled for Cleo again. While the palomino was trotting over to him, he found the rifle he had dropped. He checked the barrel to make sure it wasn't fouled, then reloaded it too, before he slid it back in the saddle boot.

Then he mounted up and rode to the top of the ridge, stopping just short of it so he wouldn't be skylighted. From there he could see that the outlaw horde was indeed moving on to the south. They were at least half a mile away now. They had to be heading for the border, Jason thought. Juan Alba probably had a stronghold somewhere across the line in Mexico.

Jason topped the ridge, hurried down the slope, and turned the other way when he reached the flats. The pall of smoke that hung over Fury was beginning to thin. At least some of the fires were out by now.

But as Jason galloped toward the settlement, he dreaded discovering just how much death and destruction had been left behind by the raid.

Chapter 18

Jason felt sickness churning in his belly as he approached Fury and saw an overturned buckboard. The two horses that had been hitched to the wagon lay dead in black pools of blood that had gushed from their numerous bullet wounds. The poor animals had been riddled with lead.

As had their owner, who lay facedown on the ground about ten yards away, as if he had fallen while trying to flee from the outlaws on foot. The back of his shirt was soaked with blood. He had been shot at least half-a-dozen times.

His head was twisted so that Jason could see one side of his face, which was now frozen in a permanent grimace of fear and agony. Jason recognized him as Ed Willet, one of the newcomers to Fury who had arrived only a week or so earlier. Willet had planned to start a farm, and Jason guessed he had been heading to town to pick up some supplies when he saw the raiders coming. He hadn't made it to safety in time.

Not that anybody had been much safer in the settlement, Jason thought. The outlaws had swept right on into town, shooting, looting, and pillaging. Jason grew even more sickened as he reached Main Street and saw the bleeding bodies of people and horses littering the ground. Men, women, even children had been slaughtered with no thought of mercy or compassion.

Jason had been through Indian attacks and had seen their grim aftermath. In a way, this was worse. At least the Indians were fighting for what they considered their own way of life, barbaric though it might be.

This . . . this was just pure evil.

The front window of Nordstrom's Mercantile was busted out. A million pieces of glass covered the porch and the floor inside. Randall Nordstrom was slumped backward over the sill, unmoving. His chest was a gory mess, looking like someone had unloaded both barrels of a shotgun into it. Jason looked past Nordstrom's body into the wreckage of the store. It had been thoroughly looted, the outlaws carrying off everything that struck their fancy.

Across the street, the livery stable was still burning, although the flames were dying down since the roof had already fallen in and the walls had collapsed. The stink in the air told Jason that some of the horses had been caught inside the inferno and never made it out. The old man who ran the place and his Mexican hostler lay in front of the stable, both of them shot dead.

Several houses were nothing but piles of ashes, including the one where Michael Morelli had his medical practice and his family's home. Jason hoped all the Morellis had gotten out safely. He turned his head, dreading whatever terrible sight he would see next. It was Abigail Krimp's place, burned out inside even though the adobe walls still stood. Jason didn't see any sign of Abigail and wondered if she was inside.

"Jason!"

The shout made him jerk around in the saddle and reach for his gun. He stilled the instinct as he saw Saul Cohen running toward him. Saul had blood on his face, but he seemed pretty spry and wasn't moving like a wounded man.

"Thank God you're here, Jason!" Saul gasped as he came to a stop beside the palomino. He was so shaken that he reached out and grasped the stirrup for a moment to steady himself. "It was awful, just awful. Like something in a war."

Jason glanced toward Saul's hardware store. It seemed to be largely intact, although the front window was broken and it looked like the door had been kicked down.

"Saul," Jason said in a ragged voice. "Your wife, your kids . . ."

Saul nodded. "All right, all of them, thank God. I got this cut from some flying glass, but that's all."

The gash on Saul's cheek was bloody and ugly, but the glass had missed his eye and the cut wasn't life-threatening.

"What about Jenny and Megan? Have you seen them?"

Saul shook his head in dismay. "I don't know. I just don't know, Jason. I haven't seen them, but I'm sure they're all right."

Jason wasn't sure of that at all. He had seen several women lying in crumpled heaps in the street and knew that the raiders had shown no compunctions about hurting females.

But there were other things to worry about in the wake of this tragedy. "What about Ward and Wash?" He would need help putting Fury back together, and he knew he could count on those two.

"They're around somewhere," Saul replied, and Jason felt relief at the knowledge that they were still alive. "Ward took a bullet in the arm, but I don't think Wash was hurt at all. Both of them put up a fight. They got a few of the bastards."

To hear that curse from the normally mild-spoken Saul was an indication of how shaken he was. Jason dismounted and asked, "What about Dr. Morelli?"

"Trying to help the injured, the last I saw. He was setting up what he called a field hospital in the Crown and Garter."

Jason started toward Alf Blodgett's saloon when he paused and looked back at Saul. "What about Morelli's family?"

Saul shook his head. "I don't know." His voice and face were miserable.

Hoofbeats made both of them look around. Salmon Kendall's

wagon rolled toward them, with Salmon at the reins whipping the horses. His wife Carrie was at his side, clutching Salmon's arm. Carrie's daughter Chrissy peered over their shoulders from the back of the wagon. She held a gray, squirming bundle that Jason recognized as her dog Rags.

Salmon, whose first wife had been killed in the Comanche attack during the wagon train journey, had married the widow Carrie English and taken on Chrissy and Rags as members of his family as well. Carrie was a pretty blonde, but at the moment her face was tense and drawn with worry.

Salmon pulled his team to a halt and leaped down from the seat. Jason was glad to see that his friend was hale and hearty, unharmed by the outlaws. In fact, it became evident as Salmon spoke that he and his family hadn't been caught in the raid.

"We heard the shots and saw the smoke," Salmon said. "I wanted to come right on into town, but Carrie insisted on coming with me. Said with all hell breakin' loose, I couldn't leave her and Chrissy alone on the farm." Salmon's broad shoulders rose and fell. "I figured she was right. Took me a while to get the team hitched up, though."

Jason nodded. "You did the right thing. A gang of outlaws did this, and you wouldn't have wanted them to catch the womenfolks alone on the farm." Jason rubbed a weary hand across his jaw, wincing as the movement made his arm hurt. He looked down and saw several cactus needles sticking through his shirt sleeve. He was going to have to pull those out of there when he got a chance. Lord knows when that would be.

He went on. "I've got a hunch this was Juan Alba's bunch."

"You're right," a familiar voice said behind Jason. He looked around to see Wash Keough coming toward him. The old-timer continued. "I heard some o' them sons o' bitches yellin' back and forth and caught Alba's name. The bastard."

He nodded to Carrie. "Beggin' your pardon for the language, ma'am."

"Don't trouble yourself, Mr. Keough," Carrie said. "Men who would carry out atrocities such as this deserved to be called bastards and sons of bitches."

"What do we need to do, Jason?" Saul asked.

Townspeople would normally look to the mayor in times of emergency, but Jason knew they all still relied on him because he had taken over as wagon master after his father's death. He said, "The well seems to be all right. Put together a bucket brigade and get the rest of the fires out. I don't think you'll be able to save any of the buildings that are already burning, but we need to keep the fire from spreading. When you find people who are hurt but able to get around on their own, send them to the Crown and Garter. Dr. Morelli is there, tending to the wounded. Anybody who's hurt too bad to walk, put them in Salmon's wagon and he can take them to the saloon."

"You don't think there's any chance those bandits will come back, do you?" Salmon asked.

"I had a little run-in with them south of town," Jason replied without going into the details. "They were going hell-for-leather toward the border. I don't see them turning back." He added in a bitter voice, "Looks like they already got everything they came for."

The next couple of hours were like a nightmare from which Jason couldn't wake up. He moved from building to building, checking the damage, the wounded, the dead. Much of the destruction was wanton and senseless, killing and burning just for the sake of savagery. It hadn't been enough for Alba's raiders to clean out the settlement of everything valuable. It was like they had tried to drive a stake into the very heart of Fury.

Ward Wanamaker caught up to Jason while he was making

his grim tour of the town. A bloodstained rag was wrapped around Ward's left arm, but he shrugged when Jason asked him about the wound.

"Didn't bust the bone," Ward said, "so I'm not gonna worry about it."

"You'll worry about it if it festers and you get blood poisoning," Jason warned. "Go over to the Crown and Garter and let Dr. Morelli take a look at it."

"Aw, damn, Jason—"

"Go on," Jason insisted. "It shouldn't take long." He looked around at the devastation. "And I'll be at this chore for a while, figuring out just how bad things really are."

As he continued his inspection of the town, he looked for his sister and Megan. He hadn't seen either of them so far, but at least he hadn't found their bodies. He could tell himself that they were still alive.

Cyrus Valentine had his wagon out and was gathering up the bodies. There were so many, he didn't have room for all of them in his undertaking parlor. Jason glanced into the yard behind the building, and shuddered as he saw corpses stacked up in a shed like cordwood.

"I'll get to everybody as quick as I can, Marshal," Cyrus promised.

"Grab a couple of men to help you," Jason said. "Tell them I said for them to give you a hand."

Cyrus nodded and hurried off to implement Jason's suggestion.

Jason moved on to the Crown and Garter. The saloon's tables had been turned into makeshift hospital beds by spreading blankets over them. A couple of wounded men were lying on the bar itself. Michael Morelli was fishing around in the chest of one of them, evidently looking for a bullet. The doctor's sleeves were rolled up, and his arms were smeared with blood to the elbows.

Morelli glanced over as Jason came up beside him and muttered, "This is almost as bad as Shiloh, damn it."

"You were there?"

"That's right. I was one of those butchers who lopped off arms and legs until the piles of them were so big they almost forced us out of the hospital tent. Lost more than half the men we operated on. But we saved some of them. We saved some of them, damn it."

Jason put a hand on Morelli's shoulder and squeezed. "Do what you can, Doc."

"Ah!" Morelli lifted the forceps in his hand and tossed the misshapen chunk of lead he had just removed from the wounded man's chest into a basin, where it rattled around with at least a dozen more bullets that had been taken out of human flesh. The man on the bar began to breathe a little easier.

Jason started to move away, but Morelli stopped him. "Marshal," the doctor said, making a visible effort to control his emotions, "have you seen any of my family?"

Jason had to shake his head. "Afraid not."

"I . . . I saw the house. One of those . . . those bastards must have tossed a torch into it. Some of them had torches . . . they threw them all over town . . . didn't seem to care what they were burning down . . ." Morelli stopped and passed a shaking hand over his face. He straightened his back, squared his shoulders, and turned to Alf Blodgett and a couple of other men. "I'll close up this fellow. As soon as that's done, you can move him to one of the tables and bring me the next man who needs surgery."

Jason left Morelli to go about his bloody business. As he went back out into the street, he saw Carrie Kendall coming toward him, along with Chrissy and the two older Morelli children. Carrie was carrying a blanket-wrapped infant.

"Is that the Morelli baby?" Jason asked, very relieved to see that Constantine and Helen were all right anyway.

Carrie nodded. "It is. Constantine got them all out the back of the house when it caught on fire." She smiled down at the boy. "He was very brave."

"What about Olympia?"

Carrie shook her head. "She sent the children out, but stayed behind to try to save some of Michael's medical supplies. I . . . I don't know what happened after that."

Jason nodded and glanced toward the smoking ruins of the Morelli house. He was afraid they would find Olympia's charred remains in there.

"Take the kids on into the saloon," he told Carrie. "I'm sure the doc will be happy to see them."

Morelli would have to face the loss of his wife, but Jason knew he would carry on as long as his services as a doctor were needed. That was the sort of hombre he was.

More hoofbeats made Jason look around. Matt MacDonald and some of his men were riding into town. Jason noticed that Bill Rye and the other gunslingers weren't with them. Matt had a frantic look on his face as he hurried over to Jason and dismounted.

"We saw the smoke and knew it must be coming from town," Matt explained. "Got here as fast as we could. Where are Jenny and Megan?"

"I don't know, Matt," Jason said, putting aside at this moment all the hostility and outright dislike he felt for the man. Right now Matt was scared for his loved ones, like everybody else in town who didn't know for sure what had happened to their families. Jason went on. "I've looked pretty much all around the town, and I haven't seen them. But at least I haven't found their bodies."

"That's not enough, damn it!" Matt turned to the men who had ridden in from the ranch with him. "Spread out! Find my sister and Jenny Fury!"

But Megan and Jenny were nowhere to be found, and as the afternoon waned, Jason called a meeting in the marshal's office—which had been untouched by the outlaws for some reason—with Ward, Saul, Wash, Salmon, Matt, and Dr. Morelli to take stock of the situation.

The ashes of Morelli's house still hadn't cooled completely, but several men had risked burns to sort through the rubble. To Jason's surprise, they hadn't found any sign of the doctor's wife.

Nor had an exhaustive search turned up several other citizens of Fury. Everyone was accounted for except Megan MacDonald, Jenny Fury, Olympia Morelli, and Abigail Krimp.

"We got to face it, Jason," Wash said. "If them women ain't here in town, dead or alive, then there's only one thing that could've happened to them."

Jason looked around at the grim faces of the men and knew they had all reached the same conclusion he had.

Megan, Jenny, Olympia, and Abigail had been kidnapped. The band of vicious outlaws led by Juan Alba, the Scourge of the Borderlands, had carried them off when they left Fury after the raid.

And as for where they were taking the women and what fate was intended for them . . .

Only God knew.

God, and the devil called Juan Alba.

Chapter 19

"What are you going to do, Jason?" Matt demanded in a voice that was taut with strain and worry.

Jason pinched the bridge of his nose and closed his eyes for a moment. He was "Jason" again to Matt, rather than the disdainful "Fury."

But he couldn't afford to dwell on things like that. Not with his sister and the young woman he loved in the hands of vicious outlaws.

"Only one thing to do," he said as he opened his eyes. "We're going to go after them and get them back."

"That's gonna be mighty easier said than done," Wash pointed out. "That gang o' desperadoes is like a small army, and they're probably well on their way to the border by now."

Jason shook his head. "I don't care how many of them there are, and the border means nothing to me. We'll hunt them down, wherever they are."

"Just so you know what you're gettin' into," Wash said with a shrug.

Dr. Morelli leaned forward and clasped his hands together between his knees. Deep lines were etched in his kindly face. "Someone will have to loan me a rifle," he said. "I'm afraid mine was destroyed when the house burned up."

Jason shook his head and said, "You're not going, Doctor."

"Damn it, they have my wife!" Morelli's voice trembled from the depth of his emotion. "I *have* to go!"

"You're the only doctor in town. You're needed here. Some of the folks who were wounded may not pull through if you're not around to take care of them."

"I'm sorry about that, but Olympia is more important—" The physician broke off his argument and slumped back in his chair. "You're right, of course, Marshal. I know you're right. I swore an oath, and I have to live by it. But at a time like this . . . it's hard. By God, it's hard."

Ward reached over and squeezed Morelli's shoulder. "We'll get your missus back safe and sound, Doc, along with those other ladies. You just wait and see."

"You're not going either, Ward." That was a more difficult decision for Jason to make, but he didn't see that he had any choice. As Ward turned a surprised face toward him, he went on. "Somebody has to stay behind to maintain law and order here in town. You've got a little experience at that, and you're wounded to boot."

Ward lifted his injured arm, which now sported a proper bandage, courtesy of Dr. Morelli. "This little scratch? Hell, Jason, it don't amount to anything!"

"It might if it's not cared for properly. Anyway, I think you'd have to stay here even if you weren't injured, to look after the town. That bullet hole just makes the decision a little easier."

"Easier for you maybe," Ward muttered.

"Well, *I'm* going," Matt declared, "and you'll just be wasting your breath if you try to talk me out of it."

Jason nodded. "I figured you for one of the members of the posse. What about your men?"

"That'll have to be up to them. I can't order them to go chasing after a bunch of bandits."

That made sense to Jason. They would be setting out on a

highly dangerous mission. Anyone who went along would have to do so voluntarily.

"Count me in too," Saul said.

"And me," Salmon added.

"Both of you have families," Jason pointed out.

"And if it was our wives missing, all of y'all would be willing to help," Salmon said. "We've got to stick together, Jason. When those outlaws raided our town, struck at us in our own homes, they hurt all of us, whether we actually took a bullet or got our houses burned down. We're all wounded in a way, and we got to get the sons o' bitches who're responsible."

Jason understood what the mayor was saying, and he had to agree. Everybody in Fury had a stake in this rescue mission.

"All right," he said. "You'll need good saddle horses, guns, and plenty of ammunition. Spread the word. Any man who wants to come along should be out in front of the office here in about an hour. The sooner we get on that gang's trail, the sooner we get those ladies back."

He didn't mention the fear that was uppermost in all of their minds. The outlaws would probably keep moving until they reached their stronghold, wherever that might be, but once they stopped, their thoughts would turn to the women. On the frontier, most men, even hardened outlaws, wouldn't think of molesting a decent woman. But based on the evidence they had left behind in Fury, the members of Alba's gang weren't men at all. They were animals, vicious, unrelenting animals, and they would be fully capable of abusing their female captives, even to the point of death.

That was why time was of the essence.

Jason hoped it wasn't a fool's errand they were setting off on. On the surface, it appeared to be. He didn't know how many men he would be able to recruit for the posse, but it was almost certain they would be outnumbered. And they would be facing a highly formidable group of foes too. It was possible they would fail to rescue the women, and might even all die in the process.

But the risk had to be run. The alternative was to sit back and do nothing, to not even try to make things right, and that was unacceptable to all of them.

Jason pushed himself to his feet, looked at the grim faces of the other men, and nodded. "Let's get started," he said.

Within an hour, approximately thirty men and even more horses were milling around in the street outside the marshal's office. The extra mounts would be taken along in case anything happened to some of the saddle horses. Also, when the women were rescued, they would need mounts too. Might as well be optimistic about it, Jason thought as he looked over the group.

In addition to Saul, Salmon, and Wash, several other men from the wagon train had joined the posse, including Zachary Morton, who had ridden in from his ranch north of town. A gunsmith by trade, Zachary was an old-timer with plenty of years under his belt, but he was also tough as whang leather and a good shot. Jason was glad to have him along.

Alf Blodgett was there too, which surprised Jason a little because the Englishman was such a newcomer to the settlement.

"This is my home now," Blodgett replied when Jason questioned his presence, "and an Englishman's home is his castle! Can't have those damned barbarians thinking that they can come in here, sack the place, and get away with it, now can we?"

"What about your saloon?"

A grin spread across Blodgett's beefy face. "You mean Dr. Morelli's hospital? It'll be fine. My girls will look after the place while I'm gone."

"Well, then, if you're sure, we're glad to have you."

Jason moved on, spoke briefly to some of the other men, assuring himself that everyone was there of their own free will and understood the perilous nature of the mission they were about to undertake. Satisfied that they were and did, he raised his hands to get their attention and addressed all of them.

"Thank you, men, for turning out. You all know what we're doing. We're going to rescue the ladies who were taken from here as prisoners, and we're going to teach Juan Alba and his gang that they can't attack the town of Fury and get away with it. I won't lie to you. Some of us won't be coming back. If you don't think this mission is worth risking your life, nobody will think any worse of you if you decide not to go. I know that a lot of you men have wives and children, and you'll be risking their futures as well."

"Stop trying to talk us out of it, Jason," Saul said. "What sort of future will our families have if they have to live in constant fear of outlaws? If we smash Alba's band, then lawbreakers will think twice about coming to Fury from now on!"

Cheers of agreement went up from the assembled posse and the townspeople who had gathered to watch the group get ready to ride.

A faint smile touched Jason's face. "All right, Saul," he said. "I reckon you made your point." He raised his voice. "Everybody mount up!"

The posse did so, but before they could move out, someone called, "Riders comin'!"

An air of tension swept over the crowd. After what had happened today, everybody was scared and suspicious. Even though it was unlikely, the raiders might be coming back for more bloodshed and destruction.

Instead, as Jason sent Cleo trotting down the street so that he could meet the newcomers, he recognized them as Ezra Dixon and several hands from the Slash D. Dixon reined in and motioned for his men to stop as Jason rode up to him and halted about twelve feet away. Jason spotted several men he hadn't seen before, including a lean, dark-faced man in black clothing, including a black Stetson with silver conchos on the band. He wondered if he was looking at the notorious Flint

Gallister and some of the other gunfighters Dixon had hired for the looming war with Matt MacDonald.

"What do you want, Dixon?" Jason asked.

Dixon thrust out his jaw, as belligerent as always. "Heard about the trouble you had here in town. Never would have happened if you hadn't squatted here in the first place and drew Alba's attention to you."

"You got anything useful to say, or did you just come to be unpleasant?"

Dixon scowled. "Come to offer my help. I got no use for them damn *bandidos*. If you're ridin' after 'em, me and some o' my boys will go along."

The offer took Jason by surprise. As opposed as Dixon was to the very existence of the town, he had supposed the rancher would be glad to hear about the devastation Alba's gang had wreaked. But Dixon still had *some* human feelings after all, it looked like.

Jason turned his head to look at the man in black. "You're Gallister?" he guessed.

The man smiled. "You've heard of me, Marshal. I'm impressed."

"Don't be," Jason snapped. "Are you coming along too?"

Dixon answered before Gallister could say anything. "Flint and his pards are stayin' on the Slash D. I can't afford to go off and leave the place defenseless. If I did that, those hired guns o' MacDonald's would probably move in and take over whilst I was gone."

Matt edged his horse forward from the posse. "Damn it, Dixon," he said, "if you think I care about our feud right now, you're crazy! Those bastards have my sister and the woman I love!"

"Yeah, but I don't believe in takin' chances," Dixon replied. "Flint and the others stay behind."

"Then so do Bill Rye and his friends," Matt said. "I was going to stop by the ranch and get them, but I don't trust you.

I'd come back to find every building on my place burned down and all my stock slaughtered."

Dixon just grunted. But he didn't deny the charge, Jason noted.

These developments were a little disappointing. Having ten or twelve professional gunmen along would have increased the odds of success against Alba's gang. But on the other hand, such men could never be fully trusted either. As it was, with the addition of Ezra Dixon and four or five of his regular ranch hands, the posse now numbered almost three dozen men. They would still be outnumbered by the outlaws, but the odds weren't overwhelming. With a few lucky breaks, the posse stood a reasonable chance of rescuing the prisoners and getting back to Fury alive. Some of them, anyway . . .

"All right," Jason said, "if that's settled, we've got an hour, maybe two, of daylight left. Let's put it to good use. Is everybody ready to ride?"

All the men nodded, and a few called out agreement.

"Move out!" Jason shouted as he waved a hand forward. He and Wash took the lead, and he felt almost like he was in command of a military patrol. He had missed out on all the action during the war, but now his time had come. Everyone was relying on him.

And instead of wondering, as he usually did, whether or not he was up to the challenge, he pushed any doubts out of his head. This rescue mission was going to succeed. He could feel it in his bones.

The only question remaining was how high a price they would have to pay to get those women back alive.

Chapter 20

Megan MacDonald had never been so scared in her whole life. She had seen violence before. She had been there when the Comanches attacked the wagon train and when the Apaches tried to lay waste to Fury. Those experiences had been terrifying, but they had also been so hectic that Megan hadn't had time for the fear to really soak in on her.

That wasn't the case now. The outlaws had visited more death and destruction on Fury than even the Apaches would have. These men were more savage than the so-called savages. And since Megan had been their prisoner for hours now, she'd had plenty of time to think about the perilous situation in which she found herself.

Jenny's quiet sobbing didn't help matters. The younger girl hadn't stopped crying ever since the outlaws had ceased their breakneck flight and pulled their horses back to a steady, inevitable, ground-eating lope that carried them farther south, inexorably toward Mexico. The man who had Jenny in front of him on his horse's back didn't seem to mind her sobs. In fact, he acted like he found her terror amusing.

Megan was trying very hard not to let herself cry. She didn't want to show any weakness, not with the ordeal she and the other prisoners had facing them. Her captors might assault her, might even kill her, but they wouldn't break her, she vowed.

Brave intentions, but they might prove difficult to live up to.

The man who had grabbed her up off the street as she tried to reach safety during the attack on the settlement still carried her in front of him on his horse. His left arm was looped around her, not particularly tightly now, but she knew that if she tried to escape, his grip would clamp down on her like an iron band.

Earlier, he had fondled her breasts, squeezing them until she wanted to gasp in pain. Thankfully, he had seemed to grow bored with that, and now just held her on the horse. Her fear had eased a bit, and as it did, she realized that there had been something familiar about him when she caught a glimpse of his face as he jerked her up off her feet and dragged her onto the horse. She hadn't realized who he was, though, until he said, "Don't you fight, little one, and Flores will treat you nice."

The outlaw was the man Jason had arrested a couple of weeks earlier for wounding Wash Keough in Abigail's place. Megan wondered if the other two men who had been with Flores were also part of this bandit gang. It made sense that they would be. In fact, as she thought about it to distract her mind from her own desperate plight, she realized that the three hardcases must have ventured into Fury to scout out the settlement. To decide if it would be worth Juan Alba's while to raid it.

Obviously, the answer had been yes.

She knew the leader of the gang was Juan Alba, the so-called Scourge of the Borderlands, because Flores liked to talk and his chatter had included several references to the notorious bandit chieftain. Megan had heard stories about Juan Alba, and knew that he was reputed to be without mercy. As long as they were in his hands, she and Jenny, along with Mrs. Morelli and Abigail Krimp, were facing a terrible fate.

Even though Olympia and Abigail weren't riding right alongside her as Jenny and her captor were, Megan had caught glimpses of the two older women. She didn't know if any other prisoners had been taken from Fury. She hoped not. It was bad enough that the four of them were captives. The fewer prisoners there were, she thought, the easier it would be for Jason to rescue them. Megan had no doubt that Jason Fury would come after her and take her back to safety.

If he was still alive . . .

She refused to consider the possibility that he might not be, that he could have been killed in the fighting. As far as she knew, he hadn't even been in town when the raid started. He had ridden out to either Ezra Dixon's Slash D or Matt MacDonald's ranch, to try one more time to bring about peace between the feuding factions. She hoped he hadn't returned in time to be gunned down like so many others.

The thought of the dying she had witnessed made a little shudder go through Megan's body. Flores felt it and said, "Getting tired of riding? We'll be there soon."

Megan didn't know where *there* was. They had traveled so far already that she felt certain they had crossed the border and were in Mexico. On the other hand, she wasn't really sure how far it was to the border. It was possible they were still in Arizona Territory, she supposed.

In that case, there was a chance a cavalry patrol might come along. She prayed it would happen that way. She knew from the things she had heard that she and the other prisoners couldn't expect any help from the Mexican *rurales*. The so-called police force was corrupt, and the local commander was probably being paid off by Juan Alba to leave the bandits alone.

Megan's head was spinning with possibilities, a few good, most overwhelmingly bad. She told herself to hang on to the hopes she had, slender though they might be.

The sun had dropped below the horizon a short time earlier, and the light left over from its setting was fading in a hurry. Megan didn't know if the outlaws would continue pressing on to the south after darkness fell, or if they would stop and make camp for the night. Nor did she know which of those things to hope for. She was exhausted and sore from being forced to ride astride, and stopping meant that the gang would no longer be putting more distance between themselves and any rescue attempt.

But stopping also meant that the outlaws would have a chance to turn their full attention on their captives. Megan knew that most Western men, even the disreputable ones, respected women. But she wasn't naïve enough to think that these . . . *animals* . . . would respect anything. As soon as the gang got a chance, she and Jenny and the two older women would be raped, probably repeatedly.

She could survive even that, she told herself. The important thing was to stay alive, no matter what else happened.

But as she thought about how Jason would look at her in the future, knowing how soiled she was, she wondered if it wouldn't be better to just die in captivity. . . .

A short time later, the outlaws called a halt. Dread grew inside Megan as Flores chuckled and said, "Now you get a chance to get down and stretch your legs, eh, little one?"

He dismounted first, and then reached back up to take hold of her and lift her down from the horse. When he let go of her waist, he grasped her wrist instead and said, "Don't try to run."

"I . . . I'm not going anywhere," Megan managed to say. She wanted to appear cooperative, so as not to anger him.

But in the fading light, she found herself looking at the butt of his gun where it stuck up from the holster. If she could get her hands on it, she thought, she could put a bullet through his head and then press the barrel to her own temple and pull the trigger—

No. Jason would come after her. She couldn't allow herself to lose hope.

Megan, Jenny, Olympia Morelli, and Abigail Krimp were herded together. As far as Megan could tell, they were the only four prisoners. She was glad no other women had been dragged away from the settlement. Olympia put her arms around the sobbing Jenny and tried to comfort her. Megan found herself standing next to Abigail. Both of them had red hair, but the resemblance ended there. Abigail was at least ten years older and was both taller and heavier, with a voluptuous figure that drew many admiring—well, lustful, to be honest about it—glances from the men she encountered. The outlaws were no exception.

"Stay close to me," Abigail said in a low voice to Megan. "If any of them start trying to bother you, I'll do my best to distract them."

"But then they'll just—"

Abigail's low, humorless laugh interrupted her. "They can't do anything to me that hasn't been done plenty of times before, except kill me. If that's what happens, then so be it."

"You can't mean that."

"No? The life I've led, I always expected to die young. Women like me don't get old unless they're lucky enough to find some man who wants to marry them, no matter what they've done in the past. It happens more than you might think, but I was never that fortunate." A wistful tone came into Abigail's voice. "If some young fella like Jason Fury felt about me the way he does about you, then I'd have something to live for. As it is . . ." She shrugged. "Just stay close to me, like I said. I'll do what I can for you."

"Thank you," Megan whispered. She didn't know what was going to happen, but it helped somehow to have Abigail close by.

She didn't have to wait long to find out what their captors had in mind. One of the men jerked Jenny away from Olympia and started running his hands over her body. She cried out and struck wildly at him with her fists, but he just laughed and pushed her down onto the ground.

"Go ahead and fight me, you little honey," he said with a lecherous sneer. "I don't mind. Fact is, I like it better that way."

Olympia moved between Jenny and the man. "Leave her alone," she said. "You can have me instead. I won't struggle."

"Forget it," the outlaw said. "Didn't you just hear me say I like it when a gal tries to fight? Besides, I want me some o' that young stuff."

The man grabbed Olympia's shoulders to shove her out of the way, but before he could do so, a gunshot roared out. The outlaws who were standing around tensed and reached for their guns, but they didn't draw. Instead they stepped back as a huge man strode up, looming like a mountain against the last of the red light in the sky.

"I told you, no one bothers the women yet!" the man bellowed. He was at least six and a half feet tall, with legs like tree trunks and massive arms and shoulders. A bristly black beard jutted out from his heavy chin. He wore a sombrero with silver balls dangling from the edge of the brim, and a blood-red serape was thrown back over his right shoulder so that he could easily reach the holstered revolver on his hip.

The aura of unquestioned command about the man, and the way the other outlaws drew back from him a little, as if he were a volcano about to erupt, told Megan that this was Juan Alba, the Scourge of the Borderlands.

"You all know that we have plans for the prisoners, especially these two," Alba continued, gesturing with a hamlike hand toward Megan and Jenny. "Any man who harms them in any way will answer to me!"

It was obvious none of the outlaws wanted that. They drew back to a respectful distance around the prisoners, while still remaining close enough to keep them from having any hope of escaping.

"We will let the horses rest for half an hour, then push on." With that order issued, Alba jerked his head in a curt nod and turned away. He didn't look back to see if his commands were being followed. He didn't have to. None of the men, not even the rugged and vicious Flores, would cross him.

"Thank God," Megan murmured. She sank down on the ground to rest. Abigail sat beside her, as did Jenny and Olympia. Tears still ran down Jenny's face, but at least she was crying quietly now.

"Don't get too comfortable," Abigail said, keeping her voice low enough so that only Megan could hear her.

"What?"

"The leader stepping in like that was the first bit of luck we've had, but it's just a reprieve. It won't last. So don't start thinking this is over, Megan. I'd be willing to bet that it ain't. Not by a long shot."

"But he said for the others to leave us alone."

"Only because he's got other plans for us . . . especially you and Jenny," Abigail added. "Just what do you think those plans are going to be?"

Megan swallowed hard. She had no idea.

But whatever it was that Juan Alba had in mind for the captives, it wouldn't be anything good. . . .

Chapter 21

Jason was glad to have Wash Keough along as a member of the posse, since the old mountain man had a reputation as a good tracker. That skill might come in handy before this job was done.

But starting out, anyway, a blind man could have followed the trail left by the outlaws. Fifty galloping horses left plenty of sign, even on hard ground. And Alba's men weren't even trying to cover their tracks.

Why should they? Jason asked himself. It was doubtful that any force in the territory, short of the army itself, could stand up against them in battle. Even some cavalry patrols would be outnumbered and outgunned against the bandit horde.

As the sun set and the light began to fade, Matt MacDonald brought his horse alongside Jason and Wash and said, "We're going to push on even after dark, aren't we?"

Jason looked over at the old-timer and asked, "What about it, Wash?"

"I ain't sure." Wash chewed on his mustache as he thought about the question. "It's mighty hard to follow a trail at night. I ain't sayin' it can't be done, especially if there's a moon, but you run the risk o' losin' the trail good an' proper."

"Don't be ridiculous," Matt snapped. "We know which way

they're going. They're headed almost due south. They're making a run for the border. All we have to do is steer by the stars and keep going the same direction."

"That's all well and good," Jason said, "*if* they keep going the same way. What if they veer off some other direction?"

"They can't go east," Matt pointed out. "They'll find themselves running into Tucson or Camp Grant if they do. And there's nothing the other way but a hell of a lot of nothing."

Wash muttered, "That's pretty much what they'll find south o' the border too. Plenty o' desert and a few mountain ranges, less'n they plan on goin' all the way to the Gulf o' California."

Jason frowned in thought. "How far is that, Wash?"

"To the Gulf? Shoot, I don't know. Ain't never been across that way. I'd say eighty, ninety miles."

"Close enough they could reach it in a few days of hard travel, in other words."

"Yeah, but it'd be hard travel, all right. Sonora's a mighty inhospitable place. Ain't much water to be had."

Matt put in, "They'd have plenty of water once they got to that gulf you were talking about."

"Yeah . . . salt water." Wash turned back to Jason, ignoring the resentful flush that spread over Matt's face. "Now, like I was sayin' . . . there's water in the mountains and probably a few tanks in the desert where you could dig down and find more. If they was careful, and if they knew what they was doin', I reckon they could make the Gulf without too much trouble. Why would they go there, though? Chances are they'll hole up somewheres in the mountains instead. That makes a heap more sense."

Jason nodded. "Yes, I know. The other was just a thought."

But the idea stayed with him, even when he called a halt to let the horses rest. He gathered the most trusted members of the group around him to discuss their options.

"We can stop for the night and wait until morning to push on. That way we'll be sure of not losing the trail."

Salmon said, "That gives those damn outlaws more time to, ah . . ." His voice faded as he looked at Jason.

"You don't have to watch what you say, Salmon," Jason told him. "We all know what they're liable to do to the prisoners. That can't be a consideration now. We're just trying to get those women back alive, that's all."

Matt MacDonald came up in time to hear Jason's comments. He snapped, "Speak for yourself, Fury. My sister is one of those captives, damn it."

"And so is mine," Jason said, making the necessary effort to keep his irritation under control. Matt always rubbed him the wrong way, but he had to ignore that for the time being. "We have to be realistic about this. Saving their lives is the first priority. Anybody disagree?"

He looked around. The others met his gaze with solemn stares, but no one argued with him, even Matt.

"All right," Jason went on. "Why don't we wait here until the moon comes up, then we'll try to push on and see how much trouble it is to follow the trail that way. If it looks like we're in danger of losing it, we'll call a halt until morning. But if we don't have to do that, at least they won't have gained a whole night on us."

One by one, the men nodded their agreement. Jason added, "We'll be relying a great deal on you, Wash. You'll have to tell us if we're going astray."

"I'll try not to let you down, son."

Matt continued to grumble, saying that they ought to just head for the border as fast as they could without worrying about following the trail, but Jason tried to ignore him. He knew Matt was wrong, and so did most of the others.

But not all of them. As they waited for the moon to rise, a group of men approached Jason, and one of them said, "Marshal, how come we're dillydallyin' around here when we could be chasin' them outlaws?"

Jason explained that they were waiting for the moon to come up, so they could follow the tracks left by the bandits.

"Hell, there's no need to do that!" the spokesman responded. "We should just light a shuck for Mexico. That's where they're headed."

"You know that for sure, do you?" Jason responded in a cool voice.

"Hell, yes. Why, MacDonald said—" The man stopped short, as if he had blurted out more than he intended to.

"Don't worry," Jason told him. "You didn't give anything away. I figured Matt was behind this." He turned, his eyes searching through the shadows for Matt MacDonald.

When he spotted the young rancher, he walked over to him and said, "You know, on the high seas, inciting a mutiny is a serious crime."

Matt's jaw jutted out. "What in blazes are you talking about?"

"I'm talking about the way you're questioning my judgment and trying to turn this posse against me," Jason shot back. "I don't like it, and I won't stand for it."

"This is still a free country, damn it. I've got a right to say whatever I want."

"You don't have a right to put those prisoners in even more danger than they already are." Jason looked around and raised his voice so that everyone could hear. "Listen to me! We're waiting for the moon to rise so that we can follow the trail those outlaws left, and as soon as it does, we'll be pushing on. Anybody who doesn't agree with that can turn around and ride on back to Fury, and good riddance!"

Maybe he was reacting too strongly to Matt's challenge, he told himself, but he didn't care anymore. He was tired of Matt MacDonald always second-guessing him and disagreeing with his decisions. That conflict went all the way back to the wagon train journey out here, and Jason was sick of it.

"Yeah, that's just like you," Matt said with a sneer. "So high-and-mighty, lordin' it over everybody else just because you've got that damn tin star on."

"Oh? Is that all it is?" Without thinking about what he was

doing, Jason reached for the badge on his chest and unpinned it from his shirt. He slapped it into the palm of a startled Saul Cohen and said, "Hang on to that for me, will you?"

"Jason, you shouldn't—" Saul began.

Jason knew he shouldn't, but he had gone too far to back down. Besides, Matt didn't give him the chance. Without waiting for Jason to turn around, Matt lunged at him, swinging a roundhouse right at his head.

Jason twisted as Matt's indrawn breath and the scuff of his boots on the ground warned him. Just in time, Jason ducked so that Matt's punch went over his head. He stepped in and hooked a short but powerful blow to Matt's midsection. Matt grunted and moved back a step, his back hunched against the pain. He didn't double over, though, and he was ready when Jason tried to follow the right with a left cross. He blocked it and shot out a left jab that landed on Jason's jaw and rocked his head back. Jason's hat fell off.

He caught his balance and struck swiftly, boring in to pepper Matt's body with quick punches. Matt roared in anger and threw a looping right that would have taken Jason's head off if it had connected. Instead, Jason was able to jerk back so that he felt the wind of Matt's fist passing right in front of his face.

Even though Matt missed, he didn't let that throw him off balance. He launched a kick at Jason's groin. Jason twisted aside and took the impact on his thigh. It was hard enough to knock him backward. Matt lunged, taking advantage of the opportunity to tackle his opponent. His arms locked around Jason in a bone-crushing grip as he bore Jason backward.

Both young men went down, landing hard on the rocky ground. They rolled over and over. Since they were just about the same size and weight, neither had an advantage over the other when it came to wrestling. Matt had the edge in viciousness, though. He drove his knee into Jason's belly. The blow sent pain blossoming through Jason's body and forced the air out of his lungs. He gasped for breath, but before he could drag any air down his throat, Matt's hands closed around it, choking off the life-giving air.

Desperation exploded in Jason's brain as a red haze slipped down in front of his eyes. He balled both hands into fists and slammed them in the sides of Matt's head. The blows must have made Matt's ears ring and rattled his brain in his skull, because he shook his head and loosened his grip enough for Jason to break free. Heaving and arching his back off the ground, Jason flung Matt off to one side.

He only took the time to gulp down one big breath before he threw himself after Matt. As Matt tried to get up, Jason met him with a pile-driving right that sent him sprawling on his back. With an animal-like spring, Jason landed on top of him and hammered a blow into his face. Two more punches crashed against Matt's jaw before Salmon Kendall and Alf Blodgett caught hold of Jason's arms and hauled him upright. They dragged him back away from Matt's now-senseless form.

"Take it easy, Jason," Salmon said. "He's an annoyin' son of a bitch, I'll grant you that, but you don't want to kill him."

"Don't be . . . so sure about that," Jason panted. He shrugged free of Salmon and Blodgett and dragged the back of a hand across his mouth, leaving a red smear on the skin from a bleeding lip. He stood there with his chest heaving as he glared at Matt.

Saul knelt beside the young man, took hold of his jaw, and moved it back and forth. "Doesn't seem to be broken," he announced. "I think he'll be all right when he gets his wits about him again, except for a headache."

Jason looked around at the others. "I meant what I said," he told them. "I'm in charge of this posse. If you can't abide following my orders, you need to leave." He took another deep breath. "But I'll tell you this. Stick with me and we'll get those women back. I give you my word on it. And we'll kill as many of those damned raiders as we get a chance to as well."

That brought mutters of agreement and support. Nobody said anything else about wanting to leave or going against Jason's decisions.

A couple of men helped Matt to his feet. Matt spat blood for a moment, then looked at Jason. "All right," he said, his voice distorted a little by swollen lips and a sore jaw. "You beat me. But that doesn't mean you're right."

"I don't give a damn if you agree with me," Jason snapped. "Just follow orders. That's all I care about."

"Fine, fine," Matt muttered. He started looking around for his hat, swaying and stumbling as he did so.

Wash Keough chuckled. "If you boys're through waltzin' around and providin' some entertainment, take a look at that."

Jason turned and saw a three-quarter-full moon edging above the eastern horizon, spilling silvery illumination over the plains. The light was growing brighter by the second as the moon rose.

It was time to get back on the trail of the outlaws.

Chapter 22

As it turned out, Wash was able to follow the tracks by the light of the moon. They were so easy to see, Jason figured *he* could have followed them if he'd had to. That showed how confident Juan Alba and his men were about being safe from pursuit.

By morning, though, Wash was convinced that they hadn't really cut into the gang's lead by much, if any.

"Reckon they pushed on most o' the night, just like we did." Wash broke the news to the others when they stopped to let the horses rest and to refill their canteens at a creek that wasn't much more than a tiny trickle of water winding its way across the mostly arid flats.

"Aren't we still going south?" Matt wanted to know.

Wash shrugged. "Yeah, pretty much."

Matt glared at Jason. "In other words, if we had pushed on when I wanted to, instead of waiting for the moon to come up, we might have closed in on them."

Jason wasn't going to dignify that comment with a denial or an argument. He didn't have to, because Salmon snapped, "That didn't cost us all that much time, Matt, and you know it. You just don't like playin' second fiddle to anybody, and some of us are gettin' a mite tired of it."

Matt flushed with anger. Saul moved between him and Salmon to forestall any more trouble, even though the hardware store owner was nearly a head shorter than both of them.

"Let's just take it easy," Saul suggested. "What do we do now, Jason?"

"Only one thing we can do," Jason said, "and that's push on after them."

Wash said, "Well, see, now, that's gonna be a problem. We stopped to let these horses blow several times durin' the night, but they need more rest than that. We don't have enough extra mounts for everybody to switch out and keep movin' at the pace we have been. We need to stay here for an hour at least, maybe two."

"Two hours!" Matt said. "That'll let those outlaws get that much farther ahead of us."

Jason shook his head. "Not necessarily. They won't want to ride their mounts into the ground either. I'm betting that they stopped somewhere up ahead too."

"It's not your life you'd be betting. It's Jenny's and Megan's."

"And Mrs. Morelli's and Miss Krimp's," Saul reminded him. "But I agree with Jason and Wash. We can't do those ladies any good at all if we wind up afoot."

Matt gave a snort of contempt. "What does a Hebrew storekeeper know about things like that?"

"It's just common sense," Saul said.

That was something that Matt MacDonald was sorely lacking, Jason thought, but he didn't say it.

Ezra Dixon spoke up for the first time in this council of war. "We got ten extra horses that ain't been ridden all night. Ten men could take them and push on, maybe close in on them bandits a mite."

"Ten men can't fight fifty," Jason pointed out.

"No, but they can scout out the situation and see what's what, so that when the rest o' our bunch catches up, we'll have it figured out what to do to rescue them women."

Jason frowned in thought as he considered the old rancher's

suggestion. Sending out a group of advance scouts wasn't a bad idea. Something else occurred to him, and he said, "If five men took the ten extra horses, they could switch mounts from time to time and move even faster. And five men could do that job just as well as ten."

Wash nodded. "I was just thinkin' the same thing. And you never know, there might be a chance for us to Injun our way in there and grab the gals away without them bandits knowin' what's goin' on, where a bigger bunch wouldn't have a chance o' doin' that."

"You'd be risking their lives to do something as chancy as that!" Matt protested.

"Their lives are already at considerable risk," Jason said. "I like your suggestion, Wash. Question is, who's going with us?"

"If you're bound and determined to do this, I'm going to be one of the five," Matt declared. "I have a right to be included."

Dixon said, "It was my idea, so I reckon I ought to come along. Besides, I got a hankerin' to kill some o' those varmints. Might get my chance sooner this way."

"We don't want to get in a shooting war with them," Jason cautioned. "Not if we're outnumbered ten to one. We'll wait for the rest of the posse to catch up before we try to rescue the prisoners, unless, like Wash says, a perfect opportunity presents itself."

"Then who's the fifth man?" Saul asked. "Me or Salmon?"

Jason shook his head. "Neither of you. I need both of you to stay with the main bunch, to keep everyone organized and moving as quickly as possible." He looked around, studying the other members of the posse, and said, "Mr. Morton? How about you?"

Zachary Morton grinned. "I was sort of hoping you'd ask, Jason."

"Him?" Matt said. "He's an old man!"

"I ain't no spring chicken myself, and neither's Dixon

here," Wash said. "But don't you worry about us, sonny. We can keep up and tote our share o' the load."

"Damn right," Dixon put in.

Zachary just smiled, licked his thumb, and ran it over the front sight of the rifle he carried. Jason knew that Zachary was a crack shot, and the message in the old gunsmith's gesture was plain—Zachary just wanted a shot at those bandits who had stolen the four women.

"All right," Jason said with a nod. "Let's get our saddles on those spare horses. *Now* we're wasting time."

He hated leaving Cleo behind, but the palomino had done valiant work during the pursuit so far and Jason didn't want to ride her into the ground. He also didn't like the idea of taking Matt MacDonald along as a member of the small group of scouts, but he knew that arguing with Matt would just be a waste of time, breath, and energy. Anyway, by taking Matt along, Jason could keep an eye on him and make sure he didn't ruin their chances of success through incompetence, impulsiveness, or sheer contrariness.

Jason wasn't too fond of the idea of Dixon being a member of the group either. The rancher equaled Matt for arrogance and was used to giving orders, not taking them. Besides, it had only been a couple of weeks since Matt and Dixon had been trying their damnedest to kill each other. So far, they had seemed to call a truce during this emergency, but how long would it last before they blew up at each other again?

Dixon had one thing going for him that Matt didn't, though—experience. Dixon had lived on the frontier for a long time. He had fought bandits in the past, as well as Apaches. You didn't have to like a man to be able to depend on him in a fight. Jason knew he could depend on Dixon not to cut and run, no matter what the odds.

With each man riding one of the spare horses and leading another, the scouts moved out after only a short rest. None of them had slept any the night before, but they were all too keyed up to worry about that. Fear for the lives of the captives and hatred for the scavengers in human form that had descended on Fury would keep them going.

The temperature rose along with the sun. By mid-morning, they were baking as they followed the trail left by the outlaws. The vegetation had grown more sparse, and for the most part the landscape was an ugly gray, brown, and tan. Jason set as fast a pace as he dared. Under these conditions, extra care had to be taken with the horses.

Jason thought they were angling more toward the southwest now, and when he asked Wash about that, the old-timer confirmed it. Pointing to some rugged hills in the distance, he said, "Them's the tail end o' the Cimarron Mountains. Won't be long now before we get to the border. You still figure on crossin' it?"

"We're going wherever Alba goes," Jason replied without hesitation.

"Might be hope for you yet, boy," Dixon commented. "A real man does what has to be did, without worryin' all the time about rules and shit like that."

Jason frowned. "I never said people shouldn't follow rules. But sometimes you have to think more about what needs to be done."

"That's what I said, ain't it?"

Jason didn't continue the debate. He wouldn't have anyway, but he was spared the necessity of doing so by Wash saying, "Take a look over yonder, Jason. See that dust?"

Jason saw it, all right. The plume of dust rising to the east was large enough to signify quite a few riders, but it was in the wrong place and not large enough to be coming from Alba's band of thieves and killers.

"Who can that be?" Jason asked with a frown.

"We keep goin', I reckon we'll find out. Our trails are gonna cross 'fore too much longer."

"What if they're Apaches?" Matt asked.

Dixon snorted. "You won't find that many 'Paches on horseback."

"Could be that some of Alba's men split off from the main bunch," Zachary Morton suggested, "and now they're comin' back."

That was a good example of why Jason had wanted Zachary to come along. The old man was cool-headed and had an insightful way of looking at things.

"What do you want to do, Jason?" Wash asked.

"We'll push on," Jason decided. "But if they're Alba's men, we'll have a fight on our hands." Grim-faced, he added, "We can't afford to let any of them get away and warn Alba that we're back here. We want him thinking that no one is pursuing him."

"Kill 'em all, you mean," Dixon said.

Jason nodded. "That's what I mean." It was a ruthless plan, but by raiding Fury as they had and carrying out such wanton slaughter, the outlaws had lost whatever right they might have had to any consideration. As far as Jason was concerned, they were mad dogs and had to be dealt with that way.

However, as the two groups of riders converged, it became obvious that a battle wouldn't be in the offing. Wash pulled a spyglass from his saddlebags, pulled it out to its full length, and studied the other bunch. "I see blue uniforms," he announced. "Them are soldier boys. Looks like a cavalry patrol."

"That's good news!" Matt said. "They can help us hunt down Alba's gang."

Jason's instincts told him not to be so sure about that. With the other riders closing in from the east, he raised a hand in a signal for his companions to halt. They waited there for the cavalry to come up to them.

That took only a couple of minutes. The blue-clad riders emerged from the dust with the officer leading them calling a halt just as Jason had. He rode forward slowly and brought his mount to a stop about ten feet from Jason's.

Without any preamble, the lieutenant said, "Who are you men, and what are you doing out here?"

"We're part of a posse from the town of Fury," Jason said. "I'm Marshal Jason Fury. We're chasing a band of outlaws led by Juan Alba. They raided the town yesterday and kidnapped four women. The women are still prisoners, and we aim to rescue them."

"Just the five of you?" the lieutenant asked.

"Another thirty men are coming up behind us. We're advance scouts." Jason looked at the fifteen troopers behind the officer. "We'd surely be pleased to have your help, Lieutenant. Your force and ours combined would a match for Alba's gang."

The lieutenant snapped, "I can tell you right now, Marshal, that's not going to happen. We're not going after Alba, and neither are you."

Chapter 23

For a couple of seconds, Jason was so shocked that all he could do was stare at the officer. When he recovered his voice, he asked, "What the hell are you talking about?"

Before the lieutenant could answer, Matt MacDonald spoke up. "I could have told you you were wasting your breath talking to this stiff-necked little tin god, Fury. He doesn't do anything unless it's right by the book."

The lieutenant gave Matt a thin, cold smile. "Mr. MacDonald, isn't it? I recall how incensed you became when I refused to interfere in a purely civilian matter."

Dixon glared over at Matt. "You tried to sic the cavalry on me?" he guessed.

Jason slashed the air with his hand. "Never mind about that now. Are you refusing to help us, Lieutenant? Because you can't say *this* is a purely civilian matter. American citizens have been kidnapped!"

"That's a matter for law enforcement, not the army."

"Damn it, Fury was invaded! Alba's a Mexican, and so are some of his men!"

"They don't represent the government of Mexico, however, so their raid doesn't qualify as an act of war requiring military intervention. As I said, this is something for law enforcement to deal with."

"But you just said we couldn't chase Alba either!"

"Not any farther, no." The lieutenant turned his head. "Sergeant Halligan, how far are we from the border?"

The grizzled old sergeant seemed reluctant to answer, but he said, "About a mile, sir."

The lieutenant turned back to Jason's group. "So, I suppose that technically, you can pursue the outlaws for another mile, but then you'll have to stop. You're not allowed to cross the border into Mexico."

"But they've got our women, for God's sake!" Matt burst out.

The lieutenant shook his head. "That's unfortunate, but it doesn't make any difference. The border is still the border."

Wash glared at him. "Who's gonna stop us?"

"I am, of course," the lieutenant replied. "In fact, I'm going to ride along with you, just to make certain that you men don't attempt to make an illegal incursion into Mexican territory."

Jason struggled with the urge to pull his gun and blow the officious little son of a bitch right out of the saddle. That might make him feel better for a second, but the next second those troopers would probably riddle him with bullets, so it wouldn't accomplish anything except to get him good and dead. And dead, he couldn't help Megan, Jenny, Mrs. Morelli, and Abigail Krimp.

But he couldn't allow the lieutenant to prevent them from going after Alba's bunch either. Maybe they ought to pretend to turn around, Jason thought, then cross over into Mexico later after the patrol had moved on elsewhere.

That could cause a considerable delay, though, and Jason wasn't sure they could afford to do that. Already, every moment that the prisoners were in the hands of the outlaws gnawed at Jason's guts, and he knew the other men felt the same way.

"Lieutenant Carter," Sergeant Halligan said, "beggin' your pardon, sir, but I just spotted somethin' in them hills over yonder." The veteran noncom pointed at some low hills several miles distant.

Lieutenant Carter raised himself in the stirrups and peered in that direction. "What was it, Sergeant? What did you see?"

"Some flashes o' bright color, red and blue mostly. Like the sashes and headbands them 'Paches we're chasin' would wear." Halligan took a pair of field glasses from a pouch attached to his saddle and lifted them to his eyes. He peered through them for several moments, then said, "Yep, definite Apache sign."

Carter held out a hand and snapped his fingers. "Let me see those glasses."

Halligan handed them over. Carter raised himself in his stirrups, pressed the lenses to his eyes, and squinted through them. He moved his head from side to side as he searched the hills. Finally, he said, "I don't see anything except rocks and dirt and a few ugly bushes, Sergeant."

"Yes, sir, but you know what they say 'bout 'Paches. When you don't see 'em, that's when they're most likely to be there."

Carter frowned. "Yes. Yes, of course. Let me take another look." He studied the hills some more and then said with a tone of rising excitement in his voice, "Yes, I see what you mean, Sergeant. There are definitely Apaches up there!"

Jason glanced over at Wash and saw that the old-timer was struggling not to grin. Even under the circumstances, Jason felt the same way. Lieutenant Carter was so anxious to find some Apaches and ride to glory in battle that he was willing to make himself *believe* that he saw Apaches in the hills, whether there were really any there or not.

"What're we gonna do, Lieutenant?" Sergeant Halligan asked.

Carter handed the field glasses back to him and frowned, obviously torn between imposing his will on the posse from Fury and giving chase to the Indians he thought were in the hills.

"Our orders were to seek out and engage the hostiles," he said at last. "Therefore, it's clear that we should proceed to the hills and find those Apaches you spotted, Sergeant." Carter turned a stern glare toward Jason and the other scouts. "But I'm giving you men firm orders not to even approach the border between the United States and Mexico, and under no circumstances are you to cross that border. Is that understood?"

"Understood," Jason said. He hoped he sounded solemn enough to fool the lieutenant. Just because he understood the orders Carter had just issued, that didn't mean he had an intention of following them.

"All right then." Carter turned to Halligan. "Sergeant, are you and the men ready to proceed?"

"Ready, sir," Halligan replied.

Carter lifted a hand and waved it forward. "Patrol . . . *ho-o-o-o!*"

As the troopers trotted their horses past the posse, Halligan glanced over at Jason with a twinkle in his eyes. He quirked one corner of his mouth in a half-grin and lowered the eye on that side in a wink. Jason gave him a brief nod of gratitude, fully aware of what the sergeant had done for them.

"Ain't they purty?" Wash muttered as the soldiers rode past. "All they need's a brass band playin'."

"If they do ever find any Apaches, that shavetail will probably get them all killed," Jason said when they were out of earshot.

Wash shook his head. "Naw, that ol' sarge'll find a way to keep most of 'em alive anyway. If it wasn't for fellas like him, the whole damn army'd fall apart."

Jason knew what the old-timer meant. Even though he had been an officer during the war, and a paper-pusher at that, he had seen enough of military life to learn that experienced noncommissioned officers like Sergeant Halligan were the glue that held the whole thing together.

They watched until the patrol had ridden out of sight; then Jason lifted his horse's reins and said, "Let's go. We've still got some outlaws to catch."

Unlike the Rio Grande in Texas, the border between Arizona Territory and the Mexican state of Sonora was just another hot, sandy stretch of ground. In fact, Jason didn't even know they had crossed it until Wash said, "Well, I reckon we're in Old Mexico now."

"We sure are," Dixon agreed. "I've chased rustlers down here more'n once. Bastards'd raid from below the border, wide-loop some o' my cows, and chouse 'em back down here." He gave a snort of disdain. "I didn't let no damn border stop me from chasin' them varmints neither."

Jason asked, "How far into Mexico have you been?"

"Well, not more'n a few miles," the rancher admitted.

"Then you don't know what's up ahead?"

"I can make a pretty good guess." Dixon waved a hand at their surroundings. "More o' this."

"Leastways until we reach the Gulf," Wash added.

There wasn't much to see. The hills, which hadn't amounted to much in the first place, had been left behind on the other side of the border. Except for an occasional depression, the landscape was completely flat, covered with tufts of tough bunchgrass, scrubby mesquite trees that looked more like bushes than actual trees, and clumps of cactus. Here and there, one of the big saguaro cactuses lifted its arms toward the silvery-blue heavens. The heat was oppressive, the sun like a giant fist pounding down on them.

"Those poor women," Jason muttered as he rode. "They must be burning up in this heat."

"So am I," Matt said. "We need to find some shade and let the animals cool off."

Jason figured Matt was less concerned about the horses and more about himself, but that didn't make what he said any less true. Their mounts would wear out even faster in the heat. The problem was, there was no shade to be found anywhere in this wasteland.

By the time the sun was directly overhead, they had stopped and switched mounts a couple of times. All of the horses were tired now, so Jason called another halt and said, "We'll rest here for an hour."

"An hour!" Matt said. "We can't afford to waste that much time."

"You were the one who said we needed to stop for a while," Jason reminded him.

"Yeah, if we could find some shade. What good is it going to do sitting here in the sun?"

Matt might have a point there, but Jason was damned if he was going to admit it. He said, "Everybody dismount. Give your horses a little water. Better not drink any yourselves, though," he added as he watched Matt pulling the cork from the neck of a canteen. "No telling when we'll find drinkable water again."

Wash, Zachary, and Dixon hunkered on their heels in the shadows cast by some of the horses. Jason and Matt followed the example set by the older men. It helped a little.

Jason was fighting off weariness, and the lassitude brought on by the heat didn't help matters any. He hadn't slept since before Juan Alba, the Scourge of the Borderlands, rode into Fury, shooting and burning and killing. It would have been easy to stretch out on the ground, hard and rocky though it might be, and go to sleep. Instead, he forced himself to stay awake as the time dragged by.

Finally he said, "That's enough," even though he knew it might not be. "Let's get moving again."

"Better wait a while yet," Wash advised. "The horses are just startin' to get their wind back."

Jason frowned but nodded. "All right. I'm ready to ride, though."

"I hate to agree with you about anything, Fury," Matt said, "but so am I."

Jason looked over at him, then at Dixon, and said, "Don't you think that if the two of you can work together like this, you ought to be able to get along?"

Dixon's response was hard and immediate. "I'm here 'cause I got no use for bandits and I want to help them women. It don't have anything to do with this damn squatter."

"I'm not a squatter," Matt said. "I have just as much right to that land as you do, Dixon. More, since I plan to file a legal claim on it, when I get around to it."

"Ain't you ever heard o' open range?"

"I've heard of it, but those days are soon going to be over."

"Not if I've got anything to say about it," Dixon declared with an ominous scowl.

"That's just it," Matt said. "You *don't* have anything to say about it, not legally. That's what I've been trying to get you to understand."

Wash said, "You two knock it off, why don't you? For God's sake, anybody who can squabble in heat like this has got to be one o' the stubbornest, contrariest critters on the face o' the earth."

"You can call me stubborn and contrary if you want to," Dixon said. "I don't give a damn. I'm just standin' up for what's rightfully mine."

"So am I," Matt said. "Only I'm right and you're wrong."

Dixon's hand edged toward the butt of his gun. "Why, I oughta—"

"Stop it, the both of you," Jason snapped. "If you want to

tangle with somebody, I'm sure Alba and his cutthroats would be glad to oblige."

That quieted them down, and a few minutes later, as if by mutual consent, the men rose and started switching saddles from the horses they had been riding to the extra mounts.

It was time to get back on the trail.

Chapter 24

Jenny still sniffled from time to time, but at least she had gotten over the worst of the crying. Megan was grateful for that. She didn't blame Jenny for being scared, but bawling didn't help anything.

The outlaws had spent a second night on the trail, and from things Megan had overheard them saying, she knew that they were well across the border and deep in Mexico. She didn't think that would stop Jason and some of the other men from Fury from coming after them, but it would prevent the would-be rescuers from getting any official help, say, from the army.

Would a posse of citizens be enough to stand up to Alba and his men and free the prisoners? Megan didn't know. She could only hope and pray that it would be.

Since the night before, when Alba had ordered his men to leave the women alone, things had gotten better. Flores still sneaked a hand over Megan's breasts every now and then as they rode, and he liked to press his arm against the underside of them. But there was no blatant molestation carried out against any of the prisoners.

Their main concerns now were exhaustion, exposure, and the terrible heat. Megan saw that Jenny, Olympia, and Abigail were all badly sunburned, and she could tell from the way her face felt that she was too. None of them were accustomed to such arduous conditions. Thirst was a constant demon torturing them, and their muscles ached from all the riding.

On the afternoon of their third day of captivity, Megan husked through her parched throat, "When are we going to get where we're going?"

Flores chuckled. "You are anxious to arrive, little one?"

His amusement made some of Megan's usual fire return. "I'm anxious to get off this damned horse," she said, "and away from you."

"Do not be so sure of that. Maybe when you find out what Juan Alba has in store for you, you won't mind old Flores's company so much, eh?"

Megan wouldn't have thought it was possible under these blistering conditions, but a chill went through her at his words. *"What Juan Alba has in store for you . . ."* What could that mean?

Megan didn't know, but obviously it wasn't anything good.

A short time later, she began to notice a difference in the air. It was still hot, but maybe not quite so oppressive. Knowing that she shouldn't but unable to stop herself, she ran her tongue over her dried-out lips and realized to her shock that she tasted salt on them. That taste hadn't been there before. A breeze picked up, blowing toward them, and it had an unidentifiable smell to it, a faint tang that was odd but somehow slightly familiar.

They were approaching a large body of salt water, Megan suddenly realized. She wasn't that knowledgeable about the geography of this region. What could it be? The Pacific Ocean? It didn't seem possible that they could have reached the Pacific in three days of riding.

She cast her mind back to the maps she had seen her father and brother studying before the family began its journey west. It seemed to Megan that she recalled some sort of large bay or gulf in Mexico, separating most of the country from a peninsula that jutted down south of California. She wasn't that good at telling which way they were going by looking at the stars, and anyway, the past two nights she had been too tired to study those celestial guideposts. But she *thought* they were going south by southwest, which would take them toward that gulf she recalled from the maps. . . .

"We're almost there, aren't we?" she said.

Flores stiffened. "What you mean by that? How do you know where we're going?"

Megan didn't answer him. Let him wonder about something for a change.

Flores muttered in Spanish under his breath, but didn't press her on the issue. The group pressed on, not moving as fast now as they had at first. Everyone was tired—the men, the horses, and certainly the prisoners.

The land had been flat and featureless for a long time, but now Megan saw something shimmering up ahead of them and thought for a second that they had reached the sea. It wasn't water she saw, though, she realized as they drew closer, but rather sand. White sand. Great hills of it that rolled and shifted with the wind. The land dropped off some so that only the tops of those sand hills were visible from where the riders were, but as they approached Megan got a good look at the dunes. They were quite impressive, stretching out in front of the group for miles and miles.

"Good Lord!" Abigail exclaimed from the back of the horse she shared with one of the outlaws. "You can't intend to take us across that wasteland!"

"It's not as bad as it looks," the man told her. "We'll be out of the sand hills by nightfall."

"Anyway," Flores put in, "there's water out there, if you know where to find it, and Juan Alba does."

The pace became even slower as the horses slogged out into the shifting sand. The group of outlaws stretched out into a long line, riding two or at most three abreast so that they could stay on the harder-packed dirt of a trail that twisted and turned sinuously through the dunes as if it had been laid out by a demented snake.

Megan became aware of an odd sound. It was a low-pitched, never-ending hiss, something else that put her in mind of a snake. After a while, she figured out that it was the sound of the sand moving, millions and millions of the tiny grains sliding over each other as they were pushed here and there by the eternal wind. And it wasn't really a hiss either, but more of a whisper.

Whispering sands . . . telling bloody secrets that only the endless dunes knew. The thought made a shudder go through her. Flores laughed and tightened his arm around her.

"Men go mad when they are lost out here on foot," he said. "But that won't happen to you, little one. Flores will take good care of you."

Megan didn't doubt that. The monstrous Juan Alba would probably kill Flores if anything happened to the valuable prisoner he was guarding.

Jenny began to sob again while they were in the sand dunes. Megan ignored her. She loved Jenny like a sister, but she had run out of patience with the younger girl. They were all in this terrible predicament, not just Jenny, but Olympia and Abigail weren't crying all the time, even though they probably felt like it.

The sandy wasteland ended as abruptly as it began. The riders emerged from the dunes onto a broad, grassy slope that led down to a series of rocky cliffs overlooking a vast, rolling sea. Of course, it wasn't really the sea, but rather the gulf Megan remembered from the maps. The Gulf of California, was that what it was called? She thought that was right.

The salt tang in the air was even stronger now. The moisture was a blessed relief to her blistered lips and skin.

Reaching the gulf meant there was nowhere else for them to go. This had to be their destination. And as that thought went through Megan's brain, she saw the stone house rearing itself on the cliff, rising like some sort of medieval castle to overlook the endless waves that pounded on the rocks below.

"There it is," Flores said. "The *casa* of Juan Alba. Your new home, little one, at least for a short time."

Megan didn't know what he meant by that, but again . . . it couldn't be anything good.

She had no idea who had built the massive, brooding house, but it couldn't have been Juan Alba. The place had an air of antiquity about it that said it had been here long before Alba's loathsome presence had taken it over. And it would remain standing long after these outlaws had ceased to sully it.

None of which helped Megan, Jenny, Abigail, and Olympia one bit. No matter how long the house had been here, no matter how long it would remain after they were gone, right now Alba was the master of this *casa*. His word was law.

The women were taken from the horses, hustled into the house through a courtyard, and led down a narrow flight of stone steps that ended in a dank hallway with several small chambers on either side. Each of the rooms had a heavy door with only a small barred window in it.

As soon as Megan laid eyes on the cells, she knew what was about to happen. She and the other captives were about to be locked up here. At that realization, a new terror welled up inside her. She hadn't realized that she had such a fear of small, enclosed spaces until this moment. But it was all she could do not to scream as Flores forced her into one of the chambers.

She turned on him, unable to contain her terror. She had been so calm, so cooperative, during her captivity that her sudden movements took him by surprise. One of her hands shot at his face, the fingernails clawing for his eyes, while the other hand fumbled at the butt of the Colt on his hip.

Flores let out a curse and recoiled from Megan's unexpected attack. He gasped in pain as her fingernails drew red streaks down his face. She felt the walnut grips of the gun, and had just closed the fingers of her other hand around it, when something exploded in her face. Pain filled her head so that she was barely aware of being knocked backward. She slammed into the stone wall of the cell and bounced off, falling to her knees. Landing on the hard floor like that caused her even more pain.

"What the hell!" Flores exclaimed. "You gone crazy, little red? You like to put Flores's eyes out!"

She looked up at him, panting from pain and anger. "I wish I had, you bastard," she grated. "I wish I'd gotten your gun and blown a hole in you!"

Flores took off his bandanna and dabbed at the bloody scratches on his face. In a worried voice, he said, "Don't tell Juan Alba I punched you, all right? You took me by surprise. I didn't expect you to fight. You got more sense than to think you can get away." He glanced around at the close confines of the cell. "Oh. You don't like it in here, no? Don't worry. There are no rats or anything like that, and you got a window you can look out." He pointed to a small opening, barred like the one in the door, that was high on one wall. "You can even see the water. It won't be so bad. And it won't be for too long."

"Then what?"

Flores shook his head. He wasn't going to tell her anything else. He kept his hand on the butt of his gun as he backed toward the door.

"Somebody will bring you something to eat and drink later. You rest now."

Megan wasn't sure she would ever rest again. As Flores moved out into the hall and began swinging the door shut, gibbering devils ran along her nerves and through her brain. She closed her eyes, squeezed them tight shut, unwilling to see the barrier to her freedom closing.

But she heard it. Lord help her, as the heavy slam of the door went through her like a shot, she heard it.

Chapter 25

By nightfall of the first full day of pursuit, Wash estimated that the scouts from the posse had cut into the lead, but the outlaws of Juan Alba's gang were still well ahead of them.

"I didn't figure on them pushin' so hard once they crossed the border," Wash commented as the group stopped to rest their horses and once again wait for the moon to rise. "Fact is, I sorta thought they would've got to their hideout by now."

"They're headed for the Gulf of California," Jason said, putting into words the hunch that had been dogging him for quite a while.

"Why do you say that?" Matt asked with a skeptical frown.

"I don't know. It's just a feeling I have."

Matt's snort testified to how much faith he put in Jason's feelings.

"You might be right, Jason," Wash said. "I don't think there's much else in this direction *except* the Gulf."

They pushed on when the moon rose. As they followed the trail left by the outlaws, Zachary said, "I hope the rest of the men were able to get across the border without that stiff-necked cavalry lieutenant stopping them."

"I reckon Sergeant Halligan led that patrol on a merry

chase through the hills," Wash said with a chuckle. "He knew that we're the only chance those gals have."

Matt said, "It would have been easier if those soldiers had come along with us. I intend to pay a visit to Camp Grant and have a word with Lieutenant Carter's commanding officer when we get back. He's neglected his duty for the last time."

Jason didn't think talking to Carter's commanding officer would do a bit of good, because according to army regulations, the lieutenant had been right to refuse to cross the border, or to let civilians cross it when they were looking for trouble. Such things could cause international incidents, if someone cared about that.

Which Jason didn't right now. All that mattered to him was getting Megan, Jenny, and the other two women back safely.

The scouts were able to push on through the night, but in the morning exhaustion finally caught up to men and horses both. While they were stopped to allow the animals to rest, the men took turns sleeping. No one got more than a couple of hours of slumber, but as tired as they all were, even that much sleep was more than welcome. No one felt really rested when they took up the trail again, but at least they didn't have the blind staggers anymore.

Late that afternoon, they came to some sand dunes that stretched out in front of them apparently endlessly. The tracks left by the gang's horses led right up to the edge of the waste-land and then vanished. Jason let out a groan of despair as he reined to a halt.

Wash shook his head and muttered a curse. "Reckon the wind wiped out their tracks within an hour or so o' them ridin' through here. The way that sand moves in the wind, nothin' looks the same for very long."

"What do we do now?" Matt asked. "We've come this far. We can't just give up."

"Nobody said anything about giving up," Jason responded. "Wash, let's assume that they headed through these dunes on a relatively straight line. Can you do the same thing?"

Wash frowned and tugged on his mustaches. "Thing is, you can't go straight across dunes like this. Horses'll bog down in the worst of it. You got to find the places that're packed the hardest and follow them. I reckon I can do that, but if it'll bring us out in the same place them outlaws wound up . . . well, I just can't say about that, Jason."

"We don't have any other choice. Has everyone still got water, in case we're stuck in there for a while?"

The men checked their canteens. Each of them still contained at least some water, sloshing back and forth as the men shook the canteens.

"At least it'll be dark after a while," Dixon said. "We won't have to cross that hell durin' the day, when the heat would be at its worst."

"Yes, we should be thankful for small favors," Zachary put in.

"I'll be thankful when we have those women back," Jason said. "Let's go."

As darkness fell, the landscape around the five men took on an eerie aspect. The dunes rose like humpbacked monsters, and the sand muffled the horses' hoofbeats until they couldn't be heard. The night was not silent, however. It was filled with the ceaseless whisper of sand shifting in the wind. As the moon rose, the dunes shone like silver. Blistering hot at first, they gave up that heat quickly in the dry air, so that the wind took on a chill that raised gooseflesh on Jason's skin. He was going to be very glad when they got through these towering hills of sand.

Although the dunes seemed endless, they weren't, of course. Sometime far into the night, the riders came to the far edge of the wasteland. They found themselves at the top of a gentle, grassy slope. As they reined in, Wash said, "Listen."

Jason heard the rumble and roar of waves. "The ocean," he breathed.

"The Gulf anyway," Wash agreed. "It ain't far off."

Matt spoke up with a note of excitement in his voice. "Look over there, to the right."

The rest of the men looked in that direction and saw a faint yellow light, like the glow of a candle through a window. It appeared to be about a mile away, maybe a little less.

Jason turned his head, peered in the other direction, and saw nothing but darkness as far as the eye could see. Facing northwest again, because that was the direction in which the glow lay, he said, "That light must be coming from Alba's hideout. There doesn't seem to be anything else along this coast."

Matt urged his horse into motion. "Come on!"

"Hold it a minute," Wash said. Matt reined in, but he did it with an impatient glare at the old-timer. Wash went on. "We can't just go gallopin' up to the place. We got to approach it careful and quietlike."

"Alba's bound to have guards posted," Jason added. "If they spot us, we won't stand a chance, and then we won't be able to help the prisoners."

"Speaking of that," Zachary put in, "once we make sure that light is coming from Alba's hideout, how will we lead the rest of the posse here?"

Jason pondered that for a moment and then said, "Somebody will have to go back across the dunes to meet them and lead them through. Wash, I reckon that'll be your job."

The old-timer bristled. "Why me?"

"Because you're the best man for that chore, and you'll be more likely to be able to carry it out than the rest of us."

"You're just tryin' to cheat me out o' my share o' the fightin'," Wash grumbled.

"I hope there won't be any fighting until you get back with the rest of the posse," Jason pointed out. "If there is, it'll mean that everything's gone wrong."

"All right, all right. I guess the first thing we need to do is make sure that's the place we're lookin' for."

Jason heeled his horse into a walk. "That's right. But we'll take it slow and easy."

The thought that they were probably within a mile of the prisoners chafed at Jason and made him want to go charging ahead recklessly just like Matt would if there was no one there to restrain him. He reined in that impulse and forced himself to remain calm and cool.

They followed the top of the slope, with the sand dunes to their right and the cliffs that lined the shore of the Gulf to their left. When they were within a few hundred yards of the light, Jason stopped his horse and signaled for the others to do likewise. He swung down from the saddle, as did the other four men.

They were close enough now to make out the dark, looming shape of a huge house perched on the cliff, overlooking the water. "Probably built a long time ago by some Spanish grandee who had a ranch in these parts," Wash whispered. "Either it was abandoned and Alba took it over, or he killed all the folks who lived there and moved in."

The light came from a window in a tower at one end of the building. As Jason stared at it, he couldn't help but wonder if the prisoners were locked up in that tower. He decided it was unlikely—they were probably down below in a dungeon; that gloomy pile of rocks looked like it ought to have a dungeon—but the thought went through his mind anyway.

"Now what?" Matt asked.

"We get closer on foot," Jason said. "Wash and I do anyway. The rest of you stay here and look after the horses."

Matt shook his head. "I'm coming along too."

Jason didn't trust Matt not to do something that would give them away, so he said flatly, "No, you're not. You're staying here with Dixon and Zachary. I don't want to have to worry about you stumbling over your own feet and warning those outlaws that we're here."

Matt's breath hissed between his teeth, and his voice was tight with anger as he said, "One of these days, Fury, you and me are going to settle this. I'm sick and tired of you and your insults."

Dixon chuckled. "You've just got scores to settle with everybody, don't you, boy?"

"That's enough," Jason said before Matt could reply. "If we start fighting among ourselves, we won't have any chance of getting those women out of there. Both of you just let it alone until we get back home."

Matt and Dixon glared at each other for a few seconds before Matt shrugged and turned away. "I'll stay here," he told Jason in a sullen voice, "but I don't like it."

"You don't have to. Come on, Wash."

They gave their horses' reins to Dixon and Zachary, then started down the slope toward the big house on foot. There was no cover here, and although the moon was low, it still gave off quite a bit of light. Anybody studying the grassy slope might spot them approaching the house. Jason and Wash dropped to their hands and knees, and then a little farther on, to their bellies. The grass was tall enough to give them some concealment.

They crawled to within fifty yards of a pair of heavy wooden gates that opened into a courtyard. They were close enough to hear some drunken laughter that floated through one of the windows from somewhere inside the house. Wash had brought along his spyglass. He pressed it to his eye as they lay there silent and motionless.

A few minutes later Jason saw movement in the courtyard. Wash nudged him in the ribs and handed him the spyglass. Jason pressed his eye to it, and in the moonlight he saw a man in a big sombrero walk across the courtyard. The man had a rifle canted over his shoulder, and bandoliers of ammunition were crisscrossed over his chest.

Wash put his mouth close to Jason's ear and breathed, "Fella's got to be a guard."

Jason nodded. He kept the spyglass trained on the courtyard, and about ten minutes later he saw another man stroll across the open space. This one was an American, or at least he wore a high-crowned Stetson. He also carried a rifle.

"Alba's probably got several more men posted around the place," Jason whispered. "We can't attack the place without them knowing that we're coming."

"And if we can't take 'em by surprise, they'll fort up in there and we'll never get 'em out."

Jason knew that Wash's gloomy prediction was right. He thought as hard as he could, his brain racing, as he tried to come up with a way to rescue the prisoners. He would have loved to wipe out the band of outlaws in the process, to settle the score for what they had done to the town of Fury, but that might not be possible. Saving the women had to come first.

"There's only one way to have any element of surprise at all," he decided at last.

"How's that?" Wash asked.

Jason nodded toward the fortress-like house. "Somebody's got to get in there, free the girls, and then provide a distraction that will allow the rest of the posse to have a chance of overpowering Alba's men."

"Sort of like stickin' your head right in a hornet's nest, ain't it?"

Jason nodded. "That's why I intend to do it myself."

Chapter 26

By reaching up and grasping the bars in the window, Megan could pull herself up on her toes far enough to see out the opening. From there, she could see the blue-gray waves rolling in from the Gulf and the sun lowering toward them, but that was all. She strained to lift herself even farther, until she got her chin over the sill and pressed her face against the iron bars.

Space fell away below her in a dizzying drop. She couldn't see the rocks at the base of the cliff, but she heard the waves crashing against them and knew that there was nothing outside this window except several hundred feet of empty air with death waiting at the bottom. There would be no escape this way.

Not that she could have gotten out through the window anyway, she told herself. It was so small that the only way she would have fit through it was if every bone in her body was crushed.

When the muscles in her arms began to ache and tremble from supporting her weight, she let herself down to the floor of the cell again. Since there was no bunk, she slumped all the way down to a sitting position and propped her back against the hard stone wall.

Overwhelming feelings of despair and helplessness threatened to swallow her whole. She couldn't escape, and no one would come to save her. If by some chance Jason Fury managed to follow the gang all the way from Arizona Territory, he wouldn't stand a chance against Juan Alba's men, even if he brought a posse with him. The settlers were just ordinary men; they couldn't survive a fight against a wolf pack like Alba's gang.

It was just luck that she and the other women hadn't been assaulted repeatedly already. That luck couldn't last. Now that the outlaws had arrived at their destination, it was only a matter of time before they would take their pleasure with the helpless captives.

Maybe it was a good thing she couldn't fit through that window, Megan thought. If she was able to, she would be tempted to squeeze out through the narrow opening and launch herself into the empty air. A few seconds of terror as she fell, and then it would all be over. She was sure she would be killed instantly when she landed on the rocks below.

But that wasn't going to happen, she reminded herself, so she might as well not even think about it. Instead, no matter how hopeless things looked, she ought to be trying to think of some way to get out of this mess.

Despite her intentions, she surprised herself by drifting off to sleep. She had no idea how long she drowsed there, leaning against the wall, but when the sound of loud, hollow footsteps approaching the cell jolted her awake, the light was gone from the window and utter darkness shrouded the chamber.

Megan's heart hammered in her chest. Even though the footsteps were just footsteps, there was something ominous about them. She knew that whoever was approaching the cells didn't have anything good in mind for her or the other prisoners.

She could tell now that there were several sets of footsteps in the corridor. A light appeared, outlining the little window in the door. One of the visitors had to be carrying a lantern. The footsteps came to a stop, and a second later a key rattled in the padlock that held the door closed. Megan heard the lock snap open. The door swung back, creaking on its hinges.

"Come out, little red," Flores ordered. "You will not be harmed if you do as you are told."

Megan put her hands against the rough stone wall and pushed herself to her feet, but she didn't make any move toward the open door. She couldn't see the men in the corridor, but the light cast by the lantern formed large, grotesque shadows that Megan could see. When she didn't emerge from the cell, Flores leaned into the doorway, holding a gun in his hand.

He grinned when he saw her shadowy form huddled against the wall. Crooking a finger on his empty hand, he said, "Come on. I'm not going to hurt you. I promise."

"Wh-why should I believe you?"

He pressed his open hand to his breast as if he were offended. "Have I spoken a single falsehood to you, little one? In the time we have been together, have I lied to you?"

They hadn't been "together." She had been his prisoner. That was all.

But it was true that he had promised she wouldn't be harmed if she cooperated, and so far that had been the case.

"What about the others?" she asked warily. "Will they be all right too?"

"Of course. I have come to fetch all four of you. Juan Alba wishes to speak with you. And there will be food and drink as well."

Megan hadn't realized just how hungry and thirsty she really was until he said that. She took a step toward the door without even thinking about what she was doing, then stopped short.

"Come on," Flores said again, grinning at her. "You know you can trust me."

Megan knew nothing of the sort, but even if this was some sort of trick, she doubted that she could be worse off than she already was, stuck in this cell with no food or water or even a blanket.

She took a deep breath and walked out into the hall.

Half-a-dozen men were gathered there besides Flores. One held the lantern while the others all gripped rifles. Megan allowed herself a smile and said, "You must think four defenseless women are mighty dangerous."

"My orders are to take no chances with you," Flores said. "You and the others are very important to Juan Alba."

Megan couldn't imagine why four women from a small settlement in Arizona Territory would be of any importance to the bandit chieftain, but she supposed if she were patient she would find out. Flores had said that he was taking them to see Alba, after all.

While Megan stood there with the other outlaws keeping an eye on her, Flores unlocked the other cells. Olympia Morelli and Abigail Krimp came out without much hesitation. They must have overheard Flores's conversation with Megan and knew that they weren't in any immediate danger.

But Flores had to go into Jenny's cell and carry her out. She fought him every step of the way, and screamed until he clapped a rough hand over her mouth and shut her up that way.

Megan took a step toward them and said, "Don't hurt her."

Flores thrust Jenny at her. "You calm her down, then! If I take her to Juan Alba acting like this, he will be angry!"

None of them wanted that, Megan realized. She put her arms around Jenny and held the younger girl in a tight embrace. Jenny struggled against her for a moment too, before she seemed to realize that it was now Megan who held her and not the outlaw.

"It'll be all right, Jenny," Megan said. "Just settle down. I won't let anything happen to you."

She hoped she would be able to keep that promise.

Flores and the other men herded the prisoners along the corridor and up a different flight of stairs than the one they had come down earlier. The staircase twisted back and forth on itself until Megan realized that they were climbing into some sort of tower. When they reached the landing at the top, they emerged into a large room dominated by a long, heavy table. Platters of food and pitchers of water and wine sat on the table, tantalizing the hungry, thirsty prisoners. The massive Juan Alba stood at the far end, his hamlike hands clasped behind his back.

"Ah, Flores," he said, "you have brought our guests."

Guests, Megan thought bitterly. That was a joke. They were prisoners, plain and simple, nothing more and nothing less.

Alba waved a hand at the heavy chairs around the table. "*Señoras y señoritas,* please to sit down. The food is for you."

The others hesitated, but Abigail said, "Hell, I'm not going to turn down food. Lord knows when we'll get a chance to eat again."

She went to the chair at the end of the table on Alba's left. Olympia sat next to her, and Megan and Jenny took the first two chairs to Alba's right. The outlaw leader lowered himself into a big chair at the head of the table.

Flores remained in the room, standing at the far end of the table in an attitude of respect, but the other men left. Clearly, the two men thought they could handle any problems with the prisoners. They would be right about that too, Megan admitted to herself. Either of the bandits would be a match for all four of them.

The platters contained baked fish and chicken and strips of roasted beef, along with tortillas and beans and peppers. Everything tasted wonderful to Megan as she and the others began to eat. An Indian woman came into the room from somewhere and poured cups of wine for them. Abigail drank hers down and held out her empty cup for more. She grinned across the table at Megan and Jenny and said, "Whatever's coming, maybe being drunk will help it go down easier."

Alba ran his blunt fingers through his jutting black beard and asked, "Have you been harmed, any of you?"

"You mean besides being dragged away from our homes and families and forced to ride for scores of miles with a band of greasy, stinking outlaws?" Olympia asked, surprising Megan a little with her spirit.

Flores grinned, but Alba scowled and said, "Yes, besides that, I mean."

"I'm fine," Olympia replied with a defiant tilt of her chin.

"Me too," Abigail said.

Alba turned his massive head toward Megan and Jenny. "And the *señoritas*?"

"Your men haven't molested us," Megan said, feeling her face grow warm as she did so.

Alba nodded. "*Bueno*. If any of those dogs had touched you, especially you two, I would have strung them up over a fire and stripped their skin off while they still lived."

That image made Megan a bit queasy, but she shoved the feeling aside and asked, "Why are we so important?"

"I can tell you that, sweetie," Abigail said before Alba could answer. "It's because you're virgins." She looked at the outlaw leader. "Isn't that right, big man?"

Alba's broad, burly shoulders rose and fell in a shrug of agreement.

"That means you'll fetch a higher price," Abigail went on.

"A . . ." Megan had to swallow. "A higher price?"

"Right. When he sells you to whoever he's got lined up to buy a couple of young white virgins."

Alba scowled at Abigail. "You are a crude woman."

"I just tell the truth as I see it. And I worked in enough whorehouses to know that the young, inexperienced girls always fetch the highest prices . . . especially the ones who have never been with a man before. You can still get a good price for women like Mrs. Morelli and me—no offense, Olympia, I'm not calling you a whore."

"None taken," Olympia murmured.

"Because we're white and still fairly young and good-looking, if I do say so myself," Abigail went on. "But we don't compare to a pair like these two."

Jenny's bottom lip started to quiver, and Megan was afraid she was going to start crying again. That wasn't going to help matters. She was relieved when Jenny took a deep breath and seemed to get hold of herself.

"Is all this true?" Megan asked.

Alba said, "Tomorrow morning, a ship will arrive. On it will be men from China—warlords, they call themselves—who have arranged to purchase American women to take back to their homeland. You four will be the first, but if the warlords are satisfied with the arrangement, it will continue." A grin stretched across the bandit's bearded face. "There are enough young women in Arizona Territory to make me a very rich man before I am through."

"To make all of us rich hombres, eh, Juan?" Flores put in.

Alba nodded. "You understand now why I ordered my men not to harm you."

Abigail said, "You didn't want to hurt the price you'd get for us."

"But what about after you turn us over to the Chinese?" Megan asked.

Alba's smile broadened into a grin. "After that, I will have my money, *señorita,* so what happens to you then will be no concern of mine."

This time, Jenny couldn't contain her sobs. She put her head down on the table and her back shook. Alba looked irritated.

Megan put an arm around Jenny's shoulders and told her to

stop it. "It won't happen," she whispered into Jenny's ears. "Jason and Matt and the other men from Fury will come to save us. You'll see."

But even as she spoke the words, she wasn't sure she believed them. In fact, she thought the chances of that happening were so slim that she found herself considering that leap from the window she had thought about earlier.

Plummeting hundreds of feet to her death was looking better all the time.

Chapter 27

The five men from Fury hunkered on their heels, back in the sand dunes a short distance so that there was no chance of them being spotted from Juan Alba's stronghold.

"You can't sneak in there by yourself, Jason," Wash argued. "You'll get caught, sure as shootin'."

"One man has more of a chance of not being noticed than two," Jason pointed out.

"Then let me go. I lived with the Injuns. I know how to move around quietlike."

"We need you to go back across the sand dunes and bring the rest of the posse."

"Damn it, send Dixon or Zach!"

Jason shook his head. "Like I said before, you're the best man for the job, Wash."

Matt spoke up. "Keough's right about one thing. It's too big a risk for you to go in there by yourself, Fury."

Jason looked at him and asked, "How do you figure that?"

"When the posse launches its attack, those men won't stand a chance unless something distracts the outlaws. And if you get caught, you won't be able to provide that distraction."

Jason frowned. Much as he hated to admit it, what Matt was saying made sense.

"Two men sneaking in doubles the chances of being caught, all right," Matt continued, "but it also doubles the chances of one of them succeeding."

"Boy may be a damn squatter, but he's right about that," Dixon said.

Matt was about to make some sort of angry retort to the rancher's acerbic comment when Jason stopped him with a curt gesture.

"Let it go, Matt. I guess you've got a point. Who's going with me?"

"I am," Matt said without hesitation. "I'm younger, and I can move faster if I have to."

Zachary said, "I hate to admit it, Jason, but I'm not as spry as I once was. I think Matt's right again."

Twice in one day, Jason thought. That had to be a record.

"Dixon, what do you think?"

"Well, we already know he's good at sneakin' around—"

"Damn it," Matt grated.

"All right," Jason cut in. "I guess it's settled. You and I will try to get in there somehow and provide a distraction. If we can find the women and set them free at the same time, so much the better."

"What sort of distraction?" Matt wanted to know.

Jason had to shake his head. "I can't tell you. I guess we'll just have to play it by ear."

"We better figure out some sort o' signals," Wash said, "so you'll know when the posse's out here ready to attack, and so we'll know when to hit the place."

Jason's mouth curved in a thin smile. "You'll know when to attack, because it'll be when all hell breaks loose inside the house. But you're right, we don't need to make a move until we know you're ready."

"Wait until dawn if you can. That's when them bastards'll be the groggiest. If I'm back with the posse, I'll take off this here red bandanna of mine and lay it out on the grass where you can see it. If it's not there, you'll know to hold off . . . if you can."

Jason nodded. It was an arrangement that was full of uncertainties and great risks, but it was the best they could do.

Jason and Matt left their hats and rifles with the other men, taking only their holstered revolvers and a knife apiece. With Jason in the lead, they crawled toward the big stone house, staying low in the grass.

Fear gnawed at Jason's mind. Not fear for himself so much, although he knew he was heading straight into a very perilous situation. He was worried about Megan, Jenny, and the other two women. Right now, he and his companions had no way of knowing if the prisoners were even still alive. His sister and the woman he loved might be dead already. Jason didn't want to let himself think that, but the possibility intruded into his brain anyway.

And if the captives *were* still alive, there was no telling what sort of degrading ordeal they had gone through. Jason tried to tell himself that it didn't matter, but he knew to some people it would. Women who had been raped were regarded as soiled, as somehow less than they had been before. It wasn't right, but it was the way things were, and he knew that the stigma would eat away at Megan and Jenny and make their lives miserable.

Worry first about saving their lives, he told himself. Other problems could be dealt with later.

When he was about fifty yards from the gate into the courtyard, Jason paused and let Matt crawl up beside him. He put his head close to Matt's and whispered, "We can't get in there. There are guards in the courtyard. We'll have to circle the place and look for some other way in."

Matt nodded that he understood. Jason turned and resumed crawling, staying well away from the stone wall around the courtyard.

The place really did look like a castle with that tower sticking up at one end, he thought. For some reason, his eyes kept returning to it, drawn there as if by some unknown force. He wondered if it could be climbed from the outside, so that the window could be reached that way. Almost as soon as the idea came into his brain, he discarded it. Anybody trying to climb that tower would be spotted right away and would be an easy target for riflemen down below.

A group as large as Alba's gang had to have quite a few horses, and sure enough, a stable was built to one side of the big house. Jason hadn't been able to see it until now. It was a long, low building, and the smell that came from it told him what it was. He also heard the faint sounds of the horses moving around inside.

Most importantly, a passage connected the stable to the house itself. That was their way in, Jason told himself.

He tapped Matt on the shoulder and pointed, and both young men crawled toward the far end of the stable. When they reached it, Jason saw an open window. There would be guards inside. Alba was too smart to leave this way into his stronghold undefended. Being as quiet as possible, Jason crawled closer and spotted a deeper patch of darkness at the base of the wall. An opening of some sort? He moved toward it, and as he did he found himself crawling through mud and wet grass. The smell of horseshit was almost overpowering. Jason realized that the opening at the base of the wall was a drain, so that when buckets of water were sloshed across the stable floor to wash it out, the liquid would have somewhere to go.

He heard Matt gagging a little behind him, and twisted his head to hiss for silence. Sure, the smell was bad, but they would have to put up with it. This was a possible way in that the outlaws wouldn't suspect anyone of taking. No one in his right mind, that is.

Jason wasn't sure he *was* in his right mind at the moment. He was too worried about the prisoners for that.

He reached the drain opening and put out his hands to see if it was barred in any way. He almost groaned out loud when he touched iron bars that were too close together for a man to crawl between them.

But he wasn't ready to give up. The bars were set in stone on their top end, but the bottom ends were buried in the ground. How deep did they go? Jason knew only one way to find out. He started digging with his hands.

The ground was softer here, since it stayed wet a lot of the time. Matt caught on to what he was doing and started to dig as well. Both of them ignored the stench as best they could.

Jason came to the bottom of the bars about six inches deep in the ground. He and Matt cleared the mud away around several of the bars, then each of them gripped one of the bars and started to heave. They were big, strong young men, but they were working against iron and stone. The stone didn't give, but after a few arduous, teeth-gritting minutes, the iron began to bend under the strain.

Jason and Matt took a break to catch their breath, then resumed pulling on the bars. Over the next half hour or so, they bent several of the bars up and out of the way so that there was an opening just large enough for them to wriggle through it one at a time. Jason went first, being careful as he pulled himself onto the sloping stone floor of the stable that his holstered gun didn't scrape against it.

He saw a light and heard men talking at the front of the stable. When Matt was through the drain, they both edged forward until they could look along the straw-littered aisle between the stalls where the horses were kept. Two guards, both Americans, were at the far end of the aisle where the passage from the house opened into the stable. One man sat on a three-legged stool while the other leaned a shoulder against the wall. Each of the hardcases had a quirly in his mouth and a shotgun in his hands.

Not surprisingly, they were talking about the prisoners, as men always will whenever there are good-looking girls in the vicinity. Jason's jaw tightened as he listened to them trading lewd opinions about the women and detailing what they would like to do to them. None of that mattered now, he told himself. What was important was figuring out a way to draw the guards down here so that they could be disposed of without any noise or fuss, nothing that would give the alarm to the men in the house. Once they were taken care of, Jason and Matt would be able to get into the stronghold.

"Too bad those Chinamen will be the only ones who get to enjoy them gals," one of the guards complained.

Jason and Matt exchanged a silent glance. Chinamen? What Chinamen?

"Maybe we could talk the boss into not sellin' the redhead," the other outlaw replied.

"You mean the young one? Alba'd never let us have her. Damn yellow bastards've promised too much money for the likes o' her."

"No, I mean the older one, the whore. Hell, as much as she's been used, she can't be worth a whole lot, even to a Chink."

They were talking about Abigail Krimp, and even though Abigail made no bones about what her profession was, it angered Jason to hear the men talking about her in such a callous fashion.

"Yeah, the boss could've let us have a little fun with her and the other older one, instead o' makin' us keep our hands off like he did with the two young ones."

Was it possible? Jason asked himself. Could it be that none of the prisoners had been molested yet? All because Juan Alba was planning to sell them to some unknown Chinese?

Jason's brain was whirling as he tried to sort everything out, but he knew one thing—they would take any stroke of luck they could get. He glanced at the window and saw that the sky outside was still dark, without even a hint of gray yet. Dawn was still at least a couple of hours away. He hadn't been sure about that, because it seemed like it had taken him and Matt hours to crawl to the house and find a way in through the stable.

He wished the two guards would talk about where the prisoners were being held, but it seemed like they had provided all the information they were going to provide. They started reminiscing about some particularly sordid adventure in some cantina in Nogales instead. Jason knew that he and Matt couldn't wait here forever. It was time to make their move.

He could see across the aisle into one of the stalls. A big rangy dun horse was standing there, munching at some hay. Jason slipped a bullet from one of the loops on his shell belt and whispered to Matt, "If only one of them comes down here to see what's going on, you take him. I'll get the other one."

Matt nodded, and Jason was thankful that for once Matt wasn't going to be argumentative. He drew back his arm, took a deep breath, and threw the bullet across the aisle, hoping that his aim was true.

It was. The bullet hit the horse in the head and bounced off, rattling a little as it hit the floor and rolled across the stone. The horse jerked his head up, let out a startled whinny, and shifted in the stall.

"What the hell?" one of the guards said.

"Something spooked one of the horses. Maybe a snake got in here or something."

"I guess I better go see." The man who was already standing sighed and started walking toward the far end of the stable.

Jason drew his knife, looked at Matt, and gave him a grim nod. Matt had his knife out and ready as well. Hidden from sight by the wall of the stall next to them, they rose into a crouch.

The guard's footsteps echoed against the low ceiling as he approached. Without looking toward the little alcove where the drain opening was located, the outlaw looked into the stall at the dun and asked, "What's got you spooked, boy?" Then he shook his head and added, "Whoo-ee, what's that stink?"

Jason and Matt exploded into action.

Chapter 28

Matt lunged out of the alcove first, throwing himself across the aisle toward the man who stood in front of the dun's stall. The outlaw heard him coming and tried to turn, but he was too late. Matt's left arm looped around his neck and jerked him backward, and at the same time Matt drove the knife in his right hand into the man's back.

Jason burst into the aisle right behind Matt. He had the tougher job. The guard who had been sitting on the stool leaped to his feet, a startled look on his face, and swung his shotgun up.

Jason's right arm drew back and flashed forward. The knife left his hand and flew through the air, turning over twice in its flight so that the light from the lantern winked on the shining blade. An instant later, the knife struck the guard in the chest with a meaty *thunk!* Jason had put all his strength behind the throw. The only question was whether or not it would be accurate enough.

It was. The blade sank deep in the outlaw's chest. The painful, shocking impact was enough to drive him back a step. His mouth hung open as he stared down at the hilt of the knife where it stuck out of his body. The shotgun slipped from his fingers and fell butt-first to the floor.

Jason was already moving even as the knife whirled through the air. By the time the guard dropped the shotgun, Jason was close enough to dive forward and reach for it. All their efforts would be for naught if the scattergun discharged. That twin boom would warn the rest of the outlaws in the house that something was wrong.

The butt of the shotgun thudded against the floor, practically stopping Jason's heart. But it didn't go off, and he wrapped his hand around the double barrels before the weapon could topple over. He hit the stone floor and rolled over, coming back up on his feet.

The outlaw with the knife in his chest was swaying back and forth, but he hadn't fallen yet. His left hand made feeble pawing motions at the knife, but his right struggled to pull a revolver from its holster.

Jason didn't give him a chance to complete the draw. He stepped closer and smashed the shotgun's butt into the man's face, breaking bones and sending blood spurting from crushed nose and pulped lips. The outlaw went over backward, his face a crimson ruin. He didn't suffer long from the pain of that injury, though. He spasmed a couple of times and then lay still, his final breath rattling in his throat. The knife wound in his chest had finally claimed his life.

Turning toward the other end of the stable, Jason saw that Matt had lowered his man to the floor. As Jason watched, Matt pushed the knife even deeper in the outlaw's back. The man twitched a time or two as he died.

The whole thing had been accomplished in near-silence. The only sounds had been grunts of pain and effort, the scuffling of boot leather on the stone floor, and the butt of the shotgun hitting the floor, Jason knew those noises couldn't have been heard in the house.

He dragged his man into the alcove by the drain and motioned for Matt to do likewise. Then he said, "We stink to high heaven. That's liable to give us away inside the house. We'll take the clothes from these two. That might help a little."

Matt grimaced. "They've got blood on them."

"Better blood than horseshit. It doesn't smell quite so bad."

Matt shrugged in acceptance. Moving as fast as they could, they stripped the clothes from the dead men, took off their own reeking garments, and pulled on the trousers and bloodstained shirts of the guards. They took the outlaws' hats as well.

The man Jason had killed had worn a cowhide vest. Jason pulled it over the crimson stain on the shirt as best he could. The bloodstain on Matt's shirt was on the back, so it might not be seen right away.

"We'll keep our heads down," Jason said. "Maybe if anybody sees us, they'll take us for these two hombres."

"What if some more guards show up?" Matt asked.

"I'm sure they will sooner or later, but I'm hoping not until dawn anyway. As late as it is, these two probably had the night shift."

Matt nodded. "I'm ready if you are."

"Keep your eyes open."

"Where do you think the prisoners are?"

"I don't have any idea," Jason answered. "We'll just have to look around."

Carrying the shotguns, they moved into the passageway between the stable and the house. The door at the far end was closed. Jason eased it open while Matt stood by with his shotgun at the ready. An empty corridor was on the other side of the door.

They made their way along the corridor in swift silence. At the far end, they came to a staircase that led both up and down. Jason tried to estimate their position and figured they were at the end of the house where the tower was located. He wondered if Juan Alba's chamber was up in that tower. Since Alba was the leader of the gang, that seemed to be the logical place for him to stay, above everyone else.

Jason's knew that if there was a dungeon in this place, it would be down below. He pointed down the stairs and nodded to Matt, who returned the nod. With Jason going first, they started descending.

Before they reached the bottom, they heard the soft murmur of voices. Jason slowed to a creeping pace, placing each foot with extreme care before he let his weight down on it. The staircase reached a landing between floors and turned back on itself. Light shone at the bottom.

Jason stopped where he was still out of sight of the men who were below and listened to them talking, trying to make out the words. It was difficult, because their voices were obscured by a constant noise that Jason soon recognized as the sound of the waves from the Gulf. They were close to the long drop; that was why he could hear the pounding of the surf on the rocks below.

He caught a few references to the prisoners, and his heart thudded harder when he heard one of the men say something about letting them out of their cells in the morning, before the ships arrived.

Those ships would be carrying the Chinamen who planned to purchase the women from Alba, Jason guessed. And the mention of cells made him think that he and Matt had come to the right place. The prisoners were close by. He could feel it in his bones.

He moved back up a couple of steps to whisper to Matt about what he had overheard. Matt tensed and whispered back, "Let's go get them, damn it. They have to be right down there!"

"We don't know how many guards there are," Jason argued. "We might not be able to get rid of them without making a racket and waking up the rest of the house."

"So what do we do? Wait?"

The scornful tone of Matt's whisper made it clear what he thought of that idea. Jason would have continued the discussion if at that moment he hadn't heard footsteps somewhere on the stairs above them.

And those steps were coming down, straight toward them.

He and Matt exchanged alarmed glances. Now they had no choice. They couldn't just wait here on the stairs to be discovered.

"Follow my lead," he whispered to Matt.

Then he tugged the brim of the borrowed hat down as far over his face as he could and started down the stairs at a normal pace, making the turn at the landing and clattering down to the corridor below as if he didn't have a care in the world, as if he was supposed to be there.

Matt followed, also assuming a nonchalant gait.

When they reached the bottom of the stairs, they found themselves in a corridor similar to the one above, only this one was shorter and had a pair of heavy doors on each side. The small, barred windows in each door identified the rooms beyond as cells where prisoners could be locked up. The presence of two men standing guard in the corridor told Jason those cells were occupied.

The two outlaws looked surprised but not alarmed. Jason knew they had taken him and Matt for fellow members of the gang. He had known that changing clothes with the dead men in the stable was going to come in handy. He whistled a flat little tune as he walked toward the guards.

"What are you fellas doin' here, Ford?" one of the outlaws asked. "I thought you and Fargo were posted out in the stable tonight."

Jason made his voice rough and hoarse as he replied, "Change of orders. We're takin' over here."

The other guard frowned. "Nobody told us— Hey! You ain't Ford and Fargo!"

Jason hadn't expected the deception to work for very long, just long enough to get close enough to the guards so that he and Matt could strike in silence. But that had failed, so they had to try another tack.

He brought the shotgun up and eared back both hammers as he pointed the twin barrels at the guards. Both men froze in the act of reaching for the guns on their hips. Staring into the gaping double maw of a scattergun had that effect on folks.

"Freeze," Jason grated. "At this range, if I pull these triggers, the buckshot will smear you boys all over the walls."

The outlaws didn't move, just stared at Jason and Matt in shock and anger.

"Take your guns out slow and careful-like," Jason went on. "Bend over, put them on the floor, and slide them over here."

One of the guards sneered. "The hell with you, mister. I don't know who you are, but if you pull those triggers, you'll have everybody else in the house down on you in about five seconds. Kill us and you're dead too."

"Yeah, well, that won't help you any, will it?" Matt said. He had stepped up beside Jason and leveled his shotgun at one of the guards. "I'm aiming right for your face, you son of a bitch. There won't be enough of your head left for your own mama to recognize you."

The tense standoff continued for a couple of heartbeats until a face suddenly appeared at the barred window of one of the doors. "Jason! Matt!" a ragged voice cried. "Oh, thank God!"

Jason recognized Jenny's voice, but managed to keep his gaze locked on the two outlaws. Matt didn't have that much self-discipline. His head jerked to the side as he choked out, "Jenny!"

"Take 'em!" one of the guards yelled as his hand dipped toward his gun in a hook and draw.

Now it was too late to do anything except kill or be killed.

Chapter 29

Jason moved as fast as he had ever moved in his life. He lunged forward, thrusting the shotgun out in front of him, aiming the barrels at the closest guard's face. The barrels struck the man in the mouth, which was open to shout a curse. The impact shattered the outlaw's teeth and drove them back in his throat, choking him. At the same moment, Jason barreled into the man, knocking him off his feet.

Matt tried the same tactic as Jason, but wasn't quite fast enough to pull it off. The second guard managed to get his gun out of its holster and twist aside from Matt's rush. But before he could pull the trigger, Matt cracked the shotgun barrels across the wrist of his gun hand. The man yelped in pain and dropped the revolver.

A few feet away, Jason came down with a knee in his opponent's groin. The outlaw tried to scream, but the sound couldn't get past his mangled mouth. Jason lifted the shotgun and brought the butt down hard against the man's jaw. He felt the satisfying crunch of bone. The guard jerked and then stiffened, either dead or out cold. Jason didn't know which and didn't care.

He glanced over and saw Matt wrestling with the second guard. Matt had a hand clamped around the man's throat to keep him from shouting a warning to whoever was coming down the stairs. He didn't see the man pull a knife from somewhere and raise it high, poised to bring it down into Matt's back in a killing stroke.

Jason saw it, though, and threw himself across the intervening space. He grabbed the man's wrist as the knife started down and wrenched it to the side. While Jason was doing that, Matt snatched up the revolver the outlaw had dropped and slammed it against the man's head. Matt struck twice more, the blows falling with savage strength, and when he pulled the gun back to hit the outlaw again, Jason said, "Forget it. He's dead."

Matt blinked, then swallowed hard as he looked down at the outlaw's misshapen skull. The blows had caved it in and left it distorted grotesquely.

Jason pushed himself to his feet, grabbed Matt's arm, and hauled him upright too. By now the other three women were at the doors of their cells, peering out into the corridor like Jenny. Jason saw the relief on Megan's face and wanted to go to her, but there was no time.

Someone was still coming down the stairs, and whoever it was, they were close now.

There was no place for Jason and Matt to hide in the corridor, so they would have to meet the trouble head-on. "Stay here!" Jason hissed at Matt. "Protect the women!"

Then he ran toward the stairs and bounded up toward the landing, taking the steps two at a time and drawing his knife as he did so.

He reached the landing at the same time as the man who was coming down, and as they suddenly faced each other, both of them froze for a second in surprise. Jason was shocked to find himself staring into the face of Flores, the man who had shot and wounded Wash Keough at Abigail Krimp's place back in Fury, what seemed like an eternity ago. As for Flores, he was startled into immobility for a second by finding an intruder in Juan Alba's stronghold.

The two men recovered from their surprise at the same time. Flores clawed for the gun on his hip, but before the weapon could clear leather, Jason had stabbed him in the belly. Using the strength in his powerful arms and shoulders, Jason ripped the blade to one side and then back the other way, opening up Flores so that the man's guts spilled out. Flores groaned in pain and fell forward, crashing into Jason.

Unable to keep his balance under Flores's weight, Jason went over backward and tumbled down the steps. Flores fell with him, losing more blood with every bounce. The two men wound up at the bottom of the stairs, tangled together in a gory mess. Jason grimaced as he shoved the bloody corpse to the side and scooted away from it. He was so shaky when he got to his feet that he had to put a hand against the stone wall to steady himself.

He looked down and saw that he was covered with blood, but all of it belonged to Flores. Jason was unhurt.

He drew in a ragged breath, and then hurried back along the corridor to where Matt was bending over the bodies of the guards. Matt came up holding a ring of keys he had taken from one of the men.

"One of these ought to open those locks," Matt said as he brandished the keys.

He went to the door of Jenny's cell and began trying the keys in the padlock. While Matt was doing that, Jason hurried over to Megan's cell and asked her, "Are you all right?"

"I'm fine," she said. "None of us are hurt, just scared. They . . . they let us alone because Alba plans to sell us to some Chinese warlords."

Jason nodded. "We overheard some of the outlaws talking and figured it was something like that. Thank God all of you are all right. Now we just have to get you out of here."

"Did you and Matt come alone?"

"The two of us are the only ones who snuck into the house, but there are more men waiting outside." He didn't tell her that, right now, only Ezra Dixon and Zachary Morton were nearby, unless Wash had gotten back with the rest of the posse. She didn't need to know yet that the odds against them might still be incredibly long.

Jason wanted to press his face to the bars too and kiss Megan, or reach through the bars so that he could stroke her red hair. He wanted that physical contact to assure himself that she was real. But she would be out of that cell soon enough, he told himself. He turned to Matt, who was still fumbling with the lock on Jenny's cell.

"Isn't the key there?" he asked.

"I'll find it, I'll find it," Matt snapped. "I didn't think it would take this long— Ah!"

Jason heard the lock click open. He looked across the corridor to the other cells, where Olympia Morelli and Abigail Krimp were watching with anxious expressions on their faces. "It'll just be a few minutes and then we'll have you out of there, ladies," he assured them.

Matt tossed the keys over to him. Jason caught them and began trying them in the lock on Megan's cell. He was luckier than Matt had been; the third key he inserted into the padlock opened it. He swung the door open and Megan rushed out to throw herself into his arms. Jason hugged her tightly for a moment, burying his face in her thick hair.

As wonderful as it felt to embrace Megan like that, he knew he didn't have any time to waste. He turned away from her and hurried across the corridor. Abigail's door was closer, so he went to work on it first, searching for the right key.

This one took longer. While Jason was doing that, Megan picked up one of the revolvers that had been dropped by the dead guards. She averted her eyes from their corpses and stepped over to Matt and Jenny, who were still hugging each other.

"Jenny, you'd better get one of those guns," Megan said. "We may have to shoot our way out of here."

"Sh-shoot?" Jenny said. She looked at Matt.

He nodded. "Alba won't let you go without a fight. You've been through Indian battles before, Jenny. You'll be all right."

Jenny managed to nod. It was true that she had been on hand for the fights with the Comanches and the Apaches, but she had spent her time loading guns for the men, not using them herself.

Megan picked up the other guard's revolver and pressed it into Jenny's hands. Jenny clutched it tightly and swallowed. Her eyes were big with fear.

Jason got Abigail's door open. "Give me one of those shotguns," the older redhead said as she emerged from the cell. "If any of those bastards gets in my way, he'll get a double load of buckshot."

Jason unlocked the door of Olympia's cell and gave her the other shotgun. With two Greeners and four handguns, they made a pretty formidable group, at least under normal circumstances. That much firepower wouldn't do much good, though, in the face of Alba's bandit horde. If it came to a pitched battle before the rest of the posse arrived, the six of them wouldn't have a chance.

Jason gathered the others around and said, "We need to find an out-of-the-way place to hide you women until the sun comes up. That's when the posse will be moving in. Matt and I have to figure out some way to distract Alba and his men when that happens."

"Why don't you try to take Alba prisoner?" Megan suggested. "His room is at the top of the tower."

That confirmed what Jason had guessed earlier, but unfortunately, it didn't do them much good. "Alba's probably got several bodyguards close by," he said. "We couldn't get to him without raising a ruckus, and that would alert the rest of the gang. We were mighty lucky to reach the four of you without having anyone spread the alarm."

"Why don't the women wait right here?" Matt suggested. "The guards probably won't be changed until morning, so no one will discover that they're free. And they can cover the bottom of those stairs with the guns they have, no problem. If anybody starts to come down them besides us, they can blast 'em."

Jason thought it over for a second and then nodded. He'd had plenty of problems with Matt in the past, but he had to give the other young man credit where credit was due. Matt's words made sense.

"That's a good idea. We'll drag these corpses all the way to the end of the hall, where they can't be seen from that first landing."

The women turned their eyes away from the gruesome spectacle of Jason and Matt hauling the bodies of Flores and the two dead guards down to the far end of the corridor. They couldn't do anything about the blood Flores had spilled onto the stairs during his tumble down them, but if any of the outlaws started to descend, they might not notice that. Jason figured plenty of blood had been spilled in this old stone heap of a house since it was built many years earlier.

"All of you get in one of the cells," Jason told the women. "But first close all the other doors and hang the padlocks on the hasps so that they look like they're still fastened. Then pull the door of the cell you're in almost closed. If you're quiet, you'll be able to hear if anyone starts down the stairs a long time before they get here."

Abigail nodded in understanding. "Don't you worry about us, Marshal," she said. "Any of those bandits come anywhere near us, we'll blast 'em."

Jason didn't doubt it for a second. He knew Megan and Abigail were capable of keeping their wits about them and fighting for their lives. He thought Mrs. Morelli probably was too, and even Jenny seemed to have settled down some. She held onto the Colt Megan had given her, and her hand wasn't shaking anymore.

Jason hugged his sister and kissed her on the forehead, then turned to Megan and drew her into his embrace for a kiss on the mouth. Knowing that they might never see each other again, they each packed plenty of passion into the kiss. A few feet away, Matt was bidding farewell to Jenny in similar fashion, leading Abigail to smile and say to Olympia, "I'll bet you wish your husband was here, hey, Mrs. Morelli?"

Olympia shook her head. "No, I'm glad Michael's not here. He's a healer, not a fighter. I wouldn't want him getting hurt by those outlaws."

"Yeah, I guess that's true. Everybody contributes in their own way."

Once the good-byes had been said, Jason and Matt headed up the stairs while the women retreated into one of the cells. Both of the young men glanced back one last time before they went out of sight.

"They'll be all right," Matt said.

"Of course they will," Jason said.

Both of them sounded like they were trying to convince each other, and themselves.

They had to put any thoughts of the women out of their heads as they climbed to the ground floor of the old stone house. They heard men's voices and laughter coming from somewhere nearby, and went the other way, trying to avoid whoever was up at this early hour of the morning. Probably an all-night drinking session or poker game, or both, was going on, Jason thought.

They slipped along dark hallways. Candles were lit here and there and stuck on wall sconces, but the flickering light they cast was soon swallowed up by shadows. Jason found a window and peered out. The sky was gray now. It wouldn't be long until dawn.

Matt put a hand on Jason's arm to stop him and sniffed the air. Jason did likewise and noticed the same thing Matt had— the smell of coffee brewing and biscuits cooking. Somewhere not far off, someone was in the kitchen getting breakfast started. The new day would be beginning soon, and with it would come the arrival of those ships bearing the Chinese warlords. Jason thought it likely those warlords would have a considerable number of fighting men with them. He and the other rescuers really needed to be out of here with the women before those potential reinforcements for Alba arrived.

Jason tried an unlocked door, and felt his pulse quicken as he peered into a dim room that had quite a few crates and kegs stacked around it. Those containers might hold food or other supplies, but as he picked up one of the kegs and carried it out where he could get a better look at it in the light of the hallway, he saw that he was holding a keg full of gunpowder, at least according to the markings on it.

Matt hissed a warning and pushed Jason back into the room. "Somebody's coming!"

They retreated into the room and Jason pushed the door nearly all the way closed, leaving it ajar only a tiny crack. If the men who were approaching stopped at this storage room, the jig would be up. Jason and Matt would have to fight and probably die.

From the sound of the footsteps, the group included several men. They were talking among themselves, and Jason heard one of the men address another as *jefe*—chief.

That would be Juan Alba, Jason thought. If Alba was down here, that meant he wasn't up in his tower room any longer. Jason reached out in the dark room, touched Matt's arm, and whispered, "Grab a couple of those kegs of powder. We're going up into the tower."

They waited until Alba and the other men had passed the room and moved on out of earshot. Then Jason eased the door open, saw that the corridor was empty, and motioned for Matt to follow him. Each of them carried two kegs of powder as they retraced their steps back toward the staircase that ran between the tower and the basement corridor where the cells were located.

This old house was a warren of twisting and turning passageways, so a few times Jason was worried that he and Matt had gotten lost. Finally, though, they came to the staircase and recognized it as the one they had been on earlier. They started climbing, being as quiet about it as they could in case someone was up in Alba's room at the top of the tower.

The big room was unoccupied when they reached it. Large windows commanded a great view on all four sides of the tower. They could see far out into the Gulf, as well as down to the stable and the courtyard in front of the house.

Jason saw something else too. At the top of the grassy slope leading to the sand dunes, something red fluttered a little in the dawn wind. Wash's bandanna, Jason thought. He pointed it out to Matt and said, "That means the posse is ready to attack. All they're waiting for is our signal."

Matt had set down one of the powder kegs. He patted the other one and said, "I reckon this is it?"

Jason nodded and said, "That's right."

The sun was about to come up like thunder.

Chapter 30

Jason raised the window overlooking the courtyard while Matt tore strips off the sheet on Alba's opulent bed and twisted them together to make a fuse. Jason used his knife to gouge a small hole in the top of the keg. When Matt forced the strip of twisted cloth through the hole, it made a crude fuse. An oil lamp was burning on the table next to the bed, its flame turned low. Matt carried the keg over to it and looked at Jason.

"Ready?"

Jason nodded. Matt held the end of the fuse in the flame until it was burning. Then he tossed the keg to Jason, who stood beside the open window.

Jason caught the keg, turned, and threw it out the window, putting plenty of strength behind the throw so that the keg sailed high over the courtyard, arching through the air. As he watched it, he wondered if the members of the posse could see the burning fuse. Even if they couldn't, they would know soon enough that the time had come to launch the attack.

The keg hit the ground, bounced a couple of times, and rolled to a stop against the gate. It was a perfect landing, exactly how Jason wanted it, except for one thing.

The fuse had gone out before it reached the powder.

"Damn it!" Matt exclaimed. He had hurried over to the window to stand next to Jason. "What do we do now?"

Jason spotted movement in the courtyard below. One of the bandits, a Mexican in a big sombrero, was walking toward the gate. The man must have seen the keg fall and wanted to find out what was going on.

Jason jerked his pistol from its holster. He wished he had his rifle, but he had left it with his horse. The Colt would just have to do.

"We'll have to set it off this way," he said as he lined up his shot. Beside him, Matt got the idea and yanked his own gun out. Both of them aimed at the keg and fired, Jason first, but Matt so closely behind him that the two shots sounded almost like one.

Down below, the *bandido* recognized the keg for what it was, heard the shots, and let out an alarmed yell as he tried to turn and run.

He was too late. The powder keg exploded with a thunderous roar and a gush of smoke and flame. The heavy gates were blown outward and ripped off their hinges, and the force of the blast picked up the fleeing outlaw and flung him ahead like a rag doll. His sombrero flew in the air and his arms and legs flailed helplessly for a second before he slammed face-first into the wall of the house. The impact burst his head open like a melon. He left a bloody streak behind him as he slid down the stone surface.

Jason and Matt looked toward the sand dunes and saw the members of the posse gallop into view, racing toward the house. Outlaws poured out of the stronghold in response to the explosion. As they gathered in the courtyard in consternation, Jason said to Matt, "Throw another keg down there!"

Matt grabbed one of the powder kegs and heaved it out the window. Jason tracked it with his Colt and squeezed off two shots, missing with the first one. But the second bored into the keg and set off the powder inside just as it landed in the middle of the startled outlaws. Several of them were blown to pieces by the blast. Arms and legs and other body parts flew high into the air, trailing a shower of blood. Others were cut down by the deadly spray of splinters from the wooden keg. Most of the men who weren't killed outright by the explosion were knocked off their feet.

Jason saw Wash, Dixon, Zachary Morton, and the other members of the posse as they charged through the blasted gates into the courtyard, firing all around them as they galloped in. Most of the outlaws who were caught in the open were still too stunned from the explosion to put up much of a fight. The men from Fury cut them down. Bullets scythed through the ranks of the bandits.

Not all the members of the gang had come charging out into the courtyard, though. Some of them were still in the house, and they opened fire on the posse. Jason saw a couple of the men topple from their saddles. The others leaped off their horses and hunted cover. Within moments a pitched battle had developed, the posse men laying siege to the old house and the remaining outlaws defending it.

Matt grabbed Jason's arm and yelled, "Look!" He pointed out the big window on the other side of the room, toward the Gulf.

Jason turned and saw the ship sweeping over the waves toward the shore. It had to be the vessel belonging to the Chinese warlords. Jason didn't know much about sailing, but he estimated that it wouldn't be long before the ship reached the stronghold. There had to be a dock of some sort at the base of the cliff, with stairs leading up from it. If the warlords and their men charged up the stairs and entered the fight on Alba's side, that would swing the odds and put the members of the posse in even greater danger than they already were.

"We've got to end this fight in a hurry," Jason said. "Grab those kegs and come on."

Caught up in the excitement of battle, Matt forgot about his natural inclination to argue with Jason and did as he was told, picking up the kegs and following Jason down the staircase.

They met several of the outlaws charging up the stairs. Some of the gang must have figured out that there were enemies in the tower and were coming to flush them out, not knowing that Jason and Matt were already on their way down. As the two groups almost collided, Matt called out, "Fury! Get down!"

Jason dropped out of the way as Matt heaved one of the kegs downward as hard as he could. It crashed against the chest of the outlaw in the lead and knocked him backward. He got tangled up with the other men, and suddenly all four of the bandits were tumbling down the stairs.

Jason and Matt followed, the guns in their fists flaming as they fired into the group of outlaws. With all that lead flying around, Jason hoped a stray slug didn't hit the powder keg Matt was still carrying. If it did, they would both be blown to Kingdom Come.

They leaped over the sprawled, bloody bodies of the outlaws, all of whom were either dead or wounded so bad that they were out of the fight, and continued down the stairs. Jason picked up the keg Matt had thrown and carried it with him. When they reached the ground floor, they followed the sound of shooting to a large chamber where the outlaws were using windows and rifle slits to fire at the members of the posse.

Jason and Matt paused just around a corner to reload, then exchanged grim nods. They leaped out and rolled the powder kegs across the room toward the outlaws. Their shots added to the deafening roar of gunfire in the room.

That roar turned into a tremendous blast a second later as both kegs exploded when the bullets fired by Jason and Matt slammed into them. The two young men from Fury jumped back just in time. When they looked around the corner, clouds of smoke and dust blinded them, and their ears were ringing so much from the explosion they couldn't tell if anyone was still shooting or not. Gradually, though, the dust settled and their hearing came back, and then they could tell that the double explosion had cleared the room of defenders. The bodies of the outlaws littered the floor, some whole, some in pieces, but all bloody and motionless.

The battle was over.

"Go tell Wash and the others to gather their horses and get ready to ride!" Jason told Matt, not really aware that he was shouting because his hearing wasn't completely back to normal yet. "I'll get the women!"

Matt nodded and ran through the devastation toward the door that led out into the courtyard. Jason went the other way, toward the staircase that would take him down to the cells.

He kept his eyes open as he hurried along the stone passageways. There could still be outlaws on the loose inside the house, although it seemed certain that most of the gang had been wiped out by the three explosions and the battle with the posse.

When he reached the stairs, he clattered down them with his gun clutched in his hand. He ducked around the last landing, crouching low in case an enemy was waiting for him. The staircase was empty, though, so Jason hurried on down to the corridor where the cells were located.

"Megan!" he called. "Jenny! It's me! Hold your fire!" The women might be pretty jumpy and trigger-happy by now, and after all the danger he had come through safely, he didn't want to get shot to pieces now by the very people he had come to rescue.

There was no response from the cell where the women had taken refuge, which made a worried frown appear on Jason's face. Maybe they were afraid that he was a prisoner himself and was being forced to call out to him with a gun at his head.

"It's all right," he assured them. "I'm alone. The fighting is over. Most of Alba's men are dead. We need to get out of here, though, because that Chinese ship is offshore—"

He had reached the cell as he spoke, and now took hold of the door to open it. It was jerked inward, pulling him with it. A massive hand, with incredibly strong, sausagelike fingers, clamped on the back of his neck and flung him across the cell like he was little more than a rag doll. Jason opened his mouth to yell but before any sound could come out, he slammed into the wall with stunning force.

He was barely aware of bouncing off the wall and collapsing on the floor of the cell. His gun was gone; it had slipped out of his fingers and he didn't know where it had gone. He forced himself to lift his head, and give it a groggy shake in an attempt to clear away the cobwebs from his brain. His vision was blurry, but as a giant shadow loomed over him, it cleared and he looked up into the fierce, bearded face of Juan Alba, the Scourge of the Borderlands himself.

"Oh, hell," Jason said.

Chapter 31

Alba grinned down at him. "So, you think you have won, gringo," the bandit chieftain said. "You think you have defeated Juan Alba. But you are wrong."

Let the man lord it over him for now, Jason thought. He wanted to make sure the women were all right. He looked around and saw the four of them huddled against one wall of the cell. The shotguns and pistols were on the other side of the room where Alba must have thrown them after he had disarmed the women.

"I'm sorry, Jason," Megan said. "We tried to stop him, but he . . . he's a monster!"

Alba thumped himself on the chest with a big fist. "Too strong to be brought down by women," he said with a scornful sneer. "Strong like the bull."

But now Jason noticed for the first time that there was blood on Alba's shirt under his fancy jacket. At least one of the women had gotten a bullet in him. The wound hadn't been enough to bring him down, but it might weaken him.

"He . . . he had Jenny by the neck," Megan went on. "He said he would snap it if we tried to warn you."

Jason looked at his sister and saw the ugly bruises on her

neck. One more score to even with Alba, he thought. He pushed himself to his hands and knees.

With no warning, Alba lashed out at him, aiming a kick at his ribs. Jason twisted and rolled out of the way and scrambled to his feet, his chest rising and falling as he tried to catch his breath. He knew that the other members of the posse upstairs would be unaware of this deadly showdown going on below them. It was up to him to defeat Alba and get the women out of here before the warlords arrived.

"Now," Alba said, still grinning, "now I will kill you. No matter what happens to me, you will die, gringo, and these women with you before I will let them go. You can go to your death knowing that your mission was a failure."

"What do you plan to do?" Jason asked with a sneer of his own. "Talk me to death?"

Alba's grin disappeared, and with a roar he charged, lumbering forward like a grizzly bear. Also like a bear, he moved faster than it seemed a man of his massive size ought to be able to.

Jason got out of the way just in time. As Alba went past him, he clubbed his hands together and smashed them into the back of the big outlaw's neck. Alba didn't even seem to notice. He swung an arm like the trunk of a young tree in a backhanded blow that crashed into Jason and threw him against the wall.

Megan darted forward, making a try for one of the weapons on the other side of the room. Alba spotted her and swatted at her like she was nothing more than an annoying insect. That was enough to make Megan cry out in pain and go spinning off her feet.

"Megan!" Jason shouted. With a red haze of anger half-blinding him, he slammed a right and a left at Alba's head. Both punches connected, but again, they seemed like nothing more than the bite of gnats to the huge bandit. Alba's left fist crashed against Jason's breastbone, numbing him and making him gasp for breath. Alba swung again, a roundhouse right this time that would have broken Jason's neck if it had connected with his jaw, where Alba aimed it. Instead, Jason weaved his body so that the blow skidded off his right shoulder. That was enough to make that arm go numb and render it useless.

Alba charged again, arms outstretched. Jason knew Alba meant to catch him in a bear hug and crush the life out of him. Alba would probably laugh in his face as he did it too. Jason stumbled out of the way just in time. As he did so, he kicked one of the revolvers and sent it skidding across the floor toward Jenny, Olympia, and Abigail. Megan was still crumpled on the floor, either unconscious or dead.

Jenny reached the gun first, scooping it up just as Alba rushed Jason again. This time, the treelike arms closed around Jason before he could avoid them. He was jerked off his feet. The arms tightened just as he had known they would, and he felt his ribs creaking under the pressure. They would snap at any moment.

The shots slammed out, one after the other, the explosions painfully loud in the close confines of the cell. Jason felt Alba's body shuddering under the impact of the slugs as Jenny emptied the Colt into him at close range. It occurred to Jason that the bullets might go all the way through Alba and strike him too, but he was too numb to feel it if they did.

Alba's eyes widened in pain and shock. He was strong enough to withstand one bullet or maybe even two, but Jenny had buried at least five slugs in him. His lips drew back from his teeth in a grimace. Blood trickled from the corner of his mouth, a crimson trail that lost itself in the tangle of thick black beard. Alba staggered to one side, but his grip on Jason didn't loosen.

"B-before Juan Alba dies . . . he will crush your bones to dust . . . gringo," gasped the Scourge of the Borderland.

"Jason, duck!" Abigail cried. She shoved the barrels of a

shotgun against the back of Alba's skull and pulled both triggers as Jason lowered his head and pressed it against the big outlaw's chest.

Alba's arms didn't let go until his headless body hit the floor. Jason writhed loose and crawled away from the gruesome corpse of the bandit chief. He grabbed Megan and lifted her, pulling her against him.

"Megan! Megan!"

Her eyes, her beautiful green eyes, fluttered open. "J-Jason?" she said in a husky voice.

He cradled her in his arms, murmuring, "It's over, it's over."

A rush of footsteps sounded in the corridor. Jason glanced up, wondering what was going to happen now, and felt relief flood through him as Wash Keough and several other members of the posse appeared.

"Everybody all right in here?" the old-timer asked. He let out a whistle of surprise when he saw what was left of Alba. "Everybody but that big bastard, that is?"

Jason struggled to his feet, lifting Megan as he did so. "We're fine," he said, although every bone and muscle in his body ached terribly. "We've got to get out of here—"

"Yeah, Matt told me there's some Chinese fellas comin' that we don't want to meet. Come on, we got the horses ready to ride."

With the strong hands of the posse men steadying them, Jason and the four women stumbled out of the cell where they had almost met their doom. Within minutes they reached the courtyard, where most of the men from Fury were already mounted. The women were helped onto the extra horses, except for Megan, who would ride with Matt since she was still dizzy. Jason would have taken her with him, but he wasn't in very good shape himself.

Good enough to ride, though, and they all galloped out of the courtyard toward the sand hills before the ship made landfall. Jason thought it highly unlikely that the warlords would pursue them across a strange land, even if they could round up enough of the gang's horses to do so. Some of the posse members had opened the stable doors and sent the horses scattering up and down the coastline.

Jason glanced back at the dark hulk of Alba's stronghold as the riders entered the dunes. It squatted there on the cliff like some unclean beast, and Jason wished they'd had time to use the rest of the powder kegs in the storage room to blow the place off the face of the earth. He supposed they would have to be satisfied with rescuing all four of the prisoners and wiping out Alba's gang, including the bandit leader himself. Alba wouldn't raid any more settlements in Mexico or Arizona Territory.

The Scourge of the Borderlands was no more.

They made it through the dunes by midday. Jason and Wash paused their horses at the top of a high dune near the edge of the sand hills and looked back toward the Gulf, waiting there as the others rode past, searching for any sign of pursuit. Horses' hooves didn't raise a cloud of dust in the sand, like they did on normal dry ground, so they couldn't go by that. But they could see a long way into the wasteland from where they were, and they didn't spot any movement. Riders would be easy to see against the sweep of sand, which was bright in the midday sun.

"Reckon when them Chinamen found everybody dead, they got back on their boat and sailed away," Wash said.

Jason nodded. "That was my hope anyway. Of course, we couldn't be sure that all of the outlaws were dead. We got out of there too fast to check all the bodies. Some of them could have been hiding out in that old heap of a house too."

"Couldn't be more'n a handful, if that many," Wash said. "And with Alba dead, they ain't gonna give chase, Jason. They'll just slink off somewhere's else like the mangy coyotes they are."

"You're right." Jason turned his horse. "Let's catch up with the others."

One member of the posse had been killed in the fighting. His body was draped over his saddle and tied into place. Jason didn't even know the man's name; he had been a newcomer to the settlement.

Several others were wounded, including Saul Cohen and Alf Blodgett. None of the injuries were serious, though. They had been cleaned and patched up. The wounds would need medical attention from Dr. Morelli when the posse got back to Fury, but they could wait that long without doing any more harm.

Jason wondered how Michael Morelli was doing. Knowing the physician as he did, Jason was sure that Morelli was going about his business and tending to the sick and injured in town to the best of his ability, even though worry about his wife's fate had to be eating away at him. Jason was looking forward to seeing the expression on Morelli's face when he realized that Olympia was all right.

They paused to give the horses a short rest soon after leaving the dunes. Slogging through that sand had been hard on the animals. Saddles were removed from the horses that seemed to be in the worst shape and placed on some of the spare mounts. There were fewer of them now that the prisoners had been rescued, but that was a good thing.

Jason sought out Saul Cohen and Salmon Kendall and asked, "Did you run into a cavalry patrol before you crossed the border?"

The two men shook their heads, and Salmon said, "No, but Wash told us about how that green lieutenant tried to stop you. I'm glad we didn't meet up with them. It would have gone against the grain for me to defy the army . . . but I wouldn't have let those troopers stop us either."

"Nor would I," Saul put in. "Imagine, representatives of our own government taking the side of a foreign country over the interests of American citizens."

"It's a disgrace, that's what it is," Salmon agreed. "If it ever gets to where it's that way all the time, I tell you, this country won't be a fit place to live."

Jason didn't think they'd have to worry about that. Americans in general had more common sense than that, even the politicians.

He hoped that was the case anyway.

Putting such things out of his mind, he went over to Megan and took her hand. "How are you doing?" he asked.

She managed to smile. "Not too bad, I guess. My head doesn't hurt anymore from that clout Alba gave me. It was terrible seeing what Jenny and Abigail did to him, but at the same time, I can't feel too sorry for him, knowing what he planned to do with us."

Jason didn't feel sorry for Alba at all. The bastard had gotten what was coming to him.

But he didn't say that to Megan. Instead, he just squeezed her hand and said, "We'll be home in a day or two. I'm looking forward to it."

She smiled at him. "So am I."

Jason noticed that Jenny and Matt had their heads together most of the time. Even though Matt had made a worthwhile and courageous ally, Jason still didn't like him much. He knew that Matt's basic nature hadn't changed. Matt was still an arrogant, willful troublemaker. That was why Jason hated to see him and Jenny fawning so over each other.

But his sister was a grown woman—well, nearly—and she had long since passed the point where she listened to her big brother's advice. And Jason had to admit that when you came right down to it, Jenny had shown a lot of backbone, grabbing that gun and emptying it into Alba. From what Megan had told him, Jason knew that Jenny had been nearly hysterical all the time during their captivity, but she had overcome that fear when she really needed to.

Jason supposed she could make up her own mind about

Matt MacDonald . . . and whatever she decided, he would just have to live with it.

When the horses had had a chance to rest for a short time, the group pushed on again. They stopped several more times during that day, then took a longer rest that evening as they waited for the moon to rise. Even though everyone was exhausted, they were anxious to get back to the settlement and see their families. No one wanted to stop and camp for the whole night, so as soon as the moon came up and they could see where they were going, they resumed their northward trek.

Jason and Wash kept an eye on their back trail the entire time, but never saw any signs of pursuit. By the middle of the next afternoon, they were across the border, back in Arizona Territory, and Jason was finally willing to admit that no one was chasing them.

He said as much to Saul as they rode at the rear of the group. Wash and Salmon were up front at the moment, with Wash leading the way home.

"You know that we were awfully lucky, don't you?" Saul asked.

"Can't help but know that," Jason admitted. "But my father taught me to take my luck wherever I could find it."

"A wise man, Jedediah Fury."

Jason was about to nod in agreement when he saw Wash spurring back toward him and Saul at a gallop. The old-timer waved for everyone else to stop as he passed them.

"Now what?" Jason muttered. He supposed it would have been too much to expect for them to get back to Fury without running into more trouble along the way.

Wash confirmed that a moment later as he reined in and said, "I hate to tell you this, Jason, but there's some sort o' ruckus goin' on ahead of us. I heard gunshots a minute ago."

"Can we go around it?" Jason asked.

"Reckon we might . . . but then there might be trouble right behind us, and we wouldn't know what it was."

"You're saying we should go take a look?"

"It'd be the smart thing to do."

Jason sighed, not surprised by Wash's answer. He knew the old-timer was right. For a while there, peace had been wonderful. . . .

But the sound of distant gunfire that now drifted to his ears through the hot, still air told him what he already knew.

The only peace that lasted came after a man was dead.

Chapter 32

The stubby red butte stuck up from the arid landscape about a quarter of a mile from the little rise where Jason and Wash were stretched out on their bellies, studying the situation. They had passed Wash's spyglass back and forth several times, and there was no getting around what they saw through it.

A group of cavalrymen were holed up in some rocks at the base of the butte. Arrayed in front of them, taking advantage of every bit of cover no matter how small, was a band of Apache warriors. The Apaches had rifles they had probably looted in previous raids, and they kept the soldiers pinned down in the rocks. From their vantage point, Jason and Wash had seen a couple of the troopers lying motionless on the ground behind the rocks, and they figured those men were either badly wounded or dead.

"You think that's Lieutenant Carter's patrol?" Jason asked.

"More'n likely," Wash replied. "He found his Apaches, but I'm bettin' that right now he wishes he hadn't. If he's still alive, that is."

"What do you think the chances are that they can hold off the Indians?"

Wash frowned. "Considerin' that they likely ain't got no water 'cept what's in their canteens, and they'll be runnin' out o' ammunition sooner or later, their chances ain't good. An Apache can outlast pert' near anybody. Them Injuns'll squat out there till doomsday, content just to pick off a trooper ever' now and then whenever one of 'em gets careless."

"When they've been without water long enough, they'll go mad and try to break out," Jason predicted.

"Yep. That's what them 'Paches are countin' on."

"Speaking of counting . . . how many of the Indians are there?"

Wash gnawed on his mustaches and looked through the spyglass some more. "Hard to say," he finally declared. "They slide around from bush to bush and rock to rock, lookin' for a better angle to shoot at the troopers. But my best guess is about twenty-five."

"So we outnumber them," Jason said.

Wash looked skeptical. "Twenty-five Apaches ain't like twenty-five normal jaspers. I wouldn't feel confident goin' agin 'em unless I had ninety or a hundred men."

"We can't just ride around them and leave those soldiers to be slaughtered."

"I was afraid you'd say that," Wash replied with a sigh. "And you're right, o' course. Anyway, they might spot us, and when they was through with them soldier boys, they'd come after us. Best to deal with 'em now, when they ain't expectin' it."

Jason nodded and started sliding back down the rise. "Let's go tell the others and figure out what to do."

When they got back to the posse, which was waiting a few hundred yards away, it didn't take long for Jason to explain the situation. He wasn't surprised when Salmon Kendall spoke up right away and said, "We've got to help those cavalrymen."

Ezra Dixon leaned over in his saddle and spat to the side. "Them bluebellies got themselves into this fix. Let 'em get their ownselves out of it."

"They would come to our aid if we were the ones who were trapped," Saul argued. "I vote we help them."

Matt said, "Putting it to a vote, are we? In that case, I vote that we help them too." He glared at Dixon, all but admitting that he had chosen that course because the rancher advised against it.

"Nobody said anything about voting," Jason snapped. "I'm still in charge of this posse, and I say we help the soldiers. If you don't like that, Dixon, you're free to ride on by yourself . . . but don't look to us for help if the Apaches start stalking *you*."

Dixon grunted. "Never said I wouldn't go along with it. I just figure it's a piss-poor idea, that's all."

Jason turned back to Wash. "How do you think we should do this?"

"Well . . . we can ride right up on 'em from behind and go to shootin', but they're gonna hear us comin'. We'll get some of 'em, but they're liable to scatter and some o' those bucks will get away. They'll go back to their camp and get some more warriors and then dog our trail all the way back to Fury."

"Yes, and they'll pick off some of us if that happens too," Jason said. "We need to make sure none of them get away." He looked at the butte, which was still visible from where they were. "I've got an idea about that."

Sweat trickled down the back of Jason's neck and dripped into his eyes. He paused for a moment, with his hands wrapped around jutting little projections of rock and the toes of his boots wedged into small openings in the rock face, and blinked to clear his vision. The sun's heat blasted down on the butte.

But it had to be even worse among the boulders on the other side of the butte, where the cavalry troopers were pinned down. At least on this side, nobody was shooting at Jason and his companions.

Four men had accompanied him on this mission, circling far around the butte so that the dust from their horses' hooves wouldn't give them away as they approached from the north. They had tied their mounts to scrubby mesquite trees, slung their rifles on their backs by makeshift slings fashioned from lengths of rope, and started to climb. The rugged face of the butte provided enough handholds and toeholds to allow the men to make the ascent, but it was hot, hard, grueling work.

Once they reached the top, though, they would have a commanding field of fire. They would start picking off the Apaches as the rest of the posse attacked from the rear and flushed the Indians out of their hiding places. It was up to Jason and his companions to make sure that none of the Apaches escaped.

As he resumed climbing, Jason glanced over at the other men. He had picked what he hoped were the best marksmen among the group, but he had only their word for that in some cases since he didn't know all of the men. He was confident in his own abilities and those of Wash Keough, but the others were unknown quantities.

One of the volunteers, surprisingly, was Alf Blodgett. The burly, middle-aged Englishman had explained that before becoming a saloonkeeper, he had been in the British Army in India. "Best shot in the Khyber Rifles, and that's sayin' a bit," he had declared proudly.

Blodgett's claims might well be true, but he was so red in the face that Jason worried he would have a seizure before he reached the top of the butte. Blodgett climbed pretty well for an overweight, middle-aged man, but he was still an overweight, middle-aged man.

The Englishman made it, but by the time the five men pulled themselves onto the flat top of the butte, he was puffing so hard and wheezing so loud that Jason was worried that the Apaches would hear him from all the way down on the flats. "Are you going to be all right, Alf?" he asked.

"Oh . . . sure," Blodgett replied as he struggled to catch his breath. "It was hotter that day . . . in the Khyber Pass . . . when our lads took on . . . a group of rogue Sikhs."

Jason didn't have any idea what the Englishman was talking about, but he nodded anyway and said, "All right, stay low while we're crawling over to the other side."

The butte was only a couple of hundred yards wide, but that seemed like a long way to the men who were crawling over it. Tufts of grass grew here and there, as did a few small bushes, but for the most part the top of the butte was flat, rocky, and arid.

The popping of gunfire continued from the rocks below, but it seemed to Jason that the shots were fewer and farther between now. He wondered if the troopers were already running low on ammunition. It probably wouldn't matter to the Apaches if they did; the savages would continue to play their cruel waiting game.

Jason, Wash, Blodgett, and the other two men didn't unsling their rifles until they were almost at the butte's brink. When they had the weapons ready, they eased forward, being careful not to let the barrels protrude too far over the edge. They didn't want the Apaches to notice that they were up here until they were ready to fire.

"Pick your targets," Jason said, "and make your shots count. We'll only get one chance to take them by surprise."

From up there, he could see several Apaches lying in shallow depressions they had scooped out of the sandy soil. Others crouched behind rocks or bushes, making themselves smaller than seemed humanly possible. Jason picked a fairly difficult target for himself. He could see about half of the Apache's head behind a rock. A strip of red cloth bound the warrior's raven-black hair. Jason drew a bead on that tiny bit of bright color.

"Everybody ready?" he called to the others, and received four affirmatives. "Let 'em have it," Jason said as he began to take up the slack on his rifle's trigger.

The weapon cracked loudly and kicked against Jason's shoulder. As he worked its lever, he saw the Apache he had aimed at thrown backward by the bullet, a red spray of blood exploding from his head. The warrior landed on his back with his arms and legs outflung and didn't move again.

Along the rim of the butte, more shots rang out. Those shots were the signal for the posse to charge into the battle from the rear, led by Saul, Salmon, and Matt. The four women would still be far in the rear, guarded by several of the wounded men who were left behind for that purpose.

Jason fired again, and saw an Apache's arm jerk and then dangle uselessly, probably broken by the bullet. At that moment, the posse came galloping into view, yelling and shooting. Jason scooted forward until he could look down into the rocks at the cavalrymen who had been trapped there.

"Hold your fire! Hold your fire!" he shouted. He didn't want those troopers blazing away at the Apaches, because any of their shots that missed might pose a danger to the men from Fury who were attacking from the rear.

Jason spotted the wiry little sergeant kneeling behind a boulder. The lieutenant was sitting beside him with his back propped against the rock. A bloodstained bandage was wrapped around the young officer's shoulder. At Jason's shout, Sergeant Halligan twisted around and craned his neck to look up at the top of the butte. Jason snatched his hat off and waved it in the air so that the sergeant could see it and know that they were white men up here, not Indians.

Halligan grinned and waved back at Jason, then bellowed an order for the rest of the patrol to hold their fire. Jason resumed firing. The Apaches were scattering now, just as he had figured they would. The posse men rode some of them down, and blasted others with rifles and handguns. Jason and his sharpshooters picked off others. The fight didn't last long. Within minutes, all the Apaches were down. All but a couple of them were lying motionless, either already dead or mortally wounded. The two who weren't hurt that bad were taken prisoner. Jason was glad to see that. He had issued firm orders before leaving the posse that none of the Indians were to be murdered if they were out of the fight, but he hadn't been sure the men would cooperate and follow those orders.

Alf Blodgett stood up, pulled a bandanna from his pocket, and wiped his sweating face. "Blimey," he said. "Now we got to climb back *down* the bleedin' hill." He grinned. "Still, 'twasn't a bad fight while it lasted. A bit unfair perhaps."

"What's unfair is not doing everything you can to survive a fight," Jason said.

"And a mite foolish to boot," put in Wash.

By the time Jason and the others descended from their aerie, the troopers had emerged from the rocks and the women and their guards had come up. As the posse members and the cavalry patrol gathered at the base of the butte, Sergeant Halligan helped Lieutenant Carter forward. The wounded lieutenant looked around at Jason and the other men from Fury, and then his gaze lingered on the four women. Not out of admiration, though, as he made clear when he said, "You men are all under arrest."

Jason stared at him, unable to speak for a moment. When he regained his voice, he said, "What the hell are you talking about, Lieutenant?"

"I know I owe you a debt of thanks for coming to our aid," Carter said, "but I can't ignore the presence of those women. Obviously, you men ignored my orders and entered Mexican territory without permission. You invaded a sovereign nation!"

"Invasion, hell!" Jason flared back at him, too fed up to keep his temper under control. "Alba and his bandits invaded Arizona Territory first! If you're a big enough fool to try to arrest us, you can do it after we've taken those ladies back to Fury!"

"Lieutenant," Halligan said, "with all due respect, sir, you might want to think about what you're doin'. We lost a couple o' men, but I reckon we'd all be dead if it wasn't for these folks. They saved our bacon, and that's the God's honest truth."

"But they broke the law and disobeyed a direct order—"

That was all Halligan could take too. "Beggin' your pardon, Lieutenant, but were you such a horse's ass *before* they pinned them bars on you, or did you get that way afterward?"

Carter could only gape at the sergeant, too overcome by shock and anger to speak. When he was able to talk again, he blustered, "Of all the damned insubordination! I'll have you busted all the way down to private! You won't see the outside of the guardhouse for months, Sergeant!"

"Good," Halligan said. "Maybe I'll get some sleep in there."

"Now, see here—"

"No, you see! You got the makin's of a fine officer, Lieutenant. Ain't nobody doubts your courage, and you're smart as a whip most o' the time. But this ain't one o' those times." Halligan waved a gnarled hand at the posse members. "You tell a bunch of Americans they ain't got the right to protect them and their own, and of course they're gonna ignore you! You tell 'em they got to sit back and let badmen run roughshod over 'em because o' some rule or regulation some stuffed shirt back East come up with, and they're gonna tell you to go to hell! They don't care about the law near as much as they care about doin' what's right. And if they weren't that way, well, I reckon they'd've rode off today and left us here to die, instead o' riskin' their own lives to help us. You get all that through your head, and you might be more'n a good officer someday, Lieutenant . . . you might be a good man too." Halligan shook his head and blew out his breath. "That's the longest piece o' speechifyin' I ever spouted in all my borned days. I'm done."

Lieutenant Carter stared at him in silence for a long moment, then finally turned his head and looked at Jason. "You have my apologies, Marshal," he said. His voice was stiff, but he was making an obvious effort to be more human.

"And you and your companions have my gratitude as well. If there's anything I can do to repay you for your assistance . . ."

"There's one thing," Jason said. "Ride with us back to Fury. It's on your way to Camp Grant anyway, and we've got a good doctor there who can tend to your wounded."

A smile appeared on Carter's face as he nodded. "All right. Thank you, Marshal."

Jason turned to the posse members and waved them into their saddles. "Mount up, men," he called. "We're going home."

Chapter 33

It was the middle of the next day when the large group of riders came in sight of the settlement. Jason felt a wave of relief wash through him at the sight of Fury. They had made it the rest of the way without any trouble. Now all they had to do was ride in, and they would be home.

"It looks good, doesn't it?" Megan asked from beside him.

Jason nodded. There had been a time—not all that long ago really—when all he had wanted to do was leave this town called Fury behind him. Now, although a small part of him still regretted that he hadn't been able to further his education, either back East or in San Francisco, the warm feeling inside him left no doubt that he had come home.

The pretty redhead beside him probably had something to do with him feeling that way, he reflected. He looked over at Megan and smiled, and when she smiled back at him, he saw his future—and he liked the looks of it.

Jason grew puzzled, though, when no one came riding out from town to meet them. He figured someone would have spotted them coming by now, and he thought Ward Wanamaker or Dr. Morelli, at least, would want to know as soon as possible if their mission had been successful.

If he didn't know better, though, he would almost think the

settlement was deserted. As they drew closer, he didn't see anyone moving around the streets. Maybe everybody was just taking a siesta, Jason told himself.

That was better than thinking about the alternative—that something serious was wrong here.

Jason wasn't the only one to notice that there was something unusual going on—or not going on, as the case might be. With a frown on her face, Megan asked, "Does it seem to you like the town is awfully . . . quiet?"

"It does," Jason replied.

"Do you think anything is wrong?"

Despite his intentions, Jason had been thinking about nothing but that for the past few moments. He considered several alternatives. Maybe an illness had struck the settlement, a sickness so bad that everyone was in bed trying to recover from it. Or there could have been an Indian scare. Maybe everybody had packed up and left for Tucson, where they would be safer. What about a gold strike? Jason had heard of towns that literally emptied out when word of gold being found somewhere else arrived.

None of those possibilities seemed likely, though. Jason couldn't imagine an illness bad enough to make every single person in town take to his or her bed. Quite a few of the citizens of Fury had been through Indian attacks too. They were too tough and seasoned to cut and run. And he couldn't believe that everyone in town would have the gold hunger bad enough to up and leave, abandoning all they had worked for here for the mere hope of something better somewhere else.

Wash, Saul, and Salmon trotted their mounts up alongside Jason's. "Somethin's wrong," Salmon said. "Where is everybody?"

"We were just wondering the same thing. Wash, you and I better ride ahead and take a closer look."

"I'm coming too," Saul said.

"And me," Salmon added. "I'm the mayor o' Fury, gosh darn it. If something bad's happened, I should've been there."

"You had your hands full helping to rescue those prisoners," Jason pointed out. "And if there's any danger in town, I want you and Saul out here to help handle these folks, Salmon. Don't let them go charging in, no matter what you see or hear."

"What could it be?" Megan asked. "Where has everyone gone?"

"We'll find out," Jason promised. "Come on, Wash."

As they rode toward the settlement, Wash said, "I notice you didn't ask me if I *wanted* to come with you, Jason."

"I figured you would," Jason explained. "You've never been one to avoid trouble, Wash. You usually gallop right into it. But you can go back to the others if you want."

"Hell, no! And miss all the fun?" Wash snorted. "Just ask me next time, all right?"

"Sure," Jason promised.

They were close enough to town now to see that a couple of wagons were parked in front of the mercantile, and several horses were tied at the hitch racks. So Fury wasn't completely deserted, after all. But no one was moving around, that was for sure. Jason hadn't seen a soul on the streets so far.

They reached the edge of town and started riding slowly along Main Street. An eerie silence hung over the settlement. Not even a dog barked anywhere.

"Oh, now," Wash said in a hushed voice, "I really don't like—"

A man suddenly burst into view, running from an alley into the street and shouting. Jason barely had time to recognize him as Ward Wanamaker and realize he was calling, "Jason, go back! Get out of town!" before a shot rang out.

Ward jerked, stumbled, and went down. Jason and Wash reached for their guns, but before they could draw the weapons, the barrels of numerous rifles and pistols appeared in open windows and thrust over the tops of roofs. A voice ordered, "Hold it, Marshal!"

Jason's hand froze as it hovered over the butt of his Colt. In a tense voice, he said, "It looks like they've got the drop on us, Wash, whoever they are."

"Yeah," the old-timer agreed. He lifted his hand away from his gun, and so did Jason. To do anything else would be to invite getting shot to pieces.

A couple of men sauntered through the batwings of the Crown and Garter. Jason stiffened as he recognized them as Bill Rye and Flint Gallister, the gunslingers who led the opposing factions of hired guns working for Matt MacDonald and Ezra Dixon.

At least, they had been opposing factions when the posse left Fury. Now Rye and Gallister looked downright friendly with each other as they strolled toward Jason and Wash.

"Marshal," Rye said with a nod. "Might as well get down from your horse and make yourself comfortable. You're not going anywhere."

"What's going on here?" Jason demanded without dismounting. "Where is everybody?"

"Oh, don't worry. They're around," Rye said.

"They're just lying low for now," Gallister added. "Until they see whether or not you and the rest of that posse are going to act sensibly."

With an effort, Jason restrained his anger and impatience and asked in a low voice, "What the *hell* are you talking about, Gallister?"

"That's Marshal Gallister," the gunman said. "And this is Mayor Rye. We're running this town now."

Wash let out a whistle. "Lord have mercy! You coyotes decided to get together and take over!"

"Insulting a public official," Gallister said. "Got to be a hefty fine for that, doesn't there, Mayor?"

"That's right," Rye agreed. "We'll figure it out later, though. For right now, you old buzzard, just ride out there and tell the rest of your bunch what's happening. If they want their former marshal to live—"

"And if they want to keep their own families from coming to any harm," Gallister added.

"They'll ride in and turn over their guns to us," Rye went on.

"Just like that?" Jason said. "You take over a whole town just like that?"

Rye smiled and nodded. "Just like that, Fury. Flint and I decided there was more money to be made this way than by working for those two stupid, feuding ranchers. Don't worry, you'll get your town back—eventually."

After the wolf pack had looted it of everything that was valuable and gotten tired of tormenting the citizens, Jason thought.

He looked past Rye and Gallister and saw that Ward Wanamaker had pulled himself to a sitting position and was now scooting toward the hardware store, dragging a bullet-ventilated leg behind him. At least Ward hadn't been killed. That was something to be thankful for.

Jason turned his angry gaze back to Rye and Gallister and said, "You're insane, both of you. There are only about twenty of you. You can't take over a whole town."

"That's where you're wrong, Fury," Gallister said. "It don't matter how many people are in this settlement. They're no match for men like us. They're sheep. They're too afraid for their lives to fight back. Hell, they're afraid of being made uncomfortable! They'd rather give in and let us have whatever we want."

Rye laughed. "That's right. Before you start thinking about fighting for them, Fury, you'd better consider this. They ain't worth it."

"Just throw your gun in the dirt, Fury," Gallister ordered. "There's no shame in being a sheep when all the other folks in your town are."

Jason lowered his head and stared at his saddle horn. Rye, Gallister, and the other gunslingers wouldn't have been able to take over the settlement if there wasn't some truth to what they were saying. The citizens had given up too easily when it looked like their lives and their property would be endangered.

But they had just made a mistake, Jason thought. It was easy enough to do. And he couldn't believe that they hadn't realized that by now. He couldn't believe that they wouldn't fight if they got another chance.

He was about to stake everything on that hope.

"Wash," he said quietly as he lifted his head again, "ride back out to the posse, tell them what's going on, and tell them I said to come in with all guns blazing."

Rye and Gallister stared at him in amazement. "What the hell's wrong with you, Fury?" Gallister demanded in an irritated voice.

"What makes you think we'll let this old buzzard go anywhere?" Rye added.

"Because I'm about to kill the both of you," Jason said.

The gunslingers' amazement lasted only a heartbeat after those words came out of Jason's mouth, and then they both reached for their guns, their hands flashing toward the holsters.

Jason was drawing at the same time, remembering everything he had learned and all the time he had spent practicing before Juan Alba's raid on the settlement had disrupted everything. His mind was clear, and his eyes had never seemed sharper. All his senses had expanded in this frozen second of time. He smelled the dust of the street, felt the warmth of the sun on his face, heard Ward Wanamaker cry, *"Nooooo!"* He was aware of Wash Keough whirling his horse around and jabbing his heels in the animal's flanks. The horse's hooves thudded against the ground.

Gallister's gun was out of leather now and rising. Rye was even a little faster; the barrel of his Colt had almost come level.

But Jason's fingers were wrapped around the smooth walnut grips of his gun and it was free too, his thumb on the hammer as the revolver came up, drawing it back, the cool metal of the trigger against his finger as the muscles of his hand contracted and took up the slack. . . .

The shots rolled out, one-two-three-four-five, so close together they were like one continuous roar, exploding in the time it took for a man's heart to beat three times. Jason fired twice, the first bullet going into Flint Gallister's chest and knocking the black-clad gunman back off his feet. The one shot Gallister got off clipped the brim of Jason's hat and sent it sailing off his head. Jason swung the barrel of his gun and fired at Rye.

But between Jason's first and second shots, Rye had fired, and he didn't miss. Jason felt the bullet pound into his body. The impact made him slew sideways in the saddle. The fact that he almost fell was the only thing that saved his life, because Rye's second shot would have hit him in the throat if he hadn't. As it was, the slug burned a fiery path along the side of Jason's neck.

His muscles no longer responded to his mental commands. He felt himself sliding out of the saddle and couldn't do anything about it. He crashed to the street beside his horse, which was spooked by the gunfire and danced around for a second before bolting, luckily missing Jason with its iron-shod hooves. Jason lay there with a terrible coldness filling him, unable to move.

But his eyes still worked, and he saw Bill Rye lying a few feet away, eyes wide open. Rye's gun had slipped from his fingers. A black-rimmed hole just above Rye's left eye showed where Jason's second bullet had gone. He was as dead as Gallister.

But the other gunslingers who had thought they could waltz in here and take over the town were still alive, and they began firing from windows and rooftops as Ward Wanamaker pushed himself to his feet and staggered over to Jason. Jason was aware of Ward grabbing him under the arms and dragging him toward the mouth of a nearby alley. Ward grunted as he was hit again, but he stayed on his feet and kept moving.

Jason heard something else—angry shouts. He found that he could move his head again, and when he looked around he saw fights spilling into the street as the citizens of Fury attacked the wolf pack with fists, clubs, pitchforks, shovels, anything they could lay their hands on. The people were fighting back, as Jason had known they would if they got another chance to do so. Some of them might die, but they would take back their town from the evil ones.

Ward slumped to the ground next to Jason, breathing heavily. He pulled Jason's shirt aside and gasped, "Lord! You're hit bad, Jason!"

Jason didn't care. There was a smile on his face as he heard the sounds of the struggle around him, and it widened into a grin as pounding hoofbeats and a fresh volley of gunshots told him that the other members of the posse had arrived to finish cleaning up the town. The people of Fury would finish the job, no matter what happened to him.

Confident in that belief, he let the onrushing tide of blackness that swept toward him claim him and carry him away.

Jason didn't expect to wake up, but he did. He became aware of a tight pressure around his chest and a warmth clutching his hand. When he forced his eyes open and looked down at himself as he lay in a bed somewhere, he saw that the tightness came from the bandages wrapped around him.

The warmth came from Megan MacDonald's hand. Her fingers were intertwined with his, holding on as if she never intended to let go.

She wasn't looking at him, though. Her head was down, and her eyes were closed and her lips were moving as if she were praying. Jason hated to interrupt her, but he wanted to talk to her. He whispered, "M-Megan . . ."

Her head jerked up, and her green eyes flashed open. "Jason!" she cried. "Jason, you've come back to me!"

"Didn't know . . . I'd gone anywhere."

But if that was true, he suddenly thought, then why did he remember talking to his father again? Why did he remember, plain as day, Jedediah Fury telling him that his work wasn't done yet, that he needed to get back to the settlement?

Jason couldn't answer those questions, and he didn't have the strength to worry about them. It was enough to know that he was here and that Megan was with him and that evidently life went on in a town called Fury.

Chapter 34

All the gunslingers were dead, and so were half a dozen of the townspeople. It was a high price to pay. A high price in blood and loss and sacrifice. But from time to time, that was what life demanded of those who dared to live it.

Within a month, all the buildings destroyed by Juan Alba's bandit horde had been rebuilt. Flowers had begun to bloom on the fresh graves in the newly established town cemetery. Marshal Jason Fury and Deputy Ward Wanamaker were both back on their feet, although they were still getting around a mite gingerly. Wash Keough had stayed sober and acted as the town marshal while both lawmen were laid up, assisted by several volunteer deputies including Alf Blodgett and Saul Cohen. Wash had proclaimed that month of sobriety to be the worst month of his life, and warned Jason that he'd better find somebody else to take over before he got himself shot up again.

An uneasy state of truce existed between Matt MacDonald and Ezra Dixon. They still didn't like each other, not even a little bit, but working together on the posse had forced them to develop a grudging respect for each other. Jason was convinced that sooner or later things would flare up between them again—they were both too stubborn and prideful for it not to—but he hoped any trouble would take its time about getting here.

Anyway, Matt had enough to worry about at the moment, what with the wedding date he had set with Jenny rapidly approaching. Jason sighed when he thought about that—even though it hurt the healing bullet hole in his chest—but he wished his sister well in her marriage.

A laboriously scrawled letter arrived from Sergeant Halligan. After helping the posse clean up the last of the gunslingers who had terrorized the settlement, Lieutenant Carter and the patrol had returned to Camp Grant. According to Halligan's letter, the lieutenant's official report of his last patrol contained no mention of any civilian force making an incursion into Mexican territory. "There's hope for the boy yet," the sergeant's letter concluded.

Jason was sitting in a straight-backed chair in front of the marshal's office, leaning back against the wall, when Dr. Morelli strolled up, accompanied by Wash, Saul, and Salmon. Jason lowered the front legs of his chair to the ground and asked, "Is this a committee of some sort?"

"No, we just all happened to be coming the same way," Morelli replied. "I'm here to check on that wound."

"It's fine," Jason said. "Time for you to quit fussing over me, Doc."

"Yeah," Salmon said with a grin. "He's got Megan MacDonald to do that. Say, Jason, I'll bet if you got busy, you could talk that girl into marryin' you in time for you to have a double weddin' with her brother and your sister."

Jason winced. "Don't remind me. And don't go messing in things that are none of your business, Mayor."

Wash said, "I'm on my way down to Abigail's for a drink. Don't let on that I told you, but I think that gal's gettin' a mite sweet on me, even if I *am* old enough to be her pappy. Course, she'd throw me over in a minute if she could have you, Marshal."

Jason didn't say anything to that. Some things were better left alone.

Saul put his hands in his pockets and rocked back and forth on his heels. "More people moving in," he commented. "Looks like new settlers aren't going to be scared off by what happened here. The raid by Alba and the trouble with those gunslingers, I mean."

"No need for folks to be scared," Salmon said. "Alba's dead, his gang is wiped out, and we all saw what happened when those gunnies tried to take over. Our marshal put a stop to that. Slapped leather against both Bill Rye and Flint Gallister, Jason did, and killed 'em both. Hell, our marshal's the most famous gunfighter in the territory now! Nobody's ever gonna try to cause trouble in these parts again!"

Jason looked out into the street and smiled. He wished he could believe that. He really did.

Johnstone Justice. What America Needs Now.

From William W. Johnstone and J.A. Johnstone comes a special holiday gift for devoted fans of the Jensen saga— a warmhearted story of burning justice, blazing bullets, and other Jensen family traditions . . .

AN ARIZONA CHRISTMAS

It's that time of year when families gather together to celebrate the holidays, and the Jensens are no exception. This year, since half the clan is scattered across the American West, they've decided to split the difference and meet up in Tucson. Matt and Luke will be there for sure and maybe Ace and Chance, too. That leaves Sally, Preacher, and Smoke Jensen, who've reserved three seats on a westbound stage to make sure they don't miss out on the festivities.

They won't be traveling alone, however. A reporter with a nose for trouble, a mail-order bride with a wandering eye, and an old woman with a surly young grandson are on board—along with a freshly minted cargo of cold hard cash. What could possibly go wrong?

Mother Nature is the first to strike, dusting up the trail with a sandstorm as blinding and deadly as any northern blizzard. Then come the Apaches who ambush the stagecoach, forcing the passengers and drivers to seek shelter in a cave. Even if Smoke and Preacher manage to shoot their way out of this, they have another big surprise waiting—a ruthless gang of outlaws after the cargo of cash, happy to slaughter any man, woman, or child who tries to stop them. If the Jensens hope to save Christmas this year, they'll need to save their own lives first . . .

Coming in NOVEMBER 2017
wherever PINNACLE BOOKS *are sold.*

Live Free. Read Hard. www.williamjohnstone.net

Chapter 1

Smoke Jensen dropped to one knee and fired twice. Flame licked from the muzzle of the Colt in his hand.

On the other side of the main street in Big Rock, Colorado, the man Smoke had just shot staggered back toward the plate glass window of a store. He pressed his hand to his chest. The palm was big enough to cover both bullet holes. Blood welled from the wounds and dripped between his splayed fingers.

He went over backwards in a crash of shattering glass.

That didn't mean the danger was over. A slug whipped through the air only inches from Smoke's left ear. He dived forward, off the boardwalk, and landed behind a water trough. Bullets thudded against the other side of the trough. A few plunked into the water.

Smoke had seen four other outlaws besides the man he had shot. From the sound of the guns going off, all of them were trying to fill him full of lead.

Hoofbeats pounded in the street. A man yelled, "I got the horses! Come on!"

They believed they had him pinned down, Smoke thought. They figured if they kept throwing lead at him, he couldn't do a thing to stop them from getting away.

They were about to find out how wrong they were.

No doubt spooked by all the gunfire, the horses stomped around in the street, making it more difficult for the outlaws to mount up.

Smoke thumbed more cartridges from his shell belt into the .45's empty chambers. Then he rolled out into the open again, tipped the Colt's barrel up, and fired.

The outlaws had managed to swing up into their saddles. Smoke's slug ripped into the chest of the man leading the gang's attempt at a getaway. He jerked back in the saddle and hauled so hard on the reins that his horse reared up wildly.

The man right behind him tried to avoid the rearing horse but was too close. The two mounts collided and went down, spilling their riders.

Smoke pushed himself up and triggered again. His bullet shattered the shoulder of the third man in line and caused him to pitch out of the saddle with his left foot caught in the stirrup. As the horse continued galloping down the street, the wounded outlaw was dragged through the dirt past Smoke.

The fourth man fired wildly, several shots exploding from the gun in his hand. Smoke didn't know where the bullets landed, but he hoped no innocent bystanders were hurt. To lessen the chances of that happening, he took a second to line up his shot and coolly put a bullet in the outlaw's head.

That left one man in the gang who wasn't wounded or dead, the one who had been thrown when the two horses rammed into each other. He scrambled to his feet as soon as he got his wits back about him, but as Smoke's gun swung toward him, his hands shot in the air, as high above his head as he could reach.

"Don't shoot!" he begged. "For God's sake, mister, don't kill me!"

Smoke came smoothly to his feet. He was only medium height, but his powerfully muscled body, including exceptionally broad shoulders, made him seem bigger. His ruggedly handsome face was topped by ash blond hair, uncovered because his brown Stetson had flown off when he threw himself behind the water trough.

The gun in his hand was rock-steady as he covered the remaining outlaw. From the corner of his eye, he saw his old friend Sheriff Monte Carson running along the street toward him. Monte had a shotgun in his capable hands.

"One in the store over there," Smoke said, nodding toward the building with the broken front window. "The others are all here close by, except for the one whose horse dragged him off down the street."

"I'll check on them while you cover that hombre," Monte said. "Not much doubt that they're all dead, though."

"How do you figure that?" Smoke asked.

"You shot 'em, didn't you?" A grim smile appeared on the lawman's weathered face.

Smoke knew the question was rhetorical so he didn't answer. He told the man he had captured, "Take that gun out of your holster and toss it away. Slow and careful-like. You wouldn't want to make me nervous."

The idea of the famous gunfighter Smoke Jensen ever being nervous about anything was pretty far-fetched, but not impossible. He had loved ones, and like anybody else, sometimes he feared for their safety.

Not his own, though. He had confidence in his own abilities. Anyway, he had already lived such an adventurous life, he figured he was on borrowed time, so a fatalistic streak ran through him. If there was a bullet out there somewhere with his name on it, it would find him one of these days. Until then, he wasn't going to waste time worrying about it.

The surviving outlaw followed Smoke's orders, using his left hand to reach across his body and take out the iron he had pouched when he mounted up to flee. With just a couple fingers, he slid the gun from leather, tossed it aside, and thrust his hands high in the air again. Then he swallowed hard. "No need to shoot me, Mr. Jensen. I done what you told me."

"How do you know who I am?" Smoke asked with a slight frown. Although he had spent quite a few years with a reputation, first as a notorious outlaw—totally unjustified charges, by the way—and then as one of the fastest men with a Colt ever to buckle on a gunbelt, he was still naturally modest enough to be surprised sometimes when folks knew who he was.

"Who the hell else could you be?" the captured outlaw asked. "You shot four fellas in less time than it takes to tell the tale. I warned Gallagher we shouldn't try it right here in town. I *told* him. I said, Monte Carson's a pretty tough law dog to start with, and Smoke Jensen lives near Big Rock and we'd be liable to run into him . . . into you, that is, Mr. Jensen . . . and I said that's just too big a risk to run, and sure enough—"

"What's this varmint babbling about?" Monte asked as he walked back up to Smoke with the scattergun tucked under his arm.

"Claims he didn't want to pull this job and warned the boss they shouldn't do it," Smoke explained with a trace of amusement in his voice.

"Well, he must not have argued too hard. He's here, ain't he?"

"In the flesh," Smoke agreed.

The frightened outlaw looked at both men. "You reckon I could put my arms down? They're getting' sort of tired."

Monte shifted the Greener and covered him. "All right, but if you try anything funny, this buckshot'll splatter you all over the street."

"No tricks, Sheriff. You got my word on that." The man licked his lips. "I just want to take what I got comin' and get outta this without bein' hung or shot."

"Behave yourself and you won't get shot. As for being strung up, well, that's up to a judge and jury, not me." Monte glanced over at Smoke. "The other four are dead, by the way, just like I figured. The one you shot in the shoulder might've lived if he hadn't gotten dragged down the street with his head bouncing until it busted open."

Smoke was reloading the Colt. He left an empty chamber for the hammer to rest on then slid the gun back into its holster. "Bad luck tends to dog a fella's trail when he starts riding the owlhoot."

"What were these varmints after, anyway?"

"Don't know," Smoke replied with a shake of his head. "I saw them come running out of the freight company office while I was on my way down to the train station." He nodded toward several canvas bags the outlaws had slung on their saddles as they tried to make their getaway. "I'd check those bags."

Monte squinted over the shotgun's barrels at the prisoner.

"Or I could just ask this varmint, and if he knows what's good for him, he'll answer."

"Money, of course," the outlaw volunteered quickly. "We got a tip that a fella named Reilly was having a payroll brought in by freight wagon, rather than on the train. He figured it'd be safer that way, since nobody would know the money was hidden in some sacks of flour."

Monte frowned. "Jackson Reilly, the rancher? He's sort of an oddball. That sounds like something he'd do. You know him, Smoke?"

"Met him once or twice," Smoke said in his usual laconic fashion. "Wouldn't say I know him all that well. He's been in these parts less than a year."

"I've heard him say he doesn't trust banks. Appears he doesn't trust the railroad, either."

Now that the shooting was over, quite a few of the citizens who had scrambled for cover earlier were coming back out to gawk at the sprawled bodies of the outlaws and stare at Smoke, Monte, and the prisoner. A ripple of laughter suddenly went through them. The man walking toward them was covered in white powder that clung to his clothes, his hair, and his mustache.

Smoke recognized Angus Mullen, one of the clerks from the freight office. He smiled and said, "Angus, you look like you got caught in a snowstorm."

"There'll be snow soon enough," Mullen said as he slapped at himself and raised a little floating cloud of white. "This is flour! Those scoundrels were cutting bags open and throwing them around the office."

Smoke nodded. Now that he took a closer look, he could see that some of the bandits were dusted with flour as well, although not nearly to the extent that Mullen was.

"Who the hell had the bright idea of hiding money in flour sacks?" the clerk went on.

"You should check your manifests," Smoke suggested. "I'll bet those sacks were being held for Jackson Reilly."

Mullen grimaced and scratched his jaw. "Yeah, now that you mention it, I reckon that's right," he admitted. "I'll have to have a talk with Mr. Reilly. The freight company has rules about this sorta thing, you know!"

"You do that, Angus." Monte jerked the shotgun's barrels in a curt gesture to the prisoner. "You march on down to the jail now. Smoke, thanks like always for lending a hand. You sure keep the undertaker busy."

"Not by choice," Smoke said. "I'm a peaceable man."

Monte just snorted and prodded the prisoner into marching toward the jail. Smoke returned to the errand that had brought him to Big Rock. He had come to meet the westbound train, which would soon be delivering his wife Sally to him.

He'd been early, so he had parked the buckboard at the station and walked back up to Longmont's Saloon for a cup of coffee and a visit with his old friend Louis Longmont. As the time for the train to arrive had approached, Smoke had said his good-byes and started for the depot again.

He had spotted the outlaws and recognized trouble in the making right away. When he'd called out for them to hold it, a man across the street, who had probably been posted as a lookout, opened fire on him.

Smoke hadn't wasted time asking any questions. Anybody shot at him, he regarded it as a declaration of war and proceeded accordingly.

And anybody not prepared to back it up hadn't ought to slap leather in the first place, as far as Smoke Jensen was concerned.

A thin overcast hung in the sky, thickening into darker clouds over the mountains. Avery Mullen was right. There would be snow soon enough. But that was expected in the fall in the Colorado high country. Smoke had seen plenty of snow and never minded it. The brisk nip in the air felt pretty doggoned good, in fact.

The shootout with the would-be thieves had delayed him some, but the train still hadn't rolled in. As he walked out onto the platform after crossing the station lobby, he heard the locomotive's shrill whistle in the distance, heralding the train's arrival.

A few people on the platform were waiting to board, others looked more like they were there to meet someone . . . like Smoke was. He smiled and nodded pleasantly to several he knew.

It was impossible not to notice a few folks whispering to each other behind their hands. Smoke wasn't so full of himself that he assumed they were talking about him, but given the recent ruckus, it made sense if they were.

Smoke knew he was famous—or infamous, depending on how you looked at it—but it wasn't anything he had ever set out to be. All those years ago, in the hardscrabble days right after the war, when he and his pa Emmett had left the farm in Missouri and headed west, all young Kirby Jensen had been interested in was getting by from day to day. That was before he'd met the old mountain man called Preacher, who had dubbed him Smoke because of his speed with a gun, and before he'd set out on the vengeance quest that had changed the course of his life forever.

Smoke preferred not to dwell on that.

Anyway, the train was pulling in, with smoke puffing from the diamond-shaped stack on the big Baldwin locomotive, and as it came to a stop he looked toward the passenger cars, eager to catch a glimpse of the woman he loved.

There she was! Sally stepped down from one of the cars, graceful as always. She looked up as Smoke came toward her, and a smile appeared on her face, making her more beautiful than ever.

Then she was in Smoke's arms and his lips were on hers, and he wasn't going to waste one bit of time or energy thinking about anything else for a while.